'Liz Fenwick's writing is vivid, sat~~isfying a~~

KT-408-281

Liz Fenwick, award-winning author, ex-pat expert, wife, mother of three, and dreamer turned doer, was born in Massachusetts, and at the age of twenty-six moved to London where she fell in love with an Englishman. After nine international moves, she now spends her time in Cornwall with her husband and her mad cat, writing stories inspired by the beautiful Duchy.

Find out more at www.lizfenwick.com or follow her on Twitter @liz_fenwick

Also by Liz Fenwick

One Cornish Summer

LIZ FENWICK

ORION

First published in Great Britain in 2018
by Orion Books
This paperback edition published in 2018
by Orion Books,
an imprint of The Orion Publishing Group Ltd
Carmelite House, 50 Victoria Embankment
London EC4Y 0DZ

An Hachette UK Company

1 3 5 7 9 10 8 6 4 2

A CIP catalogue record for this book
is available from the British Library.

ISBN 978 1 4091 6215 5

Typeset by Deltatype Ltd, Birkenhead, Merseyside

Printed in Great Britain by CPI Group (UK) Ltd
Croydon, CR0 4YY

www.orionbooks.co.uk

For Chris

✵ Prologue ✵

'Don't ever speak of this to anyone.'

He rolled over, and I saw who was under him.

My body began to shake. I opened my mouth to speak but words would not form as I watched her pull on her clothes. He remained in the bed with a sheet covering his nakedness. My brain wouldn't lose the image of what I'd seen. It was stuck on repeat as she walked past me without a word or a glance. The last thing I saw was the friendship bracelet on her ankle.

PART ONE

❋ One ❋
Hebe

June 2015

T he beach below is empty and we begin down the path. Your excitement about your new project proposal explodes into your words and it catches me.

'You need to expose them to the power of the metaphor. No one does this better than Donne.' I turn to you and your smile is radiant. '*Yet nothing can to nothing fall.*' I take a breath. '*Nor any place be empty quite ...*' I can't recall the rest and I stumble. You take my hand and give it a squeeze, not releasing it. Doubt fills me again.

The sound of a bell carries on the breeze. A church nestles in the sand just out of sight. In front of us the water flashes turquoise, which startles me. My steps falter yet we go forward, openly hand in hand, down to the sea. I have not been here with you before. For nine years I have kept you separate from something that is so much a part of me. Maybe the decision to come was reckless, but I hope here in this remote part of the Lizard we can be invisible. That we can simply be us ... before it is gone.

The path ends. Sunlight bounces off the damp stones. The clarity of the water hurts my eyes as the blues and greens glisten jewel-like while a breeze stirs the surface. You've never been to Cornwall before and I can see the wonder on your face.

'I told you it was lovely.'

You turn to me. 'You did, but you were lying.'

I tilt my head and study you. 'I haven't lied to you.' But I know I haven't told you everything either. I glance away. How much longer will I know what I have and haven't told you?

'You have.'

I shiver and look away. Your hand waving as if caressing the beach catches my eye, drawing me back to you. 'This isn't lovely ... it is so far beyond that. It is almost too beautiful.'

I laugh and pull you into my arms. We are alone with only a seagull for company. The freedom of being away with you is intoxicating. June sunshine beats down on our heads and I allow myself to forget that this is all wrong. I kiss you, then pull free, running along the sand like a child. The sea laps at the bottom of my jeans and you begin to race with me until we reach the rocks that mark the end of the beach. You swing me into your arms and we spin around until we fall onto the damp sand.

'I love you, Hebe Courtenay.'

I open my mouth to speak, to silence you, but you place a finger on my lips.

'I know you don't want to hear it, but I'm going to shout it anyway. I want the world to know.' You stare into my eyes, and all the love you have for me is reflected there. 'I, Rory Crown, love you!' You pull me to my feet. 'I love you.' You shout it to the cliff, and then turn to the sea and do it again.

I look around, ready to run. No one else is here and I am safe in your arms. We have time here away from the world, just me and you. No one cares who we are, or why we are together. For this moment, I can pretend that we are normal.

I am sleepy from the wine and the heat of the log fire. Despite the strength of the sun during the day, the evening is cold. I shudder and you look up from the computer. I should be working too, but I can't focus. The doctor said this would happen more and more. Right now I am too tired to fight it, but I must. Do you see the difference in me, I wonder, or is it just that now that I know ... everything fits?

'Can you take a look through this passage?' You stand and bring your laptop to me. 'I'm not sure it's concise enough, or maybe the wine is affecting the words.'

Smiling, I pick up my reading glasses. You've highlighted the text in orange so that I know what to review. I glance up at you but you are staring into the fire. The flames are mesmerising, but I force myself to read your words. Yet no matter how many times I read them, their meaning evades me. I tighten my grip on the laptop, trying to force my brain to work, but it won't pull sense from your sentences. It must be the wine. It has to be the wine.

You yawn and I do as well. 'Are you struggling with it too?' You take the computer from me. 'Let's both look at it with fresh eyes in the morning.' Closing the laptop, you hold out your hand. 'Come.' I take it, remembering the day you came into my life almost nine years ago.

*

Come, madam, come, all rest my powers defy

Just then the door opened and you walked in. 'Sorry.'

My breath caught. Your dark hair fell in curls on your neck. Your shoulders were broad but not yet fully fleshed out as a man. It was as though Thomas Grylls had stepped out of the portrait on my wall and into my classroom wearing jeans and a grey T-shirt. I closed my eyes for a moment. I shouldn't turn into a puddle of lust because of you. I had seen more than my fair share of handsome young men and none had ever tempted me to cross that line.

But you.

'Sorry. I was locked out of my room and had to wait for the porter to let me in.' Your voice softly Scottish.

'We were just beginning.'

You nodded and took a seat in the front.

'As I was saying.' I glanced at you, leaving the sentence unfinished, then started to hand out sheets of paper. 'Before we begin, here's the reading list and the next assignment.' Your hand touched mine as you took the pages from me. I froze. I could barely look into your eyes. My glance fell to your mouth. Your full lips lifted as if you knew what I was feeling.

Turning from you, I picked up the book and opened it.

7

'Who would like to read Donne's Elegy XIX, "To His Mistress Going to Bed"?'

Silence. Worried glances travelled from student to student, then you raised your hand, looking at your peers. 'I'd be happy to.' You smiled.

'*Come, madam, come, all rest my powers defy,*
Until I labour, I in labour lie.'

The words rolled from your tongue and I clung to the edge of the desk. The women of the group were as enraptured as I was. You continued.

'*The foe oft-times having the foe in sight,*
Is tir'd with standing though he never fight.
Off with that girdle, like heaven's zone glistering,
But a far fairer world encompassing.
Unpin that spangled breastplate which you wear,
That th'eyes of busy fools may be stopped there.
Unlace yourself, for that harmonious chime
Tells me from you that now it is bed time.'

Audible sighs brought me out of the trance I was in. Dear God, listening to you was as if Thomas Grylls had appeared in the flesh. In fact I'd written such a scene just days before, where Thomas was alone with his fiancée Lucia and he undressed her slowly, worshipping her with kisses. My face flushed and I turned from the class, looking out of the window at the September morning. Sunflowers had rotated upwards, burning in the heat of the sun.

'*Those set our hairs on end, but these our flesh upright.*
License my roving hands, and let them go
Before, behind, between, above, below.
O my America! my new-found-land,
My kingdom, safeliest when with one man manned.'

Your performance of the lines was as skilled as an actor's. Your burr caressed each word. Flesh tingled back to life. I longed for you to stop, and yet I didn't.

'*There is no penance due to innocence.*
To teach thee, I am naked first; why then,
What needst thou have more covering than a man?'

'Thank you …' The words stuttered from me. As I looked at you, the room disappeared. Your glance met mine; you gave me an apologetic half-smile then shook your head.

'Sorry.' I cleared my throat. 'Time to leave the magic of Donne's words behind and delve into the gritty reality of the seventeenth century.'

*

You sneeze, and suddenly I am back in this isolated old cottage and not standing at the front of a dusty classroom with twenty students waiting. I crawl into bed beside you, remembering while I still can. I pull you close and fall asleep to the sound of your heart beating.

❈ Two ❈

Lucy

26 September 2016

'Hello.' A voice whispered from behind Lucy and a hand brushed the base of her spine. She shivered. Ed. She raised the camera to her face, covering the rush of colour to her cheeks. Lucy had to play this cool. She couldn't let him distract her from her job.

Through the viewfinder she saw a Member of Parliament chatting to one of the teenage volunteers for the literacy charity. The camera shutter sound was muted and Lucy captured the images leaving them all unaware. That was best. She saw the real but created an illusion. Not fake, but certainly an altered reality. The discussion between the two was heated, but looking through the twenty images she'd taken in quick succession, she'd caught what looked like a beaming smile. The teen had made a winning point in the argument, but taken out of context it was charming, not victorious.

All the young volunteers attending had signed release forms before the guests had arrived. They were keen to help raise awareness, and so was Lucy. Today she was working for no fee. She knew what it was like to struggle to read being dyslexic, but she'd had the benefit of the best schooling available. The girl she had photographed was eighteen and angry. For years she had been written off as stupid, but she was far from it; Lucy had seen that in their chat earlier. The teen wore her emotion like a tattoo across her unlined forehead. Yet in the photo she appeared sweet. But Lucy knew the truth. The girl would soon acquire the skill that all women learned at some point in their lives: hiding their emotions from the world. Another year or two and she would have buried the anger. It would still be there – if invisible – and it would drive every move she made, but she would forget it was the anger navigating her choices. Lucy sighed.

By the window stood Daisy, an old school friend. Her face was the picture of concern as she listened to an older man. Lucy framed the image, making sure Daisy looked her best. The goal was to encourage others to want to donate and to be a part of something good. Although this was similar to much of the work she did for magazines – capturing in pixels the great, the good and in some cases the far from good – the kids in attendance gave the event an interesting edge. The challenge of telling this story was that it was important and not just people launching a new product or simply having a good time. For once it was a story Lucy wanted to tell.

She slipped unnoticed through the guests, not being drawn into conversation. It would have been so easy to stop and talk. She knew these people and they knew her. Hell, she'd attended enough of these events as one of them, without a camera in her hand. But she much preferred it with one.

Over the past nine years as a professional, she'd become a master of the flattering shot, even if for some subjects this was challenging. They relied on her to take the perfect picture, or at least one that wouldn't make them appear worse. She understood how the world worked. It didn't have to be real these days, it just had to look good.

By the window she saw Mrs Talworth with the princess and composed the shot. That photo with the afternoon sun shining on Mrs Talworth's highlighted hair would make the centrepiece for the society pages and might even hit tomorrow's papers. With the golden tone of the light she had dropped a good ten years off the woman, and the princess looked as unchanging as ever.

'Lucy, darling.'

She lowered the camera as the editor of a glossy magazine appeared.

'Surely you've got what you need and can knock off and enjoy yourself now?' The woman smiled. 'We haven't had a proper gossip in ages. Who are you with these days?'

'No time for gossip if you want the pics first thing in the morning.' Lucy looked at her watch. She'd need to edit these and send the best off tonight.

'True.' The editor sipped her champagne. 'I'll see you at the weekend.'

Lucy frowned, reviewing her schedule in her mind. Was she shooting a wedding? It wasn't like her to forget a job.

'At your parents'.'

Lucy rolled her eyes then nodded. A weekend in the Cotswolds with her family was exactly what she didn't want. Why had she agreed to this? Emotional blackmail. It was her brother Michael's birthday. 'Forgot.'

Ed brushed past and slipped a piece of paper into her hand. He despised most of this crowd but knew it was important to be seen supporting the charity.

The editor wandered away in the direction of the princess and Lucy fled to the ladies. Locking the door, she opened the note. She hadn't seen Ed since last week. Most of the time this was exactly what she wanted, a man with limited access. No emotional demands, just mental and physical stimulation – hers but not hers. In short, Lucy wanted the impossible and had found it with a married man. The irony wasn't lost on her.

Sheila's gone to her mother's. Meet me at mine at eight. Use the rear entrance. X

She flushed the note down the loo, knowing she could never be too careful. It was now 5 p.m. She had work to do, then he would be a reward for good behaviour.

Lucy's stomach rumbled. The problem with working these events was that she never had a chance to eat. Glancing at her watch, she thought about stopping and picking up a sandwich, but she was late getting to Ed's already. She hoped there was some food in the flat, but she doubted it. The last time she'd visited there had been a mouldy loaf of bread and a bottle of champagne. His wife didn't do domestics – or marriage, for that matter, from what he'd told her.

Reaching the back of the building, she sent him a text. The pong from the bins reacted with her empty stomach. She loved the no-ties relationship they had, but the subterfuge had begun to pall. Just as her gut rolled uncomfortably, Ed met her at the rear entrance and they climbed the stairs in silence. Once through the door, he reached for her and Lucy allowed the passion to rise, trying to ignore her hunger pangs. While Ed was pulling at her shirt, she was scanning the counter for a piece of fruit, anything she could eat. It was devoid of anything but a bottle of wine. The only thing that marred the bare room was a calendar with the days circled in red taped to the fridge.

Her stomach growled.

'Hungry?' He ran a hand over her backside.

'Yes.'

'Hopefully for me.'

She laughed. His ego knew no bounds. 'Food.'

'A takeaway later.' He nibbled her neck.

'Yes.' She'd heard that before but he had never followed through. Maybe it was too intimate to sit and eat in front of the television. Her skirt dropped to the floor and she brought his face up to meet hers and kissed him. His lips stilled, and he pulled away and led her to the bedroom.

He was focused on one thing and Lucy wouldn't complain. He wanted her. That was clear. As she fell onto the bed, she spotted a copy of Enid Blyton's *Five Go Off to Camp* on the bedside table. What the hell was he reading that for? As her body began to respond, her mind was in a damp tent in Devon, or was it Wales? She couldn't remember.

Ed rolled over and lit a cigarette, then checked his phone. His smoking didn't fit with the pristine state of the flat. Nothing was out of place except for their clothes on the bedroom floor. On the chest of drawers there was a black-and-white picture of Ed and Sheila at the register office. They'd been married ten years. What did they have to show for it?

'You wouldn't believe what Sheila texted me as she stormed off to her mother's.'

'Probably not, but tell me anyway.' Lucy stretched out her legs, trying not to think that she was currently naked in Sheila's bed.

'That she was only staying with me for the benefit of my career.'

Lucy frowned. 'Well that's what you told me when we met.'

He turned to her. 'Did I?'

She nodded. 'Yes, you said the marriage was all but finished except that it was politically expedient.'

He grinned. 'It is.' He stubbed out his cigarette. 'That's why I need you. You're clever, beautiful and ask nothing of me ... and you are great in bed.'

'Not sure about the first three, or even the last ...' She ran her hand along his chest.

'But you are.' He kissed her. 'That's another thing she just doesn't understand.'

Her hand slipped lower. 'Really?'

'We haven't had sex in years.'

Lucy couldn't imagine that. 'Poor you.'

'I know.' He nuzzled her. 'Pity me. I'm neglected by my wife, who doesn't love me.'

'*I* don't love you.'

'But you at least want me.'

Lucy kissed him and showed him that was true.

❊ Three ❊
Hebe

26 September 2016

The waiting room was empty. Hebe crossed her ankles, then uncrossed them. She checked that she had her notebook in her handbag, then settled the bag beside her feet and crossed her ankles again. Pulling at the hem on her dress so that it reached her knees, she saw *Country Life* on the table beside her. She picked it up and flipped through the pages, looking at the properties. Her hand stilled. Helwyn House. She ran her fingers down the page. For sale by auction. The north front with its distinctive loggia stared at her. She knew it so well. Desire. She looked up. The receptionist wasn't there. She ripped the page out of the magazine and slipped it into her bag.

'Dr Courtenay, Mr Phelps will see you now.'

She stood and straightened her dress. This wasn't going to be fun even if she wanted to pretend otherwise. As she entered the room, the consultant was standing by the window. He turned and smiled. Was that a good sign?

'Take a seat.' He came back to his desk and she wished he would sit down too, but he walked back to the window holding a clutch of papers. This wasn't OK. Some things had gone already, but her ability to read body language hadn't disappeared.

'Your test results show a marked deterioration.'

Hebe pulled her notebook out and wrote down *deterioration*.

'I know this doesn't surprise you, since you mentioned you had felt it yourself.'

She nodded.

15

'We've spoken in the past about your plans as the disease progresses.'

She wrote down *disease progresses*.

'What care arrangements do you have in place?'

Looking up at him, she frowned. Surely they were not at that stage yet.

'You never bring anyone with you and yet I recommended this right from our first appointment.'

'I don't want to.'

He cleared his throat. 'Hebe, this shows clearly that your decision-making process is impaired and has been for some time.'

She flattened her lips.

'You will need help.'

She let the words sink in as she wrote it down. *Need help*.

'If not today, then in the very near future.' He came back to the desk and sat down. 'Promise me you will bring someone to your next appointment?'

She nodded and continued to write down everything he said, but she wasn't thinking about it. Helwyn House was being auctioned in a few days' time. She would buy it. There were things she needed to do.

'Hebe, have you written down what I said?'

She looked down at her notebook.

Buy Helwyn House.

'Yes.'

'Good.' He pushed some papers across the desk. 'As you can see, there has been a marked decline in the cognitive area.'

The lines went down sharply. She had felt this. 'How long?'

'How long what?'

'How long until I don't know who I am, let alone anyone else.'

He raised his hands. 'If we look at the time since your first appointment ...' He pointed to the starting point on the graph. 'If your ability declines at that rate, you may have six months of good cognitive ability, but it might not even be that long.'

Hebe looked at her notebook.

Buy Helwyn House.

'You have been in decline for years.'

'Years? How many?'

'At a guess, based on where you are now, ten. But you have developed coping mechanisms. Those will begin to fail. You need support.'

'Yes, thank you.'

'Your next appointment is in a month.' He tapped the papers so they all came together and slipped them into a file, then closed it.

'Yes.'

'Please remember to bring someone with you.' He stood. 'This is important, Hebe.'

'I know.' She smiled. 'Thank you.'

Walking out of the door, she stopped at the receptionist's desk. Lying on the table beside the chair was the magazine she'd torn the page from. She knew what she was going to do.

'Can I help you, Dr Courtenay?'

'Yes, I can't make my appointment next month. Can you cancel it and I'll give you a call when I have my diary with me.'

'Certainly. Should I ring to remind you?'

Hebe's mouth flirted with a smile. 'No, I've written myself a note. Thanks.' She strode out of the door, down the steps and into the September sunshine, trying to remember what was next on her list of things to do today.

Hebe looked at her wrist. Her watch wasn't there and she couldn't remember where she'd left it. She didn't know this restaurant, with its white tablecloths and flickering candles. The chair opposite her was empty. Rory. Was he late or was she early? Today was special but she couldn't recall why. It was the feast of St Colman Elo, Irish. But he wouldn't know that.

He'd made a fuss on the phone and he'd left three notes on Post-its stuck to the fridge, the door and the bathroom mirror. He'd also emailed. She guessed she must have forgotten to meet him last time. That would explain it.

He could arrive any minute. Pulling out her lipstick, she

reapplied it then checked her phone for messages. It was exactly seven o'clock. She was early. He wasn't late. She took her notebook out of the bag.

Doctor's appointment notes.

Deterioration.

Which she knew …

Prognosis bleak.

Why had she bothered going? Wouldn't it be better to live in ignorance? Though she wasn't ignorant; she had been in … in something. The word would come later, much later when she didn't know why she'd wanted it in the first place. Denial. That was it. She must do something but wasn't sure what. The picture of the end she faced was so bleak she was glad she wouldn't be aware it was happening. But what of the others who would witness it?

She closed the notebook and put it back in her bag. In there she found a folded page from *Country Life*. The last time she'd read the magazine was when her sister was the frontispiece thirty years ago … or was it less, or maybe more? She closed her eyes, trying to remember her sister's name, but at this moment it was gone, just out of reach like so much else.

Laying the page flat, she pressed the creases out. The loggia. There was only one house with that architecture in Cornwall. Helwyn House, Thomas Grylls's home. He was a lover, a hero, a royalist, a model Cavalier.

Her phone lit up announcing a message.

On my way. X

That was good. She would hate to have to leave the restaurant without eating. That was what they were for after all. Glancing at the paper again, she traced it with her fingers. She knew the details so well. She had written so much about this house and visited it many times trying to capture it in words … those elusive things, and more so now than ever before. Before, they had been friends and tools. Now they were things to lose and stumble over.

Helwyn House to be auctioned on 30 September 2016.

She should buy it. Then she could take the portrait of Thomas

Grylls and return it to where it belonged. That would be perfect, in fact the perfect end. Almost as good as her mother's. Cornwall.

Looking up, she noted a handsome man chatting with the maître d'. He was holding flowers. Red roses. She knew him. She frowned. Today was the twenty-sixth of September. Tucking a stray hair behind her ear, she wondered whether there was something special about that date. The notes, the flowers, they meant something. Did she have time to pull out her diary? That would tell her the significance of the day ... but he was already walking towards her with a smile. Rory. Her heart raced.

'Hebe.' He kissed her, then presented her with the bouquet. 'Happy anniversary, darling.'

She blinked and a memory ran swiftly, too swiftly, through her mind. It was gone before she could capture it. She coughed, willing her brain to give up on its game of hiding key facts from her.

They had been together for a while. But she had no idea how long this handsome man opposite her had been her lover. The waiter came over with a bottle of Prosecco. She jumped when the cork popped; her mind had wandered to Rory's neat hands. Linen shirt, blue. Jacket, tan.

She looked down at her own hands. There was an age spot just south of her ring finger knuckle, but she wore no rings.

'How did it go today?' He studied her.

'Boring.' She smiled and raised her glass to him. 'Happy anniversary.'

'Yes, cheers.' Their glasses touched and another memory raced by and disappeared. She was becoming weary of chasing these fleeting things. Why wouldn't they stop?

'Your day?'

His phone flashed and she watched him read the words. Who was texting him? Her breath caught as jealousy soured the wine in her mouth.

'Nothing new, just another round of first years and a meeting with a promising student in her final year.'

She sat up straight. Why did that off-hand comment niggle?

His attention returned to her. 'You start tomorrow, yes?'

She swallowed. Did she? She hadn't taught today, from what she could remember. She nodded and took another sip. Maybe the bubbles would clear the clouds in her mind.

'What do you want to eat?' He reached across the table and touched her hand. 'You haven't been eating much lately.'

This was true. If he wasn't with her she didn't bother, and of late he hadn't been with her much. Her clothes were all too loose. 'You choose for me.' She smiled.

'Fine.' He let out a long breath.

Was he cross? It didn't matter. The wine was going to her head. She wasn't sure if she had eaten today. Moving her foot under the table, she rubbed his ankle. He looked up. There were crows' feet around his eyes. She didn't remember them, but she itched to touch them.

'Not tonight, of course, but I was wondering if you could have a read through my latest paper before I submit it?' He smiled at her.

She looked down. Why not tonight? Of course. It was their anniversary. They would eat dinner, go to his and have sex. No time for reading.

❊ Four ❊
Lucy

27 September 2016

The phone on the bedside table beeped. Lucy opened her eyes. Ed stirred and reached for it.

'Shit. She's on her way back.' He sat up and pushed the hair out of his eyes.

'Great.' She frowned as she watched his glance dart about the room. The empty wine bottles were on the chest of drawers but the glasses were nowhere in sight. It had been quite a night. It was still a few hours before he was due in Parliament and it would take Sheila some time to reach London from Surrey. She stretched and ran her fingers down his spine.

'You'd better leave.' Ed looked at his phone again.

She stopped. There was a note in his voice that was new. Impatience. 'Is something wrong?'

He turned to her with a smile. 'Nothing.'

Lucy climbed out of bed and collected her clothes on the way to the bathroom. He was lying. She was positive. Maybe it was the smile. After dressing, she did her best to repair her face. The dark smudges of yesterday's mascara wouldn't shift, so she grabbed a bit of loo roll and wetted it. When she opened the bin to drop it in, there lying on top was a pregnancy test. She stood, staring at it, trying to register what it meant.

Returning to the bedroom, she wanted to scream at him, but he was now on the phone. So much for a dead marriage. That positive test told her it was alive and kicking. Bastard. She cursed herself for believing his lies, then laughed, looking down at herself in yesterday's clothes. There was no sense in dwelling on it. What didn't kill you made you stronger.

She stormed off to the kitchen, where she'd dropped her bag last night. As if for the first time, she looked around, seeing what was actually there. The calendar on the fridge made sense. Those circled days weren't key debates in Parliament, but the days Sheila was ovulating. Bloody fool. Lucy didn't love him, so what did it matter? But it still hurt. She grabbed a stale croissant from the bread bin, then pulled out her phone and texted him.

It's over. Didn't anyone ever tell you not to lie? Congrats on the news of your wife's pregnancy.

Before she could leave the building, he was beside her. 'What are you doing?'

'I would think that was blatantly obvious. I'm leaving.'

'Don't say a word to anyone.'

Lucy stopped and stared at him, then began to laugh. Don't say a word to anyone? No one knew about this affair. No one except the two of them. She had been the ideal mistress, and the key to that was being totally and utterly stupid. She'd believed everything he'd said.

Turning away, she walked out to the lobby with Ed hot on her heels. She moved faster until she was out of the front door, where he grabbed her arm. She turned to him. 'You lying bastard.'

'You've got me wrong.'

'No I haven't. You're an asshole with a big sex drive and I'm an idiot for believing your lies.'

'No, the marriage is broken.'

As Lucy turned away, she clocked a stranger and the reporter for the *Daily Mail* who lived in the same building holding up their phones. Her stomach dropped. They were both recording the whole thing. She turned to Ed. 'You've just dug your own grave.' Walking away with her head held high, she said, 'Morning, Tom.'

'Morning, Lucy. Up to your old antics, I see.'

'Not quite.'

She flagged down a passing cab. Ed had fled back inside the

building. He was going to have a fine time explaining this to Sheila. Poor woman. Poor child. And what a bloody mess Lucy had landed herself in.

By the time the taxi reached Lucy's flat in Pimlico, there was a photographer waiting. Word had spread fast. No doubt the footage was online and would make the breakfast news. She clenched her jaw. This was not good. She tapped on the dividing glass. 'Change of plan. Can you take me to Cheyne Walk, please.'

'Sure.'

'Thanks.' Lucy sank back into the seat. She could only hope that reporters weren't camped out in front of her parents' house. It was now 7 a.m. She tried to repair her hair before arriving, hoping her mother might not assume the worst. She always looked for the positives even if there were none. Lucy's father was a case in point.

As the taxi neared the house, she saw a sole photographer leaning against a lamp post and her mother opening the door to pick up the paper. At least the affair wouldn't be in there. That joy would be saved for tomorrow morning, unless the world imploded. She had to hope that the *Telegraph* had something better than her name to splash across the front page, or her father would never let her forget it. Who was she kidding: he wouldn't let her forget it no matter what. She was a constant reminder to him of what an absolute shit he was. Some things could never be forgotten or forgiven.

'Keep driving and take the next left,' she said. The driver gave her a funny look as they went past the address she'd given him.

'Here will do.' She jumped out and paid before dashing through Mrs Hill's gate and into her garden. There was no light on in the kitchen, so no one would witness her unusual behaviour. Her father, Giles, would say that it was always questionable, but she would reply that she'd learned it from him. This time, though, she'd better think of something quickly. Explanations would be asked for, but they wouldn't make any difference. She knew her father asked only to see her squirm. But she'd refused to squirm for years.

As gracefully as she could in a pencil skirt, she climbed the back wall. She hoped no one was watching, because by the time she'd finished, her skirt was around her waist. Things were descending from bad to worse. Her mind raced but it wasn't getting anywhere without coffee. The aroma of a fresh brew came from her parents' kitchen. It would be just how her father liked it, and she could only hope he wouldn't be there waiting.

She slipped in through the open garden door. The television was on and Kate Trevillion, her mother, stood pressing down the cafetière and reading the paper. The cat jumped down and came to weave through Lucy's legs. Her mother looked up. Sadness deepened the lines round her eyes and the ones from her mouth to her chin. In that moment she looked not forty-nine but eighty-nine.

'Dear God, Lucia Anne Trevillion.' Her glance went to the television and back to Lucy. Then she reached into the cupboard for the white china cups that Lucy's father preferred. Lucy thought the plain old mugs did a far better job.

Scooping up the cat, Lucy nuzzled her nose into his ginger fur. He purred. At least someone was pleased to see her.

'A married man.' Kate set a cup and saucer down with a thud. 'Do you still take your coffee black, or has that changed along with becoming a home-wrecker?'

Ouch. Her mother wasn't putting a positive spin on this one. Lucy caught her own reflection in the glass of the French windows. She looked guilty. But at least she had dumped him before they had been caught. His marriage was broken, he'd said ... but now she knew differently. He was simply a typical man, a lying bastard. Her fingers clenched. She should have known better. She was an idiot and she didn't feel sorry for him. He was getting what he deserved for lying to her, though she felt terrible for poor Sheila.

'So how do you plan to get out of this mess?' Her mother sighed onto the surface of her coffee before leaning back against the spotless white counter. Unlike Lucy's, her coffee was laced with cream. The rich glossy surface rippled with her breath.

'I don't know.' In the taxi, Lucy had considered her options and hadn't found any that worked. She put the lack of choice down to the hangover and caffeine deprivation.

'Nothing new in that.' Kate pursed her lips.

Lucy stared back at her mother. Kate was loyal, blind to her husband's serial infidelity. Maybe Lucy was more like her father. Her mouth twisted into a scowl. That was nothing to be proud of, but given the choice, she would rather be like him than the saintly doormat her mother was.

'By the look of you, you haven't been home.'

'No.' That sounded like an admission of guilt. 'Look, Mum, it's not what it seems.' As soon as the words were out of her mouth she regretted them.

In the corner of the room, her father's parakeet plucked out a feather, which fell to the bottom of the cage. The cat circled below. Kate tapped the bars and the bird looked at her with blank eyes.

'It never is with you.'

'Mum ...' Lucy's phone rang. It was Samantha, her agent. 'I have to take this.' She walked into the dining room but kept away from the front windows.

'What the hell were you thinking?' Samantha asked.

'I don't know.' Running her finger along the gleaming surface of the table, Lucy pictured the years of elbow grease that had created that sheen and protected the wood's beautiful surface.

'Where are you?' Samantha's voice was quiet, which Lucy knew from the nine years they had been working together meant that things were bad. She paced the room, then stopped dead when she heard a key in the front door. Her day was about to get worse. Her father was back. Then the landline rang. She could hear her mother's voice rising in tone.

'I'm at my parents'.' She rubbed her temples.

'You're an idiot.'

'I know.' She picked up a bowl from the sideboard. It was a delicate thing of bone china covered in spring flowers. It had belonged to her great-grandmother. It looked so fragile, but here it was without a chip or hairline fracture some two hundred years after it had been fired.

'We've already had two cancellations and it's not nine o'clock yet.'

Lucy winced. 'Ouch.'

'There will be more.'

'I know.' Lucy pressed her lips together, thinking what a fool she'd been.

'Will you make a statement?'

She frowned. Face the press? 'Not sure.'

Samantha sighed. 'Why did you do it when you could have had any man? It's not even as if Ed is good-looking.' She paused. 'Earnest, I'll give you.'

Lucy's mouth twisted into a half-smile. 'It's best not to comment.'

'You know what this means, don't you?'

Lucy drew in a deep breath, then forced herself to speak. 'Yes.'

'I hate to do it. You're brilliant, but this isn't going to work.'

'I know.' She bit her lip. 'Sorry.'

'Next time, think. No man is worth risking your career for, believe me.'

'True.' An awkward laugh died on Lucy's lips. 'Should have thought of that sooner.' She rolled her eyes.

Samantha sighed. 'Talk later.'

'Yes.' But both of them knew it would be a long time before anyone would consider using Lucy again. She was tainted goods.

She hesitated in the hallway, listening to her father's voice. Escape through the front door was impossible, and now the back door was blocked too. She would have to face the music sooner rather than later – which was her preferred option.

Walking into the kitchen, she saw her mother step away from her father and put down her coffee cup. 'I thought you would have grown up by now.'

'You've had enough time to do so.' He was a fine one to talk. Clearly he'd seen the early news and come to discuss the situation. She stared at them both. They hadn't a clue. Unable to see what their dysfunctional life looked like from the outside. Maybe she should have photographed it for them so they would have no choice.

The phone rang again and Kate answered, walking out of the room as she spoke.

Shaking his head, her father said, 'And really, a Labour minister, what were you thinking? The best you can hope for at this moment is a war, otherwise I'd say you'll be a top news item for days.' He glanced back down at the paper, then turned the page. Lucy glared at him. No one deserved to die for her sexual misdemeanours. She wasn't that needy; in fact she wasn't needy at all, which was why she had turned to a lover who offered only limited access.

Her father seemed to work on the same premise, though occasionally he appeared in the middle of the family he had created. Pontificating was his speciality. Lucy had ceased answering back long ago. It was a waste of her breath and time. Speaking of time, she glanced at her phone. A text from Ed appeared.

Call me asap.

She walked into the utility room, leaving her father in full flow. She debated whether to reply to Ed or not. Nothing she could say would help.

I don't think that's wise, she texted.

It was seconds before the reply arrived.

Bugger wise.

She laughed. He was good at making her laugh. She would miss that.

If you must.

She waited for the response.

I need you.

Lucy held her breath. Everything inside her was curled into a tight ball. She tapped in her reply with more force than was needed.

No you don't. You need to apologise to your wife, then the public. Eat humble pie. Save your marriage and your career. Think of your child. Think of someone other than yourself. You do not need me.

She didn't write that he was a lying toad. Maybe she should have.

I do.

She looked at the neatly lined-up shirts hanging on the rail. Why was her mother still with her father? Was she nothing more than a laundry service? She shuddered. As beautiful and kind as her mother was, Lucy would never become like her.

Her phone beeped again. She replied.

You want me. You do not need me.

The laundry room was pristine. Not an odd sock in sight.

I love you.

She closed her eyes. Ha. Love. Bet he said the same thing to Sheila.

Enough. Goodbye.

She shut off her phone. What was that about? She and Ed had been about sex and conversation but never about love. Love buggered everything, to use Ed's expression. It made the world unbalanced, unfair even. Love made prisons, even if they were comfortable ones. The neatly starched shirts flicked in a gust of air. The front door had opened again. Leaning against the wall, Lucy took several deep breaths, thinking about his wife and the positive pregnancy test. At least that was something she'd never have to worry about. Her body had made sure of that.

It had been quite a morning so far, but things couldn't get any worse. She stood up straight and walked back into the kitchen, searching her mind for a plan.

❈ Five ❈
Hebe

June 2015

The Milky Way fills the sky above us as we walk from the pub. Once out of sight of the village, I tuck my arm through yours. Soon we are in darkness and you reach for the torch in your pocket.

'Don't.' I touch your hand. 'The stars will be dimmed by it.'

You pull me close and our pace slows as we look heavenward. 'There are so many stars.'

I nod and rest my head on your shoulder, looking up. You point, and we both hold our breath as a star shoots across the sky.

'*Go and catch a falling star,*' you begin.

'*Get with child a mandrake root ...*' I pause.

'*Tell me where all the past years are.*' Your voice rumbles in my heart. I catch my breath and can't remember the next line. Where *are* the past years?

'*Or who cleft the Devil's foot.*' You chuckle, and it reassures me. 'I love the imagery.'

'Yes.' Donne captures ... captures the unexplainable, making it clear ... somehow. I should know that. I should know many things, but right now I can only think of you and your warmth beside me. I must hold onto the here and now and not worry about the past or the future. Live. That's what I should do for now.

'Did you make a wish?' you ask, scanning the dark mass above.

I laugh, trying to remember why I would make a wish.

Looking up at the swathe of stars, I remember the shooting star. 'Yes, that I were at least twenty years younger.'

'You wouldn't be you if you were younger.'

I frown. 'I was still me twenty years ago.'

'But the things that have happened in those twenty years have made you into the woman I love.' You pull me closer. 'Look, there's another shooting star.'

My heart sinks. I do not believe in wishes or even prayers. It is too late for all of that.

'I made another wish.'

I take a deep breath. So did I, but I cannot tell you. I wished for you to find love, love from someone worthy of you.

We walk along the lane in silence until the cottage comes into view. I was wrong to have let you into my life all those years ago. At first I was worried about my job if someone found out. But now I know that what I have done is far worse. Having an affair with you is stopping you from living. But am I strong enough to let you go?

'Thanks for your notes on the article.' You kiss my hair as you unlock the door. 'They made perfect sense, and you are right, of course. Donne's use of love in the poem is multi-layered, even ambiguous, but I hadn't looked at it in that way before.'

I frown, trying to remember what I said or even what poem we were discussing. You stare at me, expecting a response, and I turn away.

'You know, even after all this time, I still struggle to accept that God and the devil were so present in people's lives. I remember how you tried to immerse us in the reality of that fact.'

'Yes.' I take a deep breath. That I can remember. Those facts have not disappeared. God and the devil were in almost every breath they took and every word they uttered. Devil. Your eyes are smiling.

'*Love, any devil else but you,*' you say.

'*Would for a given soul give something too.*' My heart trips, thinking of when we crossed the line. I close my eyes and I am back in my flat in London, opening the door and trying not to stare.

You stood with a bottle of wine in your hand.

'I wanted to say thank you.'

I frowned, still keeping the door partially closed, half hiding me from you. But I saw all of you, especially your bright eyes inviting me to say yes. The question wasn't spoken, but it was there on your lips. I hesitated. 'For what?'

'The extension on this week's assignment.' You held out the bottle, wrapped in white tissue.

'Not necessary. The research material you needed wasn't available until next week.'

'You didn't have to.' Turning your head, you revealed a strong profile with defined chin and straight nose. My neighbour looked at you appraisingly as she headed for the stairs. Her glance accused me, but I'm not sure of what. We were just assessing each other.

I swallowed, then pulled the door open, revealing my jeans and man's white dress shirt. Your glance missed nothing. I was so different here from in the classroom, where I wore my uniform of wrap dress and modest heels.

'I wondered if I might ask you a few questions that we didn't have time for earlier,' you said, stepping across the threshold, holding the bottle out to me. If I accepted it, things would change. It was seven o'clock on a warm evening. I took the bottle. I was forty-four and I should have known better. But I was about to take a lover less than half my age, a boy who looked exactly like the one in the portrait hanging above my bed.

By our first strange and fatal interview,
By all desire which thereof did ensue.

*

I wake. Panic. Lists. What must be done? Where am I? Dawn. Birds. You. I sigh and roll closer, staring at the beams on the ceiling. My mind chases round and round. I must finish the book but I don't know how. You. I must leave you and I must

31

leave work. But then what? I will be alone. My breathing slows and panic subsides. Alone is good.

Crawling out of bed, I try not to disturb you, but then smile at myself. Nothing wakes you, not even your alarm most of the time. Throwing your sweater over my nightgown, I walk to the kitchen and pull out my notebook. The doctor said lists would help. I knew they wouldn't hurt.

Write outline for last Thomas Grylls book, then begin research.

I stand then go and put the kettle on before I flip the note-book over. You mustn't see what I am writing. Somehow I have kept that secret from you just as I have kept you as my secret. I turn my notes over again once I've made my coffee. Underlining *Thomas*, I think of the portrait. I miss it. The final book is something I must finish while I'm still able. But of course I'm missing something ... I tap the pencil on the paper, hoping the repeated activity will let my mind catch up and remember what it is. Nothing.

I sip the coffee, dark and bitter. I don't know what happened to Thomas after the restoration of Charles II. Despite my research, this has remained a mystery. My temples throb at the thought. It isn't a secret. No one is withholding the information from me. It is lost and probably never to be found. I will have to trust myself and make up the end. Isn't that the joy of writing fiction? I can write the end the way I want it to happen. I am God in the world I have created and I only have to abide by the historical fact where it is known.

I hear footsteps and turn over the notes. You appear shirtless and barefoot. Lost, not quite awake. You hold out a hand and I can't resist.

'Come back to bed. It's too early.'

I smile, taking your hand. 'The birds are up.'

'Good for them, but I want you beside me.'

We fall under the still warm duvet and you mumble Donne's words. '*Dear love, for nothing less than thee, would I have broke this happy dream.*' Your need for me is more awake than you are.

And as you settle back into sleep, I recall the final lines of 'The Dream'.

Thou cam'st to kindle, goest to come; then I
Will dream that hope again, but else would die.

The sea stretches before us and the sun is beginning its descent.
It was your idea to come and watch the sunset on the longest
day of the year. You mentioned holding onto every moment. I
study your profile and wonder if you know.

'The landscape is so stunning, yet so industrial.' You point
to an engine house in the distance. I nod, looking down to
the waves crashing below. Deep in the earth, the minerals still
linger. Their rising and falling value shaped Cornwall and her
people. The Grylls family owned mines here on the north coast,
yet their home, Helwyn, was in the gentle valleys of the east.

You pour mint tea from the thermos. The steam rises in the
evening air. Because of my sleeplessness, you have taken me off
caffeine after ten in the morning. You have seen the changes
in me. Although my body isn't showing it, the signs that my
brain is ageing appear by the hour. I feel it. A few moments
ago, you were talking about Cadgwith and our visit there. I
looked at you blankly, I know I did. My face coloured when
you mentioned mermaids. Only then did yesterday come back
to me.

*

Teach me to hear mermaids singing
Or to keep off envy's stinging
And find
What wind
Serves to advance an honest mind.

Her eyes followed you to the bar. I knew what she was thinking. She saw your beauty and wondered why you were with me.
I wondered the same. Yet you returned with my wine and your
pint and you didn't see her, only me. I still couldn't believe that
this was happening. I couldn't trust my own thoughts, because
when you weren't with me, I lived with fear embedded in the
pit of my belly. Looking at her, I envied her youth, her beauty.

Wiping the tears from my cheek, you say, 'The beauty of the sunset makes you cry?'

The corners of my mouth lift. I wish it were so simple and I could tell you the truth, but what scares me most is that if I did tell you, would I remember it tomorrow?

I open my eyes and I'm on the ground. As I focus, I see you running towards me. Your face is white. My head hurts. I reach up and touch my temple. Blood covers my fingers.

'Are you OK?' Your glance tries to encompass all of me.

I shift.

'Don't move.'

I frown. 'Why not?'

'You might have broken something.'

I shake my head and it throbs. I close my eyes again. I don't know how or why I'm here on the ground.

'I tripped,' I say. I glance at you, then look away so that you can't see I'm lying.

'Does anything hurt?' You brush my hair out of my eyes.

'My head.' Behind you flowers are blooming and I can smell their fragrance but can't recall their name. You give me a lop-sided smile and my heart tilts.

'I can see that,' you say. Taking my hand, you help me up, then lead me into the cottage. You sit me down, then you clean the cut, kiss my head and hand me a glass of water. Our roles have reversed. A chill covers my skin despite the bright sunshine streaming through the window.

'Yesterday you mentioned going to Pendennis Castle.'

I take a deep breath. I might well have done so, but right now I struggle to remember where Pendennis Castle is. Something inside me stirs. Thomas Grylls. The Prince of Wales. My shoulders slide down to a more comfortable position. 'Yes. Interesting.'

'Yes, you wrote extensively about it.'

My head flicks up. How do you know?

'Several chapters in your book on Cornwall and the Civil War.' You put the kettle on. 'Have you thought about updating it and producing a new edition?'

I open my mouth. How can I? I've thought about it, but I'm having enough trouble writing articles, let alone tackling a book. You watch me as you hand me a cup of tea. It is milky and sweet. It tastes odd. I don't take sugar. My mouth puckers.

'I felt you needed a little energy. You're looking pale.'

'Am I?'

'Yes, you haven't been yourself.'

'No?' My stomach turns.

'I think you haven't been yourself for a bit.' You blow on the surface of your own tea, frowning. I hold my breath. 'Not since April.'

'April?'

'Yes, when you came back from your cousin's funeral.'

I draw in a deep breath. My cousin. She was thirty-nine. Tragic. Alzheimer's. Early onset. Genetic. I stand, spilling my tea.

'Yes, I caught a virus while I was there. Maybe I haven't shaken it.'

Your eyes narrow. I don't like the way you are looking at me, assessing me. I have assessed you many times, but you have always just loved me. A sob escapes me and I dash to the loo and lock the door. As I lean against it, I can hear you waiting on the other side. I am lucky, I tell myself. It has waited until I'm over fifty to manifest in me.

'Hebe?' Your voice is pleading. I must resist until I can control my emotions. The consultant said this might be harder as the disease progresses. He couldn't tell me how long, only that with my family history I have done well. *Well.* It is a slippery word.

'Hebe?'

'Yes.'

'Are you OK?'

No. I am far from OK. 'Yes, fine. I'll be out in a moment.'

❖ Six ❖

Hebe

27 September 2016

The bell of St Mary-le-Bow chimed the hour, and the words of John Donne floated through Hebe's mind as if they were being whispered to her.

No man is an island, entire of itself...

She thought of Cornwall. Cut off yet part of the whole.

... every man is a piece of the continent, a part of the main.

Were we all really connected? Couldn't she disconnect, step away?

Any man's death diminishes me, because I am involved in mankind. And therefore never send to know for whom the bell tolls; it tolls for thee.

It was three in the morning. Sound carried further in the darkest moments of the night. Everything was amplified, most especially fears. Hebe had taken to recording everything in detail, as well as attempting crossword puzzles to keep her brain working. But neither activity had helped her hold on to words. They were leaving her in droves, and nothing seemed to stem the tide.

> *The feast of St Mark, martyr of Antioch*
> *I spent much of the day in the library, avoiding*
> *colleagues. I printed out my notes for tomorrow's*
> *lessons. Today went badly and I lost my place too*
> *frequently ... something to do with TIA, transient*
> *ischaemic attack. It sounds like something from out of*
> *space, not from within my body. The stroke and TIAs are*
> *all signs of*

She hesitated; she would not write that down.

I can't ignore this any more. I forget your name and your face when you're not with me. What happens if I do this when you are beside me? I'm scared.

She had delivered her notice of immediate resignation to the chair of the history department yesterday, or she thought it was yesterday. Reaching into her bag, she searched for the printout she had made, but instead her hand fell on the page she had torn out of *Country Life*. Helwyn House was to be auctioned on Friday. A smile spread across her face as a plan began to develop. She had wanted this house for as long as she could remember. Now it could be hers. There was no time to waste.

She sighed and looked at the bed where her lover turned in his sleep. They had celebrated ten years together yesterday. The duvet slipped down, revealing his naked form. The night was muggy. She closed her eyes as an image from the past, her past, came to her – his chest the first time she had touched it. No hair had marked its surface. He had been young then, so very young.

Rolling her shoulders, she flipped back a few pages in her journal. Whatever it was that she was seeking, she couldn't find it. Turning back to what she'd written, she knew with her whole being that she must protect him from what lay ahead. She owed him that and so much more.

Opening the desk drawer, she found a sheet of paper and an envelope. She would write to him to explain her actions. The pen hovered over the page. What should she say; what *could* she say? She pulled out another sheet. On the first she would write everything in her heart, then on the other she would write what needed to be said.

Her pen at last moved swiftly across the page, not hesitating as everything poured out of her. Things she'd never had the courage to utter were now set down in bright blue ink. She blew on the paper to dry the marks of her own tears. The bells announced four in morning. She folded that sheet and began the second.

I am leaving. This is for the best. Where I am going, you cannot follow. Do not try. If you love me as you say you do, then please just let me go. We've had ten good years. Hold onto that and then step forward to something new.

Hx

She placed the note into the envelope and propped it on his desk, then slipped the other sheet into her handbag and switched off the lamp. Dawn would soon come, and not long after that she would leave, but for now she couldn't face the darkness on her own. Her lover slept on. With a sense of watching the whole thing as if she weren't really there – and recently she often wondered if she was – she crawled back into bed beside him for the last time. Her hand moved across his abdomen, pulling him into her arms. He murmured, 'Come, madam, come,' and nestled close to her. Words. Troublesome things. He should have walked out last night when she'd called him Thomas. It would have made what was ahead easier.

Hebe opened her eyes and pulled her hand out from under the warm body beside her. She had pins and needles. In the dim light, she looked at her hand as she shook it to bring it back to life. He groaned and turned over. Where was she? This wasn't her bedroom. Closing her eyes, she tried to find what she was looking for, but nothing was there. Nothing familiar except the man next to her. She loved him. Everything in her called out to him. Her heart was full of him – from the contours of his arms to the way the shadows carved his features. She must remember his face.

Getting out of bed carefully so as not to wake him, she saw the note. Yes, that was what she was doing. He would forget her quickly, she hoped. But she wouldn't worry about that now. Picking up her knickers, she put them on. Her dress was over by the bookcase. She slipped it over her head and only then found her bra on top of a chair. She shoved it in her bag, then pulled out her lipstick. If he woke, she wanted to make sure that his last glimpse of her was when she looked her best.

Moving the note so he couldn't miss it, she prayed that would be enough. It had to be. It was best this way, a clean break. How could things ever have ended any differently? She'd been foolish even to dream that they could.

She scanned the room to be sure there was nothing left of hers. Her glance fell on the bedside table, where a copy of Donne's *Elegies* sat. She had given it to him years ago. As she picked it up, it fell open to Elegy V.

Here take my picture; though I bid farewell
Thine, in my heart, where my soul dwells, shall dwell.
'Tis like me now, but I dead, 'twill be more
When we are shadows both, than 'twas before.

Her mouth lifted into a smile as she touched his pencil marks in the margin. He had become a great scholar of Elizabethan literature. Now he read Donne for pleasure, and for her. And there was such pleasure to be had in the words. She plucked out the photo of them together, then glanced at the inscription on the back.

To my heart's desire xx

She closed the book, then slipped it and the photo into her bag. This was the right thing to do. It would save him.

✳ Seven ✳
Lucy

29 September 2016

Her brother Michael was leaning against the counter and as much as Lucy loved him, the last thing she needed was a little-brother intervention. Or a family one, for that matter.

'I know you're an attention-seeking cow, but this is a step too far.' He crossed his arms. No welcoming hug. So that was the way it was going to be. Full-on tear Lucy to shreds.

'Lovely to see you too, and I'm surviving, thanks. Oh, and happy birthday.' She and her brother were, in her mind rather unimaginatively, named after the saints' days they were born on – or more correctly, in Michael's case, the avenging angel.

'You're a selfish bitch.'

'Michael, that's a bit harsh.' Their mother looked up from the napkins she was folding with precision.

Her father closed his paper and laid it on the table. 'Not harsh enough. She's twenty-eight. It's time to grow up.'

Lucy looked at the three of them. They were her immediate family, yet they couldn't see past the headlines to think of her. She shouldn't be surprised, but it would have been nice to have their support in some way.

'I'm not sure what we can do about this situation you've got yourself into, but whatever happens, you must not speak to the press.' Giles stood.

Lucy pressed her lips together. It took everything in her not to walk out of the door and give an impromptu interview. Her father had that effect on her. She glanced at the door.

'Don't even think about it.' Michael moved to block her exit.

Wasn't it best to come clean, say sorry and move on? 'Look, it's my life.'

'It is, but you have ruined one family and you're not going to do any more damage to ours.' Her father's chest puffed out; his over-starched shirt had creases about the waist that reminded her of a paper fan. 'And don't tell me I have no say. It's not just you that you've taken down this time.' His smile was more of a grimace.

She opened her mouth and shut it, then sat down on the nearest chair waiting to hear what else her dear family had to say. Even if she had to listen to it, it didn't mean she had to act on it.

Having retreated into her study for ages, her mother entered the room clutching a piece of paper. 'Fate may have smiled on you.'

Lucy raised an eyebrow. There was no question: luck had not smiled on her; rather it had spat or possibly even shat on her. The only good thing about today was the gin in her hand.

'I've just spoken with your aunt.'

Lucy smiled. Her beloved Hebe would not get her knickers in a twist about this or anything. She ruled her world without fuss. That world seemed to consist almost entirely of books and a few students. Maybe that was the way forward. Not academia, but possibly a convent. The corners of Lucy's mouth lifted as she envisioned a remastered scene from *The Sound of Music*, with her family wondering how to solve a problem like Lucy. She was sure it was a chorus that her parents knew well.

'She's in Cornwall and is about to bid on Helwyn House. Utter madness.'

'It's for sale?' A shiver ran down Lucy's spine. Cornwall and that house.

'Apparently so. Michael suggested that you go down there.'

'Of course he did.' She snorted. Bastard.

Kate shook her head. 'I'm not sure why my sister thinks she can afford to buy the place, let alone cover the costs that come with a property that size.'

'She's lived a frugal life.' Giles stood and walked towards his

41

wife. He dropped a kiss on the top of her head, and she smiled up at him. Lucy stifled her gag reflex. What was all this lovey-dovey stuff? Had her own crisis brought them closer? If that was the case, then she would rue this day forever. Long gone was the time when she wished for them to be normal parents.

'Not *that* frugal, plus think of the several hundred thousand that will be required to bring it up to date, let alone restore it.' Kate straightened her back.

Lucy blinked. 'What on earth does this have to do with me?'

'I have booked you on the first train to Truro tomorrow morning. You should arrive in time for the auction, so you can stop your aunt.' Kate looked at her with that 'you will do as you are told or else' look. Since Lucy had turned seventeen, she'd ignored that look every time she saw it.

'What?'

'That way you will be out of London and this wretched mess you're in will quieten down.'

'Not Cornwall.' Dear God, anywhere but there. She stared pointedly at her father.

'You will go to Cornwall and help your aunt. You can't cause a scandal there, or if you did, no one would notice.' He took a breath, and the words '*you* did' died on her lips as he continued. 'Do something unselfish for once.' He was a fine one to talk.

But her fate was sealed. It was six in the evening. She had no work and her picture was in every paper. Cornwall it was then.

'Your aunt needs you.' Kate fixed her gaze on Lucy. She knew Lucy wouldn't say no; she would do anything for Hebe. 'I've put some of your old things on your bed. You will climb over Mrs Hill's wall in the morning and there will be a car waiting to take you to the station.' She sighed, the special sigh she reserved for moments of great disappointment. Lucy had heard many of them since she'd failed her A levels spectacularly.

'I can't believe you've done this to us again.' Giles put an arm around Kate's shoulders, uniting them as a team. Lucy wondered how long that would last as she knocked back her gin then went upstairs to her old bedroom. Cornwall. Helwyn House. Hell.

✤ Eight ✤
Hebe

July 2015

The beaches are full of holidaymakers, dividing the sand with their brightly coloured windbreaks and strange little tents. Schools are out for the summer. Our days of having this part of Cornwall to ourselves are over. I miss the isolation and I see people's reaction to us. Even now, when I no longer need to hide you, I do. I cling to that. If people don't know, then you are safe. We weave through the happy families to find a spot on the sand.

You spread a blanket while I stare at the water. Children frolic in the rock pools and a vision of my own childhood appears in my mind. I remember holding Kate by the hand as we scampered over the rocks at Dollar Cove. She was probably five. Such a beautiful child, and so clever. Much like Lucy. I shiver. I haven't seen much of Lucy recently. Kate tells me she is wrapped up in her work and, she suspects, some unsuitable man. I sigh. So much promise, so recklessly thrown away.

'Are you OK?' You slip an arm around my shoulder. I nod and settle onto the blanket. You watch me closely and I know I must try harder if I want us to continue. Some things are still within my power.

The heat of the sun soon makes us both sleepy. Your book falls to your chest and I watch it rise and fall. I have done this many times, though rarely in public. But here, far from the world that knows me and knows you, we are safe. My eyelids close and I let the heat seduce me with thoughts of you and memories of our past.

43

Twice or thrice had I loved thee,
Before I knew thy face or name.

A bottle of wine stood empty, and so did another. You were sound asleep in my bed as I stood and put on a robe. I looked from the portrait to you and back again. The resemblance was uncanny. Had I somehow created you, as if by magic; was some ancient alchemy at work to bring you from my mind and into flesh? And what flesh.

Last night was wrong, so very wrong. But desire filled me. Had I decided to let you in, or had you cast a spell over me? Were you real? Your chest rose and fell. You were perfect. If I'd created you then I should cherish you. But you weren't from my imagination – and you didn't need an affair with an old woman. What had I been thinking? I paced the room but my glance kept returning to you.

I went to my desk and turned on the light. Picking up my notebook and pen, I angled the chair so that I saw both you and the portrait. What poem had you quoted last night? Donne's 'The Triple Fool':

I am two fools, I know,
For loving, and for saying so.

My mouth lifted and I wrote down the lines. They were so powerful, so expressive. Love equalled vulnerability. I would not tread that path. Reaching across the desk, I pulled out my much-thumbed collection of Donne's work and read the poem in full.

And I, which was two fools, do so grow three;
Who are a little wise, the best fools be.

But I was such a fool because I could lose everything because of you.

A shadow crosses the sun and I wake from the bliss of the past. Clouds have begun to populate the sky above us. Putting my straw hat over your head to protect you, I know I must act. You are working towards something big, something you are thrilled about. Television. I am terrified, though. If it happens – and I'm sure it will – then we must part. I can hold you back no longer, but I need to find the strength to let you go.

The road twists and I am lost in the scenery and my thoughts. Every time I turn to you, I want to blurt out what I know, but I hold back. The less I tell you, the better things will be. I must live for now and try to remember before all is lost.

You park the car and Falmouth bustles around us. How this place has changed in the years since I first came here, digging to find out more about Thomas Grylls. In front of us is the Maritime Museum, and beyond that the great harbour.

While you deal with the parking fee, I move away from the crowds. What if someone recognises one of us? You tell me I should no longer worry about these things. The days of anyone caring about us being together have long passed, but I still feel people's glances. I feel their disgust when you take my hand, or worse, I feel their pity. As you join me and we head into the museum, I recall our first public outing.

*

The spider Love, which transubstantiates all,
And can convert manna to gall;
And that this place may thoroughly be thought
True paradise, I have the serpent brought.

We were in Hyde Park on a summer's day, under a clear sky unsullied by clouds. The city sweltered. You were sleeping at my side. A book of Shakespeare's sonnets rested on your chest. I grinned. Here in the shade of a chestnut tree we were anonymous, like hundreds of other couples around us. It was risky being out in public together in London, but in weather this blistering we needed to escape.

I scanned the crowds, holding my breath for long stretches. Relaxing with you away from my flat was still impossible. You laughed at my fear. But you refused to understand how we appeared to others. You said it shouldn't matter what anyone thought. We were two adults, you said, but I looked at your chin. You hadn't shaved in two days and there was barely a shadow on it. Your body was lanky, a youth's, although it acted as a man's and pulled my passion from me.

Turning back to look at you, I watched the rise and fall of your chest. I doubted I could ever tire of the joy of you. As much as I knew I shouldn't be here with you, I couldn't help myself. Every time I was about to end this madness, you surprised me as you had this evening, arriving with a picnic in hand. With the logical part of my brain saying it was too risky to be seen out together, I was incapable of resisting the sparkling wine, cold chicken and strawberries, and you with a sprinkling of freckles across your cheeks. So here I was, half of me loving every second and the other half afraid. We took the risk. Life was short, you said. I frowned. It was months until your twentieth birthday. I would be forty-five in September. I had lived twice your life and a bit more. Yet as I looked at you, I thought I hadn't lived at all until this moment.

Maybe it was the danger. It made me feel more alive. I was taking more and more risks. Making decisions I never would have done in the past. You were one of them. Our relationship was wrong but it felt acceptable so long as it was secret. Yet here I was on a summer's evening lying next to you for the world to see. I hoped that everyone was too wrapped up in their own affairs to notice us ... to wonder what we were doing together, whether I was your mother.

At the base of the tree a small movement caught my glance. A spider was spinning a web. The silken thread was translucent in the low rays of the sun. It was such a beautiful trap. You rolled towards me, throwing your arm around me, and kissed me. I was caught.

'I love you,' you said, and kissed me again.

*

'Hebe?' You touch my arm. I turn from the display case. 'Have you heard a word I said?'

Do I lie or do I tell you the truth?

'Yes, of course.' I smile. 'Do you see the detail on that piece of ivory?'

'Yes.' You frown and I take your hand and pull you to the next display. I must focus on the now and hope that the memory will stay with me.

❊ Nine ❊
Lucy

30 September 2016

The view should have struck her as beautiful. With the logical part of her brain (and despite what anyone in her family thought, Lucy had a logical brain), she knew the scenery was lovely. The photographer in her captured the blue sky, bluer sea and Devon's red sands. But soon the train would cross the Tamar into Cornwall and it would become more difficult to breathe. Even now her throat was constricting, making air hard to come by. Panic.

Maybe her mother was wrong and her aunt wasn't about to do something stupid like buy a house. But of course, it wasn't just any house. Helwyn House, locally referred to as Hell House. How could Hebe even be thinking of doing this? But Lucy could see her attraction to it. It was old, really old, and Hebe was a historian. But it couldn't be much more than a ruin now. Lucy's family had been the last people to rent it, and that had been eleven years ago. Old houses needed people living in them. Hell House, once a place of happy families, had become a place of shadows and dark deeds and Hebe did not need to own it. No one did.

She sighed, remembering the first time she'd seen it. Hebe had been holding her hand. It was July, and the air had smelled of honeysuckle and the house of damp. It had cast a spell over her aunt that obviously hadn't gone away in the ensuing years. But being intrigued by it was one thing; wanting to buy it was another. Had Hebe lost her mind? Why spend money on something like Hell House when there were far lovelier properties for sale elsewhere? Also, how could she possibly pay for it?

Lucy looked at the details in the brochure Michael had pointedly printed off for her.

> Helwyn House is a historic home with its origins in the monastery of St Anthony, first founded circa 1100. At the dissolution of the monasteries the property came to the Grylls family, who created a stately home to reflect their power and status. Following the English Civil War, the property changed hands and was owned by the Pendarves family.

She laughed. Even when they had rented it, it had been nothing more than a big old farmhouse with a few grand rooms. Yes, she knew the history and had climbed over the granite stones that had once made up the great hall, but it was nothing special, unlike Trelowarren, or even Pengarrock, her cousin Tristan's home.

> Sitting above the tidal creek of Gillan, the property is currently arranged with five reception rooms, a kitchen, two bathrooms and seven bedrooms. There are many other rooms that are currently unspecified on the floor plan. There are extensive outbuildings that could be converted with the proper permissions.
>
> The property is being auctioned with ten acres including the quay on the creek.
>
> This is an exciting opportunity to own one of Cornwall's most historic houses.

What was Hebe thinking, and why was Lucy sitting in cattle class on this train? No seats available in first class, her mother had said. But Lucy knew it was the headline on the abandoned newspaper on the table across the aisle that was the true cause. She pulled her trilby lower and pushed the big Jackie O glasses further up her nose.

Seriously, who was she trying to fool? She looked like someone on the run, or someone trying to deal with a hangover.

Well, the last part was definitely right. Her mother had a heavy hand with the gin and Lucy hadn't objected while the paparazzi flocked outside waiting for her to appear. Thankfully they hadn't been alerted to her inelegant scramble over the back wall and on to Paddington station for the earliest train to Truro in time to save Hebe.

The words 'save' and 'Hebe' didn't belong in the same sentence. Hebe was fiercely independent and free, unlike Kate. Being unencumbered made a lot of sense to Lucy. It was why Ed had seemed like a good idea at the time. And if she were honest, she knew part of her pleasure had been that the affair would annoy her father no end. But she'd never expected that he would find out, and certainly not like this. Ed had proved to be a mistake, the last in a long line.

She hadn't regretted any of her past flings until now. Peter: hilarious. Ben: barmy. Harry had been fun. Not that that fling hadn't caused enough problems. Her father had never forgiven her for not taking it seriously, but that was nothing new. She sighed. But if truth be told, they were all carbon copies and she was a bit bored, and that was where Ed seemed to have been the ideal answer. How could she have been so stupid? Although according to her family, stupid was her normal state.

Resting her chin in her hands, she stared out of the window. Clouds appeared, obscuring the glorious day and nearly blotting out Brunel's bridge. The water below didn't exist. They were suspended in mist. It became thicker with each second that passed, so that Saltash station was removed from the landscape as low cloud merged and moved with the fog. It was September, but this was taking the season of mists and mellow fruitfulness too far.

The headline *Amorous MP Caught with It Girl* shouted at her from across the aisle. She leaned over and flipped it face-down. Sadly there was no other news at the moment. It was as bad as August, the silly season, even though it was serious back-to-school September. Lucy had featured in the silly-season void before; in fact, she'd sought it out. But then she'd been a stupid, selfish cow, as her brother had reminded her last night.

Well, some people – Michael in particular – would say she was finally going where she belonged: to hell, or Helwyn House, at least. She grimaced at the thought of her brother's taunts. She hated him. No, not real hate, just that sibling thing. It was a competitive emotion that came and went like the Cornish mists.

Her phone vibrated and she glanced at the screen. Ed again. *Why won't you reply?*

What did he think? That she was in love with him? If he did, he had that so wrong. A day ago he'd made a perfect apology on camera, with his wife by his side. It was all over the news and the bloody Internet, so why was he texting her now? He must have a death wish.

A woman corralling a toddler with a newborn strapped to her chest joined her at the table. The toddler was in grandstanding mode and the baby grizzling. Lucy smiled at her and the woman rolled her eyes. Tiredness oozed out of every pore. Lucy pitied her, noting the sick on her shoulder.

The toddler began the one-legged loo dance. 'I need to wee now, Mummy.' The mother had just unstrapped the baby. She closed her eyes and looked as if she could both cry and scream.

'Can I help?'

Relief spread across the woman's face. 'Would you?'

Lucy nodded.

'If you could just follow us and maybe hold the baby while ...' She didn't finish, as the toddler raced down the aisle, knocking things over as he went. Lucy followed behind. The woman shoved the baby into her arms at the loo door.

The infant stared at her, then began to bawl. She could deal with this. She'd held enough babies over the years as her friends popped them out and she became the favourite godmother. Catching her reflection in the window, she saw why this one was grizzling. She slipped the glasses off and the infant settled a bit. As she waited for the mother and toddler, she hoped no one would recognise her.

'So sorry.' The mother came out holding the toddler, who was now without clothes. Things obviously had not gone well.

They returned to the table to find a man had settled there and was reading the newspaper featuring Lucy on the front page. She tilted her head down and slid into the spare seat, still clutching the baby. The mother found clean clothes and began dressing her son. The baby grabbed Lucy's hat and with one swift move pulled it off her head and dropped it on the table. The man looked up from the paper, squinting as recognition dawned.

'Home-wrecker,' he said, rising to his feet and practically knocking the mother over.

The baby gurgled in Lucy's arms and she wanted to fade into the fabric of the seat. He was right. She was the lowest of the low. The other woman. It was never going to be a defensible position. And part of her felt terrible, but she was also angry. Ed had lied to her. She was so bloody stupid. She'd believed him.

'Sorry.' The mother handed Lucy her hat as soon as she could. 'Thank you for your help.'

'No problem.'

The woman held out her arms and took the smiling child. 'You're a natural with kids.'

'Ha.' A natural she was not.

'Grab your bag, Joe, this is our stop.' She put the baby in the harness and gave Lucy one last look. She was trying not to judge but wasn't succeeding.

'Do you need a hand getting off?'

'We'll be fine. Thanks again for your help.'

Lucy watched them scramble onto the platform, where a tall man met them. He was all smiles, scooping up the toddler onto his shoulders. They appeared a happy family, if there was such a thing. The woman waved at her, as did the toddler, then spoke to her partner, who turned and looked directly at Lucy, frowning. She would need to get used to that reaction. She'd been gullible, looking for a relationship without commitment. There was no such thing. At least now she was free, and that was the way she planned to stay.

Grabbing her phone, she scrolled through her emails. She'd

sent one out to friends saying she was disappearing for a while. Not to worry and that all would be well. But she wasn't sure it would be, and she couldn't put her finger on why. Of course she was careful not to disclose her plans to anyone. She knew how these things worked. A glass or three of booze and the news of her location would be out. A short time being invisible should do the trick, and she hoped everyone would understand. But if they didn't, maybe she was due for a social-media cull.

A message from Michael popped up on her screen.

Take care. Mx

Well, she supposed he loved her in his own odd way. Despite being younger, he was always trying to be top dog. Last night had been more of the same. Her family telling her what she was going to do. Lucy had asked them if she had a choice. She'd done it knowing the answer.

'No,' they had said in unison.

The thought was giving her a headache now, along with last night's gin. She could use a hair of the dog and the dregs of her coffee didn't cut it. Outside the window the murky landscape matched the state of her grey matter. She knew what she'd been doing was wrong. Hell, she'd seen what her father's activities had done to her mother, but this had been different. Or it had been for her.

But none of that mattered now. Thanks to her stupidity, she had no work and was being sent to rescue her aunt, who she doubted needed any help at all.

Fidgeting, Lucy opened Tinder on her phone. Would there be anyone interesting, or even anyone near to Hell House? Maybe she should become celibate. She laughed to herself; she knew this wouldn't work. She swiped left and left and left, then stopped. Alone was probably better for the moment. She put her phone away.

Looking out of the window at the fog, she shivered. Too much of her past lay in Cornwall. Being alone didn't scare her, but Helwyn House did. That place held all her nightmares.

✳ Ten ✳

Hebe

30 September 2016

The heavy fog of the morning had burnt off and the sun was blistering in its intensity. Hebe loosened the scarf at her neck. She was positive it was the sun and not a hot flush causing this discomfort, but it could be nerves as well. Clutched in her hand were the details of the auction and all the paperwork she needed if she were successful. She had woken this morning sure that this was exactly what she needed to do.

Just because she'd resigned and left London didn't mean she had to stop having a purpose. For her that would be finishing her last novel. Sitting in St Anthony last night, she had let the church's atmosphere settle around her. This morning she felt the writing bug in her veins again. It was as if having put other things aside, there was finally room for her imagination to work. She hoped it would last.

Glancing at her watch, she saw it was only twelve. The auction wasn't until two. She had timed this badly, but then she hadn't remembered how long it took to drive to Truro. She'd left at 10.30, and even with the tractors on the road, she'd done the journey in less than an hour.

It had taken her a while to locate the auction house. She wasn't as good as she used to be at reading maps. That wasn't the only thing that was disappearing. A hot flush grew and she fanned herself with the papers. She had to get out of the sun. Dashing to the building, she stood in its shade waiting to cool down, but everything was becoming hotter, while her thoughts chased themselves around in her mind.

She studied the details of the sale again. Helwyn House. This was important, and she shouldn't be having doubts. She pulled out her notebook and looked at the list of positive reasons to buy the place. The first item was that she loved it and she always had. It had spoken to her heart years ago.

This was her chance. Why was she hesitating? Was it because she was early? She should head in now and register. Then she could sit down and hopefully the flush would end.

She swung around and stepped up to the door. As she pushed it open, she came crashing down hard. Things went blank for a moment, but then hands were there helping her to her feet. Her knees stung and she could feel tears threatening. She felt like a child as they led her to a sofa to sit. Was this what her world held for her?

❊ Eleven ❊
Lucy

30 September 2016

Lucy scanned the auction room but couldn't see her aunt among the suits and waxed jackets. At the front of the crowd, a photo of Hell House adorned the screen, dappled sunshine coming through the twisted overgrown trees. It looked romantic in a Gothic sort of way. For too many years it had starred in her dreams, with Lucy herself as the damsel in peril who was too stupid to live. She still remembered those novels that used to line the shelves of the house. For Christmas one year she'd even asked for one of the diaphanous nightgowns the heroines always wore. What had she been thinking? At the age of twelve she'd still believed that a hero would come and save her.

'Helwyn House has been in the same family for hundreds of years.' The auctioneer looked up from the podium and smiled.

That was obvious. Lucy studied the familiar image. No one in their right mind would touch it unless they'd inherited it. Seriously, there was a tree growing out of the roof next to a collapsed chimney.

'It is a house of real historical interest.'

She coughed. Historical it was, especially the plumbing.

'The last of the Pendarves line, Lillian, died recently at the age of ninety-six.'

Well, it didn't look like she'd done a thing with the house since Lucy's family had last rented it. Back then, it had been well worn around the edges, but not dilapidated.

'Most of the land has been sold except for the ten acres

56

surrounding the house and a stretch by the creek along with the quay, which is included in the sale.'

She smirked, knowing he was failing to mention the road that separated the grounds from the quay, and the fact that the creek was navigable only twice a day. Not exactly the ideal waterside property. The painting that Hebe loved so much came into her mind. Thomas Grylls. He'd been one of the last of the family to own the house, her aunt had told her years ago. There had been a whole series of novels written about him that Lucy had loved. When she'd mentioned them to Hebe, her aunt had dismissed them as trashy fiction. But then as a historian, she would.

A man came and stood beside Lucy. He held a paddle in his hands with the number 69 on it. She couldn't help it; her mouth twitched as she glanced discreetly at him. He was focused on the auctioneer at the front, which she should have been too. But since she hadn't spotted her aunt in the room, she assumed Hebe had had second thoughts.

'We'll begin the bidding at five hundred thousand pounds.'

Lucy's eyes opened wide. Granted, she hadn't seen the house in years, nor did she want to, but that was outrageous.

'Fine, I have a bid with me at four hundred and fifty thousand.'

The man's paddle twitched in front of his jeans. He had nice thighs and the wash on the jeans was just right. His shoes were brown lace-up brogues, very country gent. Lucy's gaze travelled higher as the bidding began in earnest. He filled his jeans well and his stomach was flat. He wore a washed green canvas jacket that had seen better days. Underneath was a blue linen shirt that matched his eyes. She knew this because when her gaze reached his handsome face, he was looking at her. She blushed.

'I have six hundred and fifty thousand at the back left.'

Lucy looked away, wondering who would be so foolish. That much for a ruin with no view. Knock a nought off, then it was about right.

'Seven hundred thousand at the front.'

She couldn't see the bidder, but her mouth opened in obvious surprise and the man beside her grinned. That was when she realised she recognised him. It couldn't be, could it? But there was no denying that smile. She was standing right next to Kit Williams, a British actor who had become a huge star in Hollywood.

'Nine hundred thousand, do I have nine hundred?' The auctioneer scanned the room, then turned to two women holding telephones. It was silly money, thought Lucy. It wouldn't get you much more than a broom cupboard in central London, but down here nearly a million pounds should buy a sea view, or at least a fully functioning roof.

The slight movement of the paddle on Kit Williams's thigh diverted her thoughts.

'We have nine hundred thousand at the front. Do I hear one million?'

The paddle stayed still. Surely he couldn't be that mad.

'Nine hundred and fifty thousand then?'

His arm shot up. He was insane.

'I have one million from a telephone bid. Do I have one million one hundred thousand?'

The auctioneer looked directly at Kit. Lucy could feel the indecision in him. He would probably have to spend that much again on the wreck to make it habitable. It would be like throwing money away.

He nodded.

Bloody hell. But then that sort of money was probably peanuts in his world.

'I have one point two million at the front.'

She craned her neck to try and catch sight of the fool who was bidding so high. But she couldn't see much. She was just grateful that Hebe wasn't here.

'I have one point three at the back of the room.'

She couldn't help it – she turned to the movie star beside her and shook her head. 'You're insane.'

He nodded in agreement.

'I have a second telephone bidder at one point four million.'

The auctioneer looked to the bidder in the front and then to Kit, whose hand clenched on the paddle.

The woman holding the phone nodded. Lucy's palms were sweaty. This was crazy. At that moment, Kit's phone vibrated. He looked at it. 'Shit.' He put it to his ear and moved off.

'One and a half million pounds.' The auctioneer looked at Kit, who was almost out of the door. 'Helwyn House is going to the telephone bidder for one point five million.' The gavel came down.

Everyone moved, and Lucy searched the room again to be sure Hebe wasn't in a corner somewhere, but she was nowhere to be found. Phew. Mum had sent her on a wild goose chase to save her aunt, and as Lucy had suspected, she hadn't even needed saving. Had it all been a ruse to get her out of London? She would have left anyway, the writing was on the wall, but she wouldn't have chosen Cornwall ... anywhere but Cornwall.

Twelve

Hebe

July 2015

Y ou're standing still on the top of Godolphin Hill with your
phone clutched to your ear. It's your sister. I can hear the
excitement in her voice, but not what she is saying. There's a
smile on your face as you say, 'Congratulations, sis, he's a lucky
man. Maybe a fool, but I promise I won't tell him that.' You
laugh.

The sun is hot and the earth has that baked smell. In the
distance the sea is blue, reflecting the clear skies above us. I feel
I can see for ever ... or at least as far as the Scilly Isles. I look
toward St Ives and slowly spin. From up here it is as if all of
Cornwall is in my sights. The world should be in yours, but
on this glorious summer's day, here you are with me instead
of drinking champagne with your sister to celebrate her happiness. She is younger than you and I have never met her, never
wanted to. That would make what is ahead more difficult. The
less we share, the less you will stumble across later. People
won't ask about me and I will fade away. Soon I will forget
you and I hope you will only remember me as a blip in your
life.

Yet as I look at you now, I am jealous of the smile that is
lighting your face. It curdles in my stomach and I remember
how it has tormented me since we began.

*

When by thy scorn, O murd'ress, I am dead
And that though think'st thee free

60

From all solicitation from me,
Then shall my ghost come to thy bed.

I was so full of rage. In the distance, you sat in a puddle of
April sunshine with the girl with golden hair. She looked up at
you from under her lashes and I knew what she wanted. I felt
it in my gut. Lust. Anger made me weak. Instead of crossing
the lawn and confronting the two of you, I stood motionless.
Shouting, screaming silently. Couldn't you see she was in love
with you?

You smiled at her and I watched you study her. You were
not immune. Your body leant in to hers, your head tilted to
match hers. You might not have known it, but you were weak.
She was tempting you and ... I couldn't blame you or her,
but that didn't stop the unreasonable rage inside me. You were
mine. You told me that daily.

Anger propelled me away. It was right that she should want
you. She was eighteen and you were twenty-three. It was natural. I was almost fifty and no longer a woman. That monthly
call had left me and taken so much. I mourned. All I was left
with was rage, impotent rage. My beauty, my power had faded
and I could not bear for you to see that.

'Stop!'

I heard your voice but continued walking faster. I had to
escape.

Your hand grabbed my arm. We were on Westminster Bridge
and I couldn't recall how I'd got there.

'Hebe, stop.'

I did as you commanded. My energy was gone. The brown
flow of water below fled to the sea.

'She loves you.'

'No.' You shook your head.

'Well, she wants you then.'

You took a deep breath. Your face told me you knew.

'She's a first-year student and I was giving her feedback on
an essay.'

I raised an eyebrow.

61

'It's not like that. She's so young, just a girl.' You sighed. 'I wouldn't go there, it would be wrong.' You looked at me and realisation dawned on your face.

I threw my head back and laughed. You were twenty-three and I was fifty. How we had changed, you and I.

You took my hand and held it to your chest. 'We are different,' you said.

I closed my eyes and tried to believe that ... at least for the moment.

*

You walk towards me, beaming. 'I'm so pleased for her.' You drop your arm around my shoulders. 'I promised I'd toast them with champagne tonight.'

'Lovely.' I smile. You hold your phone up and stretch out your arm. Just before you can take the picture, I duck away. You look at me and shake your head. I know I disappoint you daily, as I do myself. I want no evidence of us to exist.

Your shoulders droop as you walk back to the cottage. I have been watching you pace back and forth. This is so important to you. Television. Bringing literature to a wider audience. You feel that so much is lost in the curriculum taught in schools. There is too much to cover, but if you could bring it alive on the screen, as so many have done with history, then the world would be better. You truly believe that, and so do I. But I know that if you go ahead with this project, I must leave. There is no choice. I will no longer be able to be invisible in your life. The world will want you, and it needs you. Pride swells in me. Loss quickly joins it.

'Well, it's not entirely bad news.'

I paste a smile on my face. 'How so?'

'You were right, they felt the scope was too small.'

I nod, trying to recall what I said. In all my years teaching, I have tried to make the past accessible to the present, to somehow bridge the divide. I have not always succeeded, but there have been high moments when my students and I have slipped into the time machine that language and literature gives us. You understood this intuitively. You still do.

'It's back to the drawing board. I need to make the concept bigger.' You run your fingers through your hair. 'Broader, more accessible.'

'You can do that.'

You laugh. 'Yes, I suppose I can.'

'You can do anything you put your mind to.' I smile, adding silently that you seduced me despite my qualms. How they troubled me, and still do even now when they should not.

*

No spring nor summer beauty hath such grace,
As I have seen in one autumnal face.
Young beauties force our love, and that's a rape;
This doth counsel, yet you cannot 'scape.
If t'were a shame to love, here t'were no shame;
Affections here take reverence's name.

I was marking papers and you were stretched out on my sofa reading Donne with a pencil in hand, making notes. You wanted to change courses. I thought you were right. Also, it was becoming too hard to hide our relationship. I still cringed when I said it. I pretended to myself that I was not having an affair with a student young enough to be my son. You told me age didn't matter, but I looked at you and saw your youth. Age never has mattered to the young. You will live forever. But I knew my beauty was fading fast. I thought it was my confidence that drew you in. I knew who I was but in truth you confused me. I was not the woman I was a few short months ago. She would never have allowed you through the door, but I had, and I must live with that knowledge.

Thirteen

Lucy

30 September 2016

Seagulls cried as they circled in the blue sky above. It had cleared to a perfect September day and Lucy slipped her sunglasses on as she began to walk down Lemon Street. What the hell was she going to do now? Where was Hebe? She pulled out her phone and there was a text from her mother.

Did you stop her? X

She had begun typing her response when she glanced up to see Kit Williams walking past. He nodded in her direction and she didn't look back at her phone until he had turned the corner. No one else had noticed him. Maybe it was his clothing. He looked no different from any other man walking about a county town. Or maybe it was the way he carried himself, upright but not too tall. Genius really. Whereas she stuck out like a beacon, of which there were many in Cornwall, but it wasn't what she needed at the moment. For once she needed to fade into the background.

She might need to go shopping, but the selection of clothing stores in Truro was limited, unless she wanted to dress like a sailor, a yummy mummy or a teen. What did women do for clothes here? Leave was the only possible answer. And she was free to do that now Hebe hadn't bought Helwyn House. So the real question was where could she go that was cheap and would let her stay under the radar until the fuss died down? The US election was throwing up lots of controversy, which was helpful. It was all more newsworthy than an MP's sex life. This thing would blow over in a week. She frowned as she remembered that Ed was on the house ethics committee, which might prove a bit awkward.

Well, it didn't matter to her. She didn't have any work at the moment, for obvious reasons. She had some savings. It wasn't much and wouldn't last long, but it should tide her over until she found someone willing to hire her.

She stopped in her tracks as she heard someone saying, 'Thank you,' in a voice that was very proper but with a hint of West Country. Her head swung around. It was her aunt. Hebe let go of the auctioneer's arm as they reached the bottom step in front of the building, then shook his hand. Lucy squinted, making sure she wasn't seeing things. Hebe hadn't been in the room, she was certain. Yet there she stood, not a hundred yards away, clutching a folder and chatting with the auctioneer, a huge smile on her face.

Lucy began to walk towards them, trying to listen to the conversation, though thanks to a passing bus, that was impossible. When she reached Hebe's side and touched her arm, her aunt turned and gave her a blank stare. It must be the disguise, the stupid hat and glasses, she thought.

'It's Lucy,' she said.

Hebe looked at her hard, like she was trying to place her. 'Goodness, Luce, what are you doing here?' She took her arm as they began to move along the pavement.

'Mum sent me.'

'Of course,' she said, 'but I'd forgotten in all the excitement of the auction.'

Lucy looked puzzled. 'You weren't in there.'

Hebe smiled. 'No, I had a little fall on the steps up to the ...' Her hand grabbed at the air. 'You know, the ... the rooms, so I sat it out in an office and they kindly let me phone it in, as you say.'

Lucy slapped her hand across her mouth. 'Sorry, but you didn't just pay one and a half million pounds for Hell House, did you?'

'Yes, for the house and the contents I did, and I'm thrilled.'

She closed her eyes for a moment, trying to digest this titbit of information. Actually, it wasn't a titbit at all. Her aunt had one and a half million pounds in cash – or she had up until she'd just spent it a few moments ago – and she now owned Helwyn House.

'I've rented a car. Let's just get you put on the driving bit before we set off so that you can drive too.'

The driving bit? Lucy wrinkled her nose. Hebe had always chosen her words with precision. She must be overcome with her purchase. 'You're not going to the house now, are you?' It couldn't be hers just yet. Money transfers and all that stuff took time, didn't it?

'Of course not. I've rented a place from Anthony, um, you know, at Sailaway.' She smiled. 'We always rented boats from him and I thought one of those little cottages by the church would be perfect, just within walking distance for the moment.'

'Anthony Jenkin.'

'Yes, him.' She sighed. 'Perfect location.'

Perfect. Yes, in a sense St Anthony was idyllic: on the creek, with just a few buildings and lots of boats. Lucy saw it now as if she was standing on the pebbly beach skimming stones, as she had done so often as a child.

'I can't tell you how excited I am, and I'm thrilled you're with me.' Hebe looked her in the eyes. 'It wasn't you, was it, in the papers?'

Lucy took a deep breath and nodded.

'Oh dear.' They'd reached the car rental agency at the train station. 'Sometimes things happen for a reason.' Hebe gave Lucy's arm a squeeze. Lucy handed over her driving licence and hoped the woman at the desk hadn't read her newspapers too closely this week.

It was funny how forgotten memories slipped into Lucy's mind and knocked her sideways with their power. The journey to St Anthony did this at first in small ways. Reaching Gweek, she remembered Michael being sick all over her because he'd eaten a whole packet of Jaffa Cakes and wouldn't stop playing on his Game Boy. She'd never forgiven him for that, and the smell still seemed to linger in the air as they crossed the first bridge through the village. But by the time they had reached the second bridge, fear blotted out that more innocent memory.

Hebe took the left-hand turn and the tree growth became thicker and the branches more twisted, especially when she turned off the main road and took the short cut into Mawgan. In the twilight, the gnarled trunks held branches that seemed to have grown in agony, reaching downward and inward away from the wind and the rain. Lucy shivered as they passed through the village and down to the bridge over Mawgan Creek. The tide was out, revealing the mudflats and a small trickle of water working its way through the wiggly channel.

'You can feel autumn in the air. Should I put the heater on?' Hebe turned to her before Gear Bridge.

'No, thanks, I'm fine.' She wondered at her aunt's driving, though. Hebe had always been confident behind the wheel, but now it seemed she'd become very cautious. Yet even so, on a few occasions she hadn't seemed to notice oncoming cars or narrow passages.

'If I've told you before, do tell me, but on this bridge in 1648 the battle known as Gear Rout took place.'

'You may have mentioned it years ago.' The bridge was narrow, but instead of slowing, Hebe took it in third and Lucy was able to examine the orange lichen at close proximity as they sped through, missing the stones by centimetres.

'Thought I might have.' She shifted down as they went up the steep hill towards Gear Farm, then swerved for no reason. Lucy wondered if she should suggest that she take over the driving for the rest of the way. She could just about remember the route, even though she had done her best to forget everything about this place.

'When was the last time you came to Cornwall?' Hebe asked.

'Eleven years ago.' Lucy frowned, thinking of the event that had led to her swift departure.

'I shouldn't think too much has changed.' Hebe smiled.

It didn't appear to have, although Lucy noticed that a Methodist chapel had been converted and a few new homes had appeared. The Prince of Wales pub looked smarter, but as they passed the second crossroads to Manaccan, everything appeared as it had before, the old sign still pointing the way to St Anthony. A damp sweat broke out on her brow. She wiped it away, wondering if twenty-eight was too early to begin the menopause.

As the road began its downward journey to the hamlet, the first glimpse of Falmouth Bay appeared in the fading light. The evening was still and the sea flat and grey. The church tower came into sight before long then Hebe parked the car next to one of the many boats out of the water for the winter.

'I've rented the little ... one just there.' She pointed to a low granite cottage with a picnic table in front of it. St Anthony's Church still presided over the small cluster of buildings.

Lucy tried to draw on some of the happy memories of the time spent on this beach as a child, but all she could remember was the bad stuff. She'd always thought happy memories were lighter and should come to the front of the mind, but the bad ones always managed to chase them away.

'I wasn't expecting to have company, but they said it sleeps four in the ...'

Lucy frowned as the pause grew.

Hebe rubbed her temple. 'In the thing ... the paperwork I read.' She plucked her bag off the back seat and Lucy grabbed hers, which contained only three pairs of knickers, a bra, two T-shirts and a pair of flip-flops. It was apparent that she hadn't really planned for this stay, but then she hadn't expected Hebe to actually buy Hell House. This was the last place in the world Lucy had ever intended to return to. In fact she had sworn she never would. So much for keeping promises.

❊ Fourteen ❊
Hebe

1 October 2016

Opening her eyes, Hebe stared at her surroundings. Shapes loomed. Nothing was familiar. Her heart raced. It wasn't quite dark, nor was it light. It must be *uht*, the hour before dawn. Why was she remembering an Old English word now, here? She closed her eyes and breathed slowly. Cornwall. That was where she was. She could smell it. This bedroom was far from familiar, but the air, the smell of salt and herb, was. She was in a rented holiday cottage. She had done this before.

She had left *him* behind and that hurt, but it was right. He needed to let go and he never would if she left the decision to him. She was saving him, and his memory of her would remain as a woman still vibrant. She needed to make decisions while she could. Buying Helwyn House was right. It meant that from today onward, she would be busy and out of sight, buried in the wild Cornish countryside. Of course Lucy was here with her, she remembered. Everyone was looking for Lucy. Kate had mentioned it when they had spoken on the phone. Hebe had written it down.

She swung her feet out of bed. Whether having her niece here was a good thing or not she didn't know, but she wouldn't worry about it, for it was a fact. She liked Lucy – no, she loved her. Bright, stubborn and kind at the same time. Not that her family saw any of those features. Lucy kept her light well hidden, except for her looks, which she … she used. No, that wasn't quite right, but it would have to do.

As she stood Hebe's temples throbbed. *Uhtceare*, worry in

the hour before dawn. *Uht* and *uhtceare* were a part of her, a constant in her life now. This should lessen now that she was home, the home of her heart. When a professor had first mentioned *uhtceare* to her years ago, the term had stayed with her. At the time the word was in use, the church beside the cottage would have had monks saying lauds, she guessed, though maybe the hour was closer to six and it would be matins. She had always felt that had she been born in an earlier time, she would have been called to the religious life. There was something in the routine and simplicity that appealed to her. Of course, that would also have been the only way to learn.

Learning had been her life, her purpose. Helwyn House was her new purpose. It needed her as much as she needed it. Thinking of updating her lists, she was about to switch the light on, but instead walked through to the kitchen. The only sound was the hum of the refrigerator. She was tempted to unplug it. Without that noise, this moment could be the same as any time in the past few hundred years. But maybe not. The glass in the windows, for instance. She shook her head. There wouldn't have been any. There was carpet beneath her feet where there would have been hard-packed earth. The smells of animals and humans would have filled the air.

Despite the peace of the early hour, now was very different from then. She must not let things tangle in her mind. Although standing here in a cold kitchen just before dawn, with the world outside the window washed in an eerie fog-filled light, it was difficult. She turned on a table lamp, pulled out her journal, sat down and began to write.

> *The feast of St Remigius, known for his sanctity*
> *Beans on toast with half a bottle of supermarket finest*
> *claret last night. Lucy was with me. It's good to have*
> *her here, but I know this is the last place she wants to*
> *be, though I can't recall why. Sometimes it is good to*
> *face the past. Hindsight can give you clarity.*

Looking out of the window again, Hebe knew that several

yachts lay between her and the creek, but they were invisible in the mist. In her mind she saw the royalists making their way to the fort on Dennis Head, with some stopping to visit the church. Trevillion had spent his own money on building the fort to hold Cornwall for the king. It had housed twenty-six guns, or was it twenty-eight? She should know that figure but she wasn't sure. She did know that it was the only time the Trevillions and the Gryllses had seen eye to eye. The problems, the falling-out between the families, had begun long before Henry VIII gave the monastery to the Gryllses.

She closed her eyes tight, trying to find the details. Love, rivalry, wealth. But it was the building of Helwyn House that had brought things to a crisis. Helwyn House and Pengarrock were almost on top of each other. Each successive Grylls heir had made the house grander to outdo the Trevillions. Now she owned what was left of it.

She stood up and switched on the kettle, then checked yesterday's journal entry. It confirmed that she'd bought Helwyn House. She hadn't simply dreamt it. Squinting into the distance through the window, she made out the outline of the church. It appeared other-worldly, with its stones muted by the cloud clinging to the edges. Its origins were connected to monks, just like Helwyn House.

The creek would have been deeper and more navigable in those days. She stopped and listened for a moment. Drums. She could hear them. No, no she couldn't, but it was all so real to her. That wasn't surprising, given that she had studied and written about this place so frequently. But the lines between fact and fiction felt more blurred than ever before. What was real? In truth, she didn't know. There was little she was sure of any more. Except now she recalled Lucy's hands clutching her knees as they drove through the lanes. Driving. Hebe didn't like doing it any more. She didn't see things as well as she used to.

She made instant coffee and took her cup with her as she slipped out of the front door. Picking her way across the lane, she stepped over the chain enclosing the wintering boats. They loomed in the fog. Bits of rope and driftwood littered the ground. Mist swirled about her in the growing light like sand she had once seen in the desert. Everything felt unreal. The creek itself came as a surprise. She had a slightly damp left foot as a result.

Silence. No throb of a boat engine. No honk of a car horn coming around a blind bend, not even the clank of the ropes on the masts behind her. The steam from her coffee rose and twisted in the air. She had done the right thing. Here, she was safe. She could bury herself away like the many bodies that lay below the ground, unmarked, unnoticed and these days unremembered.

The sound of an oar splicing the water was dull in the heavy air. Hebe looked in the direction of the noise, but could see nothing. Then the crunch of the rowlocks, and the oars being pulled in. A louder splash, an anchor perhaps. Was some lone soul fishing on this strangely white October morning?

Taking a sip of her coffee, she thought about the day ahead. Later today she would visit Helwyn House, home of Thomas Grylls, now owned by her. The paperwork was a formality. She'd had a text last night that the money had been successfully transferred from her bank to the estate of Lillian Pendarves. Thanks to Thomas Grylls, she could afford to buy his house. She tapped her phone and a picture of the painting of him appeared. The portrait that she had bought. When? She sipped her coffee, sorting through things in her mind, trying to put the pieces together. A country house sale. Yes, that was it. Somewhere north of Launceston. Portraits were out of favour at that time. It hadn't been expensive. She'd had so little money then. But she'd bid and she'd won. Like yesterday. Yes, that was it. Buying Helwyn House at auction was fitting, in a way. Life had an odd way of twisting things.

Of course, her bank – or rather, the man who dealt with her money – would be disappointed to see so much disappear, but wasn't that what money was for: pleasure? She sighed. Not in Grylls's time it wasn't, or shouldn't have been. She closed her eyes for a moment, then opened them to refocus.

Across the creek she could just make out the house on the old quay; then a few seconds later it had disappeared, just like her thoughts. It was getting worse. The consultant had said the mild stroke she had suffered was an indication of things deteriorating. She hoped he was wrong. Fear crawled across her skin. What lay ahead? She smoothed her hair back from her face. There was no point in worrying. She must live for now, in the present. Helwyn House was hers.

The Grylls estate had been rich at the time of the Civil War, unlike many others. Supporting the king had drained the coffers substantially, but it wasn't until after the Restoration that the estate had failed, in the hands of Thomas Grylls's nephew. Thomas hadn't lived to see this happen. At least that was what the evidence pointed to, from what she had uncovered over the years. Despite all her research, she hadn't been able to find out how he had died and where he was buried. He had vanished. This was a problem. At this moment she didn't know why that was, but she knew it should trouble her. Someone else had disappeared too. Was that a coincidence? Maybe she should write it down.

She groped in her pocket for paper and pen but found nothing. She would have to go inside. Draining the mug of the last of the coffee, she looked at her hands. Water beads from the fog had built up on her fingers, magnifying her freckles and age spots. Time was passing so swiftly. But here she was, finally in the place where her heart felt most whole. Even in the thick, wet mist, love filled her.

A footstep crunched on the pebbles behind her. Hebe turned but could see no one, nor were there any more footsteps. Especially on a morning like this, with a sea mist so dense, it was a place of ghosts or lost souls – even if you didn't believe in either. So many people who lived and worked this land and fished these waters believed in both. Who was she to dismiss their convictions?

The tide was in as Hebe and Lucy walked from the cottage down the road that ran alongside the creek. Late-afternoon sunlight fell through the leaves, which were just turning colour. Right then, Hebe wanted to forget everything but the present. Sadly, her mind wasn't so controllable. She almost laughed out loud, but stopped because Lucy was walking beside her with a scowl on her pretty face. Was she thinking about her lover? It was not easy to keep love hidden. Hebe knew this well. All her life she had been good at keeping secrets. She had been a quiet child. Serious, she remembered her mother saying. So few memories existed of Frances Nance, society beauty with a wild heart and a gorgeous voice. Cornish to the core, she had sung of sadness, and when the wind moved through the trees, Hebe heard her mother.

There was nothing mournful or sad on this autumn afternoon. Excitement flowed through her like the water running under the bridge, feeding into the creek. There was happiness and joy in its energy. Poohsticks, she suddenly remembered. She had played Poohsticks here with Lucy, and sometimes with her brother. Hebe had never cared for Michael as much as for Lucy. Hopefully she had kept that a secret, too.

'Poohsticks.' She hadn't meant to say it aloud. Lucy turned to her and smiled, but her eyes were haunted. A flash of memory. Piglet. Giles, Lucy's father, was a pig. No, in truth he was just like so many of the young men Hebe had seen pass through her classes, but unlike them, Giles had never grown up. Despite his clever mind, he couldn't see what he actually had and was forever off chasing skirt. That she never understood. Kate was a gift. Loving, loyal, beautiful, a devoted wife and mother. But her sister – or to be precise, her half-sister – would never have married him if things had been different.

They reached the gate piers that led off the road. Originally they had been further from the house, but as the land was sold off, they had been moved. Now they looked like two weary hitchhikers covered in foliage and dirt. Only one nail remained holding the sign that announced the house. Turning to Lucy, she could see that her niece was pale and her expression was one of sad determination, her mouth pressed into a grim line. She was not happy, that was clear.

Hebe sighed. Impatience drove her on. Now with the house so close, she picked up her pace on the overgrown path that had once been a grand drive. She stumbled but did not fall. Had she done the right thing purchasing the house? Yes, she had; qualms were a normal part of any decision. Just as she knew that leaving him had been the right decision. Living in Helwyn House would help her to write the final book of Thomas's life.

Away from the road the sunlight disappeared, with the dense growth of trees casting shadows on the ground. In fact, nature had almost totally reclaimed the drive. To the right there was a perilous drop down to a bracken-filled pit. Wild. The sweet scent of earth, damp and rich, filled the air. She wasn't sure, but it looked like some of the fog that had concealed everything this morning lingered among the trees. Other-worldly. The souls of the past hovering in the spaces between the branches. So many souls ... from the monks who had first occupied this site to the men buried after the battles. Yes, she could feel their ghosts more clearly now than ever.

'Have I told you about the battles around here? Gear Rout?'

'You have.' Lucy gave her a half-hearted smile.

'Oh.'

This place was Hebe's to protect and to uncover its secrets. How she'd longed to do this over the years as Helwyn House slipped further into the shadows. Hopefully being here would bring light and life back, even if it didn't uncover what had happened to Thomas Grylls.

'What did you say?' Lucy's brows were drawn together.

'Nothing.' Hebe squinted into the distance. Lucy shrugged, then wrapped her arms about herself. She was a tiny thing, but somehow Hebe felt she was made of steel.

✳ Fifteen ✳

Lucy

1 October 2016

The drop in temperature since they had left the road and begun walking up the drive was marked, and Lucy couldn't help thinking it was the perfect place for ghosts. Cold, damp and eerie. The lingering clusters of mist along the drive were downright terrifying, and walking through them, she felt like she was one of the damned heroines of those Gothic novels she had loved. Going forward when she knew nothing but disaster lay ahead. Sadly there would be no brooding hunk to save her from the terrors of this place. The world today didn't work that way, though maybe that wasn't a bad thing.

There was a bitter taste in her mouth. It was anger ... with Michael, with her father and mother, who had acquiesced to his suggestion to send her here, even knowing that she hated Hell House. As she looked at the building, bile rose.

'Dear God, Hebe, have you lost your mind?'

Hebe jumped and swung around. 'No.' Her eyes narrowed as she peered at Lucy.

'You're mad to have bought this place.'

'Buying Helwyn is the best decision I have ever made.' Hebe turned her back to Lucy and Lucy felt like she had been slapped. What had she said? She hadn't meant to hurt her aunt's feelings, but she clearly had. As much as she hated it here, she would focus on Hebe and her excitement. Hebe had always been there for her, so she would repay some of the kindness now.

As they approached the house, she snuck a glance at the window of the north bedroom. Something moved. She swore it did.

'He wasn't on the inventory, but I'm sure he'll prove useful,' her aunt said, pushing aside the knee-high nettles with the folder in her hand.

'What?' Lucy looked around to see what on earth Hebe was talking about.

'Don't dawdle, it's just a goat.'

Lucy saw the strange-eyed beast standing in between the columns of the loggia. It stared at them before returning to eating the red valerian growing from the crack in the steps. This was becoming more bizarre by the moment.

Brave sunbeams caught the loggia, making it unearthly in a Narnia sort of way. Hell, the whole experience was beginning to feel that way. She was only in this place for Hebe and to get away from London until the scandal became old news. The press were moving on already and she was itching to do the same.

'It's a good omen.' Hebe stared at the animal.

Lucy frowned. She'd thought goats were OK, especially the cute little ones that filled the Internet at the moment, but a real, smelly one was another story.

'The goat repre ...' Hebe stuttered, 'repre ... stands for abundance, fertility.' She turned to Lucy, who stepped backwards.

'Fertility? Don't look at me.' Lucy stepped backwards.

'Energy, then. Vitality.'

'Also, the scapegoat,' Lucy added, looking away from the beast's weird eyes.

Hebe nodded. But Lucy didn't want that role either. She shook her head and looked back at Hell House. The loggia was the thing that had always struck her about the place. It didn't fit. Loggias were found in Italy, not damp, wet Cornwall. She and Michael had created numerous games using the pillars as soldiers, forests, aliens. In those early years, they had had so much fun.

Today, with the warm October sun finding it, it did look beautiful in an artistic, dilapidated sort of way. If one liked ruins, it worked, but if one liked houses that were warm, dry and welcoming, then you were in trouble. And Lucy knew they were in trouble. She could feel it to her very bones. She also felt the past, an unhappy past.

Decay and death spilled out of every stone at Hell House, casting shadows on the worn slabs. Trees towered above. Most things here were smaller than she remembered them, but not the trees. They almost danced with the breeze. No, she was letting her imagination run away. She turned away from the taunting branches. Her poor aunt had spent over a million pounds on the remains of a run-down house. A couple of hundred years ago, before most of it fell into ruin, it must have been jolly nice. But now …

A discreet cough alerted them to the arrival of the builder, Fred Polcrebar. Hebe had called him this morning on Anthony Jenkin's recommendation. Lucy sort of remembered him, as she had been roped into babysitting his youngest brother when she was sixteen.

'Good afternoon,' he said. 'I'm Fred.' He had grown up into a good-looking, capable sort, but the expression on his face was a picture. He was trying to contain his surprise, but it wasn't quite working.

'I remember.' Her mouth lifted at the corners, watching the reactions across his face. It read: OMG you were shagging Ed Smith.

'Sorry.' He grinned. He wasn't sorry at all, and she went full beetroot, all the way to her toes. She hadn't done that in years, probably not since she was last here. She supposed she should be used to people thinking they knew all about her life.

'Hello, Fred, I'm Hebe Courtenay and this is my niece Lucy,' Hebe said. 'Shall we walk around the outside first or just venture in?'

He looked up at the roof and the sycamore tree that was growing from the leaning chimney on the north wing. The north wing hadn't been in great shape even eleven years ago. They had rarely used that part of the house; it had been off limits for one reason or another. Lucy shivered, remembering the cold.

Fred coughed. 'It might look more promising on the inside.'

Lucy stifled a laugh. They pushed through the vegetation and she imagined them carving their way through the jungle, though in this case the jungle was made of pesky brambles and chin-high nettles.

The sun escaped behind a cloud and she pulled her coat around her as they moved towards the house. The goat shied away the closer they got to the loggia. On the step, Lucy froze. She was eleven all over again, looking up to that room. Goose bumps covered her arms and she felt the colour leave her face. This was ludicrous. Years had passed and there was no such things as ghosts, but there *were* beastly brothers in this world, namely Michael. Right at that moment, she hated him.

Hebe pulled out a huge key ring from the plastic folder. It was crammed with so many odd-shaped keys, it looked like it belonged in a museum. She turned to the massive double gates in front of her. It felt like they were about to enter a gaol or an ancient dungeon. Lucy had clearly been sentenced before the trial. Or maybe she had been found guilty in the press and that was enough.

'I'm not sure which one it is.' Hebe held up the keys, each one intricate and rusted. This gate had never been locked when Lucy's family had rented the house. She and Michael had free-ranged in and out of the house at all hours. Hebe selected the largest and tried that in the lock, but it didn't work, so she moved to the next one until finally the fifth key fitted.

'Here, let me help.' Fred put down his tool bag and pressed his shoulder against the gate. It gave way, disturbing a pile of dead leaves. The rectangular courtyard spread out in front of them, and more memories came racing back. Michael had broken his arm riding his scooter at full speed around it one year, and the summer Lucy was twelve, she had performed a one-person play to a bored audience.

Looking at it now, the air seemed to shimmer with the events that had taken place here – not just the ones her family had taken part in but the full history of the place. Facing them stood the remainder of the once great hall that marked the west side of the rectangle. Empty windows framed the sky behind it, with hair-like vines adorning the crenellations at the top of the wall. The large wooden gate below was open, looking like a mouth with one tooth missing. Stone paths crossed the open space. Lucy had walked them in her white nightie like a frightened governess as the clock in the dining room had struck midnight. Michael had laughed like a madman when he'd seen her acting out the scene from a favourite book.

Hebe's many keys jangled as she walked, surveying the wings of the house that lined the north and south sides of her new home. Columns matching the ones in the loggia supported the east wing above them, along with the wall that separated the courtyard from the outside world. Many doors were ajar to the right-hand side, while to the left, Hebe was opening one into the house. Lucy had last walked through it eleven years ago and had sworn she'd never do it again.

It was like opening a tomb or even Pandora's box as Hebe stepped across the threshold. Inside it was not so much a case of dust motes in the air but a dust storm. Lucy didn't want to think what it was made of; she was creeped out enough as it was.

On the far wall a windowpane was cracked in the upper right-hand corner. Through it a twisting tendril of ivy grew, encircling an old curtain rail before running along the ceiling to the light fitting, where a single bulb hung from a wire. It was like a weird chandelier. Sunlight penetrated the grimy window; the curtains had long since disintegrated, with only a few stringy remains bearing testament to earlier glory. The place looked like the setting for an old-fashioned horror flick. Or maybe it was just her overactive imagination.

She walked into a cobweb and squealed.

'For heaven's sake, Lucy, no need for hysterics.' Hebe glanced over her shoulder, frowning as she shoved a door open. More dust lifted. Fred coughed and pulled a torch out of his tool bag. All the doors along the corridor were closed, and daylight seeped under them, casting puddles of light grey on the dark slate floor.

Hebe pointed down the hall. 'That's the dining room.'

Fred walked to it. 'Locked.'

Hebe tried a medium-sized key, which she turned with a bit of force. More dust clogged the air and Lucy gagged. There were no curtains on the windows here, and afternoon light filtered in, revealing the beautiful wood panelling she remembered. Hebe stood stroking the wall by the fireplace like it was her lover. Lucy wrinkled her nose. Hebe and lover were words that didn't belong together.

'Linenfold,' she sighed. 'I was worried someone would have stripped it out.'

Fred shone the torch at the wall. 'It looks like woodworm have been active, but it's not too bad.' He took out his phone and began what Lucy assumed was going to be a list that would convince Hebe she was mad to have bought this place. He would say, she guessed, that the best thing to do was salvage the panelling and tear the house down and begin again. To make this place a proper home would cost more than she had paid for it.

Lucy stuck to the middle of the room by the table. It was long and narrow and she couldn't shake the image that came to mind of a body stretched out on it. Her brother's past attempts at devilish laughter bounced off the sides of her brain. He had told her that the dead would have been laid out on the table before burial. He'd also said that it had been used for surgery, amputation in particular. She shuddered. Such wonderful imaginations kids had. Michael had remained mostly revolting, only occasionally showing that he was partially human and not entirely demon.

Daylight caught the delicate strands of a spider's web on the chandelier and the rapid vibration told her that the spider hadn't yet completed its task of laying traps for the many clusters of flies tapping gently against the grimy glass in the windows. There was no escape from the room or from the spider for them. Shaking herself, she looked around for her aunt and Fred but didn't see them. Another door had been opened and she knew one thing: she didn't want to be left alone anywhere in this wretched building.

Dashing on, she tried not to trip in the gloomy light. She could hear them speaking but was unable to figure out where they were. She stopped, her heart beating faster than it should be for such minimal exertion. Above she heard footsteps, but their voices seemed to come from further down the hall – maybe the kitchen or the pantry. In her head, she was caught in a cartoon programme, and out of one of the closed doors would come a ghoul. She needed to get a grip. Just because at eleven she had thought the place was haunted didn't mean it was true. Her therapist had said it was just a rush of early hormones brought on by fear of abandonment and because her father was a dick. That, of course, wasn't the word she had used. That was Lucy's word, because that was what he was. His world, like most men's, revolved around that piece of his anatomy.

Putting one wobbly foot in front of the other, she went towards the kitchen. Cool wind blew past and the dining room door slammed. She jumped about three feet. This was stupid. She had to control this irrational fear. In the kitchen, the back door swung wide and Hebe and Fred were standing looking at the roof. The noises she had heard from above were just old house noises: creaking floorboards as the woodworm munched through them, or the wind.

Once outside, she gulped in the fresh air. They were standing in what she remembered as the kitchen garden. No one had looked after it in years. Relics of espalier fruit trees grew like they were in a jungle and not what had once been an orderly place. She tried to see it through her aunt's eyes. Hebe was smiling in a way Lucy had never seen before. Excitement oozed out of her as her gaze followed the roof line – though it was more like a tree line, or even a flower border, since several plants bloomed in the gutters and joins, along with a host of weeds too numerous to name. One of the chimneys rivalled the Leaning Tower of Pisa, yet Hebe's face showed not despair or even dismay, but love. Dear God, the woman was in love with a ruin; it wasn't a house, more a pile of stones just about holding together. Try as she might, Lucy couldn't see the attraction. Yes, it was historic, but that was the only thing about it to love.

❊ Sixteen ❊

Hebe

1 October 2016

A heron sat on the dead tree at the bend in the creek. Only a trickle of water moved through the channel out towards the sea. Hebe looked at it, thinking about it as it would have been in the 1600s, when bigger vessels could make their way to the … The word was gone, but she pictured it and it returned. Quay. The Gryllses had used boats to bring the granite stones to extend the house, in order to show their growing wealth and fend off their neighbours at Pengarrock.

She smiled. Thomas Grylls had been brave, daring and loyal. This should all have been his and Lucia's. Hebe needed to know what had happened to him. She rubbed her neck. Maybe it was something she had forgotten, along with so much else. This was important. A crow swooped low over the lane and she thought of Thomas's black clothes in the portrait then recalled his red tights. She smiled. If he was a bird he was chough rather than a crow.

Why were there no records of his death? He'd set off from Amsterdam. Of that she was certain. The ship's log noted him being aboard. They even mentioned him when they reached Normandy, but then nothing.

As she walked along the lane back to St Anthony, her thoughts circled and she could catch only a few. All around her were the dead from the defeat known as Gear Rout, and she felt the many souls buried in unmarked graves. Thomas Grylls had come back here in 1648 to ascertain support for the king, and had met with Lucia in secret. She had just been married to her cousin against her wishes, and this new husband of hers had been given Helwyn by Cromwell. Lucia and Thomas had met in the moonlit gardens outside the King's Room. Hebe knew the scene so well. She had almost lived it.

The estate had been sequestered by Parliament and anything of value was gone. In his anger, Thomas encouraged an uprising and fought bravely against the superior forces. Yet his heart was in pieces. Helwyn desolate, his love tied to another and his men defeated. They had fled. Many men had taken their chances with the rocks and the sea, jumping off the cliffs and steep banks that lined the Helford River; on their way to St Keverne. The Cornish loyal to the Crown had given so much and received so little in return. Thomas was among those who lost the most. Helwyn and Lucia was the price he paid for his support of the king. Helwyn had been in perpetual decline from that moment until the present.

'Why did you do this?' Lucy touched Hebe's arm.

'Do what?' Hebe turned and looked at her. So lovely, so fierce and so deliberately alone.

'Buy Hell House?'

She frowned. 'I've always wanted it and I could afford it.'

'Where did you get all that money?'

Her secret. 'Living carefully.'

Lucy's eyebrows rose. She didn't believe her. But it wasn't far off true.

'You can't tell me that teaching and your academic books earned enough to pay that much. Did you rob a bank?' She laughed.

Hebe tilted her head and debated. It would all become known soon enough. But not now. It could wait. She nodded and looked at the creek. 'No, it was my books.'

'OK, enough pulling my leg.'

'I'm not.'

'Maybe I should have gone to uni after all.'

'You should have. I always told you to resit.' Hebe sighed. 'You could still do it now.'

'No, I couldn't. That door is closed.' Lucy held up her hands.

'Doors are meant to be opened as well as closed.'

'I can't argue with that. But if life so far has taught me one thing, it's that a shut door is not always meant to be opened.' Lucy ran her fingers through her hair and looked out to the mudflats. Hebe followed her gaze. Two swans paddled in the twisty channel of water still heading out to sea.

'Don't judge all men by your father.'

Lucy opened her mouth, then shut it again.

'Or the man you were sleeping with.'

She pouted. 'Oh Hebe. It's a bloody disaster.'

'Married men often are.'

She laughed. 'He lied.'

'This surprises you?'

'It shouldn't.' She rolled her eyes. 'He's a politician. It's a tool of his trade.'

'So he told you his wife didn't love him and the marriage was over?' Hebe watched the expressions play on Lucy's face. Self-deprecation was the most prominent.

'And I believed it until I found the proof that the marriage was still very much alive.'

'Love note?'

'No, positive pregnancy test.'

'Oh.'

'Yeah, I ditched him and it was caught on a bloody phone, full colour video.' She laughed without joy. 'Well, there's no going back now.' Her mouth lifted into a brilliant smile.

'Always finding the bright side.'

'That's one way to look at it.' Mischief gleamed in Lucy's eyes. She was still so young, only twenty-eight. She should have packed up and travelled when she'd thrown her A-level exams. It was such a silly thing to do, but Hebe sensed that she had felt powerless in the face of her father's actions, and quitting school was the one thing she had control over. She had known it would hurt him and she had been a thorn in his side ever since.

'Hebe, where are you?' Lucy touched her arm.

Hebe squinted into the distance, then lied. 'I am thinking of the view they must have had from the roof of Helwyn when the house was built.'

Lucy laughed. 'Well, even from the roof I doubt there's a view now. Those trees are huge.'

'Yes, yes they are.' They had reached up and sought the sun, depriving the house of light and allowing the damp to take hold, but all was not lost. It turned out the house was sound, except for a few parts of the north wing, which could be recovered. Fred had assured her that it was all achievable, from the rewiring to the plumbing to the restoring. English Heritage would be out next week and they would begin to devise a plan. Now if her brain would cooperate and hold it all together just a bit longer ...

'I ... I'm just wondering if everything is OK.'

Hebe turned to her. 'Yes, everything is wonderful.'

Lucy took a deep breath. 'Maybe it's your excitement about the house, but you haven't quite been yourself.'

Hebe's gut tightened. Was she failing? She forced a smile. 'Yes, I'm distracted by the house.'

Lucy grabbed her hand. 'I'm glad to hear that. You would let me know if something was wrong, wouldn't you?'

Hebe swallowed. 'Of course.' She looked ahead of them. The lane was clear and the tower of St Anthony's Church had appeared, and so had a long-limbed man. He walked towards them with purpose, as if he knew them. She looked at her niece, hoping it wasn't one of those reporters that her sister had warned her would be seeking Lucy, but she was smiling.

'Hello.' The man stopped in front of them.

'Hi.' Lucy mimicked his stance and adjusted her hair. It was like watching a wildlife programme, with those elaborate courting rituals. Hebe could see why. The man was in his mid thirties, blonde, with good cheekbones. There was something familiar about him.

'Been to the house?' His glance moved between them.

Hebe pulled her shoulders back.

'Yes, we've just been. It's a wreck.' Lucy gave a flirtatious

86

laugh. Hebe stifled the urge to kick her in the shins. There was no need to tell this stranger anything.

'I wanted to see what I'd lost.'

'Believe me, you've had a lucky break.'

Hebe looked from one to the other.

'I don't know about that, but my bank manager is happier.' He laughed. It was a deep, pleasant laugh. Hebe studied him. The architecture of his face was excellent; there was good breeding involved in his past. His teeth perhaps were a bit too white – no doubt that was just to meet the latest trend, though she had never been sure of men who chased trends or thought too much of their appearance. But his eyes, now, they were fine. Who was it that said the eyes were windows to the soul? She should remember that. Just as she should have been able to recall who it was he reminded her of. She stamped her feet.

'Oh, sorry, Hebe. This is …'

'Kit Williams.' He held out his hand and Hebe noted that it showed no signs of outdoor work.

'Hebe Courtenay.' She took his hand, approving of the strong grip.

'The new owner of Helwyn House?'

'Yes,' said Lucy, tilting her head. 'I'm Hebe's niece, Lucy Trevillion.'

'Congratulations.' His eyes narrowed, studying them both. Hebe shifted. She wanted none of his scrutiny.

'No, I've just seen it and it should be commiserations.' Lucy grinned. 'Didn't you come to view the house before the auction?'

'No time.' He smiled.

'Filming?' Lucy tucked her hair behind her ear.

'Sadly, no.' He gazed out at the creek. 'My father's funeral.'

'Oh, I'm so sorry.' She paled.

'Thank you.' It was clear that he liked her. Hebe wasn't surprised. She was a beautiful girl even dressed as she was in jeans and an old sweater.

'So this visit now is to confirm you've had a lucky escape?' Lucy leaned towards him.

'More to test my memory – I haven't seen the place in years.'

Hebe noted that his shoulders were broad, his body lean but muscled. Why would a man of his age want an old Cornish house, and more to the point, how would he have the money to pay for it? He didn't look a city type, but nor was he a country one. He wore jeans and an old jacket that spoke of long country walks, but something didn't ring true. Although she couldn't be certain if it was the jeans or the coat that was the problem. She frowned, sensing she should be wary of him.

He cleared his throat. 'May I have your permission to look around the house and the grounds?'

A cloud blocked the sun, and in the shade, Hebe shivered. 'It's locked,' she said, touching the key ring in her pocket. Her fingers sought the cool shapes, the present reality disappeared and the one she had written appeared. His eyes ... his eyes ...

'Hebe?' Lucy touched her arm again.

'Sorry?'

'Is it OK for Kit to look around the outside of the house?'

Hebe nodded and glanced at him, then shivered again. She knew what it was now. The man had Thomas's eyes.

❋ Seventeen ❋

Lucy

1 October 2016

Lucy ducked as she walked through the door of the Shipwrights Arms. The low light and the roaring fire gave the pub a different atmosphere than she remembered. Her memories were filled with sunshine, stars, seaweed, sweet drinks and betrayal. What was in front of her seemed entirely different: a quiet, calm, embracing feeling. Strange.

Hebe strode straight to the bar and ordered a bottle of wine. Lucy had to assume that her aunt planned to drink most of it on her own. They had brought the car and Lucy had volunteered to drive, having been scared out of her wits by Hebe's driving yesterday.

It was hard for her to believe that it was only yesterday that she'd escaped London. Time had slowed down, yet when she looked at the newspapers discarded on a nearby table, she could see that she was still making the headlines.

'Hey, Luce, it *is* you?' the barman called.

She blinked and studied him. It couldn't be … 'Cadan?'

'Got it in one.'

'Long time.'

He laughed. 'No kidding. You haven't changed much.' He gave her a sideways glance as he handed her the wine then passed two glasses to Hebe. 'You know we had a reporter down here at lunchtime asking questions about you?'

'Here?' They must be desperate for news to come here. Lucy was not associated with Cornwall, but she supposed her family was.

'Yes.' He grinned.

Lucy's face coloured, and it wasn't from the warmth of the fire. There were stories from her teen years that Cadan could tell that she certainly wouldn't want in the papers, though she wasn't sure why. They were nothing like the current story. Maybe because it had been a time in her life when she wasn't in the public eye, nor had she tried to be. That came later. Back then she might even go so far as to say she was innocent, even if that was hard to believe now.

'So ... you've taken to married men, have you?' He leaned against the counter behind him.

Lucy shifted from one foot to the other. 'Is that a problem?'

'Not for me.' His glance didn't leave her. 'In touch with Alice?'

'Ouch.' Lucy winced. 'Why do you ask?' Eleven years should be time enough to let go of anger. The knot in her stomach at the mention of Alice's name told her it hadn't been long enough yet.

He raised an eyebrow. 'Just wondered.'

'What did you tell the reporter?' She swallowed.

'To sod off; we hadn't seen you in years.' He picked up a glass and polished it. 'Old Jim told him a tall tale or four then sent him away down towards Porthallow, saying that he might have seen you walking along the cliffs looking despondent.'

She laughed. 'The back road?'

'Yup, he might be stuck for weeks.' He put the glass down, grinning.

'Is Alice around?' She straightened a bar mat.

'No, she lives in London now.' He pulled two menus out. 'Now, are you ladies having dinner with us tonight?'

She nodded.

'The specials are on the board, and I can recommend the mullet; it was landed not long ago.'

'Thanks, Cadan. If anyone else comes round asking about me, I'm not here.'

'Of course, you never are.' He winked, and she remembered the kid she'd spent so much time messing about with on the river, drinking cider into the small hours. It was a blissful time, but she knew that bliss never lasted. It was best to move on before it disappeared.

Hebe settled in the corner by the fireplace. 'Was that Pat's son?'

'Yes.'

'He's a promising artist. I've seen his work ... somewhere.'

Lucy nodded. Cadan had always loved art. When she was sixteen, he'd asked her to pose nude for him. She'd thought it had been to get her out of her clothes, and was crestfallen when that hadn't been the case. He'd genuinely wanted to sketch her. His eventual painting of her had looked nothing like her, which was just as well as her father had lost his rag over the whole thing. After that, she had been a nude model any time she was short of money, which was frequently. In fact those sketches and others would no doubt appear if a bigger story didn't crop up to overshadow the current one.

She hadn't looked at her phone all day. It was the best way to remain in denial. Friends had been emailing and texting to check on her, but possibly down here carrier pigeon was best. Signal was hit and mostly miss. But she liked the ostrich approach, and being here made it easier. The Canary Islands would have been warmer, but maybe too visible. Perhaps Bali would have worked.

'Hey, Luce.' Cadan leaned on the bar. 'Are you going to be around for a bit?'

She shrugged. Not if she could help it, she thought.

'Well if you are, let me know.'

'OK.'

'Just need to be able to send the reporters in the wrong direction. You're staying in St Anthony at the moment, yes?'

She nodded. The reporters might not be able to find out where she was, but everyone here knew. Hell, she had only arrived last night. The jungle drums had been working overtime. But then nothing was secret here. Even when the population swelled in the summer, it was a small community.

'Give me your mobile number before you leave tonight so we can warn you if we need to.'

'Sure.' That was either a great chat-up line, or else he actually cared. Or maybe it was something else. And why had he brought up Alice? It was good to know that she wasn't around. She was one person Lucy never wanted to see again.

Hebe pulled a notebook from her bag and began adding to a list. Lucy could see it already had things on it like 'brush teeth' and 'call council'. She wasn't sure what one had to do with the other, unless it was a case of putting things on there that she knew she could cross off easily. Lucy had gone through a year of doing that just to feel she was at least achieving something in her life. It had been an illusion, though, and while everyone was entitled to them, she was surprised that her aunt of all people needed such tricks.

Hebe was so accomplished: a full professor so young and the leading expert on the English Civil War. Her work was her world. Lucy had never known her to be in a relationship. She guessed it would interrupt Hebe's well-ordered life. Looking at her now, she realised her aunt was beautiful in a very quiet way, and certainly never drew attention to herself. They were so different, apart from the fact that Hebe, like Lucy, had a thing about lipstick. Lucy had never seen her without it, even now when Hebe wore no other make-up that she could see. But Lucy didn't feel dressed without it either. Forget clothes, give her red lips.

'Lucy?'

'Yes?' Her stomach sank at Hebe's tone.

'I think we should be able to move into the better bit of the house by the weekend.'

Lucy shuddered. From what she'd seen of the house today, there was no way they could live there. The electrics looked like they were installed in 1600, and the plumbing facilities even earlier ... talk about the Dark Ages. Not that she had ever noticed any of these problems when they had spent their summers here. She was not sure which had changed more – the house or her.

'I'm not sure I'd agree,' she said. Tonight the temperature had dropped and there was already dew on the grass. Lucy liked the idea of central heating and hot water. Call her materialistic, but these things were essential to a happy life.

'It will be fine once I've given it a good clean. Don't suppose I could hire you to help while you're here?'

'You don't need to hire me. Of course I'll help.' She took a deep breath, thinking of the years of grime accumulated everywhere. But it would keep her mind off other things, like Ed's persistent texts. There had been ten yesterday. She'd deleted them all without replying. He clearly thought her a fool. Of course, she had been one, but not any more.

'Don't be silly. Your mother told me you were out of a job. Surely you could use the money.'

'True.' She gave her aunt a lopsided grin.

'Fred says it's only the north wing, particularly the King's Room, that is in need of urgent attention.' Hebe looked up from her notebook and smiled. 'There is running water, and I've booked the chimney sweep for tomorrow.'

Lucy squinted at her. Those chimneys would fall down if the dust was swept away. 'I think they need to be lined at the minimum. I'm not a pro, but I wouldn't think the masonry was safe.'

'It will be an adventure.' Hebe smiled.

Lucy's idea of adventure came with five stars, minimum. 'Hebe, it's not habitable as it stands at the moment.' Had her aunt gone delusional when she wasn't looking?

'It needs some love, which we will give it. And at least there is no chance of any stray reporters finding you there.'

'That's true,' she agreed. The only things that would find them there were rats and spirits of the past. Neither of which bore thinking about.

Wild, overgrown and damp. Could she love Hell House? Not likely, but cleaning it was manageable, she hoped. With a bit of luck she would be gone from here by the time it was truly possible to move in.

❊ Eighteen ❊
Hebe

July 2015

The seagulls swoop above as we stand by the harbour wall. Our ice creams are in jeopardy as the gulls dive closer. You laugh and I do too. I lick the cool, sweet vanilla, its taste taking me back years to childhood visits here, then feel it touch my nose as I duck from the birds. You put an arm out to protect me from the attack, then laugh as you look at me. My nose is covered in ice cream and you lean in and kiss it away. I shiver in the warmth of the sun, feeling passion chase through me. Your eyes are smiling. 'You look like a child,' you say.

All at once the joy stops. I will *be* more like a child as each day passes. You take your handkerchief out of your pocket and clean the last of the ice cream from my face. I try not to feel the glances directed at us, but I am useless. I step away from you, and with each step I become more certain of what I need to do. But I have decided to act before and still done nothing.

*

Stand still, and I will read to thee
A lecture, love, in love's philosophy.

Leave, I told you. You crossed your arms against your chest.
'No,' you said.
I paced the room. I was not physically strong enough to force you to go. Nor was I mentally able. But go you must. 'This isn't right.'
'What is wrong with us?'

94

I sighed.

'That there *is* an us.'

'Us is good.'

'No, it's wrong, so wrong.'

'Why? My age?' You raised an eyebrow. Your hair fell across your forehead. I could see the muscles in your arms and on your chest, under the fabric of your band-logo T-shirt. I'd never heard of them. That told me everything.

'It doesn't help.'

You laughed and stepped closer. I backed away. You moved closer still until our bodies met. 'My age helps things.' Your hips pressed against mine. Desire flared. With both hands I pushed you from me, yet my fingers didn't release you.

'Your age is wrong. *We* are wrong. You are my student.'

A slow smile spread across your face. 'So if I quit uni, there would be no problem.'

I sighed. You have won, because you know I will not concede to you quitting.

'*Come, madam, come, all rest my powers defy,*' you said, picking up the book of Donne's elegies and beginning to read. '*Off with that girdle, like heaven's zone glistering.*' You placed the book down and pulled my shirt off. '*Unlace yourself ...*' You glanced down at the page as your fingers unhooked my bra. '*For that harmonious chime tells me from you that now it is bed time.*' You undid my belt and slid my jeans down. I stood still, barely breathing.

'*License my roving hands, and let them go, behind, before, above, between below.*' Your hands moved as you said. I trembled. You carried me to bed and made me your America, your new-found-land, and I was happy with being one man manned.

*

We walk through the tourists to the museum, but my thoughts are not open to art. They are not open at all; they are simply disappearing. I turn to you, and you are squinting into the sun, watching a child play ball on the beach with his father. My heart twists, seeing the longing on your face. I have been selfish.

95

❄ Nineteen ❄

Lucy

2 October 2016

'Hi, Mum.' Lucy looked out of the kitchen window. October mornings didn't come more beautiful than this. Glimpses of blue water sparkled between the laid-up boats.

'How's Hebe?' Mum coughed. 'I had a very strange message from a man called Rory Crown who was looking for her.'

All around was evidence of Hebe having been and gone. 'She's fine, I guess. Slightly distracted by her purchase.' Lucy had always liked a bit of understatement. She'd heard Hebe up early, walking around the cottage.

'That tells me nothing. Has she mentioned this Rory chap to you?'

'No.'

Mum sighed long and loud. Lucy wondered who was unsettling her more: Hebe or Lucy herself.

'Well, I wrote down his number just in case. Can you mention it to her? She isn't answering her phone or emails.'

'I think she's focused on the house.' And the two of them living in it soon, she added silently. She was beginning to think she and Hebe were talking about different buildings. While Lucy saw the tired form of a once great house, Hebe saw a comfortable home. Even in its heyday it would have struggled to be comfortable, with the inevitable draughts, over-grand rooms, and no hot water let alone central heating. However she would allow that the windows were beautiful and the loggia spectacular, and clearly the goat thought the same.

Yesterday they had moved the goat to the walled garden at

96

the back of the house while they tried to track down its owner. Fred had no idea who the animal belonged to, but Hebe was already attached to it and calling it Henrietta. Personally Lucy thought it might be a Henry, but she wasn't going to volunteer to check.

'I don't know why she bought it, Lucy, and I have no idea where she found that amount of money.' Kate took a breath. 'If you had done what we'd asked, these questions would be irrelevant.'

'She says her books paid for it.' The corners of Lucy's mouth lifted.

'Don't be ridiculous.' She heard her mother's intake of breath. 'And even if she managed to save that much money, she can't have anywhere near enough to fix and run a house of that size.'

'I've no clue.' Hebe certainly showed no interest in the back-of-an-envelope figures that Fred was quoting. Lucy switched on the kettle.

There was a moment of silence, then she heard her mother clear her throat. 'The house was tired when we rented it but it was fine for the summers.'

Lucy bit her lip, letting the conflicting memories run amok in her head. Happy families versus totally broken ones.

'Well, keep me posted, and do take down this Rory's number and run it past your aunt.'

Lucy rummaged in her bag and found an old receipt, then dutifully wrote down the name and number, leaving it on the counter by the kettle.

'I'm sending Michael down this weekend with some of your things.'

She opened her eyes wide. Michael doing something for her? 'Thanks.' She looked out of the window again. It was so beautiful. 'Could you ask him to bring my camera stuff?'

'Of course. Have you found a job?'

'No, but you don't need to sound so surprised at the thought that I might have done.'

'I wasn't surprised, just hopeful.' Kate sighed. 'Maybe you

could work as a wedding photographer down there.'

'Oh, you think they don't read the papers or watch the news or go on the Internet in Cornwall.' She winced, thinking of her agent's words just days ago.

'Lucy—'

'Sorry, but I doubt anyone would want me to be in attendance on their big day.'

'True. You do grab the limelight.'

She tried to laugh, but it came out more of a snort. Not very attractive.

'OK, well keep a low profile. You're still in the papers, but thankfully the spectacle of the US election is taking over.'

Lucy clenched her fist. 'How much longer do you think I need to stay?' She'd only been in Cornwall a couple of days, but already it felt like years.

'Darling, I …' Kate paused, 'I don't know, but you've got plenty to keep you busy – and please keep an eye on Hebe.'

'Why do you say that?' Lucy tilted her head to the side, thinking of some of the odd things Hebe had done.

'Buying this house is why. It's out of character.'

She found herself wanting to leap to Hebe's defence, even though her mother's thoughts echoed her own. 'I suppose so, but she's always been fascinated with Helwyn and its history.'

'True.'

'OK, I'll watch out for her. Bye, Mum.'

Her mother had a point. Hebe wasn't her normal self. Distracted and obsessed with lists, she was forever jotting things down. Lucy understood the renovation was a big project. She'd offered to put it all on a spreadsheet, but her aunt had looked flustered by the offer, as if she hadn't known what a spreadsheet was.

'Morning.' Mr Movie Star was standing in the doorway, and Lucy's heart jumped so far it felt like it had leapt out to the beach.

'Hello.' She picked up the just-boiled kettle, debating whether to offer him a cup of tea. Then she glanced at her phone, making sure her browser wasn't still open on his IMDb

98

page. Of course she'd checked him out. She wouldn't have been human if she hadn't. His last film had bombed in a big way. Up until then, Kit Williams had been golden, but there were no current projects listed.

'I'd love one if you're offering.'

She plucked another tea bag out of the box and dropped it into a mug. 'Sure.'

'Thanks.' He was still hovering by the door, despite inviting himself for tea. Polite, she guessed, but weird.

'What are you doing still hanging around here?' Beckoning him in, she handed him the milk. He could sort out his own brew.

'I've rented a cottage.' He pointed to the one opposite.

'The farmhouse.' Lucy frowned. 'For how long?' she asked, trying to remember what the latest gossip magazines were saying about his love life. She knew that he'd broken up with his long-term girlfriend about a year ago. Something about careers pulling them apart.

'At least a month, maybe longer.'

'A month? Hollywood can do without you for that long?' She cradled her mug and studied the fine specimen in front of her. She could see why the camera loved him. There would be no skill required to flatter him; she would have to work hard to find a bad angle. It might be fun trying.

He looked older but far better in the flesh. Of course she wouldn't mention that she'd been watching one of his films on her tablet into the small hours of last night – no, that wouldn't do at all – but he might prove an interesting distraction if he was around for a while. A man with a sell-by date of sorts was good. She frowned, thinking of the downside. It meant that she was accepting that she'd be here for a month too – or worse, living in Hell House with Hebe. She needed to check the status of the Ed crisis. Here in this land at the edge of the world, she hadn't heard a peep.

'Did I notice your picture in the paper this morning?'

Damn. 'Did you?'

'Never wise to sleep with a politician …'

'Do you know that from experience?'

'Thankfully, no.' He smiled and her heart missed a beat, just a short one. After all, he was a movie star and that was what he was designed to do ... make hearts flutter and all that. She wasn't immune but she knew it couldn't be real. It was done for effect, and boy did it work.

'Where's your aunt?'

'At Hell House, I think.'

He raised an eyebrow. 'Hell House?'

'That's what it's called locally.' She sipped her tea.

'Fair enough, I guess.'

'Let's put it this way, kids won't go near it on Halloween.'

'Really, you intrigue me.'

She cradled her mug. 'You mean Hell House does.'

'No, you, the way you said it. It was with authority, as if ...'

'As if I believed in ghosts?'

'Your words, not mine.'

She studied him. He was more perceptive than she'd given him credit for. 'I might believe there are things beyond what we can see.'

'You've been spooked at the house, in other words.' The left side of his rather fine mouth lifted and a dimple appeared. How was a woman supposed to think straight with that so close and in high-definition reality?

Her phone beeped, and she glanced at the screen. Ed. Her stomach turned. He just wasn't going away. She switched it off.

'It's always safer to have affairs with people who are free to have them.'

Lucy looked up sharply. His eyes weren't accusing her, but they weren't far off it. She pressed her lips together. The fates had decided she was taking the fall for this one.

'I'm sure it is, but sometimes things don't work out that way.'

'I know.' He looked out of the window as a car drew up outside. The engine sounded loud in the quiet of the morning.

'Excuse me,' said a clear voice. 'I'm looking for Lucy Trevillion. Can you tell me where to find her?'

Lucy ducked down below the window, but on her way out of

sight, she glimpsed Anthony Jenkin standing by the car talking to the owner of the clear voice. She hadn't warned him to keep quiet. If the press found her, it would be harder to stay silent. Something would slip out, stirring things up. At the pub, no one had asked except Cadan. It was her business. They might discuss her when she wasn't among them, but as much as she hated Cornwall, the people were good. They wouldn't rat on her – or most of them wouldn't. She ground her teeth, thinking of the exception.

She risked a glance out of the window to see Anthony pointing up the road in the opposite direction to Hell House, though she couldn't hear what he was saying. Kit had removed himself from view, too. If the journalists couldn't find her, then he would be a brilliant consolation prize for them. And if they were found together, she could just see the headlines: *Lucy leaves MP lover and hops into bed with hot hero*, or something equally horrendous.

The car turned right in front of the cottage and she remained crouched out of sight while Kit continued to look as invisible as possible, which with him wasn't easy. There was a quality about him that shouted 'look at me', even when he was pressed to a door frame clutching a mug of tea. Lucy laughed. His eyes met hers and he grinned.

'Not a great way to live.'

'Definitely not. Hopefully Anthony sent him on a wild goose chase and I won't have to cut my hair and dye it black.'

He tilted his head to one side and studied her. 'It wouldn't be a bad look.'

'Hairdresser in your spare time?'

'Sadly, no.' The corner of his mouth lifted again.

'Just a movie star then?'

'Mostly, and sometimes an amateur archaeologist.'

She stopped, her mug in mid air. 'Is that why you're interested in Hell House?'

'In a way. A distant ancestor of mine lived there.'

'So you're related to the Grylls? Or is it the other family, that came later, after the Restoration?' She took a sip of tea.

'I'm impressed by your knowledge.'

'Hard not to know about it with my aunt being the pre-eminent expert on the Civil War in Cornwall and obsessed with the house.'

'True. Well, as it happens, I'm a Grylls, and I can trace the line way back.'

She put her mug down. 'How far back?'

'The sixteen hundreds.'

She searched his face, looking for his Cornish heritage, but couldn't see it. It was as if his years in Hollywood had erased it. Then she paused. There *was* something, something about his eyes. They were like Hebe's portrait. The boy in that painting was about seventeen, and Kit was a man of thirty-three, but there was a definite look that the two of them shared.

✳ Twenty ✳

Hebe

Hebe read yesterday's entry in her journal. She couldn't remember the cod Lucy had cooked last night, but she had enjoyed it, apparently. She knew this because she'd written it down. Yesterday she'd also attended the Communion service at St Anthony's Church. There had only been five of them. She wasn't a believer, but she found comfort in attending services, even though she spent most of them lost in the architecture of the church.

The feast of St Thomas of Hereford, excommunicated
1282 and canonised 1320
Perceptions change over time.

She put the journal down, then stood and opened the kitchen door. The air was crisp and she sucked it into her lungs. It was good to be alive on such a morning. She knew these days – the clear skies, the leaves still lingering on the trees – were numbered. It didn't matter. Helwyn House was all that was important now. No matter what Lucy had said, Hebe knew the house was habitable. It was grimy and damp, but nothing that a bit of elbow grease and a good builder couldn't fix.

Closing her journal, she tucked it into her bag with a thermos, sandwiches, and assorted cleaning materials along with her lists. Today she would begin to make Helwyn House her home, and she looked forward to the hard labour in front of her. She was going to start with the kitchen, while Fred and his team would be covering the holes in the roof on the north wing to make the building watertight until they could get the necessary permission to begin proper work.

She had looped the ring of keys onto her belt like a chatelaine of old, and they jingled as she walked along the lane. In her mind, she wore a full skirt and bodice rather than jeans and an old jumper. Many times she'd imagined what it would have been like to be mistress of Helwyn in 1640. Although Thomas never married she had often dreamed of what it would have been to be his wife, sleeping in his bed and enjoying the power of his passion. For he had been full of passion, she knew that. It was there in his words to Lucia. The poetry of the age spoke of love – heavenly and earthly – in such a way that her body trembled even thinking about it now.

Her phone beeped and the dream of being from another time disappeared. She pulled it out of her pocket.

Where are you? Why aren't you answering me?

Her heart tightened. Breathing slowly, she waited for the pain to ease. She ached for him, but this was best. It was hard for them both now, but like pulling a plaster off, it wouldn't last. Soon he would cease to text, call, email. Hebe was sure he'd been to her flat and looked for clues. But she'd had time to plan, and had tided everything away and arranged for all her post to be forwarded to her solicitor. The flat would be sold soon and there would be no trace of her left. This would no doubt force him to hate her.

Love and hate were so very close. In the end Thomas had hated Lucia as much as he'd loved her. He'd understood she'd had little choice in marrying her cousin. Did he ever recover from losing her? Was that why he never returned? Here, now, in this moment, Hebe's thoughts were crystal clear, like the blue sky above her. Love and passion leading to loss, decay.

The creek below was at flood peak and the pair of swans were by the far bank. The first cloud of the day appeared, reflected in the water along with the pines that towered above. The trees looked so at home, yet they were new additions to the landscape. Half closing her eyes, she pictured a gaff-rigged ship at the old quay in the distance. Many hands had worked to unload the stone. It was September 1615, and Thomas Grylls's father was beginning his expansion of the house built by the friars from France.

She stopped walking and turned to look for the church tower. The church had been built because of a promise to God. It had been done in honour of St Anthony, but she couldn't remember why. Something to do with a storm. She looked up. The sky was blue. No clouds, no storm. The bell tower was built of stone brought from Normandy, but the church and the first cells were local. As the community grew, it became part of the Benedictines of Tywardreath Priory. All of this was clear in her mind, but breakfast from this morning wasn't.

She stuck her hand in her pocket and found her list for today. The first item was: *Helwyn House belongs to you.*

Yes. It was not a dream. She smiled and thought about the history of her house. Henry VIII's dissolution of the monasteries had benefited the Grylls family hugely. It had been the monastery of St Anthony, but the Gryllses had decided to use the locals' name for it, Helwyn. The monks had been productive and generous to the local people, especially sharing the produce of their orchards. Hebe frowned. What was it they produced from the fruit? What fruit was it?

Her phone beeped again. She wasn't going to respond. Glancing at it in her hand, she considered throwing it into the water. In seconds it would be at the bottom of the creek, sinking into the mud. Tempting. Instead she looked at the screen. There was an email from her solicitor. She wanted to know where to send her post, and asked whether she had had the power of attorney forms signed. She must add that to the list. Having Lucy here, although not planned, was ... good.

The phone beeped yet again. Modern life had too many intrusions. She ignored it and turned her mind back to Helwyn: *Hel* in Cornish meaning generous, *yow* meaning hall. It had been Thomas's father who had taken the old cloisters and refashioned them into the loggia that still stood today. It had all been inspired by his visit to Europe as a young man.

A horn sounded behind her and she stepped aside for a white van to pass. She followed its progress to see it turn up towards Helwyn. Once boats brought men and materials, now it was white vans. She preferred the age of sail to diesel.

Fred and his team must be gathering, and she needed to increase her pace. Today hopefully the electricity would be reconnected. The question that Lucy would doubtless raise was would it be safe. That was a valid point, but Hebe had every confidence in the house. She just didn't have confidence that she would have enough time left to restore it, though at least she would have begun the process. She would have to trust Lucy to complete it, even though Lucy never stuck to anything or anyone except her photography. Perhaps her niece was the weak link in her plan.

Hebe's hands were stained with grime. Black moons waxed under her nails and her knuckles were red, but she had never been so happy. Above her the sound of banging and shouting told her of progress. The house wrapped itself around her. She closed her eyes so that she could feel it. There was a presence here. In her heart she'd always felt that Thomas had come back, but she had never been able to prove it. Something caressed her cheek and she opened her eyes to see a red admiral butterfly. Black wings with flashes of red and white. It escaped through the kitchen door.

Consulting her list, she glanced down the items to where she had written 'clean the sink'. Drawing a pencil line through it, she noted that it had been the last item for this room. She stood back and admired her handiwork. The kitchen didn't sparkle, but at least it was no longer coated in dust and mouse droppings, although the newly washed floor still scuttled with woodlice.

She shrugged, and walked up the servants' stairs to the first floor, opening each door along the way, letting what daylight there was through to the corridor. A tree surgeon was needed. Pulling her list out, she stopped to add it to the bottom, then underlined it. She wouldn't be able to take trees down without permission, but she would be able to at least pollard the ones closest to the house and let in the light. That would begin to take care of the damp plaster that blistered on the walls due to the years the house had been unoccupied.

When she came to the main bedroom, she paused to admire the south-facing window. Miraculously, the beautiful glass brought from Italy in the 1700s was all still intact. Was this Thomas's room, or had he used the one at the other end of the building? Or perhaps one of the many more that had been … The word was gone. It was exhausting. As a child, she'd always loved word-search puzzles, but now it was pure frustration. In the mass of letters, she couldn't pick out words, and each day the puzzles became harder.

She leaned her forehead against the remains of the old bed-post. Dust clung to the carving on it. The particles filled the crevices, smoothing the intricate design. Only the colour difference indicated that it wasn't as it should be. Was this what was happening in her brain? Was it becoming clogged with dust, brain dust, marring the beauty of its design? She frowned. No, the image was wrong. Everything in her mind had shifted, so that nothing connected properly any more.

She put her hand in her pocket and took out the list. Opening it, she read:

You own Helwyn House
Clean kitchen.
Begin with cupboards
Then counters
Then table
Then floor
Cooker if there is one (check)
Clean the sink
Make list of next cleaning tasks
Have Lucy sign forms
Book tree surgeon

Feeling for a pencil in her pocket, she pulled it out and

glanced round the room in which she stood. She stroked the post. Time, woodworm and vandals had taken their toll, but it could be restored, unlike her mind. She must be careful.

Looking heavenward, she studied the intricate cornicing. Most was intact, but a few parts were hanging off or missing entirely, spoiling the perfection. Repair would require a specialist, and would be painstaking and expensive. She had enough money, she thought, but did she have enough time?

She glanced out and saw Lucy pull up in the car. She had been doing the shopping. Hebe gripped the sill. Everything blanked for a moment, but only the briefest of moments. What had she been thinking about? Closing her eyes, she searched her brain, but whatever she sought was hidden from her view again.

'Hello?' shouted a man's voice.

Hebe stood straight. 'Yes?' She walked in the direction of the voice. As she passed through the salon, she noted the glorious proportions. The room would once have had a view to the creek, but now it looked on to a dense wood. Everything of the past was erased by the verdant growth of hundreds of years left unchecked.

In the north bedroom, she found Fred stranded halfway through the ceiling.

'Can you go get the guys? I think they're taking a break.'

Hebe dashed through the house, not stopping until she fell into the arms of the stranger standing beside Lucy. 'Help!'

Twenty-One
Hebe

3 October 2016

Energy drained from Hebe as she sat on a wooden bench in the dining room with her list beside her. That man was running his hands over the stone of the fireplace with a lover's touch. A great black mark scarred the top left side. His fingers caressed it. The blackness looked new and not as if it had happened years ago. But it had. It was a scorch mark. It would have been made to … to protect the house from fire. Yes, that was it. It would have been made with a tallow candle.

No one seemed to know the last time anyone had stayed in the house for more than a night since her sister ceased to rent it during those summers years ago. Its past was so chequered and marked with tragedy. People felt it was cursed, but Kate's family had had such happy times here, she wouldn't believe that. Although since Thomas had disappeared, the Grylls family had faced one disaster after another.

In past summers, Hebe used to wake at Helwyn to the sound of the soldiers marching down the lane. If she'd been the only one to hear it, she would have dismissed it years ago, but the woman who lived in the mill house was frequently woken by the sound, too. Restless spirits. Of course there would be restless spirits here too with so much history and heartbreak.

Golden autumn light filtered through the fog, casting a glow on the wooden panelling. The windows distorted the view of the north wing beyond. Each pane warped the vision in its own way.

Hebe blinked. The handsome man stood in front of her.

'Do you know the history of the house?' He glanced about the room before turning back to her.

She nodded, staring at the beautiful panelling and an ancient fire grate. In her hand she clutched a paper. She unfolded it.

You own Helwyn House.

'People seem to think it's haunted,' the man with the white teeth said.

'Ridiculous.'

'I agree.' He sat beside her. His eyes, there was something about his eyes. She tried to place what it was. Unease crawled along her skin. His eyes were familiar, but why was that? Had she met him before? Taught him, maybe?

'The house is not haunted, though if you look at its history, you can see the reason for such beliefs.' The marks upstairs by the window and the fireplace. No doubt they would find more evidence as they repaired the building. She stood. It irritated her that she couldn't place what it was about him. She should know. 'Helwyn House was originally a monastery, and any time you involve religion, you …' she flexed her hands, 'you garner mystery to a building.'

He nodded, then stood and walked to the fireplace again. Hebe couldn't recall his name. Lucy had told her it yesterday, that much she could remember, but not the fact that she wanted. Out of reach. Her fingers twitched. Why wasn't her brain like her laptop? She wanted to reboot it, but already her hard drive was beyond repair.

'Why are you so interested in the house?' She moved towards him where he was crouching over the floor of the hearth. What on earth did he hope to discover by looking at the slates? This room had been altered many times since the house was constructed. Each owner had left their mark. The most striking feature was the loggia, but there were other parts that were just as fine and of more interest historically. 'What are you looking for?'

He looked up. 'Clues.'

'To what?' Her voice was sharper than she intended.

'A puzzle my father left me.'

'A puzzle?'

'Yes, just before he died, he discovered a missing piece of our family history and indicated that there were more pieces to be found and that they would be at Helwyn House.'

'You think they will be in the fireplace?' She drew her brows together. He was not making sense. Not quite talking in riddles either, but not speaking directly.

He stood. 'No.'

'Just what are you looking for in my house?' Hebe needed to keep telling herself it really was hers, not just something she'd imagined.

'A body, maybe.' He smiled. 'Or a priest hole, smugglers' store, secret passage ... but more likely letters or a piece of jewellery.'

Hebe ran through the list. What was he really after?

'Are you related to the Pendarves family?'

'No, the Gryllses.' He paused and looked directly at her. 'I'm descended from Thomas Grylls.'

Hebe swallowed. A knot tightened in her stomach. 'Through his cousin.'

'No, directly from him.'

She shook her head. 'He had no children.'

'He did.' The man slipped his hands into his pockets.

'There is no reference in any of his papers or in any other sources. You must be mistaken.'

He leaned against the fireplace. 'I'm not.' He was the picture of ease, surety.

Hebe ground her teeth. 'I have made the study of Thomas Grylls a large part of my life's work. If he'd had a child, I would have known.'

He smiled. 'How much do you know about his time on the Isles of Scilly?'

'He was there only a short time with the Prince of Wales.'

'Yes, but he also went back several times, even during the Parliamentarian rule.'

She frowned. Thomas had been a spy as well as an emissary. A dull ache was building between her brows as those synapses that still worked tried to prove that this man was wrong. 'Again, he stayed for very short periods.'

He pulled his shoulders back like he was spoiling for a fight. Hebe knew she hadn't forgotten some long-distant heir. Thomas's life was so clear in her mind, clearer even than her own. He had not had children. She wouldn't have forgotten or missed something so vital. She lowered her chin towards her neck, then backed away towards the windows, just as Lucy walked into the room carrying a tray. The man stood with his arms lightly crossed, relaxed. Hebe swatted at a cluster fly with more force than was needed. It fell to the floor and she stepped on it.

'Thanks again for helping to rescue Fred.' Lucy put the tray on the table. The man smiled at her and Hebe turned away.

Lucy handed Hebe her tea first, then gave a cup to the man with the white teeth. Hebe closed her eyes briefly. Why didn't he just go away? Why was he here in her house, and more importantly, how could he be descended from Thomas? She wanted to shout at him and tell him he was a liar. But something inside her believed him. It was his eyes. 'What proof do you have?' she asked.

'Letters.'

She released the breath she had been holding. 'Not total proof.'

'No, but genetics are.'

'Good, but not a hundred per cent.'

'Combined with the letters it could be quite convincing.'

Hebe sipped her tea. 'How can you do genetics? The Grylls line died out.' All these years she had worked on the basis that Thomas had had no heirs, and most importantly, that he had remained loyal to Lucia.

She tried to force this new information into what already existed, but she couldn't make it work. It was like a book that wouldn't fit on the shelf even though the space looked sufficient. The historian in her told her not to believe him, to question him more. Demand to see the letters. No one knew what had become of Thomas. No one.

It was one of the questions that had plagued her research. The question that no matter how many old libraries she searched she had never been able to answer. What had become of Thomas Grylls on that last voyage? There had been rumours of sightings in Europe, but then the trail went cold. A ship had gone down off the Nare in 1660, and she had always imagined that he had gone down with it. But it wasn't the one on which he had left the Netherlands. That one had arrived in London without him on board.

The *Swallow*, however, had been caught in a fierce storm and hit the Manacles off St Keverne, then been blown onto the cliff near Porthallow. The remains had been found on the rocks of the Nare. All souls were lost. It had always bothered her that this had been his end. He had known the waters of the Lizard better than most men of his age. Living here on the creek, he had sailed almost before he could walk. His first boat was listed in his father's chattels: *Elspeth*, a gaff-rigged vessel. Thomas had taken it as far as St Michael's Mount to visit his cousins on many occasions. She'd read accounts. He knew the sea and its ways.

'May I see these letters?' There was something else. She must ask him something, but she couldn't remember what it was. Damn her mind.

'I don't have them with me.' He reached out and took his tea from the table.

'Obviously,' she said with impatience.

'Currently they are on St Mary's, where my father was living, but I'll happily show them to you when I next make the trip.'

'Thank you.' Hebe took a sip of her tea. 'I sense that you know more about Thomas Grylls than you are telling me at the moment.'

He smiled, and she wondered if the sun had suddenly come out. Then she shivered, but she didn't know why.

Mizzle blurred the shapes of the headlands and Hebe's face was more than damp. For years she had pictured Lucia coming here and awaiting Thomas's return, even after her marriage and the rumours of his death. What had she got wrong? Had their letters been false? Had their love not been true? She wiped her eyes where the beads of moisture clung to her lashes. Love. She had known its power to give and to take. She'd avoided any chance of it until words had broken her barriers down. They'd moved her. And now words written in letters could destroy her work.

Did it really matter any more if her life's work was incorrect? Didn't that happen all the time? She herself had found further evidence of the effects of the Civil Wars on Cornwall that had overturned previous assumptions. It didn't take much; simply the discovery of a new original source of information. She hadn't rejoiced that she had unpicked someone else's work so much as been relieved that she had found something that gave a ... sharper picture and a better understanding. The past was always changing. Yet she had one more book to write, and now she had no idea how it would end. Her fiction had always worked because she'd known the facts.

The man with the white teeth was related to Thomas. She felt it. The physical evidence meant she couldn't ignore what he said. When she had stomped away from Helwyn, he and Lucy were looking at the archway to the remains of the great hall. He was not an amateur. He was seeking something, something to validate his hypo ... his hypothesis. She had seen that same tenacity in herself when she tirelessly went through the archives in great houses around the country. Those often-dismissed scraps of paper might contain missing information that would turn a gut instinct into a fact.

Pushing a wet tendril of hair off her forehead, she squinted out to the bay. Both sky and sea were the same colour, and the horizon was lost. How could she find her direction when the horizon was missing? She looked up: no sun and no other stars to guide her.

Right at this moment, her goals were clear, but for how long? Her hands balled into fists. Things would continue to leave her. She reached into her pocket and felt the slip of paper. Her life had come down to this. How long would it be before she didn't know Lucy's name, or her own? Bands tightened around her chest. She didn't want to live that way. Pain, emptiness, longing tormented her when she thought of him. But those things meant that she had loved. She had lived. It hurt enough that most of the time she couldn't remember him. But maybe that was best. She turned and walked back down to St Anthony listening to the bells. It was the slow ring, a funeral.

Twenty-Two

Lucy

3 October 2016

Hebe had walked out of the house in a huff, without a word. It was odd. She wasn't the Hebe of old. Was it the menopause? Her mother had begun to act differently with it, but Hebe was older by five years. Shouldn't she be through it? Lucy frowned. When Hebe had been chatting with Kit in the dining room, she had heard the lecturer's tone in her voice, but she had also heard something new: uncertainty.

A butterfly flew through the hallway door. She turned and found it on the window grid, not moving, its colour vibrant in the light cast from the ceiling bulb. The shadow from its wings made it appear to be resting on another butterfly. She shuddered. It was as if just being here had wound her brain back eleven years. The house wasn't haunted, but it wasn't a happy place. She wasn't sure if it had ever been one, given the stories they had been told about headless monks, roaming Cavaliers and heartbroken lovers. These tales were rarely without some thread of truth in them.

What was it about kids telling ghost stories on summer nights? Sitting outside by the wall of the great hall, she had listened to gruesome tales of cadavers on the dining table and a headless army marching down the lanes. One night with a full moon, she had heard them go by, or thought she had. It had probably been a tractor working by moonlight.

Damn, now she was spooking herself. It was just childish prattle. She knew only too well that the dead couldn't hurt you, but the living bloody well could. Her father was a prime example.

The ceiling light flickered. This house was a death trap. The electrician was coming again tomorrow. She wished him the best of luck. The fuse boxes belonged in a museum, along with the servants' bells lining the wall above the door leading to the pantry. She doubted they still worked, but then remembered her father using them to alert her to the fact that they were out of tonic in the salon. He'd thought it was a laugh, but she'd felt differently. Her mother had ended up getting the tonic for him. She waited on him hand and foot and then some. Lucy never understood why. Why had she put up with his infidelity all these years?

Something thumped and she jumped. She was alone in the house. Fred and his crew had left half an hour ago. It must have been the wind, but as she looked out of the window, she saw that everything was still. It always was when the sea fog snuck across the land, damping down all movement and sound.

She had better check things out. At the top of the servants' stairs, she shoved her freezing hands into her jeans pockets. There wasn't a radiator in sight. God, it was cold.

In front of her was the bedroom she used to share with Michael. It wasn't as if there weren't enough bedrooms in the place, but they were both scared of the house because of all the ghost stories. Michael had loved telling them, but he was the one to move into her room. He only left when he hit thirteen and didn't think it was the done thing to be sharing with his older sister. In this, of course, he'd been right. Yet she had missed the comfort of his smelly boy presence in the twin bed next to hers, because Hell House made noises continuously, like it was a living, breathing beast.

She ventured into the bedroom. This room, like so much of the rest of the house, was unaltered, containing all the furnishings she remembered – including the bed linen, which was worrying. Were Michael's old comics still shoved under the bed? She wasn't curious enough to check. She looked at the worn carpet; they needed to get a hoover and a whole lot more very soon. On her phone she began a list of required equipment.

Leaving the bedroom, she came back out onto the landing.

This place was a maze. In the small sitting room she saw that the television – circa 1980 – was still there. It had barely worked back then. She added a new TV to the list, along with torches, matches, candles, firelighters and firewood. Had Hebe contacted a tree surgeon yet? Maybe Lucy should do it, as her aunt seemed to be struggling to get organised.

There was a loud thump, and the door to one of the bedrooms along the corridor blew open. Had Fred gone through the floor again? No, he wasn't here. Closing her eyes for a moment, she girded her loins and marched towards the sound. The thump had come from the north bedroom. She'd avoided it so far, but she had to face it at some point. Her steps slowed as she passed the bookcases that still housed all her past summer reading. Her excuse so far for not entering this side of the house was its safety issues, as evidenced by Fred's fall, but she knew this wasn't the real reason.

Fear crawled across her skin as she neared it, one of the grandest rooms in the house. It was said that the Prince of Wales had slept here the night before he fled to the Scillies. But several grand houses in Cornwall claimed that privilege. At any rate, it wasn't the ghost of the Prince of Wales who had whispered her name repeatedly when she'd been locked in the room for six hours. Michael, devious little brother that he was, had told her to hide there when she hadn't wanted to go to Truro. He'd said they'd never find her, and he was right. The sod had locked the door on her and it was only when Hebe came looking for something on the bookshelf that she heard Lucy's screams. Six hours in a dark, cold room were enough to fill her prepubescent mind with dire thoughts. Even now they lingered as she hovered by the door, which stood slightly ajar.

Something moved inside. It might be one of Fred's team, but she was sure they had all left. Regulating her breathing, she pushed open the door and walked in, looking up at the blue plastic sheeting covering the hole in the roof. The light coming through it cast a cold tint on an already freezing room. That hadn't changed in eleven years. Hebe had always insisted it was because it was north-facing. Lucy knew differently, not that she was going to tell anyone. People's opinions of her were already low enough.

'Lucy.' Kit was on his knees in front of the fireplace.

She jumped. 'I thought you'd left. What on earth are you doing in here?'

'Looking for clues.'

'I heard you say that to my aunt.' She gave him a sideways look. Hebe didn't trust him, but she had no idea why.

'My father always believed that there would be evidence here to finally complete the family history.'

She pointed to the fireplace as he stood up. 'In there?'

'Dad and Mum were both archaeologists, and they both made discoveries of important artefacts in places like this.'

'Oh.'

'Well, it's somewhere to start.' He looked around. 'This building is incredible.'

'That's one way to look at it. Wreck and money hole are others.'

He laughed, and she liked – no, loved – the way his eyes seemed to dance with mischief. It was a potent combination. The door to a cupboard behind her swung open of its own accord. She jumped again.

'This is the ghost room, I take it.' He looked around at the four-poster bed and the wide-open cupboard. She nodded. There was no sense in denying it. 'It does have a feel to it.' He looked up to the hole in the ceiling. 'But that could just be the eerie light.' He smiled at her and she grabbed the door behind her for stability. He was just wowing her with his Hollywood charm, which he had in abundance.

'The light certainly doesn't help.'

'Nor does being on the north side of the house. It makes the room cold, but good for sleeping.'

'For eternity maybe.' She glanced up at the plastic, which sucked in and out like it was breathing. She shivered at the thought.

'This room really scares you.' He touched her goose-bump-covered arm. She shivered again, but not from cold. She must get a grip. He took her hand and led her out of the room, and getting a grip was the last thing on her mind.

Once outside, Kit stopped in front of the bookcases. She frowned as he reached down and pulled out one of the H. J. Bowden novels about Thomas Grylls. She'd loved this series since she'd found the first book here the summer she was twelve.

'We've been linked,' he said as he ran a finger over the cover.

She slapped her hand to her mouth. How the hell had the press got hold of his name and hers and put them together? She barely knew him. Neither of them needed that at the moment.

He laughed, pointing to the bold handwriting on the title page: *This book belongs to Christopher Williams.* And under it: *And Lucia Anne Trevillion.*

She laughed. 'You're Christopher Williams?'

He nodded. 'And you're Lucia Anne Trevillion.'

'How funny! How on earth did your book end up here?' She rubbed her arms.

'Let's get you to a warmer place and I'll tell you of my first visit to Helwyn House, when I was fifteen.'

She followed him down the staircase that led outside to the courtyard, and back through the house to the relative warmth of the kitchen. Kit studied the granite lintel over the old range while she put the kettle on.

'I doubt Thomas ever set foot in the kitchen,' she said.

'True.' He ran his fingers along the stones on the sides. 'Maybe when he was a boy.'

'I'm not sure this would have been the kitchen then.' Lucy pointed to where the great hall had stood. 'So much of the original house is gone.'

He took the mug she gave him. 'Yes, I'd say it was a waste, but most of the stone was put to good use for the agricultural buildings.'

'And many of the local houses.' She smiled at their mutual determination not to be outdone when it came to knowledge of the house. 'So,' she said, taking the tea bag out of her own mug. 'You came here with your parents.'

'Yes.' He dunked a biscuit into his tea. 'They were on a dig at Gear Farm and met Lillian Pendarves.'

'So sorry about your father. Where is your mother now?'

The gleam left his eyes. 'Mum died ten years ago.'

She touched his forearm. 'Is this why finding out about your family history is so important?'

He nodded. 'I've been fascinated by the house since that visit, and those Thomas Grylls novels really brought it to life.'

'Yes, they did the same for me.' Though when she'd been alone here in the past, it hadn't required the novels to make it live. 'So how did your book end up staying here?'

He grinned. 'I was desperately searching for a smugglers' passage and must have dropped it.'

'So things haven't changed.' She cradled her mug, absorbing the warmth.

'True.'

'Are you going to tell me what your father believed was here?'

He shook his head.

'That much of a secret?'

'Not at all, and yes.'

'A riddle?' She pursed her lips.

'No, but he didn't write down everything he knew.' He sipped his tea. 'What notes I have are meticulous. We know that Thomas came back here in 1660.'

'We do?'

'Yes, it's in a letter.'

'Have you told Hebe?'

'A bit.' He paced the room. 'She's the expert on the period and has clearly researched him extensively, but she seemed ... flustered, even upset by the revelation.'

'I do wonder if she hasn't taken on too much.'

He stopped and looked at her. 'She has you.'

She swallowed. 'Yes.' But Lucy had no plans to be here for any length of time. A month if she must, but then she needed to move on. The world was waiting.

Twenty-Three
Hebe

July 2015

I study the map, pretending that I understand what I am looking for, while you take a photo of the view. Turning around, I search for a signpost, because I can't connect what I see with what is drawn on the map. I resist the urge to screw the paper into a ball and toss it into the sea below. Instead, I close my eyes and turn my face to the sun. A shadow falls across me. Your mouth touches mine. My breathing pauses for a moment and I wish this could be it. That I could stop here and now. Not take another breath.

'That beach below looks good.' You point to a path through the brambles. My head swims at the height. I can't do this, but if I say no, then you will know. My failings will be as visible as the increasing number of rogue hairs on my chin. This morning I plucked four, making myself cry. You found me in tears. I couldn't explain. I couldn't say *I am old and you are young. Leave me*. So I lied.

'Let's go. You lead the way.' Picking up the picnic basket, you stride forward and downward. I stop at the top. Should I just rush forward and jump? But then you would always remember a body splayed on the rocks below. I couldn't do that to you. I want you to remember me well, not broken.

With a deep breath, I put one foot in front of the other, only looking at the narrow path through the foliage until I bump into you at the bottom, waiting.

'It was further down than I thought.'

'Yes,' I say, not looking at anything but the curve of sand and the retreating tide. We are alone and all is fine. I can do this. But I don't know for how long.

You spread the blanket out by the rocks and I settle down out of the wind.

'I'm going for a swim. Join me?' You peel off your shirt, revealing your chest. How you have changed over the years I have had you in my life.

'Not warm enough for me today.'

You shrug and wrap a towel around your waist. Somehow you make the movement graceful, magical even, as you slip your trunks on then go to the water's edge. Looking at the sun hitting your broad shoulders, I remember when we first began our affair.

*

I wonder by my troth, what thou and I
Did, till we loved. Were we not weaned till then?

You put the book down on the bed beside me. Our clothes strewn across the floor caught the morning sun. It was a new day and everything had changed. In your hand you held a mug of coffee. Steam rose from it, blurring your features. Standing there without a stitch on, it would be easy to pretend you were Thomas Grylls, but that would be a waste of the joy of who you really were. Your glance fell on the portrait again. You saw the resemblance but you said nothing. My head was full of regrets but my heart extended my hand and pulled you back beside me. I wouldn't listen to the why nots, but only look to the whys. Surely I could be foolish for another day.

*

Startling cold drops of water tap onto my feet. I open my eyes. You block the sun. It was the wrong decision to let you cross the line from student to lover. But looking at you now, I regret nothing, even though I should. Because of me, you have lost your youth, that frivolous time when the world lets you be carefree. If I could give you anything, I would give you that back.

You kneel down on the blanket beside me. 'You look sad.' You kiss me. Your lips taste of the sea, and of tears.

Twenty-Four ❊
Lucy

8 October 2016

Michael stood at the kitchen door with a face like a slapped arse. No doubt he was concerned about getting mud on his Range Rover. The rain was pissing down, and Lucy could hear it filling the bucket in the small sitting room above the dining room. It was a problem, but on the scale of problems in this house it was not urgent, at least not at this moment. Her brother's arrival had moved to the top of her 'deal with it now' list. Not that she had been given a choice. She had been told he was coming down rather than asked if she wanted him to. Looking at his face, she didn't imagine he was too pleased about it either.

'You're a bit damp.' She stood back to let him pass.

'Your sodding fault.'

'Now that's stretching the truth too far.'

He shook himself like a dog, then looked around. 'Bloody hell, this place is dire.'

'Yep, but you know all about that.'

He put the bags down. 'Christ, you're not going to throw that at me again.'

'You scarred me for life.'

'So it's my fault you've made your life such a fuck-up?'

She crossed her arms against her chest. She was tempted to say yes, but she couldn't lay all the blame at his feet. 'No, you just began the downhill slide.'

His eyes narrowed and she braced herself. They had had this argument before, and it only resulted in him telling her to get a life. Her reply was that she had one, just not one of which he approved. Michael and Lucy had chosen different ways to react to the same situation. He, of course, felt his was the better way, but then he was a man, and life always offered better options to men.

'Where's Hebe?' He looked down at the papers on the table. Hebe had given her a bunch of documents to sign now that she had bought the house. They all needed witnessing.

'Sleeping.'

He looked at his watch. 'It's just past noon.'

'I'm aware.'

'She's OK?' He looked at the paperwork again. 'No, don't answer that. Anyone paying that amount of money for this place is not of sound mind.'

Lucy shrugged. Her mind formed words to defend her aunt and the house, but she didn't speak. It bothered her that he was right.

'Do you want me to witness these for you?'

Gathering the papers, she put them aside. 'It's OK. I asked the architect to do it, and he's popping in later today.'

'Sure. So why is she asleep at this hour?'

'The house is a big project.'

He glanced about the kitchen. His lip curled in distaste. 'Any chance of a cup of coffee?'

'As long as you don't mind instant, we have coffee.'

'I mind, but needs must.' He pulled out a chair. 'I've found someone who needs a place to crash in London for a short time. I've given them the keys to your flat.'

She looked up.

'Thought you could do with some rent coming in to cover your costs.'

'Oh, thanks.' It had crossed her mind, but then she hadn't thought she'd be here long.

'Well you're not exactly working.'

She took a deep breath. Tact was never Michael's strong point, and as she spooned in the granules, she wondered if the garden shed might still have some arsenic lying around. Even if

126

it didn't kill him, it might make him feel ill enough to take that superior look off his face. She handed him the mug.

'Can you give me a tour?'

'You don't remember?'

He gave her a sideways look. 'I do, but it's been a while, thanks to you.'

She put her hands on her hips. 'You can't lay that one at my feet.'

'You refused to set foot in Cornwall again.'

'True.' She looked hard at him. 'But that didn't have to affect the rest of you.'

He laughed. 'Not a chance in hell that Mum was going to leave you alone in London for a whole summer.'

'Nor did our dear father want me disrupting his mistress schedule.' She scowled, then a smile crept onto her lips. She had screwed it up royally for them all.

'You ruined my plans.' Michael glared at her.

'Shall I break out the violin?'

'You've always been a selfish cow.'

'I love you too, Michael.'

They entered the dining room. Rain lashed at the windows. The panes were so thin, she thought they would break with the force. Overhead, the plink-plink sound of the bucket grew louder.

'Excuse me. The crisis upstairs has, I think, grown to emergency status.'

She left her brother standing there and legged it up the back stairs. Grabbing an empty bucket, she replaced the one about to overflow. What had been a small drip was now a steady stream. Fred was needed asap. He was patching the roof above the King's Room at the moment. She turned and found Michael behind her.

'Will I need an inflatable boat to survive the night here?'

Her mouth twitched. 'Quite possibly. Let me take you to your room.'

'Is it dry?'

'Yes.' She smirked and led him through the house to the

north bedroom. As she stopped in front of the door, his face fell. She opened it, and a gust of wind passed them. The door on the large cupboard swung open.

'Not this room.'

She laughed. 'Surely you don't believe in ghosts.' She left him there while she went in search of Fred and his team of miracle men.

One night alone in Hell House and Michael had left to return to London. Lucy laughed, but she couldn't blame him. It had been harsh of her to make him stay here, but the sofa in the cottage was too small to sleep on.

She adjusted the strap about her neck. The weight of the camera felt comfortable. It nestled against her side as she walked down the path to the creek. Light was creeping into the sky and she could still hear the cry of the owls, while in the undergrowth, things moved. There was no frost despite the clear sky. Above her a few stars and planets were still visible.

All last night she'd tossed and turned, feeling guilty for putting Michael into that room. But to be fair, it was the only one that was guaranteed to be dry at the moment. Not that there had been any threat of rain last night.

A wicked smile spread across her face, and she tried to stifle it. It wasn't right that she'd wanted revenge on her brother after all these years. He'd only been ten when he'd done it, and maybe he wasn't lying when he said he'd forgotten that she was in there. But she was sceptical. Everything he did was deliberate – it always had been. It was unforgivable, yet she had forgiven him. Though obviously not quite, until she'd seen his face this morning. Something had told her to go to the house early. It was clear he hadn't slept much, but he blamed it on an urgent crisis in the office. She didn't press the issue.

She shivered even now thinking about being locked in that room. Thank God Hebe had heard her screams and, in her unique way, calmed her down. She had told her there couldn't be ghosts there, and showed her the witch marks all around the house to protect it. Lucy had liked daisies ever since she'd seen the daisy wheels on the walls. But Michael was fond of pulling flowers apart.

She did love him. He'd come down to help and he was not all bad, but there was part of him that was wicked. Wasn't that the case for everyone? Lucy herself was a waste of a human being, and maybe that was just as bad. It was a sad state of affairs she found herself in at twenty-eight.

Reaching the lane that followed the north side of the creek, she took a deep breath. Only beauty existed this morning. The tide was high, the water still. The leaves on the trees were beginning to turn. The light was soft grey. She looked up the creek to see a heron flying low to the water until it came to the dead tree, where it landed. Peace.

It was a short distance along the tarmac when she found the old path down towards the water's edge. Nearly losing her footing twice, she avoided landing in the creek by catching some branches just in time. With the water this high it was tricky to move along, but worth it as she came to the point where she could see all the way past St Anthony to the bay. Dawn had broken. A thin sliver of silver light appeared above the horizon. The colour began to bleed into the sky, catching the stray clouds that marred the almost grey canvas.

Squatting, she moved the camera from under her arm and waited. She hadn't taken any landscape shots since her A levels. She revelled in the broad sweep through the viewfinder rather than the tight angle on the subject she'd become used to with portraits.

Second by second the sky changed and the world around her went from grey to colour. Her finger twitched, but today she had brought her film camera. If she wasn't careful, she would waste the roll. She had to be patient and she wasn't good at that. This would teach her. Well, she could hope that she wasn't too old to learn.

The pair of swans she'd seen the other day appeared, disturbing the still surface of the water, swimming against the current. She zoomed in on them first, then changed focus to the water, where the pinks and yellows of the sunrise were caught on the ripples. It was beautiful, but she didn't want to be here at the back end of beyond. She knew many people sought out emptiness, but she never had. There was nothing here except two swans and a heron. Even the fishing boats were silent on this glorious morning.

In the distance the headland that guarded both Gillan Creek and the Helford river formed a dark shape on the lightening sky. She stood and rolled her neck. London. Hot water. Social life. Behind her a curlew called and she knew she couldn't leave right now. Hebe needed her. Lucy couldn't walk out when her aunt was so swamped with everything in Hell House.

Maybe it would also give Ed and Sheila time to sort themselves out, something they should have done a long time ago. She could see that now as she looked down the creek in the clear air. His texts had dwindled to two a day.

Call me.

Miss you.

Always the same two. He hadn't learned his lesson, but she had. He still wanted it all. She didn't, and she would live a solitary life like Hebe. Hebe was happy. Solo was the path to take. It led to freedom.

The sky was mostly blue now, with the rich pinks lingering on a few distant clouds. Morning had broken and so had her world as she knew it. No longer a photographer of note, no longer on every invite list. People's memories were short in one way and long in others. She was lost in the gap. There were few places in the country more remote than here, except maybe the Highlands. But the news of the unfaithful MP would surely have reached there too.

There was no escape. She was in a prison of her own making and that bothered her. She was also in a place that she hated. The people were lovely – well, mostly – but unless she found a way out, she would soon be living in Hell House. Maybe if she could convince Hebe the house was too much for her, Mr Hollywood might still want to buy it.

The tide was rising fast as she walked along what was left of the beach, reaching St Anthony, where the smell of fresh coffee filled the air. She glanced to the farmhouse beside the church. Kit stood with his hands wrapped around a mug, staring into the distance.

'Morning.' She waved.

He looked up and smiled. She tried to pretend that his smile didn't have any effect on her, she really did, but she was lying and she knew it. She went weak at the knees every single time.

'Coffee?'

'I thought you'd never ask.' She walked around to the gate and followed him into the house. She hadn't been inside since she was about ten when she'd made friends with some holiday-makers. It hadn't changed much. It was obvious that Kit was settling in for a bit of a stay, unless this holiday home came complete with a library of – she picked up several antique books on Cornwall – first editions. She put them back and went into the kitchen.

Kit handed her a mug. 'Milk?'

'No thanks.'

They walked outside together. The sky above was clear blue, with all traces of the sunrise gone.

'You're up and about early.'

She tapped her camera. 'My excuse to be up before the birds.'

He raised an eyebrow.

'OK, there was one up and about before me, but only one if we don't count the owls.'

'They are wonderful, aren't they?' He smiled. 'I'd forgotten the sounds of the country.'

'How long has it been since you lived in the countryside, let alone in the UK?'

'Too long. Ten years.'

She looked at the expression on his face and regretted her question. 'You don't have to talk about it.'

'It's complicated.'

'Tell me about it.' She blinked, then focused on Kit. What was she complaining about? Early-morning coffee with one of the sexiest men she'd ever met. If a smile could get her into bed, he'd had her at the first one, back at the auction house in Truro.

'I love it here.' He glanced around to the church, then over towards the creek.

She wrinkled her nose. 'How long are you planning to be around?'

'Good question. I've managed to extend the let through January and may take it until Easter, when the bookings they already have kick in.'

'That long?' She frowned. Here she was looking at ways to get the hell out of here, and he wanted to stay.

'Yes. Don't forget, I was planning to buy.'

'True.' She looked through the boats on the beach to the water glistening in the morning light. 'Do you still want to?'

'If I find the right property, or convince your aunt she really doesn't want Helwyn House.'

'That's a brilliant idea.' Lucy laughed. 'But I doubt it'll work. She lives for it.'

'I can see that. Do you know why?'

'Not really.' She smiled, thinking of last night when she'd caught her talking to the portrait of Thomas, which they had already hung in the salon.

'Well, the letters I have of his will be of interest to her.' He turned the mug in his hands.

'You didn't fully explain how you are connected.'

'Directly.'

She frowned. 'Yes, I heard that bit – and I'm not like my aunt, who doubts you; I'm just curious.' She sipped her coffee. 'I'm not sure why, though, as I find the pedigree thing a bit dull.'

'Your own ancestry is fairly august.'

She tilted her head to the side. 'Not really. It's more a case of younger son and second cousins. Never a big deal.'

'It must have been once.'

'So long ago that it's not worth thinking about.'

'You're still part of the Trevillion family.'

'Yes, as I said, distant cousins.'

'But Hebe isn't.'

'Correct.' Taking a deep breath, she considered this. 'How do you know my family history?'

'I did a little research when I discovered who'd bought Helwyn House.'

'Ah, that makes sense. Know thine enemy.'

He laughed. 'I prefer "opposition".'

'Me too.' She raised her mug in his direction.

Twenty-Five

Hebe

July 2015

From the start, poem by poem, you overcame my fears. They haven't gone away, though. When I'm without you, fear is all I feel. My vision clears and cold, hard facts stare at me. Silently they torment me, but when you are near, they fly away to the dark corners of my soul. Right now, your mouth moves as you quietly recite a sonnet, letting the metre lend meaning to the words. My heart races. You are speaking of love. I must be the sensible one. I must hold on to sanity, but I long to disappear into you.

You stand and stretch. The sides of your mouth lift and you hold out a hand. 'Let's take a walk. I need to clear my thoughts.'

We leave the warmth of the cottage. The air is not cold but damp and fragrant. It is a gibbous moon but I don't know whether it is waxing or waning. The landscape is muted. Details picked out in light and dark. It appears foreign and I tuck my arm through yours. You lean closer and kiss my hair. Here in this semi-darkness, details slip away and we are just any couple taking an evening walk. No one can see our ages. I remember our first anniversary.

*

He is stark mad, whoever says
That he hath been in love an hour,
Yet not that love so soon decays,
But that it can ten in less space devour;

Who will believe me, if I swear
That I have had the plague a year?

I frowned. A year. You looked no older, but I did. Time was not kind. I was forty-five and you were almost twenty-one. I would feel better when you reached that old date of maturity. Or I told myself I would. Your birthday was on the seventeenth of October – the feast day of St Ignatius of Antioch, martyr. I was still not sure why you were here in my flat and in my life, but for the moment I was grateful. You stood and walked to me, planting a kiss on my neck.

'Dinner will be ready in five. Get to work.' You went into the kitchen, passing the table you had set. Outside, I heard the bells of St Mary Abbots, taking me back to the past I looked down again at the paper I was marking. The student was struggling with Donne's words. They were such slippery things, their meaning always changing. Donne's work was the ideal platform to enter into the mind of the age. The student hadn't grasped that yet but was on the cusp of a breakthrough, an insight. I made a few notes.

'Come, madam, come.' You stood with plates in your hands, such beautiful hands. A smile lingered on your mouth. Moving to you, I kissed you while you balanced the plates either side of me. You seduced me with words today, as you did a year ago. You always seduced me with your linguini and clams. The scent of garlic and parsley drifted from the plates.

'It will go cold,' you murmured against my lips.

'Hmmm,' I said. I removed the plates from your hands and led you to the table, where we behaved like the silly lovers we were, feeding each other, you humming the music from the spaghetti scene in *Lady and the Tramp*.

*

'Hebe?' you say. 'Hebe, where are you?'

I turn to you. 'I was lost in a memory.'

'A Disney film?'

135

I laugh. You don't connect the song with our first anniversary. I'm happy that I'm not the only one who forgets.

Twenty-Six
Lucy

25 October 2016

Lucy turned the television off and Hebe peered up from her notebook. She almost always had one in her hand, but with the ever-growing list of things to do at Hell House, Lucy wasn't surprised. Her glass of wine was empty and so was Hebe's. She stood to refill them. Next to the bottle were the various notes she'd left for Hebe over the past few days; they didn't look like they'd been touched.

She frowned, flipping through them. Right at the bottom was the one with the name and number her mother had given her almost a month ago. She'd forgotten to mention it to Hebe. Picking it up, she topped up the glasses. Hebe looked up and squinted at her.

'I forgot to tell you that when Mum called ages ago, she mentioned that someone called Rory Crown was trying to reach you.' Lucy held out the notes.

'Don't worry, I forget things all the time.'

Lucy half smiled, wondering if now was the time to raise her concerns about her aunt's odd behaviour of late. 'Yes, but this Rory Crown sounded keen to reach you.'

Hebe wrinkled her nose. 'Don't know anyone of that name.' Her glance moved from the paper to the notebook in front of her. She shook her head. 'Definitely don't know a Rory Crown.'

'Odd that he would know enough to track Mum down to find you.'

Hebe tilted her head to the side. 'True. But I've not known a Rory for years.' She smiled. 'Once had one as a student, though.'

'Fair enough.' Lucy scrunched up the paper and tossed it in the bin. She'd done as her mother asked. It was ten o'clock, so she turned the television on again for the news. She hadn't dared to watch it in ages. The headlines were Brexit and the US elections. She was no longer a news item. Phew. However as the bulletin went on, it appeared Ed still was. Her hand shook a bit as she lifted her glass and watched him on the screen.

'Wasn't that the man you had the affair with?' Hebe looked up from her notebook again.

Lucy stared at her. 'Yes.'

'He's not very ...'

'Very what?'

Hebe blinked. 'Was he good in bed?'

Lucy spluttered on her wine. She'd always had an open relationship with her aunt, but this had caught her off guard. Hebe looked at her, waiting for a reply. She was serious.

'Actually, yes.'

'That makes up for having to look at that face, then.'

Lucy coughed, which turned into a laugh. 'I suppose you're right.'

'Does he have much of a ...'

Lucy waited, not sure what Hebe was about to say and not sure she wanted to know either.

'Brain ... you know – clever?'

'Yes, he's clever.' She swallowed.

'But not really, because you got caught.'

Lucy laughed uncomfortably.

'Affairs are always found out.' Hebe bent over her notebook and wrote a few more things on her list. Lucy studied her, wondering what had happened to the aunt she knew, and when she had been replaced by this woman.

The idea of buying clothes in a sports shop didn't fill Lucy with joy, but she needed some practical things, such as thermal underwear. In just a few days, they were due to move out of the comfortable centrally heated cottage into Hell House. She had tried her best to dissuade her aunt from this form of madness, but Hebe was hell-bent and determined that it would be character-building for her. Lucy quite liked her character the way it was. Hebe kept studying her whenever they discussed staying at the house, like she was trying to remember something. But she of all people knew how Lucy hated the place.

In front of Lucy were racks of clothing that would keep her warm on an arctic exhibition but might not make the grade in a house with foundations in the Dark Ages and last updated in the Victorian era. Granted, there had been a few refinements thrown in along the way, such as Venetian glass, but that offered no insulation at all. In fact it seemed to hold the cold, chilling the rooms further.

Aware that one of the other customers seemed a little too interested in her, she pulled her hat down over her eyes. Being suspicious was now a part of her life. Although she was no longer front-page news, she wasn't off the radar, and every day Google Alerts reminded her not only of this most recent incident, but of everything else she'd ever done. Friends kept her updated on the gossip. They were all still in shock that she'd been having an affair with Ed. They just didn't get it. She wasn't sure she did either any more.

Her new best friend Kit walked up to her holding a basket filled with torches, a sleeping bag, heavy socks and something that claimed to be a pillow. This was so not what she wanted. In an ideal world she'd stay in Hell House when it was listed among the small great hotels of the world and not before.

This morning she'd bagged up the ancient, permanently damp bed linen. The only things worth saving were the bedspreads. Hebe needed to buy new mattresses at some point, so a sleeping bag was the best temporary solution. Lucy would be long gone by the time the house was truly ready for new beds, when the builders and their dust were but a memory.

'Shall we step over this way?' Kit pushed her towards the fitting rooms and she found herself wedged against a mirror with him nearly in her arms.

'Fancied a quick one?' She raised an eyebrow, thinking that could be rather fun.

'Name the time,' he whispered with a smile hovering on his lips, which weren't far from hers.

She inhaled, enjoying his clean scent. There was something richer there too, but she couldn't name it. 'Wouldn't think right now was the moment.'

He laughed. 'Agreed. Don't know who that was back there, but they took a photo of you – or both of us – on their phone.' He adjusted her hat to a lower angle, then stepped back.

She studied herself in the mirror. Dressed in the old waxed jacket, green wellies and felt hat that she'd found in a wardrobe at Helwyn, she certainly wouldn't know herself. This wasn't her, Lucy Trevillion, photographer, but a lost soul. She looked more like a bag lady. Sad.

Taking the basket from Kit, she paid before anyone else could take a picture. She'd thought people would be aiming for selfies with Kit, but he managed to blend in without any apparent effort. Maybe this was method acting, because he was relaxed and no one noticed him. Yet she did. She couldn't not think about him.

Outside, she turned to him. Hebe didn't like or trust him, and maybe Lucy should be the same, wary of his charm. 'Were you serious back there, or just winding me up?'

The corner of his mouth lifted.

She laughed. 'That wasn't fair.'

'No, but it was fun. You were spending far too much time looking at long johns, which would make even the most passionate male lose all libido.'

'I totally agree they're not for seduction, and even if they were, I wouldn't want to imagine who they might attract.' She climbed into the car.

He slid into the passenger seat. 'A grizzly bear.'

'Fortunately, not a known species in Cornwall.' She pulled into the traffic.

'The beast of Bodmin then.' He grinned.

'It's a good sixty miles or more to Bodmin.'

'Fair point.' He looked out of the window at the passing scenery and she focused on the double roundabouts. She wasn't sure why he was with her today, other than the fact that her aunt had practically shoved him into the car. Hebe didn't want him at Hell House, but strangely Lucy did. There was something soothing about him that she hadn't expected when she'd first met him.

Not many people in Lucy's life had been calm. Not even her aunt. There had always been a slightly frenetic underground energy about Hebe, and since arriving here, that current had moved closer to the surface. She had applied her powerfully clever brain to bamboozling the person from English Heritage at their meeting, combining pure academic argument with charm as well as sex appeal, which Lucy had never seen her use before. By the end, even Lucy was on her side, and Lucy loathed the damn house.

All of this didn't explain why Kit was still hanging around. Yes, he had a connection to Helwyn, and documents to show Hebe. But Hebe had dismissed the letters – though Lucy supposed that might change when she actually got to see them.

'How long do you think you'll have to hide out for?' He looked at her.

She glanced at him. 'I don't know.'

'Are you sure that running away is the answer?'

She half grunted. 'Oh yes.' If it hadn't been for family pressure, she might have brazened it out. What was it her father had said? 'You have ruined one family and you're not going to do any more damage to ours.' She had raised an eyebrow at that point. Giles Trevillion should have thought about his family a long time ago.

'Why are you so certain?'

'Because ...' She closed her mouth. She didn't want to mention that her mother had told her only this morning that someone was still camped outside their house, because Lucy thought it was more likely they were there for the rock star who lived down the road.

'Because?'

'Never mind.' She bit her lip and went around the next roundabout.

'Fine.'

'Sorry.' She shrugged. 'It's complicated.'

'Life is.'

'You speak from experience.' She stole another glance at him. His mouth was set in a straight line. Gone was the heart-melting smile, and his eyes had dimmed from bright blue to a softer shade touched with grey, very moody. They had a story to tell, but she needed to focus on driving. She turned from the main road into the lane. These byways were designed for slow travel, for horses rather than cars speeding along and not paying attention. The route twisted and turned, and she held her breath, hoping that as she came around a blind bend she wouldn't meet another vehicle in a blazing hurry.

'Look it's not for me to say . . .'

The corner of her mouth lifted. 'But you will.'

'I don't know it all, but hiding away isn't the answer. You're wasting your life.'

She laughed. It came blurting out, sounding like a hyena, or at least a stunning imitation of one. He had no idea. She had already wasted her life. This hiding was turning out to be more productive than she had ever been before. 'My aunt needs me.'

'I can see that.'

She frowned. What could he see? Hebe might have been reckless buying this house, but she had been working like a madwoman to get things done as quickly as she could. She was just a bit forgetful if she had to pinpoint anything.

Lucy slammed on the brakes as they encountered a 4x4 coming the other way. All her attention focused on reversing until there was a spot wide enough for the other vehicle to pass. There was nothing quite like going backwards to give a view of things missed the first time. Hebe. Something itched in the back of her brain and she couldn't reach it. It was imperative that she lay her hands on whatever it was. Something told her it would be crucial. She shifted into gear and set off to Hell House with more speed than necessary.

✳ Twenty-Seven ✳

Hebe

30 October 2016

'Hebe, what do you think of the preliminary plans?' Hebe, hunched over her notebook at the dining room table, glanced up at the sound of the man's voice. What on earth was he talking about? Her pen stilled. She'd been sketching out a scene based on what the man with the white teeth had said … that Thomas Grylls had returned one last time to Helwyn.

'Hebe?'

She blinked, and light flashed. Where was she?

'Thought I'd lost you for a moment.' The man was holding her arm. He was the architect. Mark something. Mark Triggs, that was it.

'No, I'm fine.'

'Sure?'

She nodded, knowing she must have had what the doctor called a TIA. They might become more frequent, he'd said. These mini strokes indicated an acceleration. 'Now what was it we were talking about?'

'The preliminary plans. I've been working on them for the past few weeks.'

'Yes, they look fine.' She glanced at the papers on the table. She knew she had reviewed them, but her mind hadn't been in this century. The great hall still stood and Thomas Grylls was alive. It was a better time.

'Good. In that case we can begin the process of getting the various planning consents.'

Hebe stood and picked up her notebook. 'Yes, thank you.'

The architect stood there looking like he wanted something more from her. What had she forgotten? Whatever it was, she must not lose her train of thought on the book. She must finish it along with the house. As she glanced around, something inside tightened, and she swayed. She went to grab the back of the chair but missed. The architect caught her and held her upright.

'Sorry, suddenly light-headed.' She took a deep breath.

'Maybe you should sit.'

She shook her head. Right now, she needed to see Thomas Grylls. The portrait was in the salon, but maybe it should be in her bedroom, as it had been in London. She left the architect and made her way through the house, pausing in the entrance hall. Where was she going? Lines from John Donne's poem, 'Negative Love', came to her.

My love though silly, is more brave,
For I may miss whene'ver I crave,
If I know yet what I would have.

She was hungry. Where would she find food? She spun around, not knowing where to find the kitchen. Tears pricked her eyes, and in desperation she started down the long, dark corridor. Opening a door, she found herself in the dining room. On the table, plans were spread out. Running her fingers over them, she found the kitchen but saw that they were taking out a bedroom and making two bathrooms out of it. No. This wasn't right. The house mustn't change. It was so important to conserve it while they still could. So much history in just a few rooms, and it could all be lost.

She closed her eyes and thought about Thomas's part in the Prince of Wales's escape to the Scilly Isles. The Parliamentary forces were gaining ground in Cornwall daily. Pendennis Castle was still strong, but how long could they hold out? It was no longer safe for the prince. So by stealth on a clear moonlit night in February 1646, a small band took him by water from the fort. With Thomas in charge, they safely navigated the treacherous reefs that could catch out the unsuspecting. The tide was at its peak as they reached the quay at Helwyn.

Thomas had sent word with a trusted servant and Helwyn was ready to welcome the prince. Tapestries had been rehung, tapers lit, and a feast awaited them in the great hall. The large room off the hall, now called the King's Room, was made ready to receive the royal guest, with furniture moved so that he could meet his loyal subjects on a one-to-one basis. The north bedroom had been prepared with the finest linens. Everything was as it should be and Thomas was pleased to offer this hospitality, even knowing it was less than it would have been just a few years earlier.

'Hebe?'

She shook her head and blinked.

'Are you away with the fairies?' Lucy smiled. 'Or over-whelmed by the task that is Hell House?'

'I do wish you wouldn't call it that.' Hebe pushed her hair back from her face. 'Helwyn means bounteous hall. It is a place of welcome.'

Lucy chuckled. 'It depends on your point of view.'

'I know you have many reasons not to like the house, and I appreciate you staying here with me.' Hebe pushed the papers towards her niece. 'I just can't keep all this straight. There's so much and you've been such a huge help in the short ... time we've been here.' Looking around, she could see signs of Lucy's touch. There was even a bunch of dried hydrangea heads in a vase on the table. Helwyn was beginning to look more like a home, for all Lucy's grumbling. 'You've stocked the kitchen with food and appliances, done all the driving and kept Fred and his team on track.'

'Yes, but—'

'I need you to take over all this for me.'

Lucy couldn't meet her eyes. Instead she looked down at her phone, as if that held the answer to everything.

'I need to work on the history ... of this place ... of Thomas.'

'But surely that can wait until you've done the renovation.'

'No, it absolutely cannot wait.'

'But I—'

Hebe interrupted her. 'I know ...' Lucy's mouth stayed open as she spoke, 'I know you will do it, because you are kind.'

Lucy's mouth closed and Hebe waited for her to say yes. She prayed she would, because she knew she couldn't do this without her. Even with Lucy's help it was a mammoth task.

Lucy looked at her phone again.

'You've had another job offer?' Hebe's heart stopped. 'I'll double whatever they're paying you.'

'It's not that.' Lucy's shoulders dropped.

'What is it then?' The long-case clock chimed the hour but Hebe knew it was wrong. It was running fast. It hadn't been right since the move from London. Time was speeding up.

'It was an invitation to spend a month on Mustique with a friend.'

'That can be done any time.'

'But ...' Lucy looked down at her phone again. Hebe fought the urge to rip it out of her hands. Maybe she should try begging.

'Please.'

Lucy swallowed. 'If you really need me.'

'I do.' She pointed to the papers, and Lucy sat at the table and went through them silently. Hebe hoped that now that her niece had agreed to take over the restoration, she could get on with this last book. Thomas Grylls's final years ... but unlike the others, there was little fact on which to base the story.

Twenty-Eight
Lucy

30 October 2016

'Damn, damn, damn.' Lucy closed the cupboard, wondering if the day could get any worse. It was almost Halloween and tonight would be their first night in Hell House. How bloody appropriate. She took three deep breaths and glanced at the plans on the table next to her laptop. Project management. Joy. Instead of a few weeks lying on a beach drinking cocktails and planning how to get work, she would be layered up in thermal underwear spending time with builders.

Why hadn't she refused to take on the job? That was easy. Hebe needed her. By her own admission, her aunt wasn't doing a good job. This became glaringly obvious as Lucy looked through the plans. Hebe hadn't addressed any of the architect's questions. Of course they needed to sacrifice that bedroom for more bathrooms. It was a nightmare for a house of this size only to have two. Lucy remembered that from years ago.

She opened her computer and drafted an email to Mark and Fred. Hell House wouldn't have a phone line or the Internet for ages, so later she would have to go to the pub to communicate with the world. She could get mobile phone signal if she walked out the back and up through the fields. The problem was, she hated cows. No, that wasn't true. Cows were lovely, but they scared the life out of her. She'd been chased by one when she was five, and ever since then she had given them more than a wide berth.

She dropped her head into her hands. How was she going to do this with no means of communication?

'Hello?'

She looked up from the computer as a woman, younger than her and dressed in a tie-dyed T-shirt, walked into the kitchen.

'Hi, sorry to disturb you, but Fred left his lunch behind and I can't reach him.' She waved her mobile.

Lucy laughed. 'It would be a miracle if you could. Come in.' She stood and put the kettle on. 'Tea?'

'Lovely. I'm Peta, Fred's wife.'

'Lucy Trevillion.'

Peta smiled. Her face said it all. Everyone knew about Lucy Trevillion.

Lucy handed her a mug and took the milk out of the small fridge. Once she had figured out the plans, that was something else that needed sorting. The kitchen had a Welsh dresser and a range and a big table, but there wasn't much counter space. She needed to talk to Mark about it. A house of this size needed prep space and a much bigger fridge.

'Use the pantry next door and put a big fridge and a washing machine and dryer in there, and maybe a second dishwasher.'

Lucy frowned. 'Good idea.' Had she spoken aloud?

'Sorry.' Peta stirred her tea. 'I have this ... gift of sorts.'

'You can read people's thoughts?' Lucy pulled a face.

Peta laughed. 'Sometimes. But basically I sense things.' She looked around the kitchen. 'You're not pleased to be here.'

'That's not a secret,' Lucy said, trying not to think at all.

'Hebe needs you.'

The door opened and Fred entered carrying two mugs. Peta pointed to the bag on the table.

'What would I do without you?' Placing the mugs in the sink, he walked to her and kissed her.

Peta laughed. 'Still be drinking too much at the pub at the weekend, I should think.'

Fred laughed. 'True, but so would you.' He dropped an arm around Peta's shoulders. Lucy looked away.

'Right, I'll leave you while I try and decipher these plans.' She began collecting her stuff from the table.

'Would it be OK if I had a look around the house?' Peta pushed her blonde hair off her face.

Lucy straightened. 'Of course. Fred can take you. I think Hebe's in her room.'

'Sorry, I can't, I left Tim in charge of the drill and I've discovered he likes to put holes in everything.'

'God, we have enough holes already.' Lucy's eyes widened.

'Exactly.' He grabbed his lunch and kissed Peta again before dashing off.

Putting the paperwork down, Lucy said, 'I'll give you a tour.'

'Thanks. Fred talks of nothing but the house, but he's not very good at giving me a descriptive picture, and this is the first big project where he's been fully in charge.'

Lucy raised her eyebrows.

'Don't worry. He's passionate about what he does, and brilliant.' Peta laughed. 'I would say that, of course, but it's true.'

'Glad to hear it.' Thus far all Fred's time had been taken up with the roof, and that would be the main focus for a bit. Repairing it didn't require permissions. Lucy sighed.

'You will get there, and the house will be wonderful.'

'You think so?' She opened the door to the dining room. The windows lining the west wall were lovely, and today, sunlight filled the room. Across the courtyard she could see Fred and two of his men working on the roof above the King's Room. The windows in that room were even older than these, Lucy guessed.

'Hello.'

She spun around at the sound of Kit's voice, and a big smile spread across Peta's face. He had that effect on women – except for Hebe.

'Kit, let me introduce you to Peta ... she's married to Fred.'

They shook hands. Could Peta read his thoughts too? She looked at Lucy and winked. Lucy stifled a laugh.

'I'm just showing Peta around the house.'

'Oh, are you taking her to the north bedroom?'

Lucy frowned. 'Hadn't planned on it.'

He chuckled, and she stifled the urge to hit him. He knew the room unsettled her.

'Kit, you know more about the history of the house; why don't you give Peta the tour?'

'Really?' He took a step back.

'I want to look at where the old chapel was,' Peta said.

'What chapel?' Lucy couldn't recall one.

'Ah, there's not much left of it.' Kit shook his head. 'Just the original doorway.'

'Where?' Lucy frowned.

'Under the King's Room.'

'Then it's not really safe to visit at the moment, until Fred secures the floor.'

Peta smiled. 'Why don't you show me the north bedroom then, Kit?'

'Right this way.' He ushered her out into the hallway, and Lucy watched them go. If she hadn't seen Peta with Fred earlier, she might have been jealous, but the pair of them seemed blissfully happy together. She knew, though, that nothing was what it appeared when it came to relationships. Ed was still texting her and she was still not answering. He'd made his own bed, and while there, he'd made his own child. He needed to get his priorities straight. She shouldn't even be on the list.

Twenty-Nine ✳
Hebe

July 2015

The lighthouse behind us sends out blinding light. I stop on the narrow path and feel the force of the wind. Below the sea rages, and I feel the same inside. Emotions race, slamming against the walls of my brain. You walk ahead of me, leaning into the wind, grinning like a child. Nature is unfettered here at this lonely outpost.

You turn and point to the gull stationary in the sky. Neither moving forward nor falling back. It has managed to hold time in place. Would I stop time now, or would I go back and do something differently?

*

Now that thou has loved me one whole day,
Tomorrow when thou leav'st, what will thou say?

It was Michaelmas term again and you hadn't dallied in freshers' week. You laughed at my suggestion that you should. You asked why I would think you would want to be in crowded places with writhing bodies when you could be here with me, your love. Since that summer day when you declared your love, you had told me at any opportunity you found.

Each and every time I turned away from you, I was certain this would in turn push you away. I hadn't the strength to do more. Every day I saw my need for you grow, despite my thoughts. My weary mind told me to set you free, but it didn't want to, so it would not act. All that was left to me was to withhold the words that my heart shouted every minute. 'I love you,' it said. But you would never hear it from me unless I used the words of others. Poetry. It said what I could not.

For my sake you changed the focus of your study – no longer history but English literature. I hoped this wasn't a hardship. Of course you said it was not. You did it for me. You said you loved me. But love has never been constant and love can depart. You assured me that your love would not change. But you had no idea of the challenges love would set before you. It would not just be the nubile young women of your year, with time on their side, but those with minds as clever as mine. I did not ask you to be constant. I didn't ask you to love me. Remember that.

*

I stumble, forgetting where I am, despite the wind and now the rain that has arrived. Your hand shoots out. I glance down at the water as it is sucked out before it slams back into the cliff.

'I don't know about you, but I could use a cuppa.' You turn me around and the wind pushes us along. I have often felt like this, with little control of the direction I am heading.

It is a relief when we stumble through the door of the tea-room and away from the forces driving us there. Destiny feels a bit like that.

PART TWO

❊ Thirty ❊
Hebe

30 October 2016

Hebe pulled back the bolt and wrapped the shawl closer about her shoulders. The night was not totally dark and there was a three-quarter moon casting a silvered light among the columns of the loggia. She stroked the first two as she stepped past them. The granite was cold under her fingers while the great slabs beneath her feet were icy and damp with the dew. A chill travelled up her legs, making her feel alive. She stepped onto the grass, and the leaves and twigs clung to her toes as she walked down the drive towards the creek. Moonlight glistened on the water and reflected the waxing moon. He would come home to her on such a moon. Of that she was sure.

> Although thy hand, and faith, and good works too,
> Have sealed thy love, which nothing should undo.

All was quiet as she passed St Anthony's Church, and only the lingering scent of woodsmoke in the air reminded her that there were others about. She must be careful to disturb no one. Her vigil must be solitary. He belonged to her and her alone. She had been constant in her heart.

Cows lay in the corner of the field, the moonlight picking out the white in their hides. They didn't notice her as she skirted the field and came to the fort. Brambles caught her and scratched her legs as her foot caught on the raised root of a scrub oak. She stumbled but didn't fall. Nothing would stop her from looking out for his return.

Tonight the sea was peaceful, the wind light but constant. It was a good night to sail home. Hebe climbed down the cliff until she was just ten feet from the breaking waves. She settled on a rock. She could see the full sweep of the bay from here. Whether he came from east, north or south, he would be in her sights.

Moisture beaded on her skin, and the thin silk of her night-clothes plastered itself against her. Goose bumps covered her flesh. She felt so alive. The strength of the sea as it brought the incoming tide to the rocks empowered her. He would surely come back to her tonight. How she longed for him. His arms about her, his hands caressing her. If she closed her eyes, she could hear his voice on the breeze. Poetry. But the words, the words were lost. Only echoes of his voice as his breath touched her skin.

Syllables. Iambic pentameter reached the soul and expressed what was inexpressible, unsayable, unknowable. It spoke of things and reached things that were felt but somehow never uttered. The waves came to the rock with the same rhythm. Would her love arrive tonight? Absence made the heart fonder, but it also made it break open so that the wind whistled round it and then seeped into the cracks, pushing them wider and wider until the heart exploded.

Hebe pulled her shawl tighter still around her. She must not let the wind in. She must hold her love close and let her heart beat only for him.

Thirty-One

Lucy

30 October 2016

It was midnight when Lucy arrived back at Hell House. So much for a quick drink at the pub. Hebe had practically pushed her out of the door. She wasn't sure if it had just been because her aunt was restless, or if she wanted the house to herself.

Clouds covered the moon and the darkness now was overwhelming The torch on her phone was of little use. In fact it made the lack of light around her darker, more opaque. She reached the kitchen door and looked for the key under the flowerpot, but it wasn't there. She was regretting her decision not to let Kit see her into the house. She danced from foot to foot as her need to pee became more acute. Casting the dim light from her phone further afield, she searched again for the key, but her mind was only thinking of one thing. She needed the loo.

She looked for the most protected spot, because it would be just her luck that some wildlife photographer was camped out and would snap a pic. She shuddered, which wasn't the best thing to do when trying to discreetly pee in an old walled kitchen courtyard. Something banged and she went straight to standing, grateful that her Kegel muscles worked so well. She pulled up her jeans and stood completely still. The wind blew high in the treetops, yet there was no other sound. She couldn't tell if the noise had come from inside or out. Her head swung round as she thought she heard her name being called.

'Come on, Luce,' she said out loud. 'Don't spook yourself.'

Her voice sounded strange. What she'd heard was just the wind in the vines on the wall. Shaking her head, she tried to engage the logical part of her brain. There was nothing in the house of any value except for the portrait that Hebe loved so much. A thief would be more likely to take the builders' tools or rip out the architectural features, but midnight was not normally the hour they struck; the dead hours of three and four in the morning, when people were deep in sleep, was when locks were picked, windows smashed.

Of course this said far too much about her being awake at those hours but on the upside she'd foiled a few attempts over the years and some culprits had been caught. Maybe it was something she should put on her CV. Good at skulking about in the early hours.

Now able to think about more than her bladder, she searched again for the key. It definitely wasn't there. Who knew about it? Hebe, Kit and Fred. She went to the back door and with more hope than expectation turned the knob. There was no resistance. It was open. Why hadn't she tried this first? Then she stopped. Why was the door open when she had locked it on her way out? Directing her phone's torch, she looked to the hook where the key was kept inside. It was still there.

She stood by the door, afraid to step in further. She felt like one of those bloody too-stupid-to-live heroines, putting themselves in peril while they tried to figure out the hows and the whys. The only sound was the hum of the refrigerator. If there was someone in the house other than Hebe, what could she do about it? She couldn't even call 999. She had no signal.

Her head swam. The pints of local cider had seemed a good idea at the time, but right now she needed her wits, and they were addled. She turned on the kitchen light. The single bulb cast eerie shadows, but at least the electrics were functioning.

With careful steps, trying to make as little noise as possible, she left the kitchen and turned the hall light on. The wall sconces cast a kinder light than that in the kitchen, but at quarter past midnight, Hell House was still a creepy place. Had it ever been happy? No doubt Hebe could tell her.

She bypassed the dining room. The door was open, and from what she could see, there was no one in there. In the front hall the door was unbolted but locked. She frowned as she slid the bolt across, then turned and ventured upstairs, leaving the lights on behind her. With sweaty palms, she checked each room as she made her way down the corridor. There were no signs of life at all, including in Hebe's room. It was clear she'd been to bed, but she wasn't there now, nor was she anywhere else in the house.

Back in the kitchen, Lucy put the kettle on. She didn't know what else she could do, and tea always felt positive. It was now nearly one o'clock, and she was alone. Hebe had obviously gone out, but the car was in the drive so it had to be on foot. However, her wellies and waxed coat were by the back door. It didn't make sense. Should she be concerned? Well, she was.

Tea made, she searched for biscuits but found only marshmallows. She needed something to sop up the alcohol in her blood. She couldn't take the car to look for Hebe; she had to wait. Had her aunt left a note? All the kitchen surfaces were clear, everything in order as Hebe liked it. Where else would she leave one? Lucy's room?

Taking a big slurp of tea, she decided that had to be it. However, venturing upstairs on her own could wait another few minutes. This was what she'd been dreading. Being alone in this house in the middle of the night. Thankfully she wasn't wandering lost in a white nightgown. Her current attire, moth-eaten sweater and baggy jeans, would scare anyone off. Heck, it even frightened her.

She knocked back the rest of the tea and headed up the stairs again, leaving all the lights on. None of this made sense. When she'd gone to the pub, Hebe had been sitting by the fire in the salon reading a book. Things didn't fit, but Lucy was determined not to see anything sinister in her aunt's disappearance. Hebe was fifty-five and the most capable woman she knew. So, she wasn't wearing her coat or her boots, but Lucy was sure she owned other items of clothing that would be suitable to go out in.

Creeping past Hebe's bedroom, Lucy checked the salon again in case she had missed her aunt asleep on the sofa. Somehow she felt she should be carrying a candle rather than her phone, but it was 2016 after all. Above the fireplace, Thomas's eyes followed her. Creepy. Thomas Grylls had been a handsome youth. The style of the day made him look slightly effeminate with a big lace collar, red tights and fancy shoes, but his eyes were striking, and just like Kit's. Something snapped in the fire and Lucy jumped. She was more spooked than she wanted to admit even to herself. She needed to sleep off the alcohol and then confront Hebe in the morning, she decided.

As she turned at the end of the corridor, the door of the bedroom behind her creaked. She stopped and tried to slow her breathing down.

'Lucy.'

It was just the wind.

'Lucy.'

Her skin went cold and she raced into her room and slammed the door. Leaning against it, breathing hard, she heard her name again.

Flipping the light on, she slid the bolt on the door. There was no note from Hebe, not on the bed, the chair, the fireplace, the windowsill. Nothing. Where the hell was she? And what was Lucy supposed to do about it?

She checked her phone. No signal. No surprise. She secured the windows. The wind whistled softly. She shivered. Wrapping the sleeping bag around her shoulders, she sat in the chair. There was no way she was going to sleep a wink.

Frantic banging on her door woke her. Lucy was face down on the floor and felt like death. 'Coming.' Everything hurt as she climbed to her feet and stretched.

'Lucy?' A man's voice. It did not sound like the voice that had called her name last night. Surely that had just been her imagination, left over from childhood.

She opened the door.

'Morning.' It was Anthony Jenkin.

She rubbed her eyes and looked at her watch. It was 6.30.

'I've seen you looking better.'

'Indeed.' She pulled the sleeping bag more securely around her. 'What on earth brings you here at this ungodly hour?'

'Your aunt.'

God, Lucy had forgotten about her. 'What's happened?'

'I had a call from Mike, one of the fishermen. He saw a woman in white halfway down the cliff on the Dennis.'

'What?'

'Yeah, I thought I was hallucinating at first, but I coaxed her up.'

'Dear God, where is she now?'

'In the kitchen, drinking tea, warming up.'

Lucy frowned. 'Right.' But it wasn't right at all.

She ran downstairs with Anthony in her wake. What on earth had Hebe been doing?

'Morning, Lucy.' She was sitting at the table wearing a man's coat and sipping a mug of tea. Her hair was wild and she looked strangely beautiful.

'Morning. Nice walk?'

'Hmmm.'

'Did you offer Anthony tea?'

'No.'

'Right. I'll get the kettle on again.' She watched Hebe return the coat to Anthony. Her pyjamas were dark from the damp of the morning.

'It's OK, Luce. Best get back. Catch up soon …' He smiled in a way that told her to give him a ring.

She had thought that things couldn't get any worse, but now it turned out that while she'd been spending hours listening to every creak and moan in the house – which were too many to count – Hebe had been out wandering Dennis Head in silk pyjamas. If she had been properly dressed, Lucy wouldn't have thought much about it. She could have been researching: what did it feel like to stand on Dennis Head at midnight? What could you see, hear, smell and so forth? All things a historian might want to know. She was sure it was one of those things that hadn't changed much. Maybe just the lighthouse and the ships in Falmouth Harbour. But the fact was that Hebe had been wandering around inappropriately dressed, and Lucy needed to know why.

She began making breakfast. Everything – especially a hangover – was better with a fry-up. Bacon, eggs, tomatoes, mushrooms, and if she was lucky, baked beans and toast. After they ate, she would try and get to the bottom of her aunt's midnight stroll.

As she cooked, she stared out of the window into the darkness. It would be a little while before the morning light hit the back of the house. It would touch the top of the garden wall first, then move slowly around. It was the time of year when the sun never made it that high into the sky. Once the tree surgeon had been at work, the house would get more much-needed light. Right now, standing here in the kitchen, the cold from the stone floor seeped through her thick socks and up her legs.

'Could you make my eggs ...'

Hebe was still clutching her mug. Lucy had put her sleeping bag around her aunt. She looked entirely out of place sitting at the table in damp silk and nylon puffed fabric. She looked at Lucy blankly, then took another sip of tea.

'How, Hebe? How would you like your eggs?'

'I don't know.'

'You normally have them over easy.'

'Fine.' Her head dropped, and Lucy couldn't read her expression.

It was a good thing there were no smoke alarms yet, as Lucy forgot about the toast and the flaming ruins went into the bin. She opened the back door and noticed the overturned flowerpot. She hadn't been careful in her search for the key.

'Do you have the back-door key?' she asked.

'No.'

Lucy frowned. Hebe didn't seem to be with her at the moment. She'd experienced this with her in the past. Her mother had always put it down to Hebe being bookish. Placing a plate in front of her, along with a fresh cup of tea, she studied her aunt. They had been living together for a month, and in that time Lucy had seen both an entirely competent woman and one who wasn't really present. Like her mother, she had at first put it down to eccentricity, but now she had her doubts. Something was definitely wrong.

'Once you've eaten, I think you need to change and have a bath. With luck the old boiler will be up to the task.' Lucy wasn't too hopeful about that. There was so much that Hell House needed. Fred and his crew would be here soon. She'd have to prioritise things like consistent hot water.

Hebe's face was drawn and sadness coloured her expression. 'So what on earth were you doing climbing Dennis Head?'

'I wasn't.'

Lucy blinked. 'Anthony just brought you back.'

'I don't remember.' Hebe took a sip of tea.

Leaning against the sink, Lucy studied her aunt, looking for signs of head injury, but aside from muddy hems on her pyjama bottoms, and looking a bit cold, there were no other signs of mishap.

'You look dreadful.' Hebe nibbled the corner of her toast.

'Thanks.' Lucy rubbed her hands over her face. 'You're not looking too brilliant yourself.'

'I'm fine.' Hebe stood and cleared her plate. 'I'll see if the bath works.'

'The bath will, but the hot water might—' Before Lucy could finish speaking, there was a crash, and she raced into the dining room to find her aunt on the floor.

'What the hell . . .?'

'Sorry.'

She helped Hebe to a sitting position. 'What happened?'

'Don't know.' She rubbed her head.

Lucy watched her blink. 'Hebe, look at me.'

She turned. Her pupils were responsive and Lucy knew she couldn't have been knocked out because she was with her almost immediately. 'OK, let's see if we can get you to your feet.'

Hebe rotated onto her knees and stood, then immediately slipped again, catching her feet in her pyjama trousers. There was the culprit. The muddy hems had dragged the fabric down. Leading her upstairs by the arm, Lucy sat her on her bed, then ran a bath, which produced about an inch and a half of reasonably hot water. It would have to do.

'It's ready,' she called. 'Not a lot, but at least you can get the mud off you.'

When Hebe didn't come straight away, Lucy looked into the bedroom. Her aunt was sound asleep. There was nothing much she could do other than cover her. She would make use of the bath herself. Her head throbbed, and her back and knees ached from her awkward sleeping arrangement. This place was going to kill her. But maybe that wasn't a bad thing. It would be one way to escape from Ed and the scandal.

❋ Thirty-Two ❋
Hebe

31 October 2016

Unable to put a proper sentence together on the page, Hebe stopped typing. She couldn't remember the details of where Charles II had been during the Gear Rout in 1648. She should know this. She'd written a book about it, and the last Thomas Grylls novel had dealt with it. That was when Thomas and Lucia had last met. But what had the man with the white teeth said? Thomas came back to see Lucia again? Rubbing her temples, she glanced at her journal.

> *All Hallows' Eve*
> *I'm so angry but most of the time I forget why. I hate*
> *myself. I hate my failing mind. Without it I am nothing*
> *except emotion. Emotions plague me.*
> *Breakfast - boiled egg on toast.*
> *Meet with architect. Name?*
> *Paid builder an instalment.*
> *Emotion. Longing and …*

She went to the bookcase and pulled out the book she'd written on Charles II. The binder next to it tumbled to the floor. Pushing papers back into it, she saw her notes for the introduction to the use of literature in the study of history, or how to find a way into the mindset of the past. The pages were covered in bright orange lines. She had used a highlighter to help her keep her place. When had she started doing that? It could only have been a year or two ago, but she wasn't sure.

She ran her finger down the page, stopping at the reminder that all the calendars were different, Julian and Gregorian. She chuckled at the Michaelmas Day lore and the old Cornish belief that you couldn't eat blackberries after Michaelmas because the devil had peed on them. This always made the students laugh. It had been important that they understood that the world was different then. Everyday life was immersed in religion and superstition, even if people were not believers. So much was done to the chime of the bells.

The long-case clock in the dining room sounded. It was not yet five, but the nights were drawing in, and Hebe shivered as she scanned the first line of Donne's Elegy XIX, 'To His Mistress Going to Bed' on the page in front of her:

'*Come, madam, come.*'

Something stirred in her, but she couldn't hold it long enough to identify it. Her students thought that sex as a sensuous, free thing hadn't existed in the past. This poem always captured their attention. She laughed.

Lucy's voice carried down the hall. She was talking to the builder. The King's Room had been re-roofed and was now watertight. Hebe was pleased. Closing her eyes, she knew that another bit of the roof had been started on, the bit Fred had come through. New ... something had been needed. The deathwatch beetle had been feasting too freely.

She cast a glance at her desk, then decided to go into the salon. In the doorway, she stood looking at Thomas, so young, only seventeen. What would he have looked like when he came back? What would he have thought of the changes wrought on his home? Once it had been easy to conjure Thomas and his thoughts, but not now.

A quiet voice within her told her to read Donne. She closed her eyes and focused hard to recall a poem. '*Stand still, and I will read to thee,*' she whispered, wondering what came next.

'*A lecture, love, in love's philosophy.*'

She jumped. Standing beside her was the man with Thomas's eyes – Kit, she remembered.

'*These three hours that we have spent ...*' he paused, '*walking here, two shadows went . . . along with us, which we ourselves pro-duced.'* He smiled. 'Sadly that's all I can recall at the moment.'

'Extraordinary that you know Donne.'

'Not really. I did my thesis on his elegies.' He looked at the portrait. 'That is the only known painting of Thomas, isn't it?'

'Lucia had a gem-encrusted locket containing a small portrait of him. He sent it to her during his exile as a token of his continuing love. It was known as the Grylls Jewel.'

'Really?' He frowned. 'My father never mentioned it.'

Hebe nodded. 'Thomas had it made in France and sent it secretly to Lucia in 1646.'

'Where is it now?'

'No one knows.'

'Odd.'

'It is. But I've never been able to discover when Lucia died or where she is buried.'

'Surely there must be some record?'

'None that I've been able to find.' Hebe sighed. 'I have assumed that she . . . killed herself because . . . nothing was recorded.' She pushed her fringe out of her face. 'She is last mentioned in 1661.'

Lucy walked into the room with plans rolled under her arm.

'But why would she kill herself?' He frowned.

'A broken heart.'

Lucy snorted. 'People don't die for love. Love is a prison that sucks the life and joy out of you.'

Hebe squinted at her. 'Love isn't a prison, and no, they don't die for love, but they can – and do – die without it. Lucia's cousin, whom she was forced to marry, was a pig by all accounts. No one could stand him.'

Lucy muttered, 'Like my father, you mean.'

'So you think she killed herself?' Kit looked back to the painting as if it might provide the answers. If it had held answers, Hebe would have seen them years ago. She knew every brushstroke on the canvas.

'Yes, or possibly she died in childbirth – but there would be some record.'

167

'What if the child didn't survive?'

'Then possibly not.' Hebe looked at them both and tried to remember why she'd come into the room. Glancing about, she tried to orientate herself. It was best to go back to her room. She'd left the door open and she didn't want anyone in there.

Thirty-Three

Lucy

31 October 2016

'You have to go and see a doctor.' Lucy placed both her hands on the dining room table. Putting the facts together, she'd realised that the sounds she'd heard at night in the cottage had been her aunt roaming. Last night had just been the most dramatic example.

'No.' Hebe looked out of the window.

'You wandered the Dennis at night.' Lucy took a breath. 'You're sleepwalking and it isn't safe.'

'Fine, lock me in my room.' Hebe's arms were folded across her chest and her lips were pressed together.

She sighed. 'Why won't you see a doctor?'

'No point.'

'I agree that there's not much a GP can do, but there are specialists, I'm sure, who could help.'

Hebe shook her head.

Lucy paced. How could she force a fifty-five-year-old woman to do something she didn't want to? 'Look, you must. It's not safe.'

Hebe shrugged.

'Hebe.' Lucy came closer and reached out to touch her, but she pulled back.

'Surely my safety is my own concern.'

Lucy ground her teeth. Was this what it was like to have teenagers? She'd underestimated what she'd put her mother through. 'Not when it involves other people.'

Hebe looked away. 'So far it's only been Anthony and myself.'

Lucy wanted to shake her. Instead she looked around the kitchen, hoping to find inspiration, but there was nothing. 'Hebe, I'm worried about you.'

'I know.' Hebe's glance rested on her, then darted away. She pulled out her list and consulted it. 'The man from English Heritage is due in ten minutes.'

'Oh fuck the man from English Heritage. If we don't deal with these night-time prowls, you won't be around to find out what happens to Hell House.'

Hebe began to laugh.

Lucy rubbed her temples. She might have to summon her mother down here. Hebe was her sister after all. She might have some insight.

'Would you sleep with him to get my plans through?'

Lucy shook her head in shock. Had her aunt just asked what she thought she had?

'I think he's married; he wears a ring.' Hebe took a deep breath. 'It would be most helpful.'

'I hope you're joking.' Lucy studied her, trying to find a way to read her.

Hebe's glance darted about the room. 'Of course, but in the past you haven't actually been too fussy.'

Lucy swallowed. She couldn't really be having this conversation with her aunt. Surely she was dreaming it, brought about by four short hours of restless exhausted sleep. Hebe looked at her with a sideways glance, then walked out of the kitchen into the garden, where Fred was sorting slates to repair yet another hole in the roof. Lucy picked up the newly connected landline and dialled her mother, reaching the answerphone. 'Can you ring me back?' she said. 'Your sister is behaving very strangely.'

Hebe was talking to the man she'd wanted Lucy to sleep with. Lucy had had a quick chat with him and said all she needed to regarding what help was required with planning permission. Now Hebe and the man were deep in discussion on the history of Cornish architecture. Lucy had had her fill of it, so she took the stairs two at a time to have a little look in Hebe's room. She couldn't shake the feeling that there was something her aunt wasn't telling her.

Sunlight filled the room as the efforts of the tree surgeon this morning began to work wonders. Hebe's room was immaculate, with everything placed just so. This snooping thing would have been much easier if Hebe was chaotic, like Lucy herself. She doubted she would notice if anything was slightly out of place. But looking at Hebe's hairbrush, comb, mirror all neatly lined up according to size, she realised it wasn't going to be easy. And of course she had no idea what she was actually looking for. But she was certain there was something. If Hebe was a sleepwalker it would have been noted before. All her worldly possessions were now here in Hell House, so that would include any medical files she had. The question was, where would she keep them?

In front of the large Venetian glass window sat Hebe's desk. It was the obvious place to start. Listening to make sure no one was nearby, she tried the centre drawer. Locked. She tried the others – the same.

On the top of the desk was Hebe's collection of fountain pens, again ordered by size, as were three inkpots. She checked them all in case the desk key was hidden in one, but they all contained ink.

Moving to the tall chest of drawers, she opened the top one. Beautifully folded knickers and bras. Hebe's taste leaned towards black or red lace. She rubbed her temples. Her aunt was full of surprises. Carefully, so as not to disturb the neat order, she felt around for a key. Nothing.

Hearing footsteps, she closed the drawer and ran to the salon, where she picked up the book that was sitting next to the sofa. She made sure that it was the right way up.

'I didn't know you'd taken an interest in poetry after all these years?'

She glanced up, noting that the page was open to a Donne elegy. The only poem of his that she liked had been 'The Bait'. It was sexy as hell.

'It caught my eye.'

'Really?' Hebe's face said she doubted that her dyslexic niece would be sitting reading Donne. She had a point.

'This line here ...' Lucy placed her finger on the page. '*And there the enamour'd fish will stray.*'

'And what is your interpretation of it?'

Her thoughts raced. What the hell could she say? 'I was simply enjoying the flow of the words and the images they created in my mind.'

'Hmmm.' Hebe nodded and held out her hand for the book. Lucy's hand shook and she felt like a naughty child who had been caught reading the filthy poems that only the Latin A-level students were allowed to read. Maybe she should have focused more during her final year of school. But that was another thing altogether.

In the distance, she heard the landline ring. There was only one handset and it was in the kitchen. She raced through the house, cursing the ancient wiring system.

'Lucy, I thought you were never going to pick up.' Her mother's voice was curt.

'Ugh.'

'What sort of answer is that?'

She cleared her throat. 'The only one I have breath to make.'

'What's happening with Hebe that you leave me such a cryptic message?'

Looking around to make sure her aunt wasn't near, she said, 'Does she have a history of sleepwalking?'

'No ...' Her mother's voice trailed off.

'You don't sound so sure.'

'I was trying to remember, but no, she has never done that before.'

'Damn.'

'What?'

'Well, she is now, and if she did it as a child it might make more sense.'

'Tell me exactly what's happening.'

Lucy pulled out a chair and sat. 'Hebe went out walking to Dennis Head in the middle of the night in her pyjamas.'

Her mother coughed. 'Have you been smoking something?'

'Mum, that was something I never did.'

Kate sighed. 'True. Sorry. I'm not sure what's happening, but when I've seen Hebe recently, she hasn't been herself.'

'How recently?' There were a few moments of silence. 'Mum?'

'I think it was about a year ago that I thought things were strange enough to mention it to your father.'

'Great, why him and not me? He hates her.' If her mother were here, Lucy would throttle her.

'Nonsense. Anyway, he put it down to the menopause.'

'He would.'

'Lucy, that's not fair.' Kate sighed. 'You know, maybe it *could* be . . .' she paused, 'hormonal.'

'Maybe, but I didn't see that when I googled it.'

'Can't you get her to a doctor?' Her mother's voice had a croak to it.

'She's refused point blank.'

'Then . . . I don't know what to say.'

'Mum, I need help.'

'Let me have a think.'

'Fine, but can you be quick about it?' Lucy heard footsteps on the back stairs and hung up.

Hebe stood in the doorway with her hands on her hips. 'Who was that on the phone?'

'Just Mum giving me the latest on my disgrace.' Lucy turned to open the fridge and hide the colour on her cheeks. Why did she feel so guilty? She was only trying to help.

Lucy needed fresh air to think. It was cold, but the sky was blue. She walked up past the barns and through the field to the road to St Keverne, where she could get phone signal. She'd missed a call from her mother and one from Ed. The latter would have nothing useful to say, but hopefully her mother had called back with some information on Hebe.

'Mum.'

'Darling. It's cleared here. Is the weather as lovely down there?'

Lucy looked up to the sky. Days didn't come much lovelier, but the last thing she wanted to do was discuss the weather with her mother. 'Fine. What have you found out?'

'Well, I spoke with your grandmother.'

'And?'

'She went quiet.'

Plucking a twig from the ground, Lucy said, 'She never goes quiet.'

'I know.'

'You pressed her, right?'

'I tried.' Kate sighed.

'I need to know. I think this whole house thing is too much for her.'

'I'm sure it is.' Her mother paused. 'That's why you are there.'

Lucy rolled her eyes. 'Mum, if you wanted to give Hebe practical help, you should have sent Michael.'

'He has a job.'

'Fair point.' She pressed her lips together.

'Your grandmother will be coming down to see you soon. I'll send you the details once I know them.'

Lucy kicked a stone, wondering why her mother seemed to be avoiding the problem.

'Why aren't you coming yourself?'

'Your father needs—'

Lucy cut her off. 'What, his laundry done? Where are your priorities? Your sister is falling apart.'

'Let's see what your grandmother has to say.'

'Fine.' She hung up. Her grandmother was unique. Lucy thought it might have been her way of coping with her husband. He had been substantially older, and difficult, according to her mother. Hebe rarely spoke about him. Lucy's grandmother, on the other hand, had developed a new lease of life once he'd died. She had opened her house up as a bed and breakfast and acquired a list of 'walkers', as Kate referred to her mother's gentlemen.

As she began to walk back down the old lane, which was now

no more than a track, she could see all the way to St Mawes and to the St Anthony Lighthouse. Just at the edge of the field were the remains of the old watchtower. It must have had the most spectacular view. A cow glared at her through one of the broken walls. Rushing past before the rest of the herd took an interest, she legged it back through the fence that marked the boundary of Hell House.

From this angle, the house appealed to her. Despite the beauty of the loggia on the other side, she liked looking through what remained of the great hall. It must have been impressive when it had been two storeys high and filled a vast space. The large windows reminded her of a church and hinted at its origins as a monastery.

The sun was dropping and the light becoming golden. The grey stone glistened and softened, making the place look more like a house and less like a fortress. With her phone, she took a few shots. Another day she would bring a big camera and capture it properly, but right now she needed to prepare for the arrival of her grandmother, which meant sorting another bedroom.

Thirty-Four ✻
Hebe

1 November 2016

Hebe sat with her pen poised over the paper. The word she wanted was gone and her body ached. She was missing something and was restless because of it. Standing, she looked down at her journal. The sentences were shorter. It was mostly lists. She threw the pen down, then bent to pick it up, replacing the cap. Ink had splattered out of the nib, bleeding into the edge of the carpet. With her hankie she wiped it away.

Sitting again, she put her head in her hands. This wasn't working. According to her journal, today was the Feast of All Hallows. A sacred day. Last night the dead had walked, and the night before that so had she. Or that was what Lucy told her. Hebe looked down at her feet, which were sore. The evidence was there. This morning she had woken late in a strange bed and screamed. But it hadn't been strange. It was here. Lucy and that man with the white teeth had come running to her. His eyes. So like Thomas's. Or was she just getting things muddled in her mind? It was all too possible.

She looked at the outline she had written for this book. Thus far she had expanded it with further details, but although she had tried, she was finding it hard to string together sentences. Not just longer compound ones, but short sentences too. She had hoped that turning over the restoration of the house to Lucy would free her mind to write. But her brain was closing down. The TIAs happened frequently; they never lasted long, but each one shouted a warning to her.

The day was racing past. She must find Lucy and say sorry,

176

then tell her the truth. Her niece had a right to know. But would she leave if she did? That was the risk. Since she was seventeen, Lucy had always left when things became difficult. Hebe knew why. She remembered that much and she understood.

Lucy wasn't in the kitchen, but the plans for the house were spread out on the table, along with other computer printouts – start dates and costings. Lucy was good at this. Also on the table were photographs of the house. Lucy had captured the soul of the building. She might claim not to like it, but her photographs said something different. They mostly showed the darker, more mysterious side of the house. Hebe wondered if that came from spending time with the man who looked like Thomas.

She pulled out her list.

Lucy wanted to know what was wrong. Tell her.

The sun shone brightly through the windows on this crisp All Saints' Day. Tomorrow was All Souls' Day.

'*A soul-cake, a soul cake. Have mercy on all Christian souls for a soul-cake,*' she sang to herself. It was a day that was more associated with the old ways, but it was one that Hebe liked. Only two days until Ringing Night, which had begun in the nineteenth century in some Cornish parishes in anticipation of Guy Fawkes Night. That had been a major turning point: the Gunpowder Plot had highlighted many of the cracks leading to the Civil Wars that followed. The country had been far from unified.

She glanced down at the papers, step-by-step plans for restoration. They were wrong. They were changing things that they shouldn't be. Pulling out her list again, she looked at it for a clue to what was troubling her.

You own Helwyn House.

That was good.

Lucy is worried.

That must be it. Hebe had done something, something wrong. She couldn't remember. She swept the papers off the table, just as the kitchen door opened and Lucy walked in.

Hebe eyed her niece as she bent to pick up the mess.

When she'd finished, Lucy looked at her. Hebe saw her confusion, and it almost matched her own.

'Lucy, I'm sorry.'

'I'm sure it was an accident.'

Hebe shook her head. 'It wasn't, but that's not what I'm apologising for.'

Lucy frowned.

'I ...' The words wouldn't come out of her mouth. To voice them made it real. As long as she, the consultant and her solicitor were the only ones to know, she could pretend that everything was fine until it wasn't, and hopefully by then she wouldn't be aware. But she knew this wasn't fair.

'Yes?' Lucy glanced at her as she straightened the papers.

'There is no way to say ... this that makes it any less ... awful.' Hebe looked out of the window. The sun was already dropping behind the trees in the distance. Pink was beginning to tinge the sky.

'You're ill.' Lucy touched her arm.

Hebe nodded.

'Then we must take you to a doctor.'

Hebe gave a dry laugh. 'It's too late for that.'

Lucy stilled. 'What do you mean?'

Hebe turned to her. 'I have Alzheimer's.'

Lucy blinked. 'What?'

Hebe nodded.

'You're too young.'

She laughed. 'No.'

'But ... but Hebe, I don't understand ...'

'Nor do I.'

Lucy sank into the chair beside her. Hebe turned to the cupboard and took out the marshmallows. They went well with a cup of tea, and that was just what was needed.

'Lucy, please don't tell your mother about this, or anyone else for that matter.'

'Why?'

'Because ... because I don't want people to know.' She

pulled a pink marshmallow out of the bag. The pink ones were her favourite. 'They will think less of me.'

Clutching the bag, she left Lucy in the kitchen. She had work to be getting on with, and she needed to arrange to have her wine sent from store at the wine merchants to Helwyn House. She must enjoy it while she could.

❊ Thirty-Five ❊
Hebe

August 2015

Your phone rings on the way down to Kynance Cove. Below, the tide is out and the beach is scattered with families. I half listen to the conversation. Your television project. They need you to go to a meeting. You are resisting, not wanting to leave me or to leave Cornwall. The latter I understand, but the time is coming soon when you must leave me.

I pick my way carefully down the steep path, leaving you behind. Is there any way I can make it your choice to go? I shake my head. I have tried so many times.

Reaching the large rocks, I carefully move from one to the next, focusing on my balance, which isn't good. I look around for you but you're not there. Panic. I reach out and my hand closes on air. A young man comes along but it's not you.

'Here, let me help you.' He takes my elbow and leads me across the wobbly boulders. 'There you go.' He darts away and I turn, looking for something. The happy shouts of children chasing the waves reach me. I sink onto damp sand. I am lost without you.

But you must go. I must let you, make you. I should have done it years ago. We have always been wrong. I close my eyes, remembering how I have failed to do the one thing I needed to do.

*

Take heed of loving me,
At least remember, I forbade it thee.

You handed me my latest work. Light pencil marks indicated where you had paused to think. As I scanned the pages, I read the lines like Braille until I reached a coffee stain and a note. You had raised a question. I smiled at you and flipped through the rest. At the end you had given me an A, and I laughed at your comment.

It couldn't be an A* because you didn't reference me. Marked down for not citing all sources.

I ran my fingers over your words. We had discussed this point and eventually you had agreed that I couldn't put you in the footnotes. You told me it was fine because you loved me.

You loved me. I still could not accept it, but I did accept that I loved working when you were here. My heart sang when you read poetry to me. It would do the same if it was the phone book, but on your lips the poems came alive. It was as if you had the rhythm of the poet's heart in you. Your breath gave weight and lightness and stopped my heart from beating.

*

'There you are.' You extend your hand and I grab it. The tide has moved closer and I had been lost in thought. Standing, you draw me into your arms and kiss me, but I pull back. There are too many people here. You link your fingers through mine and we walk to a quiet part of the beach.

'Swim?' you ask.

I swallow, thinking of the cold, but say, 'Yes.' I strip away my clothing, revealing my swimming costume. Again you take my hand and we walk to the sea. I should be stronger. I must be stronger. I race into the sea knowing you are following me.

❊ Thirty-Six ❊
Lucy

2 November 2016

Lucy's hands were full of grocery bags as she walked towards the kitchen, her head laden with what Hebe had told her. Lucy had spent a sleepless night. Her clever aunt just couldn't have this disease. But she had heard it from Hebe herself, and everything she had been noticing fitted the symptoms she'd read about. Earlier, in the car, she had raged, then tears came. She'd never felt so helpless before. If this was what she was feeling, how must Hebe be coping?

She almost fell over Kit, who was on his knees looking at the carving on the gate surround. 'Drop something?'

'No.' He looked up with a smile. He pointed to the worn figure on the stone. 'Trying to figure out which saint this might have been.'

'So, praying then?'

'In a way.' He stood and brushed down his jeans. 'Let me give you a hand with these.'

'I'm fine.' She turned to the kitchen door.

'More in the car?'

'All good,' she called over her shoulder, placing the bags on the table and heading straight for the kettle, her mind running through the things she'd learned. At fifty-five, Hebe was classed as early onset. Lucy had a million questions she wanted to ask, but she wondered if Hebe would even know the answers. It was all too awful.

She sighed and turned to Kit, who had followed her inside. 'Tea?'

He nodded.

'What exactly were you looking for out there?' She opened the cupboard to get some mugs and found it all reorganised again. She shook her head.

'Clues.'

'Fine,' she huffed.

He laughed. 'You and Hebe both know that before my father passed away, he was researching our family history, in particular our connection to Thomas Grylls. His name had always shown up on the family tree, but proof was missing.' He ran his hand over the back of the chair. 'He'd moved to the Scillies to find the evidence he was certain existed.'

Lucy took the milk out of the fridge.

'I'm afraid I wasn't very encouraging, and didn't really listen to what he was saying.'

She studied him. There was a sadness in his eyes. 'I don't think anyone really listens that closely to their parents, if that helps.'

He gave a dry laugh. 'Yes and no.'

She handed him his tea. 'You miss him.'

He nodded. 'I should have come back sooner. I knew things weren't good, but I thought we had more time.' He took a deep breath. 'Instead I stayed in Hollywood to make the worst film ever.'

Lucy took his hand in hers. He looked so full of remorse.

'As a way to reconnect with him, I picked up his research, and that led me here to Helwyn House.'

Lucy blew on her tea. 'How does the house fit in, other than that it was Thomas's home at one point?'

He smiled. 'According to my father, Thomas Grylls is still here.'

'What?' She shivered.

'Not as a ghost, but one of the letters we have says that he was coming back here before returning to the Scillies.'

'Oh.' She thought of the novels. The last one had left Thomas in Europe, acting as an emissary for Charles II.

'He was never seen again.' Kit sipped his tea. 'Dad indicated that somewhere in the building there would be clues.'

'So you're looking for the body in the library.' Lucy smiled.

'Indeed, except Helwyn House doesn't have one. But it does have secrets, and I hope with Hebe's permission to find some of them out. In fact when I took a day trip to the Scillies last week, I collected my father's research and I have Thomas Grylls's letters to show her.' He pointed to a leather satchel.

Lucy squeaked.

'What's wrong?'

Closing her eyes for a moment, she debated whether she should tell him. Hebe didn't want her to tell her mother or anyone, which Lucy didn't agree with at all. But until she had more information, she would respect her aunt's wishes. But if Kit was going to be here for a while, he would need to know. Looking at him, she whispered, 'Hebe told me this morning that she has Alzheimer's.'

He took a deep breath. 'That explains a lot.' He reached for her hand. 'It's hard for you both. I'm so sorry.'

She nodded.

'Anything I can do?'

'Where to begin.' She shook her head. 'For the moment, please don't say a word to anyone.'

'Of course.' He squeezed her hand and she fought the urge to weep. This wasn't good. She had to pull herself together. Hebe needed her now. So much for a quick exit from Hell House once the renovation was well under way. She swallowed. She would focus on what she could achieve today, and not look any further forward for now.

Thirty-Seven
Hebe

2 November 2016

Hebe looked through the cupboards. Things had been moved again. She must speak to Lucy about this. But Lucy had been shopping, which was good. She just needed to put things away in the right place. Hebe began putting things back where they should be.

'Hello.' The man with the white teeth came in and put a measuring thing on the table. She frowned. He dug into a bag, then placed several plastic folders on the table.

'I brought these for you to look at.'

'What are they?'

He smiled. 'The letters I told you about.'

'What letters?'

'The ones proving that Thomas Grylls had a child.' He opened one of the folders.

Hebe's mouth dried. This was wrong. Her thoughts swam against crashing currents. Her editor had emailed. Agent. Book. Thomas unfaithful. She rubbed her temples, then looked at him. He had Thomas's eyes.

'Show me.'

With care, he pulled out several pieces of paper. Even from this distance she could tell that the writing was Thomas's. She had studied enough of his papers over the years to know the rise and fall of his letters. Taking a deep breath, she moved closer and willed her heart to slow down, but it raced forward until it threatened to leave her altogether.

My dearest Mary,

Leaving you again at this time when you are with my child tears me apart. But I must make this trip. I know you understand. I cannot leave things undone. I have broken my troth and I must tell her in person.

I can hear your voice saying that she married another. She was not true. But both you and I know that she had little choice. I fear she still holds hope that somehow we can be together. I must set her free so that I can marry you with my whole heart. This is what I want more than anything else.

Hebe's hand flew to her heart. There in front of her were Thomas's words admitting that he'd betrayed Lucia. Her thoughts raced. He was no different from any other man. But he cared enough to want to tell Lucia himself. It was there in his own writing. Again she searched her memory for anything that might help her prove that this was wrong. But nothing arrived. She didn't know if that was because there *was* nothing, or she just couldn't remember.

'As you can see, it's pretty conclusive.'

She shook her head. 'What?' The long-case clock in the corner chimed the hour, but her watch told a different time. It was ten minutes to. The clock was running fast, unlike her brain.

He sighed. 'Thomas had a child with Mary Rowse.'

That name. It stirred a memory. 'Who was she, this Mary?'

'She was the daughter of Samuel Rowse, agent for several of the governors of the Isles of Scilly.'

Hebe swallowed. Not some random woman, then. 'Did they marry?'

'No.'

She looked up from the letter. 'Why?'

'He never returned.' He shook his head.

'So your family never carried the Grylls name.'

'No.' He reached into the folder and pulled out a gold ring, which he handed to her. 'I just found this caught in my father's papers.'

She gasped when she saw the Grylls seal. Thomas's ring. It was true. 'Do you know what happened?'

He sighed. 'Sadly, no. My father was trying to piece it all together before he died.'

'I see.' But Hebe knew she didn't see at all and probably never would. Giving the ring back to him, she fought tears. She was so close to knowing what had happened to Thomas. But time and her mind were running out on her.

✳ Thirty-Eight ✳
Lucy

2 November 2016

Soul cakes? What the hell were they? Was this all part of the disease? Hebe had always been a decent cook, but the only thing Lucy could recall her baking was a king cake on the feast of Epiphany. Well, Hebe was making soul cakes now, whatever they were. Lucy had asked why, and her aunt had said it was important and told her to go away. She had done so, longing for more information.

As she came up the stairs, she found Kit studying the ancient graffiti beside the windowsill. She'd mentioned it to Hebe just this morning, asking if she wanted her to clean it up. She was sure she saw Michael's artwork among that of children from years before. Hebe had flown off the handle at the suggestion, so Lucy had made a sign and taped it to the window so some poor decorator didn't suffer the same fate. The whole incident was so unlike the Hebe of Lucy's youth. She had always taken care never to raise her voice – even when Lucy had been horrible, which she frequently had been. Of course she now knew that this was a symptom of the Alzheimer's. How many others had she missed?

'Hi.' Kit turned towards her and smiled. She grabbed the handrail near the top step. Having a movie star about the place wasn't good for her equilibrium. 'Hebe OK?' He put his pencil down.

She wobbled her hand. 'Baking. I think she's been unsettled by your revelations.'

'I sensed that too. She muttered something about needing

to make sure that the novelist used historical fact and broke readers' hearts with the truth.'

'Ah, she must be talking about the Thomas Grylls books by H. J. Bowden.' Lucy smiled, thinking of the book on the shelf containing her name alongside Kit's. Wandering to the salon door, she looked at the portrait and frowned. She had rather liked the Thomas Grylls portrayed in the books, and wasn't so sure about the man who had been revealed by Kit's letter.

He coughed. 'Where are you?'

'Sorry.' She walked back to him. 'I was thinking about unfaithful men.'

He raised an eyebrow. 'Missing him?'

She flushed. 'No. I had a lucky escape. I was actually thinking about Thomas Grylls.'

'Oh.' He leaned on the window ledge. 'It's funny, I never thought of him as unfaithful.'

'Why not?'

He tilted his head to the side. 'Lucia was married to someone else. He hadn't seen her in a while, the war had been lost, and he was in Europe with the king. From his point of view, it was over.'

'Yes, he may have felt that way.' She paused, thinking of the novels. 'But I don't think Lucia ever let go of her love for him.'

'True, but time had elapsed.'

'Typical fickle man.' She raised an eyebrow. Her father was a prime example.

Kit frowned but still managed to be gorgeous. It wasn't fair that he should look so good all the time. She would be lying to herself if she said she wasn't attracted to him, but she knew where those feelings led, and it wasn't a place she was heading. Still, she wouldn't mind sleeping with him. Lust was a far healthier thing. She ran her finger over one of the daisy wheels carved into the plasterwork.

He shrugged. 'We'll have to agree to disagree on that one.'

She half closed her eyes and turned to him. 'Have you always been faithful when you've been away from your ... your partner?' She mentally ran through every scandal rag she'd read, but there had been nothing about him cheating.

He placed a hand on his heart. 'Never been unfaithful.'

She pursed her lips. 'Even in your mind?'

'Ah, now that's a different matter.'

She laughed. 'No worries, I think we all fall down there.'

She glanced at his notebook, which lay open. He'd copied some of the graffiti into it. The daisy wheel shapes in particular. They resonated with Lucy too. They kept all evil spirits away.

'Tell me about these. Why are you so interested in them?'

'Witch marks, or more correctly, apotropaios. Ritual markings. They're fascinating.'

'How old are these, do you think?'

'Most date from just after the Reformation.'

'Why?'

Hebe appeared on the stairs. She looked at them both as if trying to focus. 'Because the old religion had been taken from the people, and although the gentry adapted quickly, the workers didn't. They looked to the past, to what they knew, to protect them.' She stepped closer and pointed to a large *VV* carved on the wall. 'They were invoking the Blessed Virgin's protection.' She turned and walked into her room and shut the door.

Lucy looked to Kit and he shrugged.

'She's right.'

She pointed to some other marks on the plaster. 'Is that a dragon?'

He grinned. 'I should think so.' His arm brushed hers as he pointed out a small figure beside it. 'St George.'

She stepped away, putting distance between them. 'Have you seen the other ones?'

'No. Where?' He frowned.

She led him through the salon, past his ancestor and into the little room to the side of the fireplace, then through another door. It shut behind them.

'So just what have you brought me into the closet for?' Kit's voice was deep and very close to her ear. She shivered. Cheeky bastard. It was a good thing it was dark and he couldn't see her face.

The light from her phone helped her to locate the door handle, then she found a piece of wood on the floor and wedged the door open. She would not be held responsible for her actions if left in a confined space with him.

'These.' She pointed to the big daisy wheels on the walls. It was only then that she noticed the rest of the writing. Kit turned on the torch on his phone. His fingers ran over the marks. What could he see that she couldn't? She frowned. 'Do you have any idea of what you are actually looking for?'

'No.' He laughed as he stepped out of the small space and looked out of the window. Now that the leaves had mostly gone, glimpses of the creek flashed through the near-naked branches. 'Do you know of any other marks in the house?'

She shook her head. 'If there are any others, Hebe might know. She's been studying this house for a long time.'

'Shall we ask her?'

'Sure.' She watched him enter the salon. 'Do you smell something burning?'

He nodded, and they both raced to the kitchen. Hebe's soul cakes.

Thirty-Nine ✳
Hebe

> *Martinmas, the feast of St Martin of Tours*
> *This was the day to slaughter the animals in*
> *preparation for the coming winter. I feel winter in my*
> *bones. Everything aches.*
> *Dinner last night was soup. I didn't feel like eating.*
> *I fell again.*

Her diary was now filled with falls. She refused to give in to the pain and looked through the notes she had written down. Outside the window the sun was setting. The low rays highlighted the upper branches of the trees. Did she really have so little time? There was so much to be done? She looked down to her desk.

There was a letter from her agent. She didn't need to read it again. It was all very polite but she was way past deadline. She folded the letter and looked at her laptop. Should she just accept defeat and tell her publisher that the last book of the contract, the last book of Thomas's life, would not be written? She dropped her head into her hands, wanting to cry, but tears wouldn't come. Empty. Slowly, everything was leaving her. First words, and now proper emotions. All she was left with was anger and desolation. She was lonely but couldn't remember why.

Pulling her laptop closer, she opened a document. It had two words. *Chapter One*. Nothing more. The cursor blinked at her, waiting. What should she write? Thanks to that man with Thomas's eyes, she knew that Thomas had lost his heart to another. But this was fiction. Couldn't she write the story the way she wanted it? That Thomas, after years of loyal service, came home to be rewarded by Charles II and finally married his one true love.

But that was nothing more than a fairy tale, and she was a historian, whose previous novels had been as much fact as they were fiction. What should she do?

❈ Forty ❈
Lucy

13 November 2016

Lucy stood on the road outside the New Inn. Hebe was talking to someone. Lucy heard her mention that today was St Brice's Day. Lucy wondered who the hell St Brice was, but let go of that thought as she looked at the moon. It was massive as it rose above the Lannarth Hills. Somewhere over there was Hell House, and she was happy to head into the warm fug of the pub. Hebe would hopefully follow soon. It was too cold to stand around outside for long.

'Hello, you,' Cadan called over his shoulder as he poured a glass of wine.

'What have you got on your face?' she asked.

'A beard, so that I can howl like a werewolf tonight.'

She shook her head.

'Not impressed, then?'

'With the moon, yes, but with the weirdly coloured beard, no.'

He scratched it. 'Yeah, who knew there was ginge in the family?'

She frowned. 'What are you doing working here rather than at the Shippers?'

He scratched his head. 'I'm broke and in debt. Will do anything for money.'

'That bad?'

He nodded.

'Your art?'

He sighed. 'Sells for peanuts if at all.' He looked to the door as it opened. 'Hi, Hebe. What can I get you?'

194

Hebe looked confused. Lucy wondered if her fall this afternoon had done more damage than she was letting on.

'Do you want red or white?' she asked, touching Hebe's arm.

'Pink.'

Lucy blinked. 'OK.' She loved rosé but she'd never seen Hebe drink it.

'What about you, Luce?'

She looked at the ciders. Nothing really appealed. 'Just an orange juice.'

'Joining us for dinner?' Cadan handed over the drinks. Lucy nodded, looking at the specials before ordering. Nothing appealed, but neither did cooking. It had been Hebe who had suggested coming to the pub for a drink and a bite to eat. She hadn't left the house much in the past few weeks. Lucy was just relieved she hadn't done any driving. Even more so now that she knew about the illness.

Her eyes narrowed as she watched Hebe sip the wine and make a face. She didn't like it. Had she forgotten that?

The door opened and a whoosh of cold air swept in along with Fred's father and mother. Lucy hadn't seen Tamsin in years. She hadn't changed much. She marched straight up to them and wrapped Lucy in a big hug. 'Hello, you. Fred's told me about all the exciting building work taking place.'

'Yes.' Hebe nodded but was subdued.

'He's wonderful.' Lucy grinned.

'He'll do.' Tamsin extended a hand to take the glass of wine Cadan had poured for her. 'How are you?'

'OK,' Lucy lied.

Tamsin looked at her and leaned closer. 'I'm around if you ever need an ear.' Had Fred noticed the difference in Hebe and mentioned it to his mother? Or had Peta sensed it and told her?

'Thanks.' Lucy twisted her glass in her hand. Maybe she should seek Tamsin out after her grandmother's visit. With everything buzzing about in her head, it was beginning to feel like it might explode.

Cadan walked past with their food. 'Shall I put this on that table?' Hebe followed him before Lucy could respond, and sat down with her back straight and hands folded on her lap. Lucy sat opposite and grabbed a chip, hoping it would settle her stomach. Chips were a panacea. In her book they solved everything from hangovers to heartbreak.

Hebe stared at her plate.

'Is something wrong?'

'I didn't order this.'

'You did.'

She pursed her lips. 'I don't like chilli.'

'I wondered that, but you did order it.'

She folded her hands on the table.

'Are you feeling OK?' asked Lucy.

'Yes.' She took a sip of her rosé, wincing again.

'Would you like my steak?'

'Yes.' Her head bobbed. Lucy's articulate aunt had gone monosyllabic.

Lucy swapped the plates. Hebe looked happier now, so it might be time to broach the subject of Lucy's grandmother, Hebe's stepmother, coming to visit. Poking the chilli to the side, she tucked into the rice at the bottom. Not as good as chips, but not bad. Fortified a bit, she began. 'I have to go to Truro tomorrow.'

Hebe looked up.

'Your stepmother is arriving on the eleven o'clock train.'

Hebe stopped with her fork in mid air. 'Sarah? Why on earth is she coming?'

Lucy swallowed. 'She's worried about me.'

'Ah.' Hebe returned her attention to the steak, while Lucy stole a chip, thinking about this reaction.

'The bruise on your head is colouring nicely,' she said.

'What bruise?'

Lucy nearly choked. Hebe was sporting an egg above her right eye that had gone from red to blue already. She was surprised no one had commented tonight, but then with the building site they lived in, maybe people took it for granted that there would be injuries. 'The one above your eye,' she replied.

Hebe felt around her left eye first, and Lucy shook her head.

Her fingers then sought out the bump and she frowned.

'You took a nasty fall. I still think you should see a doctor.'

'I didn't fall. And this will clear swiftly.'

Lucy stared at the wall. Could the fall have accelerated the dementia, or was it just a sign of things progressing?

Lucy rolled over in bed. Heartburn. With all this stress, maybe she was developing an ulcer. Joy. She sat up and slipped off the eyeshades she'd taken to wearing. There was no point putting curtains up until the building work was complete.

Cold moonlight fell into the room, cut into rectangles by the window panes. She hunted for shoes and her coat to keep warm. The temperature had dropped with the clear skies, and the supermoon was spectacular, true to its hype. It was almost bright as day. There would be a frost.

Zipping her coat, she moved to the window and stood transfixed as she saw her aunt moving across the courtyard in her white nightgown and bare feet. Her dark hair flowed down her back, catching the moonlight. Lucy rubbed her eyes. Was she dreaming? No, Hebe turned and looked over her shoulder at the gates behind her.

Propelled to action, Lucy raced down the stairs two at a time. The front door was wide open, and cold air blasted her as she ran to discover Hebe gone. The main gate was closed and locked. Lucy knew where the key was but Hebe didn't. That meant she'd gone into one of the ground-floor areas in the north wing. Damn. If Lucy thought the north bedroom was creepy, these rooms were worse, especially with no torch. In her haste, she'd left it behind.

'Hebe?' She cut diagonally across the courtyard, watching her step. The moon was high and her shadow was short, soon to be non-existent if she walked through the door that Hebe had been heading for. What would she be doing in there?

She called a bit louder, her stomach tightening. The door creaked on its hinges. Every Halloween nightmare film was at the forefront of her mind.

She couldn't see a damn thing. Stepping with caution, she

moved further into the space. It didn't feel like a room, more like she had walked into a black void. She put her hands out and wobbled forward, not sure what would happen each time she put her foot down. Then she tripped over something large and landed on her outstretched hands.

'Ouch.'

'Hebe?' Lucy righted herself. Moonlight fell through the open door and she saw the outline of her aunt kneeling on the floor. 'What in the name of hell are you doing?'

'Praying.'

Lucy took a deep breath. 'You don't believe in God.'

'I do.'

Lucy's palms were stinging. She longed to know how to handle this – whatever this was. 'OK, you believe in God now.'

Hebe remained on her knees. The stone floor was icy. 'Always.'

'If you say so.'

'I am not worthy to enter the chapel.'

'Chapel?' Lucy squinted then remembered the monks and Peta mentioning it. It had been somewhere. Why not here?

Hebe pointed to a blocked-up door. Lucy knew beyond it there was nothing but an old stone staircase on the outside of the building, leading into the King's Room. It had always struck her as odd.

'Why aren't you worthy?' she asked.

'I have sinned.'

Lucy shivered. Hebe's sins had to be far less than hers, but she didn't want to examine her past, especially not in this place in the middle of the night.

'Shall we head back inside and have a cup of tea, or maybe a hot chocolate?' The last words were lost as her teeth began to chatter.

Silence.

'Hot chocolate, Hebe?' She stepped closer. She couldn't leave her alone here.

'No. I'm not done. Go.'

Lucy backed towards the door. The moonlight picked out

the twisting vines that wound their way through the wall like an old gravestone. Looking back at Hebe, she was bent low with her forehead touching the stone floor. This wasn't OK, but Lucy didn't know what to do or how to help. Maybe her grandmother might be able to suggest something, because the situation was becoming impossible to deal with alone.

✳ Forty-One ✳
Hebe

August 2015

You are looking at a poem but you are not reading. Your shoulders are hunched, and since you've come back from London you haven't been here really. The meeting didn't go as you wanted. I am relieved. It buys me more time. If you become a television presenter, I have no choice but to end us. Maybe that is what I should be wishing for, but in my heart it is not. Yet looking at your disappointment, I long to make you happy, happy as I once did.

*

Whoever loves, if he do not propose
The right true end of love, he's one that goes
To sea for nothing but to make him sick.

It was our anniversary, you reminded me. Anniversary of what? I asked.

'Meeting.'

I looked up from my book and smiled. You held a bunch of Michaelmas daisies. Their purple colour was vibrant in the afternoon light. In your other hand was a bottle of wine. You knew me well. Simple flowers and good wine. I stood and took the flowers from you, kissing your hand in thanks.

Your eyes were filled with excitement. Tomorrow you would begin your master's. A shadow crossed your face.

'It will be fine.' I stroked your hand.

'How do you know?' You found the corkscrew in the kitchen

drawer while I put the flowers in a vase. Their earthy smell reminded me of my childhood – warm autumn afternoons and Michaelmas daisies the bright spot of colour in the garden. My mother had made me a crown out of some pale pink ones and called me her princess. I closed my eyes. I'd forgotten that. Smell. It was very powerful, because I must have only been five.

'I have had the pleasure of teaching you. It is a joy.'

'What if I'm not up to the task?'

I smiled and took the glass of wine you poured for me. 'You are more than up to it.' I touched your temple. 'Your insight scares me. Of course, if you are so clever, why are you still here?'

You raised an eyebrow, then pulled me into your arms. I laughed as I tried not to spill my wine. 'Love,' you said, and kissed me.

❋ Forty-Two ❋
Lucy

14 November 2016

Truro felt positively cosmopolitan after Lucy's weeks in the sticks. There were people and shops everywhere. Traffic was heavy near the station and her grandmother stood on the pavement waiting. She looked like she was heading to a hotel spa for a pampered weekend, rather than time at Hell House.

'Gran.' Lucy waved. The rental car was small and not what she would have been expecting. In fact Lucy hoped the rental people didn't look out of their office window, as the car was more mud than anything else. The drive to Hell House when wet was almost impassable in this little thing. She hopped out of the car to hug her grandmother and put her bag in the boot.

'Darling.' Her grandmother held her at arm's length and studied her. She would not be pleased. Lucy's hair was scraped back, she wore no make-up other than lipstick, and her jeans had seen better days. Most of her wardrobe was suited to London, not here. Her life back home felt so far away. 'You're blooming. Your skin looks wonderful.' She kissed her. 'The country suits you.'

Lucy raised an eyebrow.

'Seriously, you have colour in your cheeks, and there's a bit of a gleam in your eye.' She slid into the passenger seat. 'Does this mean you are over the dreadful MP and have found someone more suitable?'

Lucy laughed. 'I'm well over the MP, but there is no one else.'

Her grandmother cast her a sideways glance. 'Are you sure?'

Lucy thought about Kit. 'Absolutely.'

'OK, you don't need to tell me just yet.'

'Gran, seriously there isn't. I'm not in the market.'

'Nonsense. We are always in the market for love, always.'

'No, I don't agree. Just look at Hebe. She's been fine without love.'

'Has she?' Her grandmother sounded doubtful.

'Yes, absolutely.'

'If you say so, but I believe we all need love. Love is life.'

'No, love is death.' Lucy sighed. A car horn sounded as she pulled out without looking.

'Maybe we'll have this discussion when you're not driving. I'm not ready to die just yet, which is why I keep love in all its forms in my life.'

Trying to win an argument with her grandmother was useless.

'Tell me about Helwyn House.'

'Oh, it has a roof now. Of sorts.' Lucy was doing it an injustice, but they still didn't have heating.

Her grandmother frowned. 'Hot water?'

'Every second Wednesday.'

'That bad?'

'Not quite, but close.' Lucy glanced at her. 'I hope that bag is full of thermal underwear and cashmere.'

'Of course, darling, you know as well as I do that is standard equipment for any country house, unless it's owned by Americans or Arabs.'

Lucy grinned. Joy. Her grandmother was filled with it, and funny old insight.

She negotiated a roundabout. 'I still don't know why Hebe has bought this house.'

'She loves it, obviously.'

'There's that word again.' She ground the gears, struggling to slip into the right one.

'Indeed.'

'Well, love leads to stupid decisions.'

Her grandmother shrugged. 'Sometimes, but rarely is it boring.'

'I give up.' Lucy raised a hand.

Her grandmother chuckled. 'Wise in this instance.'

A half hour later she turned through the gate piers and the little car climbed the rutted drive. Gran was all eyes. Lucy tried to imagine the place as she saw it – not laden with years of hating it. Did it look as dire as she thought?

❊ Forty-Three ❊
Hebe

14 November 2016

Hebe looked in the mirror. She had no recollection of hitting her head, but the evidence stared at her. Her right eye had begun to go blue and purple under the lump. She pulled her shirt aside to see a large bruise covering her shoulder. Her knees, too, were scraped. Her diary marked each fall, so she could rely on that, but how much longer would she remember to write it down? Lucy was … Why couldn't Hebe find the word? Lucy was doing something today that Hebe didn't want. She could cry with frustration. She had no idea what it was she didn't want.

Picking up her lipstick, she applied it with care. Then she arranged her hair so it fell over her damaged forehead. There was nothing that could be done about the black eye. She stopped and dug in her make-up bag. At the bottom she found eyeshadow. Taking the brush, she applied make-up to the undamaged eye until the colour nearly matched the other. That at least looked balanced. Her diary told her she had a meeting with the architect and the builder.

She dug in her drawer until she found the Hermès scarf with the purple in it that matched her eye shadow. She must look professional. She tied it about her neck and was about to head to the dining room when she heard a car. She went to the north windows, where she saw Lucy parking. A woman dressed in black trousers and a Chanel jacket was looking up at the house. Sarah. Her stepmother.

Scanning the room to make sure it was tidy, she straightened the cover on the bed and rushed down the stairs to greet them. She couldn't remember the last time she'd seen Sarah. But of course that shouldn't be a surprise. She knew there was something else she should be doing, but it was gone.

The front door opened wide and Sarah stopped on the threshold, staring. Hebe adjusted her scarf, then remembered she was still wearing her slippers. This would not be acceptable at all in Sarah's house. Bedroom clothes were worn in the bedroom only, or to reach a bathroom. And of course they must be beautiful, not necessarily functional, which the furry creatures on her feet were.

'Darling Hebe.' A slow smile spread across Sarah's face. She walked closer and kissed Hebe's cheeks lightly. 'So this is your new home.'

Hebe nodded and looked over Sarah's shoulder to see Lucy come in carrying shopping. Lucy's face fell but she recovered quickly.

'Are Fred and Mark here?' She glanced down at Hebe's legs.

'Oh, I forgot about that.' Hebe felt in her cardigan pockets for her notebook, but it wasn't there.

'I did wonder. Hadn't you better finish dressing, dear?' Sarah smiled.

Hebe touched her scarf. She was ready for the meeting.

Sarah looked at Hebe's feet. 'We must have interrupted you.'

Hebe glanced down too. Above her slippers, her bare legs were covered in bruises and cuts. 'Yes.' She stepped backwards, then dashed up the stairs, her face beetroot. In the middle of her desk, she saw her notebook. Forgetting the notebook was one thing, but forgetting her trousers was something else.

Forty-Four

Lucy

14 November 2016

'So now you see why I'm concerned.' Lucy turned to her grandmother.

'Yes.' Sarah looked around. 'Yes, I do.'

Lucy put the bags down. 'I'd better go and have a quick chat with Fred and Mark.'

'Good plan.' Sarah studied the hall. It was one of Lucy's favourite parts of the house, except for its temperature. Cold air flowed in continuously through the pistol hole. She could see that it had been useful for spying on unwanted visitors, but there were few of those now.

'Make yourself at home. I'll bring your bag up later. I've put you in the room next to Hebe's.'

'Of course.'

Opening the door to the dining room, Lucy found Mark and Fred deep in conversation with Kit.

'Hey, Luce. Look what we found.' Fred pointed to something on the table.

'What is it?' It didn't look appealing. A dark glass jar filled with liquid.

'It's a witch jar.'

'More witches.' She put her hands on her hips. 'What is it with this place?'

'It was for protection.'

'Bloody hell, between the witch marks and this ...' She pointed to the filthy item. 'Hell House should be well looked after, but methinks something hasn't been working. Maybe they forgot to do the incantation or something.'

'Possibly.' Kit smiled. 'But we have forgotten the old ways, so it may be more down to us.'

'You mean Hebe and me.' She shrugged and then thought of Hebe kneeling on the floor the other night. 'What would the date of this be?'

'Later than the marks on the walls.' Kit picked up the jar.

'There are more markings on the beams in the attics.' Fred looked at it. 'What's the liquid?'

'Most likely urine,' Kit said.

'Great, there should be no ghosts here. Piss will keep them away.' Lucy shuddered.

At that moment, Sarah walked into the room. All the men turned to look at her. She still had that quality at sixty-seven.

'Hello, gentlemen.'

'This is my grandmother, Sarah Courtenay,' Lucy said.

'Mrs Courtenay.' Mark stepped forward and shook her hand.

'Sarah, please.' She smiled. 'I'm gasping for a cup of tea and was looking for the kitchen.'

'Sorry, Gran.'

'I'm sure you have things to sort out, but maybe you could loan me one of these gentlemen to help me find the kettle.' She looked directly at Kit.

'Happy to.' He stepped forward and offered his arm. Lucy rolled her eyes. Trust her grandmother to flirt. She supposed she herself must have learnt it from somewhere.

Her grandmother looked over her shoulder as she was leaving the room. 'Lucy, dear, you may want to go and find your aunt. She wasn't in what I assume is her room.'

'Shit.' Lucy dashed out of the dining room, hoping that Hebe had at least put trousers on before she went roaming.

'Language!' she heard her grandmother call as she raced up the stairs. Which direction would Hebe have gone? Her behaviour today had hit a new level of awful. What had she been thinking with the purple eyeshadow? It matched her black eye, but that was the best that could be said for it. Purple eyeshadow and scarlet lipstick. She had to give her aunt credit for boldness.

Stopping at the top of the stairs, she listened. Nothing. Room after room, her aunt remained elusive. She returned to the kitchen to find her grandmother surrounded by three men. No surprise there.

'No luck?'

She shook her head and took the cup of tea Kit handed her.

'After you've drunk that, would you like me to help you look?'

Lucy nodded, knocked back the tea and grabbed her coat and wellies.

'I'll sort dinner while you're out.' Her grandmother stood and took a proper look at the range. Lucy hoped she knew what she was letting herself in for, but she didn't have time to explain it, as Kit was already walking out to his car.

⁂ Forty-Five ⁂
Hebe

14 November 2016

'I am missing something.' Hebe spoke to herself as she walked the path along the creek until she reached the big pines. Part of her didn't like them. They wouldn't have been here when Thomas had been. But now these trees defined the creek. She settled at the base of the one with the biggest trunk. Sunlight picked out branches, but the water was dark and moody. From here she could see eddies swirling with mud clouds as the tide pulled the water away. A pair of swans paddled below.

Tears began to roll down her face but she wasn't sure why. She brushed them away and her hand was covered in purple sparkly stuff. Puzzled, she took a hankie out of her pocket and blew her nose. Red lipstick met with the purple sparkles. Garish. 'God, what have I done?' Picking up a stick, she tossed it into the water below. It took a moment before the current grabbed it and pulled it out towards the sea.

Her mind was like the water in the creek … disappearing. But unlike the tide, her mind wouldn't return. Each day, each hour, things were slipping away, caught on a strong current. All she had were moments when things felt normal, but they were shattered all too easily. She thought of how Sarah had looked at her, and knew what she had become, standing in the hallway with no trousers on. There had been horror on her stepmother's beautiful face.

She pulled the note from her pocket with today's list.

You own Helwyn House.

Meeting with architect and builder at two.

She looked for her watch, but it wasn't on her wrist. It was late, according to the setting sun. Hopefully Lucy had dealt with the meeting. Would she carry on with the restoration of the house, or would she sell it to the man with Thomas's eyes? What about Thomas's portrait? She looked at the list again.

Pay bills – electric and oil.

Call solicitor.

She frowned. Why must she call the solicitor? Was there a problem, aside from her failing mind? Closing her eyes, she knew she was forgetting very important things. Tears fell again. Him. She was forgetting him. Had he forgotten her yet? How long had it been? The leaves had still been on the trees when she'd bought the house, and now they were almost gone. So was she, or anything that was worthwhile about her.

Forty-Six ※

Hebe

August 2015

The train jerks and I fall against you. You steady me, whispering in my ear. '*Stand still, and I will read to thee ... A lecture, love, in love's philosophy.*'

I should be able to continue the poem, but I can't. It is gone. I shiver and look out of the window. The lighthouse sitting above the sea reminds me that that way is treacherous. Below is a vast sweep of sand with flags in the distance marking the patrolled swimming area. But I wonder, as we venture to St Ives again, if anywhere is safe for us. Yesterday a student of yours called out to you. I hid behind a stack of books. She asked about me, and you glanced up and caught my eye. You said you were here with a colleague. She accepted that, then walked away with a lingering glance at you. She wanted you.

The train pulls into Carbis Bay station and I recall your graduation.

*

Love is a growing, or full constant light,
And his first minute, after noon, is night.

I witnessed your graduation from the platform. Part of me was bursting with pride, but I kept a steady smile on my face. I shouldn't have been there, but I had been asked to fill seats. Would I have come otherwise? I don't think I would have. My gaze kept returning to you. Your grin would have lit up the world if it could have been harnessed. I knew your parents and sister were in the audience. You wanted me to meet them. I wouldn't. The idea filled me with dread. I was pleased to witness your joy as you graduated with a first. Over the years I had seen you work hard towards this. Later, much later, I would congratulate you properly and give you a gift. But for the moment I was content watching you, your joy as you climbed the steps, took your diploma and winked at me, then gave your parents a thumbs-up. In that moment, I saw how wrong this had been.

*

The train halts again and I can recall none of the journey. Is this because I was lost in the past, or because I simply can't remember why we are here?

Forty-Seven ✳
Lucy

14 November 2016

'So you're telling me that Hebe's mother had mental issues?' Lucy put the trimmed green beans in a pan and leaned against the sink watching her grandmother mash potatoes.

'I believe so.'

She glanced to the door. Hebe was in the dining room with Kit, discussing the witch jar. She took a deep breath. 'Gran, Hebe told me – in confidence – that she has Alzheimer's, early onset, obviously.'

Her grandmother stilled.

'Do you think her mother had the same thing?'

Shrugging her shoulders, Sarah turned to look at her. 'She was younger than Hebe, but maybe … yes.'

'How young?'

Sarah swallowed. 'She was thirty-five.'

'Hell.'

'Yes.' She looked down. 'I didn't behave very well.' She pounded the potatoes with more force than was needed.

'What are you saying?'

'Your grandfather was a very handsome man and quite charismatic in his way.' A smile hovered on her mouth.

'Gran?'

'I was young and foolish.'

Lucy didn't like where she thought this was heading. Nor was she sure she wanted to hear it. 'What are you trying to say?'

'I didn't see things as they were.' Her grandmother put the potatoes back on the range, then added butter and milk. 'You weren't the only one to have an affair with a married man.'

'Gran, you had an affair with Grandfather while he was still married to Hebe's mother?'

She nodded. 'Yes, I fell pregnant with your mother then too.'

'Oh my God.'

'Terrible, isn't it?'

There was nothing Lucy could say.

'You see, I told myself she wasn't treating him well. She was erratic, totally unpredictable.' Sarah shook her head. 'Clearly I know now that she was ill, but back then I was naïve and full of my own sexual power.' Tucking her hair behind her ear, she looked at Lucy. 'Frances had never been the calm sort, always wild at heart.'

Lucy's eyes opened wide. 'How well did you know her?'

'Very.' Her shoulders slumped. 'My family knew the Courtenays well. I'd had a crush on your grandfather for years.' Putting the mash into an ovenproof dish, she sank onto a chair. 'I'm not proud of what I did, but I did become the best mother I could be for Hebe.'

Lucy nodded. Hebe loved Sarah. 'Does Hebe know?'

'No, I don't think so. Frances suffered a ... tragic accident.' She sighed. 'She died just before your mother was born.'

'How?'

'A broken heart, if I'm honest, but I believe her mind was broken too.'

That didn't sound very scientific. 'Does Mum know?'

'No.' Sarah slipped her glasses off and cleaned them. 'Richard didn't want to tell the girls. He thought, rightly or wrongly, that they didn't need to know.'

Lucy closed her eyes trying to absorb everything her grandmother had told her.

'At the funeral – a small, quiet affair – Frances's aunt said something that stayed with me.' Sarah looked at her. '"Another good woman taken so young. It's a bad gene in that family, a bad gene." Frances's mother had died at forty in the same way.'

The phone rang.

'Hello, darling. Did you get my message?'

Lucy and her mother had been playing phone tag, the gist of the many messages being that Kate had decided they were all coming to Hell House for Christmas, including Michael's girlfriend. Honestly, Lucy couldn't think of anything worse than having to spend time with her father here, of all places. Why couldn't he have had the decency to spend the holiday with his latest mistress? But her mother had said that he was keen to see her. She said he'd mellowed.

'Yes. You plan to spend Christmas here. You're mad.' As the words slipped out, Lucy regretted them, and her grandmother sent her a withering look. 'The house is only just habitable.'

'Michael said the dining room is beautiful and the salon isn't bad. Besides, your father is longing to be in Cornwall.'

'Well he can have Cornwall and maybe he can buy me flights to the Caribbean.'

'Don't be ridiculous. Put your grandmother on the phone.'

Lucy handed the phone over and walked into the dining room looking for Hebe and Kit. Would Hebe be able to cope with the whole family here for Christmas? It might be too much for Lucy, let alone for her poor aunt.

❋ Forty-Eight ❋
Hebe

15 November 2016

Last night's dinner was sausage and mash with peas.
Sarah cooked. It is good to see her. Always kind.
Apparently I made a fool of myself. Lucy and the man
with the white teeth found me by the creek crying.
Breakfast this morning was scrambled eggs and two
pieces of toast.
Today the bathroom is being updated. Lucy is

Hebe put her pen down. What *was* Lucy? Hebe could see the smile on her face, but the word to say how she was feeling wasn't there. It would come later. Putting her journal away, she stood and made sure she was fully dressed. She went hot at the thought of yesterday. When Lucy and the man brought her back to Helwyn House, Sarah had helped her clean up, washing her face as if she were a child again. Talking about nothing in that calm voice, saying things like *sleep is important.*

Hebe closed her eyes, not sure what sleep was any more. She straightened the cover on the bed. She liked going to bed, but they kept telling her she didn't stay in it.

'I don't know why, but what I do know is I'm hungry.' She spoke aloud as she left her room. Out in the corridor, she saw the builders and walked past them to the salon. Thomas smiled at her. Her heart fluttered, then her stomach rumbled. She must go and find some more food.

Sarah came out of her bedroom. 'Come and show me the

gardens, Hebe.' She held out her hand. 'I'm excited about what can happen in the spring.'

Hebe took a few steps towards her, listening to the sounds of the builders. It might be good to retreat from the noise for a bit and enjoy what this November day had to offer.

They left the house by the door from the dairy. Hebe could see her breath and she pulled her cardigan around her. Sarah linked arms with her. They had done this many times.

'Now, darling, I can see things aren't right.' She pulled Hebe closer. 'Can you tell me about it?'

Hebe squinted. 'Everything is good.'

'Yes?'

'Wonderful, but I do worry about Lucy.'

They opened the gate into what had once been the formal garden, planted with roses and myrtle, but which now was more meadow than anything else. The partition walls were still there, but crumbling. Hebe thought of Lucia and Thomas courting here. They were distant relations, and Lucia had visited Helwyn for the first time when she was ten and Thomas fourteen. According to their letters, it had been love at first sight. However, it took them several years to bring their families to an agreement that they should marry, that it would be beneficial to both.

'What's wrong with Lucy?'

Hebe looked at Sarah. She'd forgotten she was there. 'Lucy?'

'You said you were worried about Lucy?'

'She's been foolish.'

'This is true.'

'But she is very good at ...' She looked at the trees that had been cut back. They were still tall and proud, catching the wind. She stopped, listening. Yes, she could hear her mother calling to her.

'Lucy is good at many things. Sadly she doesn't see this.' Sarah changed direction and they headed through a broken partition to another area.

Hebe could suddenly see the plan for the garden in her mind's eye. There was a file among her papers on its history.

The design was not unique. She rubbed her temple. It was a relic, a relic of an Elizabethan garden. She smiled.

'But Hebe, I'm sure there is something else you want to talk to me about.' Sarah bent down and ran her hand along a shrub. The scent of rosemary filled the air.

Hebe stopped walking and looked at her stepmother.

'Lucy told you.'

'No.' Sarah's gaze didn't leave her. 'She didn't have to. She was concerned, which is why I'm here, and yesterday I saw it for myself.'

'Oh.' Hebe looked to the sky, patches of bright blue between the clouds.

'You're not well.'

'No.' She turned to Sarah. She could lie, but that made things harder. 'I have Alzheimer's.'

Sarah opened her arms and Hebe let herself be hugged. In the past, Sarah's hugs could make the pain go away, but that wasn't possible any more.

✳ Forty-Nine ✳
Lucy

20 November 2016

'Gran, what are we going to do?' Lucy paced in front of the sink. Each day they had each pressed Hebe to seek help and Hebe had refused.

Sarah sighed. 'I spoke with your mother again last night.'

'And?'

'She advised me to have another try at encouraging Hebe to see a doctor. Michael had printed a great deal of information from the Interweb thing for her.'

'And?'

'She told me it made uncomfortable reading.'

'I could have told you that.'

Sarah smiled and looked at her hands. 'I feel so powerless.'

'Join the club.' Lucy huffed. 'It's so frustrating. One moment Hebe is Hebe, and then the next she's gone.'

Her grandmother nodded. 'Talking to her today, it was mostly the old Hebe, and she even confided in me, but ...' she paused, shaking her head, 'it was strange. She was so detached.'

'Her mother ... do you remember much about what she was like?'

'It's so long ago now, but she was variable, that's for sure.'

Lucy sighed. There had been one thing troubling her since her grandmother first mentioned Frances. 'Did she commit suicide?'

Sarah shrugged. 'It was the sixties. Her death was recorded as accidental. She wasn't at all herself.'

Lucy tried to process this information. After his wife's suicide, her grandfather had carried on life as normal with her grandmother. Was she missing something?

Sarah, restless like her, walked out of the kitchen door. A blast of cold air crept inside. Reluctantly Lucy followed. Mist clung to the windowless wall of the great hall. From this side, the buttresses supported the wall. But from the other side it looked like it was simply the twisted vines holding it all together.

'Hebe has always been lost in her thoughts.' Sarah sighed.

'And she lives by lists, and everything, absolutely everything, has to be in exactly the same place. Have you noticed the fridge? I'm almost afraid to use anything without making a map first, because she totally freaks if the milk isn't where it's supposed to be.'

'So sad.' Her grandmother paused and pushed her hair off her face, 'I just wish we'd seen some hint sooner. I fear ...'

'What? What do you fear?'

'That Hebe has been covering the symptoms so well that we haven't seen them, and that we are further along than we think.'

'No.' But Lucy knew she was right. The ordering was a clever coping mechanism.

Her grandmother pointed to the great slabs of stone on the ground. Kit had told her what these were. She was about to explain when Sarah tilted her head.

'Darling, do I hear a goat?'

'Yes.' Lucy listened closely, trying to figure out where the darn thing was. Earlier she had moved her to the walled garden to work on the weeds in there. She was certain she'd closed the gate. The sound came again, and she looked up. Henrietta had scaled the wall of the great hall.

Her grandmother followed her gaze. 'Oh dear.'

The goat reached the top and looked down on them, and Lucy could swear it was laughing.

'How did Hebe's mother's behaviour manifest itself?'

'I was lying in bed last night trying to think back. Trying to remember Frances when Richard married her.' Sarah paused. 'She was vivacious. No one could keep their eyes off her. Yet by the end, she was haggard.' She plucked a weed. 'Richard wasn't

221

the easiest man to live with. But then that may just have been with me.'

Lucy cast a sideways glance at her.

'I don't think I truly loved him.'

'What?' Lucy stopped walking.

'I'd been infatuated with his glamour. I was young.' Sarah sighed.

Lucy squinted at her. 'What are you telling me?'

'That Richard offered many things, but he was a challenging man.'

'Was he abusive?'

'Not in a physical way.' She pressed her lips together for a moment. 'I'm not sure he really cared for me other than in a physical sense.'

'Gran, I'm so sorry.'

She snorted a bit. 'I made my bed and I had a duty to Hebe and your mother. I loved them both with a fierceness that surprised even me.' She smiled. 'You see, I never thought I had a maternal bone in my body.'

Looking at the chic woman in front of her, Lucy could imagine that.

'I have many regrets. But now is not the time to talk about them. We need to focus on Hebe, and getting her to a doctor has to be our priority. It's vital.' She took Lucy's hand. 'Frances walked off a cliff.'

'Dear God, no. Not Dennis Head?'

'No, on the north coast.' She looked into the distance, where jackdaws circled in the pink sky, too far away for their cries to be heard.

'You're sure that Hebe doesn't know?'

'Positive. Richard told her that her mother had died of pneumonia.'

'What?'

'I didn't agree with him but he said it wasn't my business.'

'But you were her stepmother.'

Sarah nodded. 'I told you he wasn't a very nice man.'

'He certainly wasn't.' Lucy hated to think she had his genes somewhere inside her.

Kit put Sarah's bag in the car. He had volunteered to stay at Hell House while Lucy took her grandmother to the station. He claimed he could continue to try and find evidence in the house while keeping an eye on Hebe. As far as Lucy could tell, all he had done was confirm that the servants at Helwyn had been a terrified and superstitious lot. But living here herself, Lucy was becoming that way too.

Hebe hugged her stepmother and Sarah's eyes were full when she joined Lucy in the car.

'You OK?'

She gave a derisive laugh. 'No.' She looked over her shoulder at the house. In the rear-view mirror, Lucy could see Hebe waving with a big smile on her face. Sarah wiped her eyes. 'Now let's talk about something much more positive.'

Lucy shot a glance in her direction as she reached the bottom of the drive and pulled out onto the lane. 'What would that be? That I haven't been in the papers in weeks?'

'That is indeed good news but I was thinking about that rather delicious Kit Williams.'

Lucy burst out laughing. Her grandmother had been gently flirting with him the past few days and had made sure he was with them at dinner each night on some pretext or other.

'He fancies you.'

She rolled her eyes. 'Gran.'

'He's eligible.'

'Gran!'

'Darling, you are not getting any younger.' Sarah put her hand over Lucy's.

'I'm only twenty-eight.'

'I know, and what do you have to show for it?'

'Fair point.' Lucy had nothing but a stalled career. 'I don't want kids or marriage.' She felt her grandmother's stare. 'And you know that even if I wanted the former, it's not on the cards.'

'Fine. What *do* you want then?'

Lucy chewed her lip. 'It would be easier to say what I don't want.'

'I suppose that's one way to narrow it down.' Sarah cleared her throat. 'I can only offer you one piece of advice. Life is short, and without love, it's not worth living.'

'Ha, thanks.' Lucy put the indicator on. 'So you think I should start by enjoying some life with Kit?'

'There are worse places to start.'

'I can't disagree with that. He is a rather magnificent specimen.'

Her grandmother put a hand on her arm. 'Have you slept with him?'

Lucy laughed. 'No.'

'I hope you've at least considered it.'

She snorted. It was most unattractive.

'What are you doing about your love life then? Tinder?'

'Gran ... what do you know about these things?'

'I was thinking of contacting a programmer about setting one up for the older generation. But then I realised that the occasional quickie might be fun, but most of us prefer a bit more than just sex.' She sighed. 'If it's just sexual pleasure I want, I'm quite capable of taking care of that myself, and normally far better than someone who doesn't know me or what I actually like.'

Lucy was speechless. There was nothing she could say to that. Her grandmother looked at her and laughed. Lucy imagined her face was a picture.

'Don't be afraid of love, Lucy.'

She shuddered. 'I don't want love.'

'Why ever not?'

'It takes everything away from you.'

Her grandmother shook her head. 'No, it gives.'

'Ha, just look at your daughter.' Lucy felt she had won that argument.

'Not everything is as it appears. That's one thing that life has taught me.'

Lucy glanced at her. Sarah was staring out of the window, not turning from the view.

'I'll be in touch as soon as I've seen my doctor friend, Hugh.'

'Thanks.'

'No thanks needed. I love Hebe and I'm as worried as you are.' Sarah's hand covered Lucy's again, and something inside her settled.

❈ Fifty ❈
Lucy

30 November 2016

It was ten days since her grandmother had left and things were finally moving forward. Heading down the hall, Lucy danced a little. Since they had arrived, she'd been longing for a bath, a proper long soak, but had made do with a lukewarm dribble. The old boiler hadn't been up to much, but today a new combination boiler was being installed. Nothing had yet been agreed on heating the house. Wearing many layers was still a key survival technique here. Mark and Lucy were in agreement, but Hebe wanted nothing to change. So Lucy was tackling things in small steps, even the planning consents. Until she was happy with the plan as a whole, she wasn't going to submit.

On her way down the stairs, she met Fred coming up. 'The plumber's in the kitchen with Mark at the moment. Hope you don't mind, but Peta is here too.'

'Don't mind at all.'

'The van wouldn't start this morning, so she gave me a lift.'

'Great. Hopefully she'll have time for a coffee.'

He nodded and disappeared upstairs. Instead of cutting through the dining room, Lucy walked along the corridor that she'd been told had been the dairy. It would certainly have kept things cool. The walls were thick granite, with peeling plaster and a drooping ceiling. Damp, in other words.

Henrietta was outside, eating a rose bush. She must have escaped again. Lucy caught her, then walked her to the remains of what she assumed had been a pond. On a bleak day like today it was hard to imagine this place in its heyday. She tethered the goat in the middle of the empty pond and returned to the house, chilled through to the bone.

The kitchen door was open and a group stood around the table looking at Kit, who was holding another object. What was it this time, the bones of his ancestors? She gasped when she saw it was a bone.

'What the hell is that?' Everyone turned to her.

'It looks like a thigh bone, and a human one at that.' The plumber stepped back.

'It's old,' Mark said, 'but we will have to call the police.'

Lucy's stomach dropped. 'Does this mean everything will have to stop?'

Mark laughed. 'It may keep the north bedroom off limits for a while.'

'That's fine by me.' Goosebumps covered her arms.

'Thought you might say that.' Kit took a clean tea towel and wrapped the bone in it.

'Where exactly did you find it?'

'In the fireplace in the north bedroom.' He smiled. 'I heard a strange sound and went to check.'

Peta, looking a bit pale, came into the kitchen. 'His name was Thomas,' she said.

Lucy frowned. 'How can you tell that?'

Mark chuckled. 'Peta's a bit special.'

She kicked him in the shins.

'Ouch.'

'You deserved that.' She looked at Kit and then at Lucy. 'Kit, you have Thomas's eyes.'

Lucy pursed her lips. Did this bone belong to Thomas Grylls? And more worryingly, if it did, would Kit disappear now that he'd proved his father's theory?

Mark waved at the landline. 'May I?'

'Of course.' Lucy put the kettle on. 'Who wants coffee?'

'Not for me.' Peta smiled and put a hand across her stomach. Lucy raised an eyebrow. She nodded.

'I'm just going to take Peta to see the place where you found the bone. Can someone else do the honours?' asked Lucy.

'Of course.' Kit stood and pulled the mugs out.

She took Peta by the arm. 'You're pregnant?' she asked, once they were out of earshot.

Peta nodded.

'How far along?'

'Due in March.' She grinned.

'Keeping it quiet?'

'I've lost a couple, so we're not broadcasting the news.'

'I won't tell anyone.'

'I know you won't, and I know you don't want to go and see where the bone was found, but I do.'

'OK.' Lucy stepped back.

'You see only problems here.'

Lucy frowned.

'It doesn't take second sight to know that. It's all over your face, and the way you walk through the house. You'd leave right now if it wasn't for Hebe.'

'True.'

They walked on in silence. Now that Lucy was firmly out of the news, London was calling – along with several other more appealing locations.

'You're very brave,' Peta said.

Lucy stopped in the centre of the salon. 'I've been called many things in my life, but brave has never been one of them.'

'Ah, but you are.'

Peta marched on and came to the north bedroom.

'This is why you are brave,' she said.

Lucy took a step back. 'I ...'

'You don't have to say anything. It's OK ... well, it's not. Neither thing was good. But the fact that you are here helping your aunt, who needs you desperately, is wonderful.' She sighed. 'I'm going to go in, but don't feel you need to follow me.'

Was that a challenge? Lucy stood in the hallway and listened to the sound of Peta's footsteps on the wide floorboards. She knew them so well. She rubbed her bottom, remembering the hours she'd sat on them. No one had heard her cries except the spiders and other creepy-crawly things. And of course, the ghost calling her name.

'Oh.' Peta's voice sounded muffled.

'Are you OK?'

'Yes,' Peta called back. 'I just think Thomas has decided it's time to come out. I walked towards the fireplace and a skull fell down.'

Lucy rushed into the room. Her skin froze, but she pushed past her stupid fear. There were no such things as ghosts. In the grate was a skull that appeared to be bashed on one side. Thinking of all the crime dramas she'd binge-watched, she would say he was killed with a heavy blunt object.

'Yes, that's right.' Peta squinted at the skull. 'But he didn't die right away.' She squatted down and looked at it more closely.

Despite her fear, once Peta had moved away, Lucy took several photos with her phone.

'He did it because he wanted to punish you.'

Lucy shook her head. 'What?'

'Not Thomas; your brother. He felt your mother loved you more.' One side of Peta's mouth lifted in a smile. 'He was right in a way. She loves him, but to her you are special, something worth cherishing.'

'No, he's the golden boy. Sunlight comes out of his arse from my parents' point of view.'

'Not everything is always as we think it is.'

Lucy knew she'd heard that somewhere else recently.

'Your aunt needs us in the King's Room!' Peta dashed out of the door and Lucy raced after her.

Hebe was on the floor, unconscious. This time Lucy didn't hesitate. Leaving Peta with her, she ran downstairs and called 999.

1 December 2016

The feast of St Eligius, metalworker
Dinner last night was scrambled eggs on toast. No wine.
 Lucy is cross with me. I refused to go with the
paramedics to the hospital. One goes to hospital to die.
I'm not ready to die.
 Breakfast, yoghurt and a banana.
 Lucy thinks I'm low on some mineral and that
bananas have what I need. The taste reminds me of
childhood. Bananas were a treat. I can still taste it in
my mouth.
 Brush teeth.

Hebe rubbed her tongue along the roof of her mouth, feeling its furry texture. Fur in the mouth was not good. Tidying her desk, she put her pens in a neat line according to colour. When that was done, she set off into the hall, though she wasn't sure why. She had a book to write.

'Morning, Hebe,' said a man with very white teeth.

Who was he? She knew she had met him, and he was certainly attractive, but she couldn't place him. Why was he here? She turned and went back into her room. Whatever she had been about to do was gone.

Sitting at the desk, she unlocked the drawer and pulled out a notebook. She flipped through the pages, looking for something, but she couldn't remember what it was. Her computer was on the desk. Had she been writing something? As she rubbed her temples, willing her brain to work, she heard footsteps walking down the passage. That was it. The man. Kit. Supposedly a direct descendant of Thomas. She didn't believe it, but there was an echo of truth. Thomas had stayed in the Scillies, but that didn't mean he had taken up with a local woman. After all, he was devoted to Lucia.

Heart of my heart, longing of my body, each day of separation from you is torment. With each gust of wind, I try and pretend it is your fingers lifting my hair and caressing my neck. Shivers run down my body and all I can think of is lying with you.

Although she hadn't seen that letter in twenty years it was clear as day in her mind, though sadly what she had had for breakfast was not.

Where was the right notebook? This was a complete one. Summer 2015. She looked through it. It didn't list what she'd had for breakfast. It spoke of love and sex. She didn't have sex. Not now. But Thomas and Lucia must have. Hebe had written about it. Fingers running over skin. She trembled.

She looked out of the window. The sky was already darkening. Was it mid morning or mid afternoon? The branches were bare and she could see into the woods. Was it the storm last night that had taken the leaves? She squinted into the distance, but nothing came to her. She flipped through the notebook. Nothing was right. Running her finger over the writing, she tried to think. The storm had been last week. It had broken a pane of glass in the kitchen window, and one of the stones forming part of the crenellation at the top of the old wall had fallen into the courtyard. Fortunately the ground had been soft and the granite had remained in one piece. She sighed. So little of the original house was here any more. The great hall was nothing more than an unstable shadow of what had been the focus for the house.

Now the centre of the house was the old range in the kitchen. Above her she could hear the builders working on the chimney.

Soon she would have a fire to warm her room, but right now the east wind rattled the windowpanes. This wind brought change and should clear the skies, but it wouldn't clear her mind. Everything was shutting down so much quicker than she had expected. Maybe she should have gone to the consultant sooner – they might have been able to do something. But there was no point in slowing the inevitable.

She stood and walked to the great window, looking out at the bare branches warped through the hand-blown glass. A bubble marred the bottom pane. Her fingers sought it out and the cold ran up her arm straight to her heart, where it rested, taking her breath away.

❈ Fifty-Two ❈
Lucy

1 December 2016

Lucy pulled the car over to the side of the road. She wanted to have a chat with her mother without the chance of being overheard. Kit had texted to say all was well at Hell House when he'd popped in. Hebe was working in the salon. Once she had heard of the discovery of the body, it was like she had a new injection of life. Mentally she seemed more with it, and Lucy could ignore the steady depletion of marshmallows from the cupboard. She'd had to buy several more packets this morning.

The phone clicked and her mother coughed. It was that time of year when Kate became ill like clockwork. This was normally to get sympathy from Giles. Frankly, Lucy thought it just pushed him further away.

'You OK?'

'Fine. Has your grandmother been in touch?'

'Yes.' Lucy pressed her lips together, wondering if there was anything at all they could do. 'She's waiting to hear from a doctor friend for some advice.'

'That's good.'

'It is.' Lucy paused. 'Did Hebe ever talk about her mother?'

'No ...' Her mother was lying. Lucy knew that tone. 'Leave it to your grandmother. She raised her from the age of five. How much do *you* remember from when you were five?'

Lucy looked up at the darkening sky. She remembered happiness. Picnics on the beach and her mother's hugs, her father's laughter, and her brother being a pain, even then. 'Plenty. I remember your smile.'

'Lucy.'

'I'm scared for Hebe.'

'Me too.' Her mum coughed again. 'Nothing I read is encouraging. It's a good thing we'll be down soon.'

'Mum, it's weeks away.'

'It will be upon us before we know it.'

'Thanks.' She sounded ungrateful, but it was just the thought of the work involved in Christmas and how it was the last thing she wanted on top of everything else at the moment. She needed support. It wasn't for her; it was for Hebe. But sitting here in a lay-by wasn't helping anything. 'Must dash. Love you.'

'Love you too.'

She studied the signpost. Where did she want to go? Helford, Manaccan, St Anthony? She'd been in Cornwall for nearly two months, project-managing the slowest restoration ever and trying to look after her aunt. How had she ended up here? She swallowed. She'd ended up here by trying to avoid things, to sidestep the messy parts of life; by never going after what she really wanted. The key problem was that she didn't know what that was.

Lucy stood with her back to the range and her hands resting on the rail. It was bloody brass monkeys out there. Who had said Cornwall was warm? Whoever it was had lied. Her hands were raw from bringing the bags in from the car. Early darkness had settled on the house, and she hated it. No one had put on any lights and she'd tripped over a great sodding rock on her way to the kitchen door. She was not happy. Blowing on her fingers, she debated what she was, other than frozen. Actually she was numb – inside and out. Weary from sleepless nights of worry and from keeping the resident ghost, or maybe just her own personal ghosts, at bay. She looked around the kitchen, into the dark corners. This room didn't have any ghosts, at least not since the range had been fired up.

Today was the first of December. Back in London, she would be gearing up for the best parties of the season. Instead she was looking through the parish bulletin for the local bring-and-buys.

This situation was untenable. She had to do something other than stand here shivering by the range. Cooking dinner would be a start. Hebe had abandoned all housework, and even her list-making had slipped with the discovery of the skeleton.

There was a tap on the back door and she jumped three feet off the ground. Thank God this room had a high ceiling. Kit walked in carrying a shopping bag.

'Found this by your car.'

'Damn.' She shook her head. 'I'm getting as forgetful as my aunt.'

'Where is she?'

She shrugged. He put the bag on the table. 'I found her talking to the portrait today.'

She studied him. 'I've seen her do that before.'

He stepped closer. 'She was reciting poetry.'

'Donne?'

'Yes.'

'Her favourite.' She grimaced.

'Not yours.'

She turned. 'No, some of his work I like, but not his poetry so much.'

He raised an eyebrow.

'It's a bit obvious.'

'Sensual.' The corner of his mouth lifted.

'Absolutely, I get that, but ...' Words were elusive.

'License my roving hands, and let them go ... Behind, before, above, between below.'

She gripped the kitchen counter. Maybe she'd been hasty in dismissing Donne. Maybe if it hadn't been her old bat of an English teacher reading it she would have realised its power. He smiled, and she stabilised her legs. Keep sane, she told herself. The man was a professional actor; of course he would make the words sound like he was whispering them just to her, only her.

'When you put it like that, I can see some value.'

He laughed, which did nothing for her stability. Living in Cornwall was clearly not good for her. She was going soft, if cold. The single bulb hanging from the ceiling cast enough light to pick up the hint of strawberry in his blonde hair. Blonde had never really done it for her. She liked her men dark, disturbing and committed to others, but – and it was a big but – Kit had something. And she wasn't the first to realise this, judging by the number of fan sites she'd discovered when she was bored and decided to find out a bit more about her new best friend.

Another tap on the door, and her heart bounced in her chest. She was becoming very skittish. Kit answered the door, and there stood Tristan Trevillion, her third cousin once removed or something like that.

'Hi, Lucy.' Tristan smiled. 'Sorry I haven't been over before, but Jude and I have been in the States on an extended visit. Her father had a heart attack.'

'I hope he's all right.' She put the kettle on.

'All is well now.'

'So pleased to hear that. Tea?' she asked.

'Yes, thanks.' Tristan looked about the kitchen. His face didn't reveal much. 'How's Hebe?' The tone of his voice told her the grapevine had been working.

'Hasn't been on any late-night jaunts in a little while.' She watched the two men looking at each other and kicked herself. Where the hell had her manners gone? Lost when she crossed the Tamar. 'Tristan, this is Kit Williams.'

'The actor?'

'For my sins.' Kit smiled.

'Filming?'

Kit shook his head. 'Much-needed career break.'

'I would have thought the beaches of the Caribbean would be more restful.'

'Possibly for the body, but there is something about being here that feeds the soul.'

Tristan smiled. 'True. Mind you, I wouldn't have said that a few years ago.'

She handed both men mugs. Kit's already had milk in it, and she found it strange that she knew how he took his tea but didn't have a clue about how Tristan did, when she had known him all her life.

'I just popped in to say hello, and also I heard the rest of the family will be down for Christmas.'

'Jungle drums?' She raised an eyebrow.

'Absolutely. So Jude and I wanted to extend an invitation for Boxing Day. We're having what Jude calls an open house, a relaxed affair.' He turned to Kit. 'Will you be around?'

Kit nodded.

'Then please join us. Any time between twelve and four.'

'Sounds lovely.' Lucy smiled, thinking of the vast house and running riot through it with Tristan's dogs years ago. 'Many changes at Pengarrock since I was last there?'

Tristan laughed. 'Yes and no.'

'Cannons still there, I hope.'

'Yes.' He took a sip of his tea and they all looked to the hall as they heard footsteps. 'Ghosts still a problem now that you're living here full-time?'

Lucy wasn't sure which was worse: the ghosts or the full-time part. 'All's quiet these days.'

Tristan looked around. 'I've always felt there was something ... odd or uncomfortable about the north bedroom.'

Kit chuckled. 'That could be because someone was buried there, possibly even killed there.'

'Now that sounds interesting.'

'Grapevine not divulge the discovery of human bones in the fireplace?'

'Not that I've heard, but then I haven't been to the pub.' Tristan leaned against the range. 'That goes a long way to explaining the ghost. Any idea who it is, or how old?'

'Old enough that the police aren't interested but the county archaeologist is.'

'Intriguing.' He smiled, and Lucy remembered the childhood crush she'd had on him. 'Is Hebe around?'

'She's probably in her room, working.'

'I won't interrupt, but can you tell her I stopped by and that we'd love to see her?'

'Will do.'

He sent her a searching look, and she tilted her head in response. The footsteps in the hall had stopped.

❋ Fifty-Three ❋
Hebe

1 December 2016

Hebe paused in the hallway, listening to the voices. A Grylls and a Trevillion speaking amicably. How many years had that taken? Mind you, the Trevillion didn't know that the Grylls was a Grylls. This man who had become attached to them. Hebe hadn't figured out what his agenda was, but she knew he had one. Then she tapped her forehead, remembering. He was a descendant of Thomas's. There was something about a letter, and recently about DNA.

He was unnaturally keen on looking in dark corners of the house. Every time a builder cleared a bit of modern plaster or unblocked a chimney, he was there. She hoped he wasn't trying to provide evidence for listing or other nonsense. She had no plans to ruin the house or destroy its history.

The phone in her pocket rang. She looked at the screen; it was her sister. She frowned. What did she want? 'Hello.'

'Hebe, darling, how good to hear your voice.'

How was she supposed to respond to that? 'Thanks.'

'We're so looking forward to spending Christmas with you.'

Kate paused and Hebe pressed her lips together. Had she issued an invitation? She turned, about to head to her room to check her notebook, but after taking one step, she heard the line crackle. She stopped.

'Hebe, are you there?'

'Yes.'

'Well, I've just spoken with Anthony Jenkin, and it turns out that the person who had booked one of the cottages has cancelled, so we will stay there rather than all of us descending on you at Helwyn.'

'Oh.'

'Do you think you can manage to cook for us all there?'

'Yes.' Hebe could hear Lucy still chatting in the kitchen, but couldn't remember who was there with her.

'Good. I'll ring Lucy and work out more details with her, but I just wanted to say how excited I was.'

'Yes.' Hebe frowned. Her hands were cold, but the hallway was freezing so that wasn't a surprise. She must head back to her room and write this all down. Christmas.

'Good. You're really all right, are you?'

Hebe frowned. 'Yes. Why wouldn't I be? Bye.' She closed the phone and slipped it into her pocket. Once she used to keep notes on her phone, but her fingers didn't do what she wanted them to and it became useless, just like her brain. A year ago, she'd bought a simple old-fashioned phone. Now she wrote on paper.

She walked through the kitchen door.

'There you are.' Lucy stood by the doorway to the dining room. 'Tristan popped in to say hello.'

Lucy's hair was scraped up behind her head and she only had lipstick on. Such a pretty thing. Looking more beautiful each day.

Hebe moved into the kitchen. The warmth hit her. She flexed her fingers as she studied both men. What was it about them? '*I can love both fair and brown*,' she whispered, looking at one man and then the other.

'What was that?' Lucy asked.

'John Donne, I think.' The man with the blonde hair spoke. He was right. 'I can't recall it all, but ...' He cleared his throat. '*I can love her, and her, and you and you.*' He smiled. '*I can love any, so she be not true.*'

'Yes. "The Indifferent".' Hebe swallowed. '*But I have told them, since you will be true, you shall be true to them, who are false to you.*' She looked first at the dark man and then the fair.

240

A smile played around the mouth of the dark one – Tristan, she remembered.

'Poetry was never my strength, Hebe. It's just too elusive.' He half smiled.

'How so?'

'I would always think it meant what it said, and yet I would be told it never did.'

'Hogwash. Poetry is a map to the mind, *your* mind, not the teacher's or even the poet's.'

He raised an eyebrow.

'It's like a painting up close. It's simply a brushstroke or palette work on a canvas, a piece of wood, but when a viewer steps away from it they see something that relates to something in them.' Hebe looked at her niece. 'When we look at anything, it is what we think it is, or what someone tells us it is – or our experience does.'

'This is a bit deep for a December evening.' Lucy pushed a strand of hair from her face. She avoided emotion. That was why she disliked poetry. Her heart had been raw with rage. It was all clear now. Looking at her niece, Hebe tried to see beyond the broad strokes outlining her. Her socks were thick and brightly striped. She must have been wearing boots. Her jeans were faded and mostly covered by a sweater that would fit three of her.

Tristan was talking, but Hebe couldn't focus.

'I won't keep you now, but hopefully you can join us at Pengarrock on Boxing Day.'

Lucy smiled. 'That would be brilliant. It's been years since I've been there.' She moved towards her cousin, who had taken a step to the door.

'Good to meet you, Kit.'

The blonde man nodded. Hebe wondered which of the two of them Lucy would prefer in bed. Of course, one was a relative, but that had never stopped people in the past. However, she quite liked the voice on this Kit. He could read Donne to her as had ... As had who? Hebe turned swiftly and left the kitchen, heading to her room.

❊ Fifty-Four ❊
Hebe

August 2015

You lie beside me sound asleep. I stare at you in the moonlight. You are a miracle. I think of our wasted time. I could have had you with me, beside me, always, but I have resisted, and I still do. My body is content from our lovemaking. That has been good since the start. But my vision of us has been distorted.

Rising so as not to disturb you, I shiver. Goose bumps cover my naked flesh. The moonlight hides my age and I see a younger me. But I am fifty-three and you are twenty-eight: I can pretend, but that is all it would be. I love you and you love me. But if I tell you, you will never let me go.

I grab my robe and head to the sitting room. I have come to love this little haven out of time. We have two weeks left, then reality returns. Will I recall this moment, our summer of bliss? I pull my notebook to me and stare out of the window at the shadows, remembering.

*

So, so, break off this last lamenting kiss
Which sucks two souls, and vapours both away;
Turn though, ghost, that way, and let me turn this,
And let ourselves benight our happiest day;
We asked none leave to love, nor will we owe
Any, so cheap as death as saying, Go.

Your lips lingered on mine, but your mind was elsewhere. So

was mine. We spoke, but the words meant something different entirely, or I thought they did. Yet I could not bear the thought of being without your touch, be it tender or passionate. I had grown used to you. This affair was always going to be a mistake, and today I felt that chasm of love. Would you leave if I asked you to go?

You released me and walked to the bedroom. Your clothes were folded on the chair. I couldn't remember last night. But this morning I knew that you must leave. Not for my sake, but for yours. Those three grey hairs I found this morning were another sign that the gap between us was growing. No routine or comfort would be able to bridge the distance. Go, I shouted without opening my mouth. You turned and gave me a beaming smile. My heart melted all over again.

*

Closing the notebook, I stretch. I have lost all sense of the time. A bird begins its dawn serenade. I crawl back into bed beside you and breathe in your scent. Today will not be the day to push you away. I am too weary.

❋ Fifty-Five ❋

Hebe

6 December 2016

The feast of St Nicholas, Greek bishop,
wonder worker, now Santa Claus
Dinner last night was prawn

Hebe frowned. Prawn what? It wasn't curry, it was ... She shook her head. Maybe the word would appear later.

The world is covered in crystals. It shines even though
the sun is not fully up. I feel happy this morning. It was
my dream. But it is gone.

She leaned back in the chair. Her shoulders slumped. Despite the beauty that she could see out of the window, she was empty again. She checked over her shoulder; the door was ajar, but although it was 7.30, there was no aroma of coffee as there was most mornings. Had Lucy slept in?

Squirrelling her things away, she stopped and looked at the photo that poked out of the notebook. Who was that she was with? Her forehead furrowed and she tried to make the connection, but nothing happened. It was a picture of her and a handsome stranger. Her breath caught. So beautiful. So young. Pushing the picture back into the pages, she locked it away. It was no good looking at the past now. She gave a short laugh. That was an odd sentiment for a historian to have.

The kitchen smelled of toast as Hebe walked down the hall. Lucy was up after all. Coming through the door, she found her niece with her head over the sink, dry-heaving.

'Last night's prawns?' Hebe glanced around but was not sure what she was looking for. Maybe the man with the white teeth.

Lucy ran the tap, then wiped her mouth with a piece of kitchen roll. 'Must be. You haven't had any problems?'

Hebe shook her head. 'No, slept solidly last night and have woken with a huge appetite this morning.' She put the kettle on. 'Shall I make some coffee?'

'Not for me.' Lucy sank into a chair. 'Until the dodgy prawn has worked its way through my system, I think I'm restricted to water.' She looked down at the piece of toast in front of her. Hebe noticed that it had one bite out of it.

'Do you mind making your own breakfast this morning?'

'Not at all.' Hebe wondered what she could make. 'Why don't you go and lie down?'

Lucy nodded and disappeared. Hebe looked around the kitchen, opening a few cupboards. In one she found marshmallows. She placed them on a plate, then grabbed a knife and fork. It was good to have a bit of a change for breakfast.

'Does the house have any priest holes?' The man with the white teeth flashed a torch at the fireplace in the north bedroom.

Hebe pursed her lips. 'Well, it was once a monastery, but the Grylls family weren't Roman Catholics, unlike the Arundells of Lanherne, so I doubt there would be any.' Somewhere she had the family history of the Grylls, but surely this man did too. Was he testing her?

'But ...' he paused, and switched the torch off, 'wasn't the wife of Thomas's great-grandfather an Arundell?'

Hebe sighed. 'I don't remember.'

'I believe she was.' He looked at her, and she saw Thomas as a man of thirty-three, fit and virile. Was Lucy sleeping with him?

'Are you having sex with Lucy?'

Kit dropped the torch, then picked it up. Hebe watched the expressions cross his face. 'That's a rather direct question.'

'And a direct answer would be appreciated.'

He tilted his head to the side. 'No.'

'Why not? You want her.'

'I gave you a direct answer, and now we should return to the question of the body in the fireplace and why it was bricked in here.'

Hebe blinked. 'If we must.' She walked over to him. 'It would be useful if we knew ... knew ...'

He watched her, and the thought faded.

'Knew the age of the skeleton?' He smiled.

'Yes.'

'We should have that information soon.'

'You think it's Thomas Grylls.'

He nodded.

'That could work.' Hebe turned and walked out of the bedroom and went straight to her computer. While she had this idea, she must write it down.

❋ Fifty-Six ❋
Lucy

13 December 2016

The floor of the King's Room was dry, and Fred assured Lucy that all the woodworm-riddled joists had been treated and, where necessary, replaced. She looked up at the portrait of Thomas Grylls, which she had placed on the wall after she'd found her aunt staring at it in a trance two days ago. Hebe hadn't noticed that it wasn't in the salon any more.

Thomas's eyes followed her as she stepped further into the room. It was uncomfortable being watched. Was he the skeleton in the fireplace? Just yesterday the results of the DNA test that Kit had paid for had arrived. The DNA of the skeleton matched Kit's, so they knew that if Kit was a Grylls, then this man was too.

As Lucy had suspected, he had been hit over the head with a heavy object. Her hard-won crime knowledge had proved correct. She laughed. Those days of streaming Netflix were a distant memory, and now her nose was firmly in a book every night, if she could keep awake. Mostly she couldn't. She didn't know if it was the build-up of all the nights listening out for Hebe, or just the sheer volume of fresh air. Whatever it was, she was exhausted even though she was simply project-managing.

'Lucy.' Fred stood in the doorway. 'The tree you wanted cut down is on its way.'

'Thanks, appreciate the help.'

'No problem.' He looked at the sky, which was already dark. 'The biggest problem at the moment is the lack of light.'

'Today is St Lucy's Day. Traditionally the shortest day of the year.'

'Happy name day ... is it your birthday, too?'

She nodded. 'Yes, my mother lacked all imagination and named both my brother and I after the saint of the day.' No one had rung her, not even her mother, and Hebe, who normally remembered, had said nothing.

'Come to the pub and I'll buy you a birthday drink.' Fred smiled.

'Thanks, but I have too much work to be getting on with here.'

'Have you started decorating anywhere else in the house?'

'Not yet. Once this tree is up and I see what I need for it, then I can think about the rest of the house.' She pursed her lips. Although she'd enjoyed decorating for Christmas as a child, it all seemed a waste now. They weren't exactly happy families, so why pretend with a tree and all the trimmings? She could understand Hebe's desire to see the house look beautiful, though.

Helwyn, if she was fair, had come on a long way in a few months, and it was made for Christmas decorations. Hebe, despite Lucy's best efforts to keep the budget tight, kept sinking more money into it. Lucy was beginning to suspect that her aunt had a bottomless pit of funds: maybe a mysterious benefactor, or a lottery win that she'd never told them about. The splash of cash was visible in the floor beneath her feet. Each floorboard had been taken up and treated, or replaced if necessary. Now the oak boards gleamed in the fading light.

'If we set the table up, you can sort out your decorations.' Fred glanced at the folded trestle table.

'Thanks.' Lucy lifted one end of it and Fred the other. It wobbled as they placed it by the far wall.

'Needs tightening.' He smiled. 'I'll grab a screwdriver and be back in a minute.' He passed Kit and one of the builders as they appeared carrying the tree.

'Where would you like it?' Kit paused in the doorway.

Lucy put her hand up. 'Hold on a second.' She eyed the

trunk of the tree, hoping the makeshift base she'd constructed out of an old tin bucket and gravel would work. The room was a good twenty-five feet high, so she had selected a tree that she felt wouldn't be lost in the space.

'Even with that, I think you'll have to tie it to the wall.' Kit glanced at the bucket.

She nodded. 'But it could be one way to get rid of unwanted relatives.'

He raised an eyebrow. 'That bad?'

'You have no idea.'

He looked away.

She kicked herself. He would be missing his father. Holidays would be awful. 'Sorry.' She touched his hand.

Fred returned and tightened the screws in the table.

'How's Peta feeling?' Lucy said.

'Funny you should ask; she was wondering the same thing of you.'

'Ah yes, the dodgy prawn that won't go away. Please tell her I'm much better, but the little blighter still lingers a bit.'

Fred laughed. 'Will do, and she's brilliant, thanks.' His face radiated happiness. Those two might just be the exception to the rule. They were young, devoted and happy. Not words she would usually put together in the same sentence.

'OK, let's get this beast in place.' Lucy and Fred fitted the tree into the base, then Kit and Fred pushed it upright while she protected the floor and tried to get the position just right.

'It needs to come out another foot from the wall.'

'Yup.' Fred grunted. 'OK now?'

She stepped back to check. 'Yes, just.' Both men straightened and then Fred tugged a branch.

'It's pretty stable, but you might want to tie it to the wall.'

Kit laughed and looked at Lucy. 'Told you.'

'Right, you two, enough,' Fred said, smiling. 'I'll get the ladder so you can decorate this thing, and see if I have twine or wire that will do the job.'

Lucy set her phone to a Christmas playlist she'd downloaded yesterday while out, and left it sitting on the table playing with a jolly, tinny tone. The scent of the tree was enough to lift her mood, even though everyone seemed to have forgotten it was her birthday. Later she would wander up to the lane and see if anyone had emailed or texted her. She could hope.

Kit sang along to the song and she joined in on the chorus.

'Didn't know you could sing,' she said.

'Choirboy.' He grinned.

'Yes.' she paused. 'I can see you in a ruff.'

'Hmmm. It was never my favourite piece of kit.'

'I bet.' She dumped a shopping bag on the table filled with boxes and boxes of white lights. Looking at the tree, she wondered if they would be enough. The music stopped and her phone rang. She jumped. Fred walked through the door with the ladder.

'Ah, the new mast has been switched on. Hello, world.'

Lucy frowned. She didn't recognise the number. 'Hello.'

'Lucy?'

'Yes.'

'This is Hugh Jameson, your grandmother's ... friend.'

She raised her eyebrows. So this was the doctor, her grandmother's latest 'walker'. 'Hi, Hugh.'

'Your grandmother has told me about your aunt, but I'm reluctant to say anything without having seen her or read her notes.'

'I understand.'

'Your grandmother wants a word.'

'Gran?'

'Hello, darling. I'm thinking Hugh should join us for Christmas. Hebe won't go and see a doctor, so we must bring one to her.'

Lucy gave a dry laugh. 'Have to love your logic, Gran, but that means he will have to stay here.'

'Yes, of course, dear. We'll have the north bedroom. It doesn't scare me at all. Talk later.'

There was a knock on the door as Lucy washed the last of the dinner plates. Kit stood outside holding a bottle of champagne. 'Happy birthday.'

She swallowed a lump. 'Thanks.' Stepping aside to let him in, she tossed the tea towel over her shoulder. 'Who told you?'

'Fred – and your grandmother.'

'How?' She tilted her head.

'Text.'

'She has your number?'

'Yes.' He grinned.

'Bloody flirtatious grandmother I have.'

'Like grandmother, like granddaughter.'

'Ha.' She swept her arms out, looking down at her leggings with the hole in the knee and the shapeless elderly cashmere jumper she'd found in a charity shop. 'I am the epitome of sexy womanhood at the moment.'

He grinned. 'You're looking rather well on all the fresh air.'

She threw the tea towel at him. 'For that comment, you can come to the King's Room and help me decorate the tree while we drink this champagne.'

'I like the sound of that type of punishment.'

'You would.' She marched out of the room, tapping on Hebe's door as she made her way to the King's Room. When there was no reply, she popped her head into the room.

Hebe's bedside light was on and she was sound asleep in her chair with a book on her chest. Lucy tiptoed in and covered her with a blanket. Her aunt appeared so vulnerable when she was asleep. Lucy swallowed the lump in her throat. She was emotional. It was her birthday and she could cry if she wanted to. Maybe she was due one of her erratic periods, as her breasts were tender.

Through the salon windows she could see across the courtyard to the King's Room, where the lights on the tree glimmered. Magic. She heard the satisfying pop of the cork as she walked through the door. It was beginning to feel like Christmas, but not as she'd felt it before. With the lights reflecting off the old windowpanes, the room shimmered, and she hadn't even had a glass of champagne yet.

'Happy birthday, Lucy.' Kit handed her a glass.

'Thank you.' Her phone beeped. It was a message from her

mother wishing her happy birthday, saying she would call to-morrow. Her father had had a minor car accident and was in hospital. Nothing serious. Lucy sighed. She should have known it would be something to do with her father that would have prevented her mother from calling.

Kit looked down at the table, where she had spread out the array of ornaments, culminating with an elegant silver star. 'Do you start with the star? Or do you finish with it?'

Her mouth twitched. 'Hmmm, that's quite a choice. What would you suggest?'

'Well, we always had angels.'

'Did you?'

He stepped nearer. 'Yes. I have a soft spot for angels with golden hair.'

'Did this obsession begin at an early age?'

'Hours spent staring at her from the base of the tree. She was always so unattainable.'

She laughed and handed him a shiny red bauble. 'The star goes last.'

'Making me work for it.'

She gagged on her champagne. 'Indeed. It's the proper thing to do.'

The corners of his mouth lifted a bit. 'You aren't always so proper.'

She blushed. 'True, but my life has changed radically. And this tree isn't going to get decorated if you don't stop.'

'Stop what?' He opened his eyes wide, the picture of inno-cence.

She threw tinsel at him and climbed the ladder with a box of silver baubles under her arm. He kept her supplied while she worked down from the top and he worked up from the bottom. When the last one was hung, he topped up her glass.

'Who gets to do the star?'

'That would be me.' She tried to keep a straight face as she climbed the ladder once more and secured the star to the top. 'Is it straight?'

'Definitely.'

She laughed as she climbed down. 'You're terrible.'

'I admit it.' He took her into his arms and twirled her about until she couldn't think.

'Where did you learn to dance like that?' Her eyes narrowed. 'You didn't do *Strictly*?'

'Nothing so fun. Early in my career I played Fred Astaire.'

She leaned back as they moved about the floor, trying to picture him in a top hat and tails. Yes, it fitted. He was a star, but he'd become so much more real than the two-dimensional image. 'Not one I've seen.'

'Not many will have, which was a good thing. But the dancing skills acquired have come in useful at weddings.'

'I bet you're a wow at weddings.'

'Absolutely, planning on making it my new sideline.'

'Don't you miss Hollywood?'

'No.' He released her as the song ended and refilled their glasses. 'I miss some of my friends, but it was never really home.' He handed her her glass. 'What about you? London, the limelight?'

She sipped her champagne. 'I miss central heating, and the Christmas lights, but ...' she paused, 'I'm surprised at what I don't miss.' Looking down at the decorations on the table, she was amazed at her thoughts. She picked up a garland and began hanging it above the fireplace.

'Then Helwyn House is growing on you?'

She laughed. 'That may be a step too far, but Cornwall is, and ... some of the residents.'

He walked towards her holding a piece of mistletoe, which he lifted above her head. 'Kiss?'

On tiptoes she pressed her mouth to his. Something inside went *ping*. Maybe it was an alarm bell. But she ignored it as Bing Crosby began to croon, the mistletoe hit the table and Kit pulled her into his arms.

'This wasn't supposed to happen,' she whispered against his mouth.

'I know. But it has.' He kissed her again.

Fifty-Seven
Hebe

August 2015

The expanse of beach at Sennen stretches below and I am full of chocolate cake. The sunset is almost finished. I fight back tears. The end of the day has never affected me this way before. You watch me closely. I'm afraid of what you can see. Reaching out, I stroke your hand. Your fingers capture mine. We do not speak. You know I am tired and signal for the bill. I grab for my purse but you wave my hand away. I suppose you can do this now. Things have changed without me noticing.

Out in the twilight the stars begin to appear. One shoots across the sky. You kiss me. I lose my balance and cling to you. You nuzzle my neck and whisper, 'I must get you tipsy more often.' Your laughter lifts my mood and I kiss you again, forgetting that although in the dark we are still in public.

We walk along arm in arm until we reach the car. I'm grateful that you are driving. Exhaustion and wine have combined. I slip into the seat and close my eyes as the last of the daylight fades away.

*

Stars from the sun are not enlarged, but shown
Gentle love deeds, as blossoms on a bough,
From love's awakened root do bud out now.

It was St Lucy's Day and I was thinking of the lack of light in the world. I turned to you. You didn't notice me. The work in front of you engrossed you fully. I smiled. In that text, you

254

would pull out things and make conclusions, and then we would test them. You were eager to learn from me. I remembered the feeling when the world of the past had become real for me. Through you I felt that excitement again. My world was alive once more. Who was I fooling? *I* had come alive. You were the poetry that had died in my life. Each day with you was filled with beautiful words, creating a happiness in me I hadn't thought could exist.

You looked up and a slow smile stole across your mouth. My editor had raved about the new depth in my writing. She asked if something had changed. I said nothing, but everything had. You had spun my world.

You stood and walked towards me. My toes curled in anticipation. You stopped just inches from me, but didn't touch me. Everything in me leaned towards you, but I held back. Torment.

'Hello,' you said.

'Hi.'

'I missed you earlier. Did the tutorials go well?'

I nodded.

'Any promising students?'

I looked into your eyes. Promising. That was what you were. Filled with promise. 'No,' I said. 'They all require work.'

'Extra lessons?'

'Absolutely.'

You took my hand and led me to my bedroom, Thomas Grylls watching us from the portrait. I was the one who was learning new things … about myself and about you.

✳ Fifty-Eight ✳
Lucy

14 December 2016

Opening her eyes, Lucy smiled as sunshine streamed through the window. She was twenty-nine and had had the best evening of her life. Who knew that trimming the tree, laughing, singing and dancing to Christmas songs could be so much fun and so damned romantic. She touched her mouth. Kit could kiss and he could dance. Last night he hadn't been the movie star and she hadn't been the other woman. They had been simply a man and a woman. Kit and Lucy. She swallowed.

Where did she go with this? She stretched, poking her feet into the cold corners of the single bed. Kit Williams, the man with legions of love-struck fans around the world, wasn't exactly an ideal candidate to fall for. Lucy didn't believe in love, but if that was what she was feeling, it might not be so bad. Closing her eyes, she tried to think of all the negative things she knew about love, but all that was in her head was the memory of his mouth on hers.

She swung her feet out of bed. This thinking wasn't helping anything. It was just one night and a few champagne-induced kisses. Nothing more. Wrapping the duvet around her, she walked to the window. A light frost covered the ground and the sky was deepening to a bright blue. It was going to be a lovely day.

Dressing quickly, she went down to the kitchen and pulled on boots and an old coat. Golden morning light was hitting the wall, warming the granite. She grabbed her camera and raced out of the door. Her breath clouded around her as she stopped halfway up the hill. Helwyn House didn't look real, glowing in the low rays. It didn't look grey and bleak, but warm.

Through the viewfinder, the house became magical. She walked closer, feeling the pull of the building, stopping only when a reflection on the thin ice in the stone water trough caught her eye. The shapes of the windows reflected and warped, bending the blue sky. Nothing was as it seemed.

'Morning.'

She jumped, nearly losing her footing.

Kit walked up to her. His mouth stretched into a big smile. 'Sorry I startled you.' He leaned in and kissed her. Her heart, which had been racing, sped up even more. 'Shall I go and make some coffee?'

She swallowed, about to nod but then thinking better of it. 'Tea, please.'

'Sure.' Her gaze followed him into the kitchen.

A cloud sped across the sky, covering the sun. She shivered as the stones of Hell House lost their glow. The sun returned, but she didn't feel its warmth as she headed back inside. The moment had gone.

Once inside, the aroma of coffee assaulted her nose. Her stomach roiled and she raced to the loo, heaving, but there was no relief. Eventually it stopped and she leaned back on her knees. The only thing that came to her mind was something Fred had said. Peta had asked how Lucy was feeling. The dodgy prawn was nine days ago and her stomach still wasn't right. She touched her left breast. It felt full and sore.

She didn't like the way her thoughts were going. She couldn't be pregnant. She really couldn't be. Several doctors had told her there was very little chance of pregnancy with polycystic ovary syndrome, and she was on the pill.

Slowly she stood and looked in the mirror. The rosy glow everyone had commented on was nowhere in evidence. All she saw was fear and sadness. Pregnant. She could only hope she was wrong.

Fifty-Nine
Hebe

14 December 2016

Hebe looked at yesterday's entry in her journal.

> *The feast of St Lucy, martyr and bringer of light*
> *Breakfast - porridge.*
> *Dinner - roast chicken and boiled potatoes and*
> *something green.*
> *Lucy brought a tree into the King's Room, a big*
> *spiky thing. The man with Thomas's eyes was helping*
> *her put lights on it. The smell of it brought memories.*
> *Childhood. My mother holding me. Her hair was long*
> *and so dark. Happy. Why did she leave me?*

She put her pen down and wiped her cheek. There was no use in crying over something she had lost so long ago.

The light from her lamp reflected off the wobbly glass panes in the window. Her own reflection was broken up. Her forehead in one pane, her chin in another. Would she never become whole again, whole with her thoughts?

She pulled out the solicitor's letter. Everything was in place for Lucy to take over running her life. It was a relief. She laughed. It wouldn't be a relief for Lucy. Maybe she should have asked her permission, but there wasn't time now and there was no one else suitable.

Lucy would be cross. She wanted no ties, no commitments, nothing to hold her down. Except maybe the man with the white teeth. When Lucy thought no one was watching, Hebe saw her study his every move. Something stirred in her mind. She shivered. Love had passed her way once.

Her fingers weren't hitting the keys she wanted, so Hebe took out a notepad and pen.

There was no moon, yet Thomas knew exactly where he was. He could smell it in the air. Home. As he reached the bend in the creek, the wind died. The boat carried on with the momentum for a short stretch. He wondered if Lucia had received his message. Would she risk meeting him?

She put her pen down. She could see it all in front of her, but the words on the page didn't match the picture in her head. A third of the way into the novel and it felt flat, boring even. Her heart wasn't in it. This was not the way she wanted the story to end. She put her head in her hands. What should she do? *Give up*, a voice in her head said, and she knew it was right.

There was a tap on the door. Thomas's descendant stood there holding a mug of tea and a plate with three marshmallows. 'Thought you might need these.' His back was straight, and there was something in his eyes this morning that hadn't been there yesterday. Happiness.

He placed the mug and plate on the desk. Hebe swiftly closed her laptop.

'So you're H. J. Bowden.' He shook his head. 'I should have guessed.'

She took a deep breath. What should she do?

'I love your books. You brought history alive, Thomas Grylls alive. Thank you.'

Her hand shook as she reached for a marshmallow. Now someone other than her agent, her editor and her solicitor knew. She smiled; she didn't have to carry this alone.

'I don't suppose you could read what I've done so far.' She swallowed. 'I'm afraid it's terrible.'

'I'm sure it isn't, and I'd be happy to help if I can.'

'Thank you.' Hebe picked up her mug. It was good that Thomas was going to help.

Kit put the laptop aside and picked up the book of poems. 'A little Donne to clear the mind?'

'Yes please.' Hebe rotated her shoulders and settled onto the bed.

'Any requests?'

'"The Paradox", please.'

He flipped through the pages before beginning. '*No lover saith, I love, nor any other ... can judge a perfect lover; he thinks that none else can or will agree ... that any loves but he.*'

The door opened. Kit stopped and Hebe turned her head. Lucy came in with a cup of tea and biscuits. Her brow was creased and her skin pale. None of the lovely colour she'd had of late was visible. Yet yesterday there had been a brightness about her. Hebe remembered that and her heart lifted. Lucy was such a good soul.

'Hello, you ... still in bed?' Lucy came and sat on the edge. 'Hi, Kit, didn't know you were here.'

'Hebe was just telling me some history.' He closed the book and winked at Hebe. 'I'll leave you two.' He slipped out of the door.

Hebe frowned. Lucy's eyes were ... the word was gone. She was hiding something. No, that wasn't it. Lucy ran her finger over the pattern on the duvet cover. It was white on white, and from this angle Hebe couldn't see it, but she knew it was there.

Something was troubling Lucy. Hebe hoped she wasn't the cause. She never wanted that. Had she put too much on her? Lucy was so good at this restoration stuff. The man doing the work – Mark, she remembered – had said so. In fact he had wondered if she might consider working for him when Helwyn House was finished. Would it ever be finished? Did work on these old houses ever stop?

'I love you.' She pushed back Lucy's hair as she'd done when Lucy had been a child. 'If I'd dared to have children, I would

260

have wanted one just as fiery and independent as you, a product of love and passion.'

Lucy paled. What had she said?

'Are you feeling OK?'

Lucy's mouth sucked in, puckering her lips.

'You should try the pink marshmallows. They make me feel better.'

Lucy swallowed. 'I might try.'

'Do.' Something still wasn't right. 'Can you take me to Cadgwith tomorrow?'

She nodded.

'I don't think it's a good idea for me to drive myself.'

Lucy snorted.

'I'm so sorry this has landed on you, Luce.'

Lucy grabbed her hand and Hebe saw her eyes fill. Maybe it was too much, but who else could she turn to?

'Hebe, I love you too and I'm happy to help.'

Hebe smiled. 'Good.' She stood, needing the loo, and looked around. Nothing was right. 'Lucy, where is the loo. I need it now.'

Lucy jumped up and took her by the hand and through the door beside the bed. How had she forgotten that?

'I'll be fine now.'

'You sure?'

'Yes.' Hebe shut the door and rested her head against it. This was worse than she'd imagined. How much more would she lose?

❊ Sixty ❊
Lucy

15 December 2016

Lucy pulled the blanket tighter about her shoulders. She'd heard a bang, loud enough to wake her from her half sleep. She'd been tossing and turning, because she didn't want to deal with her life. Forget the ghosts, now she knew real fear. There was another thump, and she felt for the front-door key under her pillow. Hebe hadn't done any night-walking that she was aware of in a while, but she wasn't taking any chances. The key was still there.

Tapping her phone, she checked the time. Four a.m. Joy. The moon was still out and a cold light fell onto the floor from the window above her. Every nerve was on high alert. Had Hebe fallen out of bed? Had a chimney collapsed somewhere in the house? There was nothing to do but go and take a look, though the last thing she wanted was to wander the house at night.

Shivering, she left the warmth of her bed. Outside, the world was covered in a crystal frost. The ground sparkled under the haloed moon. She was stopped in her tracks by the poetry of her own thoughts. It must stem from Kit's declamations earlier. He had a wonderful gravelly voice, and a catch to his deep tones that gave it more oomph. Not to mention that it was sexy as hell when he was whispering in her ear.

She grabbed the torch from the bedside table and turned it on. Its beam picked out the lines of the floorboards and calmed her nerves. She hated this house and she hated it even more at this hour in the morning. Cold seeped through her thick socks.

She could see her breath. That was fine on a ski slope, but never a good sign indoors.

She walked down the back stairs, checking the kitchen and grabbing a little boost of warmth from the range before continuing. The door to the dining room was stuck, and she put her shoulder to it. Had something fallen off the wall and blocked it? With a big shove, it swung free, and as she stepped into the room, she thought she saw something flash. Stopping, she swept the torch around, but there was nothing except the moonlight streaming through the windows. Eerie.

Proceeding with caution, she left the dining room and walked the passage, holding her breath as the temperature dipped lower. It was only the third week of December. What was the rest of the winter going to be like, living in this wreck?

Hearing footsteps, she stilled. Hebe must be pacing her room. She reached the bottom of the stairs and listened, almost afraid to look up. The light from the moon shone through the window on the landing like daylight, casting shadow from the bars. The door to the salon was closed. Had she shut it earlier? She didn't think she had. It creaked as she reached the last step, then opened wide as she stopped.

Something went past her and touched her neck. She bit back a scream. It was all her imagination. It would only be the draught that had opened the door. That was all. She stared at the shadows, willing her heart to slow. She could hear nothing but its racing rhythm.

A few days ago, she'd greased the hinges and mechanisms on Hebe's door so that she could check on her without waking her. Thanks to the bright moonlight, she was able to switch off the torch as she entered, not sure what to expect. The curtains weren't closed and the shutters were open. There was enough light to see her aunt lying in her bed. Her breathing was regular. She was in deep sleep. Lucy's heart missed a beat when she thought about the footsteps she'd heard. Was there someone else in the house?

With small steps, so that the creaking floorboards wouldn't wake her aunt, she went to the window to have a look outside.

It was as bright as day, and the garden walls were visible. The ground was white as far as the tree line. There were no footprints on the frost-covered grass. The noises didn't bear thinking about. All was fine, absolutely fine. An old wreck like this creaked and groaned, complaining all the time. It was just more noticeable at night when the world was silent, frozen.

She took a step back and bumped into the desk. A notebook fell to the floor and something flew out. Checking to see if Hebe was still asleep, Lucy picked them up. In the otherworldly light, she peered at the photograph she'd found. Her hand stilled. It was Hebe, but with a man – no, more of a teen. He looked just like Thomas Grylls in the portrait. How weird. The two of them stood on a headland, holding hands. Lucy looked at her aunt in the bed and frowned. It must be one of her students, but why was she holding his hand? She flipped the picture over to see if it gave her any clues. But she could see nothing. She slipped it back into the notebook, hoping it was in the right place, and crept out of the room.

A cloud had covered the moon and the sharp shadows had softened. She'd liked their previous crispness, with precision edges. Now the lines blurred into the slate windowsills. Pausing at the window before the salon door, she traced the lines that mirrored the grid-like panes above. The witch marks stood out in the moonlight. Had it been on nights like this that the previous occupants had made their pleas for help and protection?

Below, the courtyard had lost its sparkle and looked like a hollow shell. The large arch surrounding the double door that had once guarded the hall spoke of wealth, power and faith. Today those words were never put together, but back when the arch was carved, they were never separated. What had Hebe said about the past years ago? It must be looked at through the eyes of faith, even if we had no belief. Faith. On a night like this, Lucy could understand its appeal.

The cloud moved and the clear moonlight cast sharp shadows again. Who was that young man in the photograph? The tall clock in the dining room chimed five. It was ten minutes fast.

Lucy doubted it was worth trying to go back to sleep. Hebe would wake soon.

In the kitchen, she snuggled against the range and saw her handbag sitting on a kitchen chair. In it sat an unopened pregnancy test. Lucy didn't want to know the answer. Pregnant. She'd never expected to have children. She'd built her life around that premise. A child didn't fit.

Blowing on her fingers, she went to the fridge and took out the milk. Hot chocolate wouldn't provide her with any answers, but it might stop the nausea. Food poisoning could linger. But who was she trying to fool? She was pregnant with Ed's child. There was only one thing she could do. She needed to terminate the pregnancy.

While the milk was warming, she grabbed the pregnancy test and went to the loo, rather than torment herself one way or the other. She needed to know for sure. Only then could she move forward. As she peed on the stick, the thought crossed her mind that if she was pregnant, this might be her only chance of having a child. She didn't know how she felt about that.

After putting the cap back on, she washed her hands and returned to the warmth of the kitchen to make the hot chocolate. Ignorance was bliss, for a few more minutes at least. Her life was upside down. She had no work. She might be at the start of something with Kit. Who knew where, if anywhere, that would go, but a child would stop it in its tracks.

She pulled a chair closer to the range and tried to think clearly. Assuming she was pregnant, she needed to see a doctor immediately. Conception would have been on the twenty-sixth of September, so she was almost three months. This was not good. Standing up, she walked across the room and turned the stick over.

❊ Sixty-One ❊
Hebe

17 December 2016

There was a tap on the door.

'Come in.' Hebe looked up from the poetry book. It was all she could focus on.

'I've found something.' He smiled, showing those teeth, but she could look past the vanity because he'd been so useful. He was helping her with the book. She would tell him what she wanted and he would write it, then read it back. They would then edit it together.

He stood beside the bed, grinning like a child. 'I was in the north bedroom again, digging about in the fireplace.'

'And?'

'As I suspected, there's a priest hole.'

She sucked in a deep breath. She shouldn't doubt him. But she did.

'And although I couldn't go into it because a beam or two must have dislodged, blocking further access … something caught my eye.'

Hebe tilted her head. 'Well?'

He was holding his hands behind his back, and she wondered if he was going to ask her to choose. She'd loved that game as a child.

He pulled his left hand forward and opened his fingers. 'The light from my torch fell on something shiny.'

Hebe gasped. Parts of it were caked in dirt, but there was no doubt. She'd read descriptions. 'The Grylls Jewel.'

He nodded.

'Do you think Lucia could be in there?'

'She went missing and we have no record of what happened to her.' He looked at Hebe. 'I've been through your files.'

'Yes.' Possible scenarios ran through her mind.

He put the locket into her hands. She lifted her eyes to his. 'Have you opened it?'

'No. I thought you should.'

She took a deep breath. Would the miniature have survived? There was only one way to find out. With shaking hands, she slipped the catch and opened it. She gasped. It fell from her fingers onto the bed.

He frowned and picked it up.

Hebe studied his expression as he looked inside. There were two portraits. Would he see what she saw?

'Remarkable.'

Hebe nodded, comparing him to the miniature. Except for the hair colour, he could be the man in the painting. Thomas was twenty-six when it had been painted. The man in front of her was older, but hadn't lived through war.

'So Lucy is related to Lucia?'

'Yes. Lucia's mother was a Courtenay as is Lucy's.'

'I hadn't realised you were so connected to Lucia.'

'It was one of the first things that piqued my interest.' Hebe glanced down at the miniatures. Thomas and Lucia had been together all along.

'Lucy resembles the Courtenays, then, and not the Trevillions.'

Hebe pressed her lips together. She would not say anything. 'Yes.'

'So assuming we find Lucia's remains in the priest hole ...' he paused, 'it looks as though whoever killed them wanted them close together but unable to reach each other.' He paced across the room. 'Whoever it was must have hated Thomas.'

'Yes.' Hebe looked at the miniatures. 'It was probably her husband.'

'True.'

'Shall we write it that way?' she asked.

'What do you think?' He sat on the end of the bed.

'He was a bastard, so let's make him a real villain.'

He laughed. 'As the lady wishes.'

'Donne, please.'

'Of course.' He picked up the poetry book and sat down beside her. She closed her eyes and let the words fill her.

Sixty-Two

Lucy

21 December 2016

There were four messages from her mother on the answer-phone, and apart from asking what she needed to bring with her for Christmas, they were all about this man called Rory Crown. He'd called enough to get under her mother's skin.

Lucy picked up the handset, dialled the number, then put it down. If she used the landline, then this Rory would have their number and know they were in Cornwall. What if he was some maniac? Even if he was a polite one (according to her mother), Lucy didn't need that hassle.

Hebe was staying in bed more and more these past few days. Not even the excitement of finding the priest hole in the north bedroom, and another body, had lifted her spirits. That sounded terrible, but for both Hebe and Kit this was an exciting find. From the size of the bones it could be a woman's skeleton. They were waiting to find out.

This past week, it was as if Hebe had given up. Many things began to make sense. The power of attorney, for one. The solicitor was away for Christmas already, and as Lucy's questions weren't urgent, they would have to wait for the new year. She could only hope that Hebe had everything in place.

Walking out of the kitchen door and through the freezing mist, she thought about how quickly her world had shrunk. She'd only ventured as far as Truro in the past three months, never leaving the Duchy. Looking around now, she waved to one of the builders as she walked up and out through the field to the road. Yes, the new telephone mast had been put up, but that moment of connection had been brief. They had only been testing. Sometime in January they would switch it on permanently. In some ways she'd come to enjoy being cut off, but she wouldn't own up to that. There was also a promise of connecting Hell House to the Internet, but she would believe that when it happened.

Leaning against a tree, she dialled Rory Crown. Who was he and what did he want with her aunt?

'Hello.'

She detected a hint of Scotland in the voice. 'Hi. Could I speak with Rory Crown?'

'Yes, speaking.'

'I understand you're looking for Hebe Courtenay.'

'Yes.' Exasperation came through loud and clear.

'I'm her niece.'

'Lucy?'

She stood up straight. How did he know that? But then it wasn't a secret. 'Yes.'

'I've spoken with your mother.'

'I know.' In the background, she could hear a great deal of noise.

'I've been a pest.' He paused. 'Look, I've ... known Hebe for ten years and she's just vanished.'

'She hasn't. She's fine and she says she doesn't know you.'

He sighed. 'I had a feeling that was the problem.'

A loudspeaker announced a flight. He was in an airport. Lucy frowned. 'Why did you have that feeling?'

'Because Hebe has been hiding and coping with her dementia for years.'

'Years?' She poked her toe in the nearly frozen mud.

'Yes, years.'

'Who are you?'

He sighed. 'I'm her lover.'

She laughed. 'Are we talking about the same Hebe?'

'Yes, she was a professor of history, she's fifty-five years old. She has a passion for pasta and likes to keep secrets.'

270

'None of that is exactly private information.'

'True. Have you become her gatekeeper? Is she not well?'

'She's OK.'

'I'd like to see her.'

'How do I know you're not some weirdo?'

'Not that it's proof of character, but go onto UCL's site and you'll find I'm an associate professor of literature there.'

'Oh.'

'Look, I'm heading to the Caribbean for my sister's wedding. I'll be back on Boxing Day. You have my number. Please call me.' He sighed. 'I'm not a stalker. I love Hebe.'

'Why don't I know anything about you?'

He laughed. 'I said your aunt liked secrets. She's kept me so secret she's forgotten me herself.'

Hebe had always been open and honest with Lucy. This didn't fit.

'They're calling my flight. Check me out and call me after Christmas. I need to see her. Have a happy Christmas, Lucy.'

She stared at her phone, thinking about the bizarre conversation she'd just had. She typed *Rory Crown UCL* into her browser, and sure enough, there he was, listed as an associate professor. There was also a link to a forthcoming television series on the great works of literature. She would read more later, but it was bloody cold standing here with a northerly wind sweeping oncoming rain into her face. She needed warmth and time to absorb what she had just heard. Hebe had a secret lover. Was there anything else she hadn't told them?

Sixty-Three

Hebe

August 2015

We are packing our bags. This summer has passed too quickly. I want to stop time, but it doesn't listen to me. Throwing my dressing gown into the suitcase, I march out of the front door of the cottage, taking great gulps of air to ward off tears. Your arms reach around me as I look across the field. You pull me against you. I feel your warmth against my back. Your proximity makes it harder to think.

Closing my eyes, I let you hold me. I allow you to love me while I think of the academic year ahead of us. Will I be able to teach? I have researched techniques to help me. I don't want to stop. I'm lost without my work. Taking a deep breath, I remember my writing. I can still write, or at least I think I can.

'Shall we book the cottage for next summer? Just you and me and glorious Cornwall.'

I turn in your arms and kiss you. There is no answer to this. I must live for now. 'Sounds good.' And it does, but I wonder if I will remember saying yes. We have work calling us both. You may be a television star by this time next year. 'Let's see what the year brings.'

*

We die and rise the same, and prove
Mysterious by this love.

Your head was bent over a book. The light cast by the table lamp picked out the highlights in your hair. It was shorter now, and your clothes were smarter. You had perfected the rumpled professor look even though you were only twenty-seven. You lifted your hand and traced the words across the page. I was jealous of that caress. I was jealous of the world. I wanted to speak but the words died on my lips as you looked up.

'This sentence is beautiful.' You read it aloud and I agreed. Looking down, I pushed my pen across the page, not conscious of the words I was writing. They came into focus, and I saw that I had written *I love you, I love you, I love you*.

❊ Sixty-Four ❊
Lucy

22 December 2016

Lucy was the second person to arrive at the local surgery. The man who came in after her kept peering over his newspaper to look at her. She wasn't sure if she was in the papers again or if he remembered her from before. But there was judgement written on his face. She looked down. So much had happened that she'd forgotten about being the other woman. Now she was the other woman who was pregnant.

'Lucy Trevillion,' a woman called from the doorway. Lucy stood and the man with the newspaper twitched. She'd made his day.

The doctor closed the door and held out her hand. 'I'm Dr Grant. How can I help you today?'

Lucy took a deep breath. 'I'm pregnant.'

Dr Grant raised an eyebrow. 'Is this good or bad?'

'Not good.'

'OK.' She looked at Lucy closely. 'When was your last period?'

'This will be a problem. It was August the first.'

Dr Grant looked her up and down. 'You don't appear five months pregnant. So, let me examine you.' She pulled a screen across the room. 'If you could remove your jeans and pants, then hop onto the table.'

Lucy stood and did as requested. A million things were going through her mind.

'How long have your periods been erratic?'

'Always. I have polycystic ovary syndrome.'

'OK.'

'They said it was unlikely that I would ever get pregnant. So I'm not sure how this happened.'

'You had sex.' A smile hovered on the doctor's lips.

'I did.'

'You don't want children?'

Lucy opened her mouth to say no. It had been years since she had even considered it as an option. 'I have no plans for children.'

'I'm just going to have a feel of your cervix and your uterus.'

'Fine.' Lucy flinched a bit, but it was not as bad as a smear test.

'You're definitely pregnant.' Dr Grant pulled the gloves off.

'How far along?'

'I'm not sure. When did you have unprotected sex?'

'I last had sex on the twenty-sixth of September. I took the pill as usual that morning and then had sex with my lover twice during the hours of eleven to four in the morning.'

The doctor raised an eyebrow.

'The problem is that due to unforeseen circumstances, I didn't take my pills for about a week after.'

'So now that you are sure you are pregnant, you plan to ...'

'Terminate.'

'Right. Get dressed, then take a seat.'

Gone was the hope that the test had been wrong. Slowly Lucy pulled on her clothes and took a seat in front of the desk. The doctor was tapping things into her computer.

'I'm sure you've thought this through and have spoken to the man concerned.'

'Yes and no.'

Dr Grant looked up and cocked her head to the side.

'It would complicate matters.'

She pressed her lips together. 'As we don't know the dates of this pregnancy for certain, you need to have a scan first.'

Lucy nodded. Her mouth was too dry to speak.

'You'll get a call ...' Dr Grant paused, 'next week. What with Christmas and New Year, getting an early appointment could be a problem.' She sighed. 'Once we have the information, we can go from there.'

Again Lucy nodded, fighting tears. Whether they were of relief or fear she wasn't sure.

'Would you like me to go through the choices with you?' Dr Grant slid a brochure across the table.

Lucy swallowed with difficulty. 'No, I'll read this later.'

The doctor flipped through the file. 'I see you're living locally.' She looked up. 'I'd like you to book an appointment with me for a month's time.'

'OK.'

'Helen at reception will sort out a date with you.' She smiled. 'There's a number on the back page if you have any questions or just want to talk things through anonymously.'

'Thank you for ...'

She nodded, and Lucy fled, clutching the brochure, without stopping at reception.

PART THREE

Sixty-Five

Hebe

22 December 2016

Hebe grabbed the bedpost. Everything went dark.

'You blacked out again.' Strong hands held her.

She nodded. His eyes showed such concern. Thomas's eyes.

'I've just come back from Truro.' He handed her a box.

She frowned. 'What is it?'

'The Grylls Jewel. I took it to the museum and they kindly cleaned it for me.'

Hebe opened the box and the stones glistened at her. All traces of their buried years removed.

'They would like to photograph it.'

She nodded.

'They would also like you to come into the museum.'

'Ha.'

'I said that you were unwell, and they mentioned that it would be good if you would write up the find.'

'I didn't find it.' She gave him a sideways glance.

'I didn't tell them that.'

She glanced out of the window. 'I want to give it to Lucy.'

'Good idea.'

'You don't object?'

'What right do I have to object?'

'You're Thomas's descendant.'

'He gave it to Lucia, and Lucy is a descendant of hers.'

'Yes, that is true.' Hebe looked down. She opened the locket and gazed at Thomas and his love. 'Will you marry Lucy?' She looked up. 'I think you should.'

The sound of tyres on gravel broke the silence in the room.

'Have I said something I shouldn't have?'

He laughed, and she smiled. Despite his white teeth, he was a good man.

❋ Sixty-Six ❋
Lucy

22 December 2016

Kit's coat was on the hook when she got back. Delicious aromas came from the oven. Lucy peeked. Shepherd's pie. There was a bottle of wine on the table and three places set. She would say he was being presumptuous, but quite frankly, she was grateful. The family would be arriving en masse tomorrow. She was dreading the holiday and wished she could have hopped on that plane bound for the sun with Rory Crown. She had to wonder if Hebe was lying when she had said she didn't remember him, or if she truly didn't. It was strange to think that the woman Lucy had known all these years had led a totally different life to the one they'd all imagined. What else had she hidden?

She picked up the landline. 'Mum.'

'Lucy. I'm just trying to finish packing so that we can set off early and avoid the worst of the traffic. Is there anything you need me to get?'

'We're fine. I've got it sorted.' Lucy leaned against the table. 'I've got the Stilton.'

'Good, though I prefer Cornish Blue.'

'Lucy, are you being deliberately mean?'

'No.' She sighed. 'Having Christmas here is hard, especially now that we know what's going on with Hebe.'

'True. I'm sorry.'

'You've always made Christmas effortless over the years, and now everyone's expecting the same. Then there's the added stress of Michael's girlfriend coming, plus Gran and her … Hugh.'

281

'Yes, dear, it's a bit much, I know, but you can do it. Your father spent a fortune on that cookery course.'

'Only to make me more appealing to some suitable man. I have never aspired to be anyone's wife.'

'I know it gives him such worry.'

'He just wants me off his conscience.' She made a fist.

'Darling, that's an odd comment.'

'Never mind, Mum. I'll be sweetness and light, I promise.' Kate sighed. 'Thank you.'

'By the way, I spoke to Rory Crown.'

'Did you manage to get rid of him?'

'No, he's Hebe's lover.'

Lucy heard the phone drop and the scrape of it being picked up.

'I'll tell you more when you get here. Travel safely tomorrow. Bye.'

So her mother hadn't known either, even though she and Hebe were close.

Lucy walked up the stairs, assuming that Kit was poking about the priest hole. He was determined to get to the bottom of the two skeletons. It was no wonder that the room had felt creepy for years. It was beginning to look like the victims had been sealed in while injured but still alive. She shivered at the thought.

On the landing, she stopped when she heard Hebe and Kit reciting poetry together again. It sounded like Donne. She could fall for Kit because of his voice alone. Who was she kidding? She had fallen.

The only way forward, with Kit or without him, was to get rid of this alien inside her. Lucy had built her life around the fact that she couldn't have kids. How could the impossible have happened? But of course, being her, it had to happen with that lying toad, and not the lovely man reading poetry to her aunt.

Peering through the door, she saw him sitting next to her aunt, who was propped up on the bed. They held the book between them. Gratitude filled her. He was so wonderful with Hebe. She looked better than she had in days, almost her old self. Kit turned and smiled at Lucy while he continued. Lucy swallowed.

They finished the poem and he closed the book. 'Lucy's back and dinner is ready.' He stood and held out his hand to Hebe. Lucy held her breath. She'd been doing everything in her power to try and coax her aunt downstairs, but nothing had worked. Things were going to be tricky if she refused to join everyone at Christmas, even if hiding in her room was exactly what Lucy would like to do herself.

Hebe put on slippers and took Kit's arm. He had charmed her; Lucy knew how good he was at that. Looking at him at that moment, it was hard to see the Hollywood star; that side of him only emerged when he was dealing with strangers. It would appear again tomorrow when her family descended. Hebe had insisted that he join them for the holiday, and he had reluctantly agreed. Personally Lucy thought he would have had more fun accepting Fred's invitation to join the celebrations at Tamsin's. Having said that, he was taking Lucy to the Polcrebars' drinks party on Christmas Eve. She'd been in two minds about it. She had begun to like the quiet life, seeing people in small quantities. The thought of virtually the whole community in one go was a nightmare.

'Oh darling, I'm so sorry.' Her mother stood outside Hell House. 'I didn't think it was as bad as you said.'

Lucy followed her gaze along the length of the loggia. With Kit's help, she had put a garland around each column. Hell House looked as welcoming as it could, with big wreaths on the wooden gates. In the end she'd done so much more than she'd originally intended to. Once she had seen the transformation, she had kept going until the place was a virtual Christmas grotto, with mantelpieces trimmed with holly and ivy, and fir cones linked with red velvet ribbons making garlands draped over and around windows and mirrors. All that was missing was the merry elf himself. One look at her mother told Lucy she didn't see any of it.

'But you look well on it. Especially your skin. The fresh air has lifted your complexion no end.'

She must have looked like death in the past from all the comments about her skin. She guessed it was the one bonus of pregnancy. She really hadn't needed much more than a bit of lipstick and mascara to tart herself up recently. Not that she'd been doing much of that. Most days it was a clean face and lip balm. How the glamorous had fallen. However, as her grandmother was due any moment, she had tried a bit harder.

'How is Hebe?' Her mother took her arm as she looked around for her sister.

'On good form.' Hebe had woken bright this morning and appeared at breakfast dressed. Lucy wondered if Hebe recalled how Sarah had reacted last time. Lucy had left her with Kit. They were spending a great deal of time together. She wouldn't be honest if she didn't admit to herself that she was a bit jealous.

Her father, wielding a crutch, had hobbled on ahead through the gates as if he owned the place. Lucy looked at her mother. She was pale under her blusher. Maybe she knew. Their time as a family here had ended so abruptly. Who was Lucy kidding? Of course she must know. Everyone here did. Alice hadn't kept her mouth shut. But maybe her mother didn't know and Lucy's silence all these years had saved her that one indignity. She could hope, even if it was futile.

They walked through the gates into the courtyard, where she had placed another tree and decorated the pillars. Her mother stood staring. Lucy followed her gaze. It was Henrietta by the far gate. 'Darling, you didn't mention a goat.'

Lucy laughed. 'She was rather low down on the list of things to talk about. I'm quite fond of Henrietta now.'

'If you say so.' Kate shivered. She was not really dressed for a grey sky with a dampness that penetrated the bones.

'Let's get you inside and warm.'

'Yes, that would be lovely.' But her feet slowed.

Lucy took her arm and pulled her close. If she could, she would have tripped her father. He was heading up the stairs without any sign of his injury, or any invitation for that matter. Bloody liar.

'Mum, if you go to the kitchen, Hebe is in there with Kit. It's the warmest room in the house and there's fresh tea.'

'Lovely.'

Lucy stepped onto the first stair. She knew where her father was going. The scene of the crime. The room that was the grave of Thomas Grylls. She put her foot on the second step. She'd dreamt of this moment for years. It was time to tell him exactly what she thought of him. This was the room that marked the death of her relationship with her father and her best friend in one blow.

Grimacing, she took another step. She'd made sure that the room looked a hell of a lot better than when she'd found him in there shagging Alice. Lucy and Alice had been seventeen. What her father and Alice had been doing was barely legal. It certainly wasn't moral. Taking three steps in one go, she ground her teeth. She'd been forbidden to mention what had happened in order to protect her mother. If he'd been so worried about her, though, he should have stayed faithful.

His behaviour had been unforgivable, and Lucy had made him pay the only way that had been in her power at the time. She'd emulated him, sleeping with teachers, unsuitable men and even a few of his friends. He couldn't say a word. She had acted just like him. She stopped on the top stair. It was all so bloody hollow. How had he spent his life like that? And why had she wasted so much time copying him? She had been a fool, an angry, powerless fool.

At the entrance to the salon, she stopped. Her father was walking without much difficulty. It was obvious he was putting on the injured act to get sympathy. He might be her father, but she didn't have to love him, or even like him. It had taken her eleven years to find the courage to tell him what she thought of him. Eleven wasted years of hating him and hating herself. And if she was truthful, hating her mother for putting up with him. Love had imprisoned her, while giving him all the freedom he needed.

As she'd expected, he went straight there. If she'd planned it, it couldn't be a better place to make him face up to what he'd done. With each step, her muscles tensed. She was ready for this. She paused in the doorway.

'Returning to the scene of the crime?' Her eyes narrowed as he turned to face her.

He stared at her, saying nothing.

She opened her mouth, but before she could utter a sound, her father held his hand up.

'Wait. I know you have a great deal to say, but let me speak first.'

'No. I've had to listen to you for years, and nothing worthwhile has ever emerged.'

'Lucy ...' he paused, 'I'm sorry.'

She blinked. There was nothing he could have said that would have hit her harder.

'I was wrong, very wrong.' He took a pace towards her and she fought the urge to step backwards. For years she'd longed to hear this.

'I was an absolute shit.'

She nodded. Words had left her.

'I won't make any excuses. There are none.'

Damn right there weren't. But she couldn't say the words aloud.

'I just wanted to apologise.' He took another step forward. She didn't move.

'I'm not expecting forgiveness.' He shook his head and gave her a self-deprecating smile. 'I just wanted you to know I am sorry.'

She pinched herself, wondering if she was hallucinating. This humble man standing in front of her was not her father. What the hell had happened?

'I think we'd better go and join the others now.' He hobbled towards the door and his hand sought hers as he passed. She didn't pull away. He walked on. She was glad of that. She didn't need him to see her tears.

286

❋ Sixty-Seven ❋
Hebe

24 December 2016

> *Christmas Eve*
> *Sarah and Hugh are very much a couple. He is very*
> *nice. They have both been kind. Sarah helped me wrap*
> *the Grylls Jewel for Lucy. She was as shocked as I had*
> *been by the resemblance between Lucy and Lucia. But it*
> *shouldn't have been a surprise in view of the lineage.*

Hebe leaned back. She hoped that Lucy would like the present. It was one way to thank her.

Tomorrow they would be eating at six and were dressing for dinner. Where were the shoes that she wanted to wear? Looking in the cupboard, she found her handbag sitting on top of the shoeboxes, abandoned since she stopped going out of the house. When had she last used it? She turned out the contents, looking for a clue. The first thing her hand fell on was a bra she'd been missing. Why on earth was it in her bag? It was caught in a folded sheet of paper.

She opened the paper. It was filled with her own handwriting.

My dearest love,

I've never been able to say what has been in my heart. I love you.

The letter fell from her hands. She didn't remember writing it. But she had. Picking it up, she let out a sound more animal than human. Love. Why couldn't she remember? Why had she kept this? Yet how could she throw it away? It contained her heart, the one she had put aside to save it.

She felt for the key on her necklace and unlocked the bottom drawer of her desk, then put the letter inside. Soon she would destroy it. It had no purpose other than to remind her of a past that she had forgotten.

Slipping the key back over her head, she went to her dressing table and repaired her lipstick. Scarlet. It was a good thing she'd left him. He should never see her like this. His love would die. The image had cracked.

Sixty-Eight

Hebe

August 2015

You frown at me as I stop the car by the opening to the field. I'm not sure why I only thought of it now, just as we were leaving. The well has been so close.

'Are you OK?' you ask.

'Yes, I've just remembered a holy well that I wanted to see.'

You shrug. Cornwall has captured you only partially if you are not intrigued by its past, its magic. I dig in my handbag and find a handkerchief. Walking with care through the field as it slopes down to a copse of trees, soon I can see the objects, the clootie, tied to the branches.

Through the leaves, I spy the remains of the well. I bend down and dip the handkerchief in the water. Rubbing my forehead with it, I'm about to tie it to the tree when I also press it against my heart. I know there is no hope for either, but I make a wish that I will at least remember you.

As I walk back up the hill, sadness fills me. How will I get through the year? You stand by the car, and as you see me, a smile spreads across your face. You are worried. I remember why. The last month of the Easter term, you had to help me organise myself.

Once inside the car, I pull out my handbag and jot down a note.

Print out lectures.

*

Therefore I'll give no more; but I'll undo
The world by dying, because love dies too.

Your look asked me questions. I could not answer them. My fear was too great. Last night you helped me print out my lecture notes and edited my last paper. I don't know why I don't know things any more. The GP assured me it was normal with age, but if this was normal, I didn't like it.

You handed me a glass of wine and squeezed my shoulder. Was it a gesture of love, or just one of those comfortable-with-each-other ones? How long had we been together? I didn't know, but what I remembered was you much thinner and me with fewer wrinkles. In the distance, I heard the bells of St Mary-le-Bow. It was the angelus bell.

Around your flat, I saw your personality in your books and in that painting you bought that weekend in Paris together. I had said it was too loud, garish even, but you laughed and haggled. Now it looked so at home on your wall, among the shelves and posters. Your flat was so different from mine. I hoped now you have accepted that living together could never have worked. And most certainly we could never have married like you wanted. I knew you hadn't understood for years.

Each day, doing things right depended on lists, endless lists. You started me on them. And you never questioned why I needed them. Many small tasks that I forgot, you did for me. Sometimes I even forgot to eat.

You placed a plate of linguine with clams in front of me. It was your … best dish. The scent of garlic filled the flat. Outside, the sky was bright. Soon it would be the longest day. I frowned. I could not remember the date. It was June. I woke to the sound of birds. Roses in bloom. I thought I had gathered as many as I could.

You sat opposite me and told me about the first-year students you were teaching. Tomorrow you would take them to the Globe. Your face was alight with passion. You loved your work, especially the teaching. Your hands gestured and shaped the air with your enthusiasm. I longed for them to touch me. Once we wouldn't have waited until after dinner. We would have loved before, during and after. Yet my desire for you waxed and waned now where it had once been constant. The one constant was your ability to make me laugh. Somehow, seeing me through your eyes, I saw not death, but joy and fear.

❄ Sixty-Nine ❄

Lucy

24 December 2016

'You look lovely, darling.' Sarah was ensconced on the sofa with Hugh. Hebe was sitting in the armchair opposite and both fires were blazing. Lucy would rather join them than head out.

'Thanks. Are you sure you don't want to come along? Tamsin said to bring any guests.'

'How kind, but I'd much rather spend Christmas Eve here with a warm fire, a good book ...' she paused and looked at the claret jug on the table, 'and a nice bottle of wine.'

Hebe looked up from her notebook. 'Have fun.'

'Thanks.'

'You look like you're heading to the death squad. Smile.' Sarah took a sip of her wine.

Lucy tried to smile, but her stomach was queasy and her tits hurt. Her appointment for a scan wasn't until the sixth of January. She would like to drink her way through the party but she had no taste for it.

'You're going on the arm of a rather handsome man.' Her grandmother grinned.

'True.' She was grateful that Kit would be with her. Her stomach flipped, but not in a good way.

'Here's the man in question.' Hugh stood.

Kit's glance met hers and her heart lifted. It would be fine. And they didn't have to stay long.

'We'd best head off. See you later and don't have too much fun without me.'

'Not a chance.' Hugh laughed and settled back next to her grandmother. Sarah had her life sorted, it would appear. It was good that one of them had. Lucy's wouldn't be sorted until the alien within was gone. She shuddered. Just thinking about Ed made her skin crawl. How had she been so stupid as to have an affair with him?

Was she cut out to be a mother? No, she was too selfish – as Michael repeatedly pointed out. Just look at the way she'd behaved for the past twelve years. Now she needed to move on, grow up and find a purpose. And being a single mum without work wasn't going to help any of those.

Outside, the air was damp and Kit opened the door for her, stopping to kiss her before she slipped into the car. Of course there was also Kit to consider. How better to kill a romance than announcing she was pregnant with another man's child.

She stole a glance at him. A smile played on his mouth and he began to hum 'White Christmas' as they drove through the dark lanes towards Tamsin's. His hand sought hers. For the first time in her life, she wanted to try and have a proper relationship. She laughed to herself. Of course, she would choose to do this with a movie star and not Joe Average. How to self-sabotage in one easy lesson.

Trying not to think of the feel of his hand on hers, she listened to the words he was singing. There was no chance of a white Christmas or even a frosty one, but it was dry. Be grateful for small mercies.

He parked and came around the car to hold the door open for her. She could get used to such niceties. 'Thanks.'

'A pleasure.'

They were not the first to the fray, as evidenced by the many cars filling the drive. He took her arm as they headed towards the sound of Christmas carols.

'OK?' He turned to her and searched her face.

'Not sure, to be honest.'

'You're not yourself.'

She shook her head. 'I'm not.' God knows what he would think if he knew the truth. She needed to take one day at a time and get through tomorrow, the Christmas from hell, or simply Christmas at Hell House.

She took a deep breath. It shouldn't be too bad. Her father had apologised, although she had no idea why, or why now. Her mother appeared happier after those first few moments at the house. There was unspoken communication between her parents, and in all it felt positive. It was as if Lucy's public disgrace had brought them closer. She was pleased if it had done some good somewhere.

'Is it your father?' Kit asked.

'Partially.'

'He seemed uncomfortable.'

'Good description.' She glanced at him. This was Kit's first Christmas without his own father. It would be hard. His mouth was pressed into a straight line. She stopped walking and kissed him. 'I don't like him, but he's mine so I have to tolerate him for the holidays. I just feel for Mum.'

'Love does strange things.'

'Yeah, I know, that's why I've made it my life's mission to avoid it.' Until now she added silently.

He stopped.

'Really?'

'In my limited experience, love makes life worse, not better.'

'I don't agree.'

They had reached the door.

'Then let's agree to disagree and head into the madness.' She held his hand.

The crowd absorbed them and in moments they had been separated. She searched for him but he was nowhere in sight. No doubt he would be in huge demand, for although no one here normally made a big thing of his celebrity, they were impressed.

'Lucy, I'm so pleased you've come.' Tamsin gave her a big hug. 'I hear you've got the whole clan down.' She shook her head. 'Just what you need at the moment. I was so sorry to hear about Hebe.' She hugged her again, then pressed a glass of mulled wine into her hands. Peta came up bearing a plate of smoked salmon on blinis. Lucy's stomach turned.

'Doesn't appeal?'

She shook her head.

'I feel the same.' Peta laughed and looked at her growing bump. 'Been off all seafood for about a month now.' She smiled. 'How are things at the house?' She wrinkled her nose. 'Your father?'

'The house is good and my father is improving. I just want to limit my time with him to short doses. All I have to do is make it through to Boxing Day, then he'll be gone.'

'True. I'd better find a place to put this tray down.'

Lucy glanced around. 'Good luck.' The place was heaving and every surface seemed to be covered in plates of food. Mark Triggs waved over the crowd and Lucy sought out other familiar faces and a place to lose the mulled wine. The stress of making tomorrow work wasn't helping her stomach. She wasn't sure how her mother had always managed to produce such wonderful meals. Most of the day would be spent cooking and clearing, and the worst thing about it all was that her father would be pontificating at the head of the table. But maybe she was worrying needlessly. Thus far he'd surprised her.

Placing her glass down, she had an idea. Who said her father needed to be at the head of the table? Hebe could be at one end and Lucy herself at the other. Done. Problem solved. She was sure this new version of him wouldn't mind. Well, there was one way to find out.

She was worrying needlessly. Maybe it was to avoid thinking about the alien. What was crucial was to keep its existence to herself. She was more than capable of handling this on her own.

'Why, if it isn't little Lucy Trevillion.'

She spun around. She knew that voice. It was bloody her. Obviously home for the holidays. 'Hello, Alice. What brings you here?'

'Always a good place to catch up with the local gossip and see what and who has changed.' She looked around. 'Haven't seen you in years.'

Lucy pressed her lips together. Her foot twitched. Even though it had happened twelve years ago, she still hated Alice.

She might be able to accept her father's apology, even if forgiveness was some way away, but forgiving her former best friend was different. Bile rose, and she needed to vomit.

'Excuse me.' She dashed away, looking for the loo. She made it just in time. Seeing Alice had not helped the nausea. All she wanted now was to head home and go to sleep. A glance in the mirror told her the same story. She was ashen. Alice shouldn't get to her like this, but having her father around too – it was all a bit much. She opened the door.

'Sorry, you looked so ghastly, I followed you to see if you were OK.'

Lucy blinked.

'So you ditched your wine and now you're throwing up. Pregnant, by any chance?' Alice raised an eyebrow.

Lucy tried to keep all expression off her face. She needed a quick, witty comeback, but nothing came. Alice laughed, but to Lucy it sounded more like a cackle.

Kit appeared from around the corner. 'There you are, Luce.'

'Oh, is this your latest shag?'

'I see you haven't become any less blunt over the years.' Lucy finally found her voice.

'No, definitely not. So, you've been hiding down here since the scandal. Clever.' Alice tapped her nose.

'Kit, let's go and find some fresh air.'

'Ah yes, I'd heard that Kit Williams the movie star had moved into the area. If Luce is less than obliging, I'll be around until New Year.'

Kit placed an arm round Lucy's shoulders and led her out to the garden. 'She's a nasty piece of work.'

'Yes, but it took me until I was seventeen to work that out.' She shook her head. 'Until then she was my best friend. I shared everything with her, and then she decided it was a good idea to sleep with my father.'

'What?'

'I know. I'm not sure who I felt more betrayed by.' She gave a short laugh. 'Sorry, it still makes me angry.'

'Not surprised.'

'I wasn't very nice to her when it happened.' Her voice was shaky.

Kit looked at her, then pulled her into his arms. 'No one would blame you.'

'Maybe not, but I got her fired and made sure she'd never get another job round here again.'

He pulled back and looked at her.

'That sounds awful, but it wasn't all me. She'd taken money that she'd intended to pay back but hadn't. I suspected she planned to get it back through my father.' She took a deep breath. 'In front of our boss I accused her of being a whore and told him to check the accounts closely.'

'So you told the truth.'

She laughed bitterly. 'That's one way to look at it, but I just wanted to hurt her.'

'I can see why you don't like her.' He stroked her cheek and gave her a lopsided grin. 'You were young and she betrayed you.'

'If I could go back, I'd do it all differently. But instead I became the classic rebel without a cause.'

'Well then, shall we blow this joint and head to mine for a quiet Christmas Eve drink?' He delivered the last line in perfect Humphrey Bogart tones. She couldn't refuse, nor did she want to.

'Yes please.' The last thing Lucy wanted was a drink, but Kit was a different matter.

✳ Seventy ✳

Hebe

25 December 2016

The house was in silence as Hebe padded through to the kitchen. The scents of Christmas wafted down the hallway. Lucy must be cooking, but all Hebe could think about was the last Christmas with her mother. Not that her mother had cooked. They had had help, lots of it. Lucy needed help to run this house. She wouldn't be able to do it all on her own. As she neared the kitchen, she heard Lucy singing. It was a joyful sound. Hebe sang along as she walked in.

'Happy Christmas, Hebe.'

'Happy Christmas.' Hebe looked for coffee but she couldn't smell any. There was a pot of tea. She frowned. How long had Lucy been up that she'd finished it all? 'Coffee?'

'Sorry, haven't made any.' Lucy swallowed. 'Couldn't face it.' She gave Hebe a lopsided smile.

'Hung-over?'

'No, didn't drink.'

'What's wrong?' Hebe could see that she'd been crying. Her bloody father, no doubt. She opened her arms and Lucy fell into them. Hebe rubbed her back as the girl sobbed. Hebe would kill Giles if she could. It would free her sister and that would be good. Kate had put up with him for too long.

'It's not me making you cry, is it?' she asked.

Lucy shook her head and the tears kept coming.

'Nothing can be this bad.' Hebe handed her a piece of kitchen roll as Lucy cried even harder. 'Tell me what's wrong so I can help.'

'No one can help.'

'People can always help.' Hebe pushed Lucy's hair back. 'Tell me.'

'Oh God,' Lucy moaned, looking decidedly green about the gills. She rushed to the sink and heaved.

Hebe stroked her back. 'Poor child. Food poisoning again?'

'I'm pregnant.'

Hebe's eyes opened wide. 'What?'

Lucy sniffed and wiped her eyes on the kitchen roll. 'Forget I said anything.'

'Isn't that something to be happy about?'

'No.' The tears began again. 'Not at all. It's Ed's.'

'Damn.'

'Exactly.'

Hebe pulled back. 'It's definitely not anyone else's?'

Lucy laughed. 'You don't have a very high opinion of me, clearly.'

'Who else have you had sex with?'

Lucy blinked. 'No one.'

'Shame. I was rather hoping you were going to say him with the white teeth.'

'Sadly, no.' She pulled the big bird out of the oven and basted it. 'The real problem is, I have no intention of being a mother.'

'No?'

Lucy wrinkled her nose.

'How pregnant are you?'

She shrugged. 'I don't know.'

'Well then, don't let it spoil today. Let's not think about it until after we get through Christmas.' Hebe went to the cupboard and took the marshmallows out. 'What time are they coming?' She looked at the clock on the wall. She didn't recognise it, but it was big and old and suited the room.

'Not until five, thankfully. They're all going to church, then to the pub, followed by a walk.'

'Leaving you to do all this on your own.' Hebe shook her head.

'Not on my own. Gran offered, and I have you.'

'I'm useless. I can't remember how to cook.'

'I'm so sorry.'

'Me too.' She shrugged. 'What about White Teeth? Would he help?'

'White Teeth?' Lucy threw the tea towel over her shoulder.

'The man with Thomas Grylls's eyes.'

'You mean Kit? You think of him as White Teeth?'

'Mr White Teeth.'

Lucy laughed. 'Love it. He'll be here after breakfast.'

'Shame he's not the father.'

Lucy sighed. 'Don't tell anyone about this, Hebe. Promise.'

'Yes, of course.' She must try to remember that this was a secret for now. 'Do remember that babies are miracles. I'm sorry I never had any.' She swallowed. 'But maybe in view of this ...' she pointed to her head, 'it's a good thing.' She laughed and ate a marshmallow. There weren't many left. 'Lucy, can you buy more of these?'

'OK. Though I'm not sure they're very good for you.'

'Doesn't matter now. Might as well enjoy them.'

Hebe walked into the dining room and stopped to look at the big fireplace. There was a knitted stocking resting on the floor. It was familiar. She knew she'd seen it before. Picking it up, she ran her fingers over the stitches. Her mother had made it for her in all her favourite colours. Christmas.

Seventy-One
Hebe

August 2015

'Is this the magical mystery tour?' You look at me as I pull into another tiny lane.

'In a way.' I smile. 'Don't know why I didn't think of it earlier.'

'Think of what?'

'This church. We've been here all summer and haven't visited.'

'Is it important historically?'

I shake my head. Important to *my* history, but to no one else's.

The lane follows the creek, and soon I park the car in front of the church. I breathe deeply. The air is scented with honeysuckle, and the bright red of the fuchsias pops against the burning blue sky.

'What's the significance of this church?'

'It's the one I was baptised in.'

'Ah.'

I turn to you, not sure what your reaction means. You are looking at the creek and I slip into the church without you. I need a moment alone. The atmosphere is cool, and light spills through the windows. I have been here so many times.

'Beautiful.'

I jump, not sure how I didn't hear the heavy door open.

You look up. 'No electric light.' You admire the brass chandeliers. Memories of a Christmas service come to me, but I let them float away. It is not what I want to hold onto. I simply want to remember my mother. And as you touch my arm, you. I want to remember you. I walk to the stone baptismal font. Solid. It speaks of ongoing life, of hope, of faith, none of which I have. I have been so wrong. Made so many terrible decisions. I know you are one of them, but I can't regret you. I think you have always hoped things could be different. But I knew they would never end well.

*

Come live with me, and be my love,
And we will some new pleasures prove.

I raised my glass of champagne and silently toasted you. Your smile told me all. You were proud, and so you should be. You had landed your first full teaching role, at Queen Mary. I was so pleased for you. They would have been foolish not to take you. I smiled. Your own cleverness astounded you sometimes, but it never surprised me. The only thing that surprised me was your love.

Despite everything I had done to discourage you, you were still here – eight years on from that fateful day when you walked into my class. Some of the sharpness of the details was gone, but the feeling remained. Menopause had taken its toll on my memory. My GP said this was normal. But then I wondered if he really listened, or maybe I hadn't told him the truth because I was afraid.

'I was thinking …' you said, reaching across the table and touching my hand.

I resisted the urge to pull away. I saw something, an earnestness in your expression. It worried me.

'Now that I'm fully employed …' You paused and sipped your champagne. Your hand grew sweaty on mine. I looked at your face. What were you about to say that you were worried about? Were you trying to tell me you were leaving me? My chest tightened. I had been waiting for this for years. In fact, I longed for it. It wouldn't take away the guilt, but it would remove the constant reminder. I was powerless to resist you and you knew that. You used it from the start. You knew my love of Thomas Grylls and you played me. I was willingly played.

'I think we should move in together,' you said.

I pulled my hand away. 'No.' I saw your hurt but I could not help it. 'That wouldn't work.'

'Are you ashamed of me still?'

I pressed my lips together, preventing myself from saying yes. I searched for what to say and the gap between us widened.

'I am no longer a boy.' You shook your head.

'No, you are not,' I said, but I was thinking that at twenty-six you were still barely more than one. Yes, you had filled out, but you were so very young.

'Then why?'

'I'm meant to live alone.' That was not a lie. You slept in my flat most nights, but it was still mine.

'We could buy something together.'

I shook my head.

'You still want to keep me your dirty little secret.' You stood up, picked up your backpack and walked out of the door of my flat.

You were right. You were my secret, and that was the only way I could have you in my life. But I had just lost you because of that.

❧ Seventy-Two ❧

Lucy

25 December 2016

Everything was ready. Kit had gone home to change, and Lucy took one last look at the dining room. Even she had to say she had outdone herself, with Kit's help. Without it the table wouldn't be laid and the gravy would have lumps, but it also would have been a Christmas that she spent mostly in tears.

Throughout the day she tormented herself with thoughts of what it would be like if this thing inside her was Kit's. She might actually consider keeping it. After all, it was probably the only chance she would have of having a kid. And as much as she'd sworn over the years that it didn't matter that she couldn't, that it was a good thing as she loved shoes more than children, the thought of this alien, this baby, being Kit's cracked something inside. But she knew it wasn't his. It wasn't the immaculate conception. The alien was Ed's.

Walking up the back stairs to her bedroom, she tried to picture said creature, even though she knew it wasn't a good idea. There was a chance of her bonding with it if she thought about it too much. As far as she knew, she didn't have a maternal bone in her body, but she also hadn't accounted for the hormones and the tears that wouldn't stop. Poor Kit had been assuming it was bumping into Alice that had triggered them.

Well, in a way that was true. Alice had looked great. Gone was the bleached-blonde hair and the nose piercing, and an elegant style had arrived. No more skirts that barely covered anything and tops that were so tight she popped out of them.

No, she had appeared a poised and confident woman. Lucy wasn't sure how and when that had happened, and in a strange way she was sad.

Stripping off her jeans and sweater, she looked for signs of pregnancy on her body. The only thing that felt different was her breasts. They were bigger. There was no sense in dwelling on it, yet her thoughts kept returning to it.

She thought about her mother. She'd done things the right way. Marriage, pregnancy, dysfunction. Her grandmother had done pregnancy, marriage, dysfunction. Lucy could see a pattern emerging. She was going to break it. First, Ed was the father. Her stomach rolled. It didn't like that thought and nor did she. Then there was this thing happening with Kit. She smiled, then frowned. It was probably best if she ended that now. Looking at her family history, it was clear they didn't do well at relationships.

Sitting on the edge of the bed, the thing that surprised her most was how much she wanted a relationship with Kit. She didn't just want to sleep with him. That was certainly there – she was a woman, after all – but for the first time ever she wanted so much more, and it scared the hell out of her.

The reflection in the mirror showed a skinny woman, looking younger than her years. At the moment she really didn't appear much different to the devastated teenager who had sat in this bedroom and cried her eyes out, vowing never to come to Cornwall again. Yet here she was: twenty-nine and about to serve Christmas dinner to her family at Hell House. She sighed.

Throwing on her slinky red evening gown, she was transformed. She looked like her old self, the London girl-about-town. It was cut on the bias and clung in all the right places. She wasn't sure it had ever looked better on her. Sweeping up her hair into a careless knot, she clipped on chunky vintage rhinestone earrings. She debated a necklace, but decided it was too much for a family Christmas meal.

Her skin, as everyone had pointed out, was glowing. She dusted it with a bit of powder, applied mascara, then completed the look with scarlet lipstick. The old femme fatale still existed despite months in exile. As she walked through the hall, she half expected the paparazzi to appear. Instead she found the kitchen empty. Only the range laden with Christmas dinner was there to admire her. How things had changed.

'Lucy, darling.' Her grandmother walked through the dining room door. 'Kit is in charge of the champagne upstairs. Everyone's here.' She kissed her. 'I've never seen you look better. Merry Christmas.'

'Thanks, Gran.' She could say the same about Sarah. The sparkly silver top and black palazzo trousers suited her, as did the gleam in her eye that had arrived with Hugh. 'You look wonderful too.'

'I feel it.' Sarah flashed her left hand in front of Lucy, and there was a stonking great ruby and diamond ring there that Lucy didn't recognise. 'I wanted you to be the first to know. Hugh proposed an hour ago and I accepted.'

Lucy gave her a huge hug.

'It was all rather romantic. He dragged me into the King's Room, where he'd put on Christmas music, then got down on one knee.'

Lucy smiled. She knew well the magic of the King's Room.

'We danced to Sinatra. I'm so happy.'

'I can see it. Where will you tie the knot?'

Sarah laughed. 'We're thinking of something silly like Las Vegas or Gretna Green.'

'I love it – this calls for champagne.'

Her grandmother tucked her arm into Lucy's. 'It does, doesn't it?'

As they climbed the stairs to the first floor, Lucy wondered if anyone would notice if she didn't drink hers. She'd have to be careful or her mother would pick up on it. She missed nothing. No doubt from years of watching for her husband's every need.

Giles went to the head of the table as Lucy had expected. She'd taken time creating festive place markers and she watched him frown. After his jovial toast to the future happiness of her grandmother and Hugh, his mood appeared to head south as he walked about the table looking for his place. She had sandwiched him between Michael's girlfriend and Sarah. Her grandmother knew how to handle him, and judging by the way he looked at Michael's girlfriend, he was beguiled by her charms. Maybe she shouldn't have done that. It felt petty now, but it was too late to change it.

'If you would all take your seats.' She fled back to the kitchen, avoiding his glare. She was definitely not the favourite child, but then she never had been. No, that wasn't true. Maybe when she had been five or six.

She grabbed an apron and was tying it about her waist when Kit came in and took another. They looked as if they had been doing this together for years. A lump balled in her throat. That thought had never appealed to her before, being a couple, being tied to someone else. But right this instant she could think of nothing better.

'You look beautiful,' Kit whispered in her ear as he put the plates, warm from the oven, onto the counter. They had had their starter of caviar and blinis upstairs with the drinks. Lucy's champagne glass, still full, sat by the sink. She thought she'd carried it off. Sarah's news had certainly helped. She did wonder if it might have stolen Michael's thunder, as he'd presented a very long face in the salon.

Looking up from carving the turkey, she smiled. 'You scrub up well.' It was an understatement. Mr White Teeth made her knees weak just looking at him.

'Years of practice.' He smiled, and it was the one she'd seen a hundred times. But now she knew the difference. It was the public smile, the movie star one, and she'd grown to love the real one.

'Red-carpet moments.'

'Indeed.' He made a face.

'You don't enjoy them?'

'They are to be endured. I love the acting, but not everything else associated with it.'

'Fair enough.'

'Shall I bring these through?' He lifted the dishes of cranberry sauce. She nodded, and he leaned in and kissed her before he disappeared.

Lucy continued carving. She had to relax. Everything was fine. So she'd messed up on the seating, but they were all adults. They would cope. She must let it go.

With a little luck, they might make it unscathed through the rest of today and half of tomorrow, then they would all disappear and life could return to normal. She paused with the knife halfway through the breast. Damn. Her normal was probably totally destroyed until she could sort out the unwanted being growing inside her. But she wouldn't think about it any more today.

✳ Seventy-Three ✳

Hebe

25 December 2016

For some reason, all Hebe could think about was a murder mystery from the television. It must be all the evening dress, particularly Lucy's. The bias cut was very thirties, and the colour was Hebe's favourite. It matched her own lipstick.

There was an atmosphere at the table. Giles was grumpy. She looked at Kate. Her sister was on edge. Hebe lifted her glass of the fine claret she had chosen from her cellars.

'I'd like to propose a toast.' All eyes turned to her as Lucy and Kit slipped into their seats. 'First, thank you all for coming to Helwyn House.' Everyone murmured and Hebe pushed on. 'But mostly I want to thank Lucy for being a star. She has kept this place running, looked after me and cooked a beautiful meal. To Lucy, the best of us.'

Giles raised his glass but didn't drink to his daughter. Rage rose in Hebe as she stabbed the turkey leg on her plate. Dear Lucy had remembered that she only liked the dark meat. How could that vile man not love her, not see her for the person she was?

'So tell me, Giles, is the wine not to your taste?' She took another sip. It was perfection. Her mind might be going, but her taste buds still worked. She noticed Lucy staring down the long table at her. She was trying to tell her something, but she didn't know what it was. She felt a kick under the table. Michael must be trying to reach his girlfriend. Such a dull little thing, perfect for him really. She took a deep sip of her wine, waiting for Giles to respond. 'Well, Giles?'

309

'The wine is excellent.' He took a sip. 'You've always had an excellent palate, and this claret proves it.'

Hebe looked into her glass. The wine in the candlelight was the colour of old blood.

'This turkey is wonderful, Lucy,' said Sarah, and Hebe narrowed her gaze.

Giles finished his glass and refilled it from the claret jug in front of him. Hebe loved the jugs; she had found them one weekend away with … She turned her glass in her hands. She couldn't remember.

'Do you like the wine, Giles?'

He squinted at her. 'Yes, Hebe, as I said, it's excellent.'

'Weren't the children adorable this morning?' Michael's girlfriend spoke.

Hebe frowned. 'What children?'

'The ones in church.' She smiled. 'You weren't with us.'

'You didn't ask me.' Hebe watched the girl glance down and play with the sausage on her plate. She filled her own glass again, then looked at Michael, who was staring at his plate. Something was wrong.

'Giles, why didn't you drink to Lucy?'

'Hebe, the wine is wonderful, but I wasn't ready to drink.'

She gazed around the table. Everyone looked odd. Was it something she'd done?

'Do you think the weather will improve for tomorrow?' Kate turned to Hugh. 'It would be lovely to have a walk along the coastal path before we go to Pengarrock for drinks.'

'When are you leaving, Giles?' Hebe cut a roast potato in half. He looked at her, then turned to Sarah. 'I asked a question.' Hebe put her glass down with a thump, and Lucy winced.

'Sooner than I intended,' he said. 'I'm no good at things … things like this. Tomorrow, possibly after breakfast.' He cast a glance at his wife.

'Oh, but it would be a shame not to spend the day here. It's been so long since we've been down, and Tristan did invite us to stop by for drinks.' Kate forced a smile.

Giles scowled. 'I can't bear to be in Hebe's presence since she's lost the plot.'

Lucy stood and began clearing plates, even though people were still eating. Kit was at her side.

'I may be losing my mind, Giles, but at least I haven't paid for another man's child.'

There was a crash behind her, and Michael's girlfriend spluttered out her wine.

'Just what are you saying, Hebe?' Giles's voice was dangerously quiet. Kate was ashen.

'You've had a cuckoo in the nest for twenty-nine years and you never saw it.'

'What the hell?' Giles forced his chair back. Sarah stood and went to Kate, who was shaking.

Hebe turned to see Lucy leaning against the door, whiter than her mother.

'Well at least you won't have to marry a man you despise to give *your* child a father, Lucy.' She smiled. 'Could you pass the wine, Michael?'

Michael looked at her. 'Have you just said what I think you said?'

'Pass the wine? Is that a problem?'

'Oh my God.' Michael put his head in his hands, while Hebe stood and reached for the claret jug. There was no accounting for manners these days.

❊ Seventy-Four ❊

Lucy

25 December 2016

The Christmas pudding was still steaming on the top of the range, there were broken dinner plates in the bin, and life would never be the same again. Kit came in and kissed Lucy's forehead. 'I'm here if you need me.'

'Thanks.' She closed her eyes and let him hold her. This wasn't the reaction she'd expected from him. He'd just found out she was pregnant. But then there was the other bomb that her dear aunt had dropped. Her father wasn't her father.

The kitchen door opened and her mother walked in. Her eyes were red-rimmed and the glow she'd had earlier from the walk and the wine was gone. Her world had shattered as much as Lucy's had in those few moments.

'I'll leave you two.' Kit held her hand for an extra moment, and the look in his eyes said that he was indeed here for her. Stranger still was the thought that she might actually want him to be. In fact it wasn't want, it was need. She closed her eyes for a moment. She needed to forget herself and think of her mother.

'Where do we start?'

Kate looked at the range. 'Perhaps with taking the pudding off the heat. Hebe would be devastated if we burnt her house down.'

'True.' With oven gloves on, Lucy slid the pot of boiling water off the hotplate and lifted the pudding out. It smelled good, the only thing that had tempted her all day, except for bacon this morning.

'You're pregnant.'

She looked down at her stomach. If she hadn't been so un-well, she might not believe it herself. 'Don't worry about it.'

'What do you mean? Was Hebe lying?'

'I don't think she's capable of lying now, which means that Giles Trevillion is not my father.'

Kate looked away.

'Who *is* my father, and why did you marry Giles and not him?'

'I didn't know who your father was until later.' Her mother's voice faded.

Sarah walked through the door. 'Sorry for eavesdropping, but I was partially to blame.'

'No you weren't, you only encouraged me to marry not forced me. And I was happy to be pregnant. I'd always wanted a family, even though you weren't planned.' Lucy's mother took her hand.

'Why did you choose Giles?' Lucy thought of all the infideli-ties her mother had put up with over the years.

Kate shook her head. 'He was the better friend. He made me laugh and I knew he would create a stable home.'

Lucy raised an eyebrow. Her idea of stable and Kate's were obviously very different. 'Why didn't you just get rid of me?' She shoved a strand of hair that had come loose behind her ear. 'Then you wouldn't have had to live this half-life, pandering to … him.'

'You're being unfair. I love him and I would never have got rid of you.' Kate's eyes were filled with tears and she was about to set Lucy off. She was sure her mother's life would have been so much fuller without her. All these years Lucy had known she loved her, but that something wasn't right. Her mother had put up with all Giles's shit because of her.

'Mum, I'm so sorry.'

'You have nothing to be sorry for … I would do it all again.'

'Why?'

'I've had a good life, full of love.' She looked at Lucy's stomach. 'You told Hebe.'

313

Lucy sighed. 'She found me in tears this morning.'

'Ed's?'

'Yes.' She shook her head. 'Not that it matters. I'm not keeping it.'

Both Kate and Sarah looked at her as if she'd announced she was jumping off the Shard.

'Are you sure?'

'Absolutely. I'm a woman without a job and with no fixed abode. That's not a good starting point.'

'What about that darling man who adores you?' asked Sarah.

Lucy frowned. 'You mean the Hollywood movie star?' She smiled, she couldn't help it. 'He is lovely, but what on earth would make you think he would want to raise another man's child? Anyway, I have no intention of marrying. It ties you down, and ...' She stopped, seeing her mother's face, and held out a hand to her. 'I'm sorry, Mum. I know you thought you were doing the right thing, but seriously, look at the life you've had.'

'Only the people in a marriage can see what it is. Giles is a good man.'

Lucy shook her head. He might have apologised for Alice, but that didn't suddenly make everything right.

'I can see it on your face,' her mother said. 'I know about Alice.'

Lucy gasped.

'I've known since it happened. Not that your father said anything until recently.'

'How can you forgive that?'

Kate gave a small laugh. 'Those without sin ...'

Lucy bit her tongue. There was so much she could say. 'Who is my real father?'

Her mother turned to look at her grandmother. Lucy leaned against the counter, waiting.

'Frank Hays.'

She blinked. 'Frank Hays, isn't he the head of the Communist Party?'

Mum nodded, and Lucy laughed out loud. 'The cuckoo in

the nest of the staunchest supporter of the Conservative Party ever to have lived is actually the offspring of a rabid communist.' Her mind leapt to a thousand scenarios. 'How ever did you meet him? Was it a one-night stand?'

'No, it wasn't. We studied history together.' She turned away. 'I loved him.'

Lucy opened her mouth, then shut it again. The growl of a car engine filled the air, and it was clear that Giles had left the building. She looked at her mother.

'What are you going to do?'

'Nothing tonight. Is there a spare bed in the house?'

She nodded. Bedrooms they had.

'Darling, don't rush to any decisions.' Her grandmother began covering the uneaten food. 'I know it's that vile man's child, but it is a child. Don't rush.'

'I can't. I have an appointment for a scan on the sixth.'

Kate hugged her. 'Time to think things through, and you know, it may—'

'Don't.' Lucy cut her off. She had a little voice of her own saying that, and she didn't need to add to it.

'Go and lie down.' Her grandmother handed Kate a tea towel. 'But first find that dishy man and give him a hug. He's been an absolute star and it's not even his family.'

'True.' Kit had been a star in so many ways.

❊ Seventy-Five ❊
Hebe

25 December 2016

Hebe sat at her desk. She knew things weren't good, but she couldn't remember why. Christmas could be a problem. Undercooked birds, soggy potatoes ... but this was something more. She unlocked the bottom drawer and pulled out a photo album. Flipping through it, she came to a picture of herself on her mother's lap, holding the knitted Christmas sock. Both of them were smiling. Her father must have taken the photo, but she wasn't sure. Her mother was so beautiful. She put the album away and pulled out her journal.

The birth of our Lord is celebrated
Breakfast - stollen bread, warm from the oven, but only
instant coffee, because Lucy is pregnant.

Hebe stopped to think about this. It was a good thing, even if it was that weasel's child. Any child of Lucy's would be lovely.

Dinner - caviar and blinis with vintage champagne.
Sarah is engaged to Hugh. She was happy. Her eyes
shone.
Turkey, stuffing, sausages.

What else was there? She couldn't remember. She went through the pages to see if Lucy had written down the menu for her. She had been bending over backwards to make things easier. It had helped.

316

There was no menu, but a photo fell out. It was Hebe and ... him. In Scotland. Christmas Day. They had both escaped from their families. They couldn't share their love with the world, for it was wrong, so very wrong.

'Hebe, are you OK?' Lucy walked into the room.

Hebe shook her head and then blew her nose. She wasn't sure why she was crying.

'Who is that in the picture with you?'

'My love.'

'Does he have a name?'

'I don't remember.' And she couldn't.

'Oh.' Lucy spoke to her like she was a child. She felt like one. 'You've had a long day. Shall I help you get undressed and into bed?'

'Yes please.'

Hebe stood and followed Lucy into the bathroom. She brushed her teeth while Lucy took out a nightgown.

'I'm tired,' she said as she slipped out of her dress and Lucy put the nightgown over her head.

'Me too.' Lucy yawned.

'Thank you.'

'A pleasure.'

'No, thank you for everything.' She went to her top drawer and pulled out the present. She had forgotten it earlier. 'This is for you.' She held it out.

Lucy frowned. 'For me?'

Hebe nodded, waiting.

Lucy took it from her and slowly undid the bow, then the paper. 'You didn't have to get me anything.'

'I didn't; in a way, the house did.'

Lucy looked up from the box. 'Now I'm really confused.'

'The man found it.'

'Do you mean Kit?'

'Yes.'

As Lucy lifted away the tissue, the gems caught the light. 'Oh Hebe, this is beautiful, and far too lovely for me.'

'Not at all. Open it.'

Lucy released the catch on the locket, then gasped. She looked at Hebe, then down at the paintings. 'Is this Thomas and Lucia?'

'Yes.'

'I see. Don't you think it should be in a museum?'

Hebe shook her head. 'No.' She walked to the bed and sat down. 'Thomas and Lucia are together, just as you and Kit should be.'

Lucy snuffled, and Hebe saw the tears in her eyes as Hebe slid between the cool sheets. She was so very weary.

'Sleep well, Hebe.'

'Can you put that picture by the bed?'

'Of course.' Lucy propped it up against the lamp. 'Light on or off?'

'On, for now.'

'OK, and thank you again for the beautiful present.'

Hebe stared at the picture, remembering love, remembering what it felt like while she could. She looked up as Lucy pulled the door closed. 'Lucy.'

'Yes?'

'I'm so pleased about your baby.' She smiled. 'I wish I had had one.'

'I'm not keeping it, Hebe.'

'Why not?'

'A child needs love.'

'Yes, it does, and you have so much love to give it.'

Lucy came back in and kissed her forehead, proving Hebe's point. 'Sleep well, Hebe.'

She nodded and closed her eyes, sneaking one last glance at the photo. Love.

✳ Seventy-Six ✳
Lucy

25 December 2016

Lucy closed the door to Hebe's room. Clutching the box containing the beautiful locket, she thought about Hebe's photograph, and what her aunt had said about love.

Everything was a mess. Lucy's secret was out. Her mother's secret was out. And poor Hebe had no idea what she'd done.

The lights were still on in the salon. So much for her idea of singing Christmas carols in the King's Room after dinner. That delusion of happy families had gone in a flash. From the salon she looked across the courtyard to the windows of the King's Room. The fairy lights glistened and she remembered the joy she'd felt dancing in Kit's arms. Now that the world, or at least her family and Kit, knew about the pregnancy, there was no joy or privacy. Nor was there any peace. Her poor mother.

She walked through the salon and down the corridor, stopping in front of the north bedroom. She thought about Giles, and felt an unexpected twinge of sympathy for him. No one deserved to hear what he had, and certainly not that way.

The sad thing was that there was nothing she could do to help either of them, though she wanted to. Was her mother right not to go and talk to him tonight? Wouldn't it be better to try and explain? Lucy was certainly no expert when it came to relationships. None of hers had lasted any length, except for the one with Ed, and that hadn't exactly been a shining example. She laughed out loud. What a fool she'd been thinking that a relationship without commitment was the ideal answer.

Her mother had chosen her father because he was a friend

and had been caring. He'd made her laugh. Yet she'd never told him the truth about Lucy. They'd both kept huge secrets from each other. What did Lucy know? Nothing. She knew nothing at all.

If she had any signal, she would send Michael a text. At least he was with her father, if she could still call him that. God knows what Michael's girlfriend thought of the family. If Michael had been about to propose or tell them of a forthcoming wedding, she must be having second thoughts.

Lucy stopped in the doorway to the King's Room. Kit was sitting in the old armchair she had moved in there.

'Hi.' He stood.

'Hello.'

'She remembered to give it to you.' His smile hitched as he walked towards her. Her breath caught.

She looked at her hand. 'Yes.'

He stopped just beside her. 'Have you tried it on?'

'Not sure I should. It belongs in a museum.'

'She wanted you to have it.'

'So she said.' She opened the box and the jewels reflected the lights on the tree.

'You look like Lucia.'

'You look like Thomas.'

He lifted the locket out of the box and held the black velvet ribbon ready. She turned, and he placed it round her neck. The locket was cold, and she shivered. The touch of his fingers as he tied the knot stopped her heart, then started it again. He slid his hands over her shoulders and down her arms until he reached her hands. He held them, resting his lips against the base of her neck. She couldn't move. She didn't want to.

The lights on the tree reflected in the old glass of the windows, and Lucy saw the image of them together, perfect. Beautiful even. Just like the couple pictured in the locket about her neck. The bias cut of her gown caught the slight swell of her stomach. She and Kit were destined to be apart, just like Thomas and Lucia. A ball the size of the clove-studded oranges she'd placed about the room lodged in her throat. She stepped away from him.

'Thank you ... for everything.' She would not cry, but just in case, she fled the room as if the ghost of Thomas Grylls was chasing her.

Seventy-Seven

Hebe

26 December 2016

Hebe pulled the shawl tight around her shoulders. The house was in darkness but still scented with food. Her stomach rumbled and she remembered that they hadn't eaten the Christmas pudding. It was always the best part of the feast.

The wind had picked up and it sang through the gaps in the window frames. It had always sounded to her as if Thomas was calling Lucia's name. She stopped halfway down the stairs, remembering that they were together and had been close beside each other for hundreds of years. All was as it should be. Their fate was finally known and she could rest.

On the bottom step, she tried to remember why she was down there, but couldn't. Through the closed dining room door she heard the clock chime midnight. The witching hour. Not a good time to be wandering.

She went back upstairs into her room. Sleep had left her. Switching on the light by the bed, she saw the photo. Why was it there? Why had she kept a picture of a student? She walked to the desk and dropped it in the bin. There were things she still hadn't done, but she was so tired now. Everything was harder, even holding a pen. Nonetheless, she would write until she couldn't.

The feast of St Stephen, the first Christian martyr
Change is in the air. It's as if candles have been
extinguished. In fact they have. I smell it. The
atmosphere is dense, and breathing is hard. This is

because my heart is heavy. I have done something wrong. No, I have done many things wrong, but I can't find them in my brain. Yet there is one thing I have done right. I have loved.

Her vision was going and she put her pen down. Maybe her end was close.

⁂ Seventy-Eight ⁂
Hebe

August 2015

We leave the church and I turn up the steps towards the graveyard. Most of the stones are upright, but not all. The warmth of the sun doesn't reach my heart as I walk by instinct to my mother's grave. My father is buried here too. But it's not him I want to see. I've left it too long to come and visit.

You are with me, but you sense that I do not want to speak. I run my fingers over my mother's name.

'So young,' I hear you say. She was, and I am lucky that I have had many more years. I close my eyes to try and pray, or to talk to my mother. But no words come. Anger bubbles and I run down the steps to the water's edge.

I don't look back for you. I don't look back to the church. Once I dreamed of marrying there in the candlelight, but it was a hopeless dream. You wrap your arms around me and I allow myself to cry.

'Tis not the bodies marry, but the minds
Which he in her angelic finds.

My need for you absorbed my thoughts. I should be looking at the letters of Prince Rupert, but all I could see in front of me was you. As I twisted the fountain pen in my fingers, I wondered if I would want you so much if I did not admire your mind. It was a clever trap. There was no piece of information that I set in front of it that it did not devour. I know that you wanted me for my brain too. I felt my face flush, remembering this

324

morning and last night. My brain was never in the equation. Except you seduced it with poetry. You knew my weakness for Donne. His words were never the same at each new reading.

I looked up to see you across the room. You were smiling as you worked. Your gaze met mine and we both looked away. I knew what you were thinking. I glanced at my watch. I had spent enough time with dead people. Right now, I needed the living.

✳ Seventy-Nine ✳
Lucy

26 December 2016

The three most important women in Lucy's life sat around the kitchen table as she stood outside in the hall. She heard her name. Did she really want to be the topic of conversation again? She walked through the door and all eyes turned to her.

'Morning, darling. Sleep well?' Her mum peered over the rim of her cup.

'No, you?'

Kate shook her head.

'Have you spoken to him?' Lucy sank into a chair.

'I've spoken to Michael. Giles is in bed with a stinking hangover.'

'Ouch.'

'How are you feeling?' She looked at Lucy's stomach.

'Other than nauseous, fine.'

'Will you tell Ed?' Hebe stood.

'No, I don't want him involved in any way.' She sighed. Everything had seemed somehow manageable when she and the doctor were the only people who knew. With Hebe knowing, it was possible that other people would find out. 'It's vital that this stays between us.'

'What about your ... Giles? And Michael and his girlfriend?' Hebe asked, playing with a fork on the table.

Sarah sighed. 'Let's hope they put it down to your imagination.'

'But I didn't make it up.' Hebe looked about the room, picking up an apron.

Standing up, Lucy put an arm around her aunt's shoulders. 'That's true, but they don't know that, and it's important that they don't find out.'

'OK,' Hebe said, then crumpled into a heap on the kitchen floor.

Lucy put her into the recovery position while Sarah called 999 and Kate raced upstairs to find Hugh.

As she sat in the A&E waiting room, Lucy's phone beeped. She wasn't going to look, but then she saw the number. Rory Crown. She'd totally forgotten him.

'Is it important?' Kate was wringing her hands, while Hugh was having a chat with the doctors.

'Yes, somehow I think it is. I'll be back in a moment.'

Outside, the air was cold and clear. It was a beautiful Boxing Day. Perfect for a long walk and leftovers, not for being here. She dialled Rory's number.

'Lucy? I just landed. How is she?'

Lucy looked heavenward and thought hard about what to say. How would she feel if she were him? Hebe had loved him once.

'We're at Treliske Hospital. Hebe passed out and hasn't regained consciousness. We should know more later.'

'I'm at the airport. I'll rent a car and be there as quickly as I can.'

'Is that wise?' She frowned.

'No, but I have to see her.'

Running her fingers through her hair, she thought of Hebe being taken away in the ambulance. 'She's stable. I'll text you once I hear something.'

'I should be down by midnight.'

She looked at her watch. 'They won't let you see her then.'

'I know.' He sighed.

She searched the clear sky for answers. 'Why don't you take the first train in the morning? You'll have had some rest and be better able to cope.'

'But—'

'Look, things shouldn't change overnight. With some sleep, you're more likely to be able to deal with whatever has happened.'

'I guess.'

'Send me a text telling me which train you are on and I'll collect you from the station.'

'OK ... and thanks.'

She walked back inside, hoping that she had done the right thing. She had no idea what was happening, but the last thing they needed was a jet-lagged man on the road.

Everyone was gathered around Hugh.

'Lucy, there you are.' He smiled. 'Hebe's still unconscious. They think she's had a stroke. We'll know more in the morning.'

'She'll come back to us, won't she?' She looked at his face, kind and serious.

'I hope so, but without knowing more, I can't say.'

She tried to swallow and couldn't. The thought of her world without Hebe wasn't bearable, but whether she was ready or not, it was out of their hands.

Lucy sat at Hebe's desk. Taking her aunt's necklace with the key on it, she unlocked the drawers. A quick peek inside revealed that everything was beautifully organised.

She began with the bottom one, where she found a photo album filled with pictures of Hebe as a baby and young child. Her mother, Frances, was a stunning woman with dark hair, and eyes that flirted with the camera. In one picture, Hebe toddled along a beach laughing. The final photo in the album had been taken at Christmas. Hebe was sitting on her mother's lap holding a sock. Lucy had seen that sock yesterday morning.

'Frances was a beautiful woman.' Sarah entered the room and perched on the arm of the chair.

Lucy peered up at her. 'You put the sock out for Hebe.'

Gran nodded. 'I found it when I was clearing out before Christmas.'

'Did she remember it?'

'Oh yes.' Sarah smiled as she touched the photo album. 'I've not seen this before.'

'No?'

'Hebe and I found it.' Kate walked in, carrying a glass of whisky.

'Where? When?' Sarah stood.

'When Dad died.'

Her grandmother frowned. 'You never said.'

'Remember how you couldn't bear to clear his things out, so Hebe and I did?'

She nodded.

'Well, we found the album and some letters.'

'Letters?'

Kate nodded. 'Hebe swore me to secrecy, but I think the time for that is past.'

'Dear God, what did they say?'

'There was one that Frances had written to Hebe, which Dad hadn't given her, and letters between the two of them.' Lucy saw Sarah swallow. 'Some of them were love letters ... right up to the end.'

'Oh no.' Sarah's hand flew to her mouth.

Kate nodded and took a deep breath. 'They were still in love, but Frances knew what was ahead. Her mother and grandmother and her aunt had all died young.'

Sarah's face lost all colour. 'You mean that Richard hadn't fallen for me?'

'I'm not sure about that.' Kate sipped her whisky. 'They also wanted to hide Frances's illness from Hebe until she was older and could understand.'

'That makes no sense. Richard didn't want Hebe to know at all. He told her that her mother had died of pneumonia.'

'That was what she believed until she found the letters.'

'So Hebe was how old when she found out the truth about her mother's death?'

'Twenty-four.' Her mother swallowed. 'It was then that she decided never to marry or have children.'

Sarah closed her eyes for a moment. 'She never said anything.' She looked at Kate. 'You never said anything either.'

'She made me promise not to talk about it.'

Sarah shook her head slowly. 'It explains so much.'

'That was when she began going to Cornwall regularly. Do you remember?'

'I do. She bought a car with money I'd given her from your father.'

'That was when she bought the portrait.'

'Thomas Grylls?'

'Yes. She swore to me that he would be the only man she would ever love. Knowing the truth about her mother's death changed her.' Kate sighed. 'I'd hoped when there'd been no sign of the illness by middle age that she wouldn't be affected.'

'I need a drink.' Sarah looked at Lucy. 'Do you want one?'

Lucy smiled. 'It sounds like a wonderful idea, but my stomach is telling me no.'

'Funny how the body takes over so quickly to protect the life inside.' Her mother smiled.

'That is so not helpful.' Lucy glared at her.

'Sorry.'

Her grandmother gave her a hug. 'I'll leave you two.'

Lucy watched Sarah walk to the salon, then turned to her mother. 'Are you OK?'

'Strangely, yes.' She gave a short laugh. 'At least it's out in the open.'

'And have you spoken to Dad?'

'I did, and we have a great deal more to talk about.' She looked at the whisky in her glass. 'But we *will* talk. He knows I didn't deliberately set out to deceive him.'

'You didn't?'

'No, I didn't know you weren't his until you were about four and I saw Frank again. You have his ears.'

'Oh.' Lucy touched her ear with a shaky hand.

'And by then I'd had Michael and we were a family. Still are.' She gave Lucy that look.

'Oh Mum. I'm so sorry I did this to you.'

'Darling, you didn't do anything. I chose my own path because I loved you from the moment I knew you were there.'

'Don't.' Lucy stood up.

'But you need to know why you exist.'

'I exist because you shagged Frank, who was obviously hot back in the day.' Lucy wrinkled her nose. 'But I still don't understand why you didn't choose him?'

'I was scared. He hated everything I'd grown up with and believed I wanted in life, while Giles represented everything I knew.' Kate sighed. 'Despite how it looks, I chose the right path.'

'How? You gave up your education.'

'So did you.'

Lucy swallowed. 'I know. I was so angry.' She gave her mother a sideways glance.

'Rightly so.'

'Did you ever confront him about Alice?'

Kate shook her head. 'There was no point. It was over, and sometimes having the answers doesn't make something more bearable.'

'He said sorry to me.'

She stroked Lucy's hand. 'I'm glad.'

'Me too.'

'He did ask after you.'

'Did he?' Lucy turned away from the intensity of her gaze.

'He loves you.'

She took a deep breath. 'Yes.' They had lost many years, but she could remember when things were good. Maybe they could be again. 'Has something else changed between you and Dad?'

Her mother gave her a funny look.

'For years you seemed to live separate lives, but suddenly, maybe because of the Ed scandal, you began acting like a couple.'

A sad smile slipped across her mother's mouth. 'I've had a cancer scare.'

'What?' Lucy stepped back. 'You didn't say.'

'It happened too quickly. A funny mole turned out to be a malignant melanoma.'

'Mum.'

'It's OK. They took it all out and there is no sign of it having spread.'

'But you never said.'

'No.' She shook her head. 'You were away on some shoot or other, and by the time you'd returned, we knew.'

'Still …'

'I'm sorry we didn't tell you, but it did make your father and me realise how important we are to each other.'

'Oh.' Lucy sank into a chair.

Her mother rubbed her back, bringing back memories of her doing the same thing when Lucy was upset as a child. Then she kissed the top of Lucy's head and left to refill her glass.

Lucy turned back to Hebe's desk. In the bin she saw the photo from the other night. Why had Hebe thrown it out? Were there any more surprises in there, and what would happen tomorrow when this Rory Crown arrived?

❋ Eighty ❋
Hebe

August 2015

The dual carriageway stretches out in front of me and I'm almost lulled to sleep. We will soon be leaving Cornwall, and the magic will leave my soul as we cross the Tamar. I turn and look at you. This summer with you has been time out of time. Should we have done it sooner? Would I have done it if I hadn't known that my days were numbered?

I reach out and rub the back of your neck as the sign announces that we have arrived in Devon. You smile distractedly at me. Your thoughts have taken you elsewhere. Away from me and away from Cornwall. I turn and look over my shoulder. My heart is back there, but it is also here with you.

*

Tears drowned one hundred, and sighs blew out two;
A thousand, I did neither think, nor do,
Or not divide, all being one thought of you;
Or, in a thousand more, forgot that too.
Yet call not this, long life, but think that I
Am, by being dead, immortal; can ghosts die?

This morning I woke beside you and felt the ghosts of my past lying here with us. The darker one was the me that had allowed you in. She smiled at me, saying, 'You have been loved,' but then the other ghost, of a paler shade, said, 'See what you have denied him. His youth and any possible children. And worst of all, you haven't given him all of you. No, you have held back the most important part.'

I took a deep breath. Both were right, and I was wrong. This relationship was never going to work out. You filled me physically and challenged me mentally; you were my world. But now, as I looked at you, I wondered where you fitted into my life. We no longer talked of books, of love or philosophy. You spoke nothing but staid dialogue written from routine. Did you love me still? And if you did, then why? I had always wondered why you loved me. Or was it now *had* loved me?

❋ Eighty-One ❋
Lucy

27 December 2016

Lucy was late to the station. She parked, then raced inside. There was no one there except a good-looking man about her own age. She couldn't place him. Pulling out her phone to check if Rory Crown had missed his train, she noticed that the man bore a striking resemblance to the portrait of Thomas Grylls. In fact he could be Kit's younger brother, though dark where Kit was fair. Maybe Thomas had spread himself about a bit more than anyone had recorded.

'Hi, Lucy?'

She jumped, wondering if he was someone she had known in the past, though surely she would have remembered him. He was too good-looking to forget. 'Er, hello.'

'How is she?'

Her eyes widened. 'Rory?'

'Yes.'

'Right.' Lucy swallowed, trying to disguise her shock. 'She's stable. Awake but not speaking.'

He nodded and followed her to the car. 'Prognosis?'

She glanced at him as they climbed inside. 'They aren't saying much, to be honest.'

'OK.'

'Before we get to the hospital, you need to know that I haven't told the rest of the family about you arriving because—'

'Because you don't know enough about me and Hebe.'

She nodded.

'Fair point. What do you want to know?'

There were a million things, the first being: how? But she knew that was rude and wrong. 'Later. We're not far from the hospital.' She took a breath. 'She may not know you.'

His face fell.

'She certainly didn't know your name.'

'To be honest, she always struggled with that.'

'Really?'

'Yes.'

She parked the car and bought a ticket. She knew that her mother and grandmother were at Hebe's bedside. Hugh would be pacing the halls and asking all the right questions when necessary. She and Rory walked through to the ward in silence. She smiled at the nurse at the desk while clocking Hugh chatting with someone further down the hall.

Kate and Sarah looked up at the sound of footsteps.

'How is she?' Lucy asked, but neither of them responded. They were staring at the man at her side.

From the moment she'd met him, Lucy had been wondering how she was going to deal with this situation. She wouldn't sugar-coat it. They all had enough to deal with at present. She'd use his own words.

'This is Rory Crown, Hebe's lover.'

They continued to stare. Rory didn't appear to notice. He sat down beside the bed and picked up Hebe's hand, then held it to his cheek. Hebe opened her eyes and looked at him, but there was no recognition.

'Let's give them some time alone,' Lucy said. Kate and Sarah looked at each other, then rose from their chairs and followed her into the corridor.

'Darling, he's young enough to be her son.' Kate glanced back into the room. 'Are you sure he's for real?'

Lucy watched Rory stroking Hebe's hand and knew he was for real.

'He looks just like the portrait,' Sarah said, glancing at Hugh, who was walking their way. 'What do you know about him?'

'Not a lot,' Lucy paused, looking into the room. Rory was

talking to Hebe, stroking her face and smoothing her hair. 'But take a look.'

Sarah covered her mouth with her hand and Lucy knew how she felt.

'I've spoken with the doctors.' Hugh stood beside them and looked in at Hebe. He raised an eyebrow.

'He's Hebe's lover, Rory Crown,' Lucy told him.

He shook his head. 'The women in this family are incorrigible,' he smiled, 'and wonderful.'

Sarah took his hand and squeezed it.

'Hebe is stable enough to go home if we can look after her.'

'What will that mean?'

'At the moment, it means doing everything. Basically, nursing around the clock.'

'Does this mean it's the end?'

Hugh nodded. 'She might return to us for a bit.' He waved his hand. 'But it's in the lap of the gods, and if you bring her home, you'll need help. Can she afford it?'

'Yes.' All eyes turned to Lucy. 'I found her bank statements in her desk. She's not short of money.'

'That's good, but it'll be tricky to access it.'

Lucy nodded. 'I think I can do that, but I need to check with her lawyer.'

'Why would you think that?'

'Hebe had me sign a bunch of papers. I didn't pay too much attention at the time as there were other things on my mind, but I think one of them might have been a power of attorney.'

Rory joined them. 'What's the latest?'

She swallowed. 'Not good, in fact totally awful.'

He nodded, and she wished she'd been a little less honest. 'Where has she been living?'

'Helwyn House.'

'The Helwyn House that belonged to Thomas Grylls?'

'Yes, the same.'

'She must have loved that.' He smiled.

A nurse approached them. 'Have you decided how you want to proceed?'

337

'We'll need to get things set up, but we would like to bring her home.' Kate looked at everyone, and they all nodded. 'Is there some sort of list of what we'll need?'

'Yes, and there are people who can help, too. I'll put you in touch with them.' Kate followed the nurse, and Lucy turned to the others.

'Let's hope the solicitor is working this week.'

'We can cover the costs for a short stretch.' Sarah looked at Hugh, who nodded. 'And of course we'll stay to help.'

'May I stay too?' Rory asked.

'Yes. I think we'll need all the help we can find.' Lucy looked through to her aunt in the bed. It didn't really look like her.

'Thank you.' Rory returned to Hebe's bedside, taking her hand in his again. Lucy wished she'd been able to contact him sooner.

❊ Eighty-Two ❊
Hebe

28 December 2016

Hebe opened her eyes and wrinkled her nose. She couldn't see very well, but she knew she wasn't at home. It didn't smell right, and she could hear the beep of a machine. She didn't want to be here.

A person sat beside the bed. It wasn't Lucy. It was a man. She tried to focus, but it didn't work. Closing her eyes again, all she knew was that she wanted to be in Helwyn House. Not here.

Another person entered the room.

'How is she?' The woman adjusted the pillow under her head.

'She opened her eyes a moment ago but immediately closed them.' There was something about the man's voice that stirred a memory.

'Hebe?' The woman picked up her hand and held her wrist. 'Hebe, I'm just going to take your pulse.' The woman moved around her and the man beside her remained. 'OK, that's all done. Isn't it wonderful that you've got this nice young man to keep you company?'

Young man. She took a deep breath. Young man, her young man. That wasn't possible.

Eighty-Three
Lucy

28 December 2016

Lucy scanned the bar at the Shipwrights, hoping to see Kit. She hadn't heard from him since Christmas Day, and she couldn't blame him. She hoped the silence was to give them space, but it was more likely that he was running for his life away from a family that was clearly contaminated. Why on earth would he choose to be involved with someone who was pregnant with another man's child and whose father wasn't actually her father? Any sane person would avoid the situation. Lucy would if she could. Yet looking at her mother, her grandmother and Hugh as they went to the table, she was thankful for them.

Coming back from the hospital, none of them had felt like cooking, so dinner at the pub was the answer. As Lucy waited for Cadan to finish taking someone else's order, she could see her mum with her tablet, doing research.

'What can I get you?' Cadan smiled.

'A bottle of the Cabernet Sauvignon and a jug of tap water, please.'

'Would that be three or four glasses?' He winked. 'I hear congratulations are in order.'

'You what?'

'Well, it's not exactly a secret, is it?'

She opened her mouth, then shut it again as he pointed to the table behind her where today's paper was lying. *Posh totty pregnant with MP's love child.* Her legs wobbled. How had that happened?

'You OK? Silly question.' He was around the bar and helping her into a seat, then pushing her head between her knees. Hugh was at her side before she was allowed to sit up.

'What happened?' he asked.

She pointed. 'This is not what I need right now.'

'Oh dear.' Her grandmother picked up the paper, which only revealed another one below it. 'Who could have done this? Only a few people knew.'

'Well, it was the talk of the pub on Boxing Day, when your father was here with Michael.'

Lucy's heart stopped. 'Who else was in the pub?'

'Oh, you know, the usual suspects.' Cadan shrugged.

'Alice?'

He nodded.

'That explains it.' She put her head in her hands.

'Oh darling.' Her mother hugged her as she stood.

Lucy needed air, cool fresh air that smelled of the sea. She grabbed her coat and walked out of the door. She hadn't a clue how she was going to live her life with the headlines she'd left behind. It had been bad enough when the scandal first broke. But now it was so much worse, and there was no way to erase the problem.

It was a long, dark walk back to Hell House. Lucy had sent a text so they wouldn't be worried. But she was. Darkness closed around her, and rather than waste her phone battery on the feeble torchlight, she stumbled along the road trying desperately to think. She needed to focus on Hebe and her needs, not on the crisis that had been created by her own stupidity. Now the nation knew she was pregnant with Ed's child. Strangely, she hadn't had a text or a call from him in ages, for which she was grateful. But that would most likely change soon.

Out in the bay she could see the lights on the tankers. One even had a Christmas tree. The world looked peaceful, but it wasn't. Her phone beeped. She almost couldn't bear to open it in case it was Ed. But it was Kit. He must have seen the papers.

Are you OK?

341

She stopped and looked up at the clear sky. Above her stretched the vast sweep of the Milky Way. She was small, so very small. She was simply a woman who had made mistakes. There were thousands like her on this planet. Fortunately for most of them, though, their mistakes hadn't been spread across the front page of the papers. That didn't make Lucy's mistakes any worse, just more public. Yet she knew that no matter how bad the things were that she'd done, she had a mother and a grandmother who loved her. Somehow she'd survive this.

She continued down into St Anthony. The lights were on in the farmhouse and she thought of Kit's text. She could use the loo and, more importantly, see a friendly face. At least she hoped it would be friendly. Opening the gate, the thought crossed her mind that he might not want to see her. Well, her bladder wouldn't let her dwell on that.

The door opened almost as soon as she tapped.

'Lucy. I've been worried.'

'Thanks. May I use your loo?'

'Of course. Cocoa?'

'Please.' She dashed to the bathroom, wondering how he knew exactly what she needed.

Heading back to the sitting room, she saw *The Times* open on the table. She'd made the second page but thankfully not the main headline.

Kit studied her as he handed her a steaming mug. 'How's Hebe?'

'Awake but not speaking.' She blew on the cocoa. 'We don't know if she can do much, or if she even wants to, but we are bringing her home.'

'She'll be happier in Helwyn House.'

'True.'

'Let me know what I can do.'

'Thank you.' She looked up at him and then down at the mug.

'How are you feeling?'

'Um. OK, all things considered.'

'Good.'

342

There were books in neat piles. She scanned the titles, impressed with the variety. 'Are these all yours?'

He smiled. 'Most, but some are my father's.'

'Is it a way to have him with you?' She slid her hand across the nearest book.

'Yes.' He stood and picked one up. 'It's like he's here in his pencil marks on the page.'

She reached out and grabbed his hand. He knelt beside her. 'I'm sorry.'

She frowned. 'About what?'

'That you've hit the papers again.'

She swallowed. 'Not ideal.'

'You didn't need it, now or ever.' He stroked her cheek. 'I have a confession to make.'

She put the cocoa down. 'Yes?'

'You're bound to find out sooner or later.'

Was this why he had stayed away? She'd assumed it was Alice who had broken the story. He was so close she could see the flecks of colour in his irises. Yellow, green, blue.

'I've been working with Hebe.'

She drew her brows together. This wasn't a secret.

'You know the books we both love?'

'The H. J. Bowden books? The ones about Thomas Grylls?'

'Those.' A smile hovered on his mouth.

'What about them?'

'Your aunt is H. J. Bowden.'

'No!' She shook her head. 'She's trashed the books every time I've mentioned them.'

He nodded. 'A good technique if you need to keep your identity hidden.'

'But why? They're wonderful, best-sellers loved by millions.'

'But if you are a professor of history ... a serious academic ...' He tucked a strand of hair behind her ear.

'Ah.' She looked down at his hand in hers, wondering if he would draw it away. 'But what do you have to do with it?'

He smiled. 'I found her struggling to write one day, and from that point on we worked together to finish the final book.'

'You've finished it?'

'Yes, on Christmas Eve, and sent it off.'

'So her work is done.'

He nodded.

'I see.' She looked at him.

'Sorry.'

She shook her head. It wasn't his fault. 'I'm grateful. I'm sure that was troubling her.'

He stood and pulled her into his arms. 'Are you really OK?'

'No.' For once she didn't have to lie or put on a brave face. Honesty was something that had been missing in her life for a very long time.

'I'm here.'

'Thank you.' She yawned, and he laughed.

'Let me give you a lift home.'

'Thank you.'

He kissed her forehead, and she was relieved that she knew where they stood. He was her friend and maybe she needed that more than anything else. Part of her longed for something more, but she knew that this was the safer option.

❊ Eighty-Four ❊
Lucy

29 December 2016

They turned through Manaccan. The sun was trying to appear but the clouds were winning. Hebe was in the passenger seat and Rory in the back. Silence surrounded them and it weighed heavily on Lucy. She fought the urge to prattle on about anything to fill the void. Though Hebe was with them, it was also like she wasn't. She hadn't said a word and might not do so again. That frightened Lucy, and sadness welled up, killing some of the joy of bringing her home. Of course she knew the damn pregnancy was playing havoc with her hormones. The sooner the alien was removed and she took control again, the better.

The creek appeared, with the mudflats glistening in the reluctant sun. Lucy spied a lone heron picking its way to the bank as she turned through the gates.

'How's the house?'

Lucy slammed on the brakes and looked at her aunt. The doctors had said that the Alzheimer's and the strokes were working together, taking Hebe from them. She could move, but not well, yet she had fed herself this morning. Rory had coped calmly with the assumption of staff at the hospital that he was her nephew. They kept staring at Lucy, but who could blame them. She was front-page news again today as another scandal broke with a Tory MP and comparisons were made with her situation.

'Are you OK, Lucy?' Hebe frowned.

'Yes, the house is good, and happy with Mum, Gran and Hugh all in residence.'

'What about … him?'

'Kit?' Lucy looked over her shoulder at Rory.

'Yes, him, White Teeth.'

'He's well.' She put the car back into motion.

'The builder?'

'We won't see Fred until the third of January.'

'The feast of St Genevieve, virgin.'

'What?' Lucy frowned, then remembered that Hebe began each entry in her diary with the saint of the day. It seemed odd. 'Hebe, how do you know that?'

'Know what?'

Lucy glanced at her. Hebe was focused on Hell House. It still looked festive in these quiet days between Christmas and New Year. In the past, she had always felt this time was the disappointing middle of the holiday sandwich, but right now it was what she needed. Quiet.

She pulled the car right up to the loggia. 'Welcome home, Hebe.'

'Home.' Hebe smiled.

Rory had hopped out of the car and opened the door. Hebe still seemed to look through him. There was no recognition on her face. It must break his heart; it certainly would Lucy's.

Her mum was at the gate. Lucy hoped they were doing the right thing by bringing Hebe home. Everything she had read said that being in familiar surroundings was best so long as they could manage the care. And she was sure they could, especially with Rory's help.

✳ Eighty-Five ✳
Hebe

29 December 2016

Hebe sat in the armchair by the range. She didn't recall that it had been there before, but then other things had moved too, like the table, which was at a different angle. But everything else was in the right place and it was good to be warm here by the range. The weather had turned cold.

Lucy came bustling into the room. Her cheeks were pink but her eyes darted about, resting on nothing. Was it because of the man who had arrived at the house? He was at the sink, washing the breakfast pans. Hebe thought it was breakfast. She couldn't remember, and when she looked out of the window, the sky was grey, giving her no hint. The sun was missing. Her head was filled with clouds. They hid everything from her.

The door to the garden opened and Mr White Teeth came in. His glance sought Lucy's first, then he smiled at Hebe.

'Morning, Hebe. I've heard from the scientist doing the dating on the bodies we found in the north bedroom and the priest hole.'

Lucy laughed. 'Were they working this week?'

'Escaping family, I think it's called.' The man at the sink spoke. His voice. It ran through Hebe, causing shivers. The clouds parted and light came in, but before she could hold it, it was gone.

'The second set of bones belonged to a woman, and the DNA was not Grylls.' Mr White Teeth sat beside her. 'So with the discovery of the Grylls Jewel, I'm pretty sure it's Lucia.' He looked up. 'We just need to check the Courtenay DNA.'

347

Hebe tilted her head to the side and tried to focus. She looked to the man at the sink. She touched her lips, then turned away. No lipstick.

Mr White Teeth walked towards Lucy. 'How are you feeling?' he asked. Lucy held out her phone and showed it to him. 'What are you going to do?'

She shook her head. 'To be honest, he isn't my top priority at the moment.'

The man at the sink hung the tea towel over the rail on the range and looked at Hebe. A slow smile spread across his face. Sunlight exploded in her mind and things were clear. She groped in her pocket and found her lipstick. With a shaky hand she applied it, then she smiled back.

Lucy gasped, looking from Hebe to the man.

Hebe turned to Lucy. 'The baby? How is the baby?' She stood, wobbling on her feet. The man was quickly beside her, taking her arm.

'No worries there.' Lucy tapped her stomach.

'A child is always a blessing.' Hebe put one foot in front of the other.

'Oh Hebe, I can't agree with that.'

She turned her head. 'Life is short, but it is precious. Mine is almost gone. Don't throw life away. Yours or that of the child within you.'

Lucy stared at her, but she kept putting one foot in front of the other until she reached the door to the dining room. Then her legs gave way.

Eighty-Six
Hebe

September 2015

The bells of St Mary Abbots ring out as I close the door behind you. I lean against it, touching my lips. I must hold that kiss and the time from this summer close. I must write down everything, so that when I forget, it can remind me.

*

Yet, love and hate me too,
So these extremes shall neither's office do:
Love me, that I may die the gentler way;
Hate me, because thy love's too great for me.

This morning the fog in my mind was gone. Everything was sharp and defined, but I knew it would not last. It might only be for seconds. I pulled out the photograph of us. Something stabbed my heart. I didn't know your name any more. The mist was blurring the edges of my mind. Even though I didn't recall your name, I knew that you loved me. I held that close as emptiness closed in. I loved you too. Did I ever tell you?

✵ Eighty-Seven ✵
Lucy

30 December 2016

Lucy couldn't avoid it any longer. He was the father of the growth within her, so she knew she owed him the chance to air his views. But she had never imagined that he'd want to meet face to face.

She had chosen a spot that was not public but that was not Hell House either. The east wind whipped down the creek, pushing against the outgoing tide, creating small white horses. Formed from two opposing forces, they were beautiful. She had given Ed specific instructions on how to find the big tree. Touching the grooves in the bark, she hoped that something this strong, this bold and this beautiful would support her. Maybe she wouldn't need support. She could hope, but judging by the more desperate texts that had flooded in this week she didn't have a snowball's chance in hell.

'Lucy, why the hell did you pick this godforsaken spot?' Ed huffed, catching his breath. He must have parked at St Anthony. It wasn't exactly a rigorous walk, but by the look of him it would appear he'd climbed Mount Everest.

'Precisely so that no one else would be here.'

'Well, that's true.' He stepped forward and attempted to take her hands. She backed up against the tree, keeping them firmly by her sides, trying to see what had attracted her to him in the first place. But right now he was just a red-faced, angry man who thought she was going to fall into his arms when all she wanted at this second was a mug of hot cocoa and a good book.

'So, what was it that you wanted to say that couldn't have been said in a phone call?'

'That's harsh.'

'Not really. Our relationship ended months ago, and even before that, it didn't extend beyond sex and a bit of conversation.'

He looked like she'd slapped him. 'Is that all I was to you?'

She tilted her head to the side. 'Yes.'

He shrugged. 'Fine, we'll do it your way. Sheila is divorcing me.'

'I'm not surprised. Look at it from her point of view. You were shagging a woman ten years her junior; she forgives you – publicly looking like a fool to save your career – then finds out you made the bitch pregnant and she is due only a few weeks after her.'

'Luce, what's happened to you?'

She thought of Hebe blurting everything out on Christmas Day. 'I dropped my filter.'

'I'm so sorry.'

'No you aren't. This so-called scandal won't really harm you, as a man. But I will never be able to shake it.'

'That's not true.'

'Oh it is and you know it, despite your public display of being a feminist.'

His feet shifted. 'You're pregnant with my child. I'm here to help.'

'No.' She shuddered at the thought.

'What?' He'd gone white.

'This . . .' she pointed to her stomach, 'has nothing to do with you.'

'I came here to offer you support. To marry you.'

She couldn't help it. Laughter bubbled to the surface. It was not nice laughter, but bitter. 'Did you? You were to be my knight in shining armour?'

'Yes.'

She shook her head. 'Oh just eff off.'

'Are you going to get rid of it?' he asked.

'What I do with my body is my business, not yours or anyone else's.'

'But the child is mine too.' He crossed his arms.

'No comment.'

'If you won't marry me, then you must terminate the pregnancy.'

She shrugged. That told her how he felt about the alien. She turned and left him standing with his mouth open. He wouldn't use her as his next headline: *MP does honourable thing*, whatever that might be.

It was New Year's Eve and Lucy had never felt less festive. Hebe was confined to bed again and mostly unresponsive. Hugh was very pessimistic which seemed to go against his positive nature. He and Sarah had set off to Devon for a commitment they had already agreed to, but promised to be back in two days' time. Kate, with a huge amount of pushing from Lucy, went to spend time with Giles. Lucy was beginning to accept that he was her father, since for good or ill, he had been the one who had raised her.

Her parents needed time to sort themselves out, one way or another. Her father had been calling several times a day, so Lucy had the feeling they would work through this. After all, if her mother could forgive him for Alice, then he could forgive the fact that he'd raised Frank's child.

She rubbed her temples. Life was so bloody complicated. Her phone was full of texts from Ed. The newspapers were having a field day with him, and by default with Lucy. The sooner she could get rid of the alien within, the better. She needed to move forward and focus on the important things, like helping Hebe.

She carried a mug of tea up to Rory. He had barely left Hebe's side. No task was too much or too awful. She paused in the doorway. He was sitting beside her aunt as she had seen Kit do, and like Kit, he was reading Donne to her. Every so often Hebe would recite a line or two, and he would continue. Was this love?

A finger ran across the base of her neck. She didn't jump. It wasn't a ghost, but Kit. She turned to find him standing there in a dinner jacket. She caught her breath. He put a finger to her lips, then took the mug from her hands and delivered it to Rory, who winked.

Taking her hand, he walked her towards her room. He was impossibly handsome.

'You're dressed up to the nines. Off on a hot date?'

'Absolutely, and right now she's about to slip into the gorgeous gown she wore on Christmas Day, while I finish preparing dinner. Meet me in the King's Room when you're ready. You need a treat.'

She might not have the energy to see the new year in, but at least she would spend the hours before it with the person who made her smile the most. For a short time she could forget that everything in life was wrong and focus on being in the now. As she slid the gown over her head, she made a vow to enjoy the evening.

Putting on a bit of lipstick, she studied her face. Her cheeks were hollow, and dark circles lurked under her eyes. That glow of well-being had faded, but maybe that was down to yesterday, standing in the cold talking to the idiot she had once found fascinating. Had the sex been so good that she hadn't seen who she'd been sleeping with?

She ran a hand over her hips, avoiding her stomach. Best not to think of that at all. Instead she would try and focus on the wonderful man who had made dinner for her. No sense in keeping him waiting.

Going through the small sitting room, she smiled. Scaffolding was in place so that come January they could repair the beautiful barrel ceiling. It would be cosy once it was finished. Walking quietly down the hall, she stopped in front of Hebe's room.

Rory had set up a table and laid out a meal for them. Hebe looked at Lucy as she stood in the doorway. Her eyes flickered with something like recognition. Lucy walked in and took her aunt's hand in hers. Rory stood, and Hebe's eyes followed him.

'Looks lovely, Rory.'

'Nothing like a quiet New Year's Eve to be thankful.'

353

'True.' Lucy kissed Hebe's hand and placed it on the table. Rory would need to feed her. That was beyond her at the moment. Thankfully, she still remembered how to chew.

'You look beautiful.' He smiled.

'Thank you. Let us know if you need anything.'

'I will. Enjoy your celebration.' He sat down at the table.

As Lucy approached the salon, the way was lit by tea lights and she heard Nat King Cole. Kit was filling water glasses as she came in. The tree, the candles, the music, the man. Magic. He'd even managed to light the fire, which she doubted had seen live flame since they roasted a boar on it.

'You look wonderful.'

She laughed. He held out his hand and drew her into his arms, and they danced cheek to cheek. This was the New Year's Eve that she had longed for years ago, but which had been pushed aside for parties, drunken kisses and stumbling home to a new year begun with a hangover.

The next song was more up-tempo, and Kit deftly swung her around till the world spun with her and she clung to him. 'Too much?'

'I feel drunk.'

'Your last drink was days ago; it must have been a good one.' He held her close until the spinning passed.

'It was. It was my birthday and it was with you.'

'So it was.'

She yawned, and he laughed. 'Shall we eat before you fall asleep on me?'

'I'm sorry.'

'That wasn't a complaint. You've had so much to contend with.' He pulled out her chair. 'It's a simple meal, but I hope it will appeal.'

'Thank you, for ...' She didn't know what to say. 'Everything' didn't really cover it. He hadn't preached at her, told her what to do or even made a comment. He'd simply been there for her. 'Just thank you.'

'My pleasure. Would you like champagne?' There was a bottle in an ice bucket.

'Just fizzy water, please. I think my champagne days are over for the moment.'

He raised an eyebrow. 'Do you miss it?'

'If you had asked me that a few months ago, I would have said yes. A day without champagne was like a day without air. I would have said the same of Snapchat and Instagram too, but much to my surprise, it's liberating.'

'I've enjoyed the freedom, too.'

'You've made yourself at home here.' She twirled the stem of her glass.

A smile stole across his face. 'I have.'

'But Hollywood will call.'

'They already have.'

She looked directly at him. She didn't want him to leave. 'When do you go?'

'I'm not. It wasn't the project I wanted. I like – no, love things here.' He took a sip of his water. 'Besides, it was a spy thing,' he added, in a perfect imitation of a particular Scottish actor.

'You'd give up the role of a lifetime to stay here?'

'Yes. And helping Hebe reminded me of what I'd always wanted to do: write.'

'Really?'

He nodded, and watched as she pushed aside the plate in front of her.

'Smoked salmon not appeal?'

She wrinkled her nose and bit into the bread. 'No, but this is good.'

'That's a relief. Should the next course be cocoa?'

She stifled another yawn. 'It may have to be.'

'This is becoming a habit.'

'Well, I must enjoy it before Hollywood steals you away from Cornwall.'

'As if they could.'

She tilted her head and studied him. 'Kit, that sounds serious.'

'It is. I love acting, but I don't like the life.'

But before she could ask more, her stomach protested and she dashed from the room and down the hall to the nearest functioning loo. Happy New Year, one and all, she thought wryly.

❊ Eighty-Eight ❊
Hebe

31 December 2016

Hebe looked from the photograph to the man helping her. She didn't know him, but Lucy trusted him. He looked after her. Had Lucy hired him? Was he a nurse? But then as he tucked her into bed, he kissed her hair. Her skin tingled.

Sitting beside her on the bed, he took her hand in his, then picked up the book and read. His voice touched her, and her eyes closed. She could hear the distant sound of St Anthony's bells. They were ringing in the New Year. New beginnings.

Eighty-Nine
Hebe

September 2015

The weeks have been busy and you remind me it is our anniversary again. How could I have forgotten? Everything is harder, but I push on. You have been helping me, reminding me. We sit together on the sofa sipping sparkling wine and marking papers. How comfortable we have become. Dinner is cooking but I can't remember what I have prepared.

The scent from the oven says it is done. I leave you on the sofa and stand still, not sure what I was going to do, then walk into the kitchen hoping I will remember.

Looking in the oven, I see the casserole is bubbling over. I take it out, wondering why I went to such trouble on a week night. You walk into the room and pull me into your arms. With my head leaning against your chest, I hear your heart beating.

'Thank you for cooking my favourite venison for our anniversary.'

I smile, and remember what it is all about.

*

When I am dead, and doctors know not why,
And friends' curiosity
Will have me cut up to survey each part,
When they shall find your picture in my heart.

❋ Ninety ❋
Lucy

4 January 2017

As Rory walked into the kitchen, Lucy looked up from the leaflet the GP had given her. His glance fell to it.

'A lot to take in?'

She nodded. Assuming she'd fallen pregnant when she thought she had, then everything was fine. It became impossible if she was more pregnant than she thought. She pushed it aside. She'd know soon enough.

Today she'd spoken to Hebe's solicitor. Her aunt had seen what was coming and in many ways had been clear-sighted. The solicitor had also confirmed what Kit had told her: that Hebe Courtenay, esteemed historian, was also H. J. Bowden, best-selling historical novelist. How had she kept that from them all these years? Calling her agent was on tomorrow's list.

'Tea?' Rory asked as the kettle clicked off.

'Just a cup of hot water.'

'Has the little blighter already taken control?'

Lucy snorted.

'Sorry, that wasn't very tactful.'

'No, but it made me laugh.'

He handed her a mug and pulled out a chair. 'Do you want to talk?'

She shook her head. 'I'm afraid if I begin I'll have no control over what comes out.'

'And that scares you?'

She nodded. 'I thought you were an English professor, not a shrink.'

359

'Teaching requires a certain amount of psychology.'

She gave a short laugh. 'True. Actually, I do have a question.'

His eyes narrowed. 'I have a feeling I might know what it is, but fire away.'

'You and Hebe. How? You said you'd been together ten years. You must have been what, eighteen?'

A slow smile spread across his face. 'I was, and I seduced her. She didn't have a chance. I fell in love with her from the moment she read Donne in my first history class.'

'So it was love at first Donne.' The corners of her mouth lifted.

He laughed. 'Yes, then, now and always.'

'So, you were a history student?'

'I was, but thanks to Hebe, I discovered my passion ... in many ways.'

'Wow.' Lucy sipped the hot water. It was soothing. 'How come we didn't know about you?'

He smiled again. 'I love that fact that you don't see the scandal.'

'I of all people can't throw stones. Though I'm not sure my mother has come to grips with it.'

'She hides it well.' He blew on the surface of his tea. 'Hebe could have lost her job. At first that was what drove her desire for secrecy, then it became something more.' He turned the mug in his hands. 'It was almost an obsession. At times it was as if she felt she didn't deserve to have love, that it was wrong.' He shrugged. 'I never understood, but I took whatever bits of her she was willing to give me.'

'I think I may be able to fill in a piece of the puzzle.'

He tilted his head.

'Hebe's mother committed suicide at thirty-five, suffering – we now think – from early-onset dementia.' She frowned. 'I don't think Hebe would allow herself to be in love, because of what she feared might happen to her. Keeping it secret meant it wasn't actually happening.' She clutched the mug with both hands.

Rory nodded, then stood and reached for a packet of biscuits from the cupboard. A bag of marshmallows fell out. 'Hebe's?'

Lucy nodded. 'My cravings are for Marmite on toast.'

He smiled. 'When they became almost the whole contents of her kitchen cupboards, I began to investigate.'

'Are you saying she lived on them?'

'Not quite, but I believe shares in the company rose.'

'What will you do?' She regretted the words as they left her mouth. He, like her, didn't seem to want to think beyond the present.

'I will be with her for as long as she needs me.'

She nodded. 'Thank you for loving her.'

'I have been the luckiest man.'

He took the packet of biscuits and climbed the back stairs. Lucy returned to the leaflet of doom and the question she could no longer answer.

While Rory was having a shower, Lucy sat on the bed next to Hebe. Days had been passing but Lucy wasn't sure that Hebe knew what day it was. Hugh said as much, which wasn't what she wanted to hear, but she didn't want her to continue like this either. She didn't know how she could have deteriorated so quickly, but Hugh told her that Hebe was amazing to have pushed through for so long. Her brain was forgetting how to live and soon it would forget to work her lungs and make her heart beat.

Was that all life was? Lucy turned away and there on the bedside table was the volume of Donne's poems. Every time she passed the room she could hear Rory reciting words of love – someone else's, but they sounded as if they came direct from his heart. She knew that if he could cut out his heart and give it to Hebe, he would. Yet Hebe had walked away from him without a word. Why? Was she so afraid of love? Was it just because she knew this would be her end?

Sarah nipped in and whispered in Lucy's ear. 'Talk to her, darling. Hearing is one of the last things to go.' She kissed Lucy's head and walked to the salon.

'Oh Hebe. What has happened to us?' Her voice wasn't

much above a whisper. She cleared her throat. 'You've always been here to help me work things through, and I could use that right now.' She picked up Hebe's hand. 'You never judged me, unlike everyone else. Thank you.' She took a breath. 'All the times you rescued me, including here at Hell House. Do you remember when I deliberately failed my A levels and you didn't yell at me? You simply asked me what my plan was.'

Hebe's eyes closed, and Lucy held her breath until she saw her aunt's chest rise and fall. 'I wish you could offer me sage advice right now. I mean, what would you say to me? What would you say of love?'

Hebe's eyes opened again.

'I know. I said the word I don't believe in, but you see, I'm falling in love and it's so damn scary.' Hebe's gaze now seemed engaged. Sarah had been right. 'I can't afford to be so vulnerable.'

Hebe's fingers moved.

'If you could change one thing, Hebe, what would it be? Would you risk it all for love?' She thought of Kit. 'I mean, if I let love in . . .' she looked down at her stomach, 'then I am open to more pain.' She sighed.

Sarah came back down the hall and popped her head through the doorway. 'Sorry to disturb. Just wanted to check. It's Twelfth Night, so we'll take the decorations down tomorrow, yes?'

'Yes, that will be fine.'

'The Epiphany was always Hebe's favourite holiday.' Sarah grinned. 'She believed good things happened on that day.'

Lucy sighed 'I need a little of that magic right now.'

Rory walked into the room with a towel around his waist. Her aunt had good taste in men. 'Thanks, Lucy. I feel a lot fresher.'

'No worries.' She kissed Hebe's forehead and released her hand. 'Thank you for listening,' she told her, 'and in case I hadn't said it before, I love you.' She took one last look at her, then left the room and closed the door behind her, leaving the two of them alone.

*

Lucy walked past the church at St Anthony. The light was fading, but she really wanted to reach Dennis Head. She wasn't sure what she thought she would find there, but it called to her. Was this what had happened to Hebe when she walked through the darkness?

She reached the top of the hill and looked out into the twilight. Neither the twinkling lights on the tankers nor the fresh breeze could lift the sadness in her heart. As the information in the leaflet ran through her mind, love and hate battled within her. Was this her only chance at having a child? Was it selfish to want it? Was it selfish not to?

If she kept it, if she made that choice, then that was the end of any possibility with Kit. He hadn't said as much, but the fact that he'd avoided the whole subject told her all she needed to know. So what was she going to do? Given what her doctors had always said, it was a miracle that she had fallen pregnant at all. Would it ever happen again? If she could wish on a star and make everything happen that she wanted to, what would she choose? She laughed. Stupid thought. It was as if her mistakes were tattooed on her face. Even if she tried to remove them, she was scarred forever. She laughed aloud. All her adult years she had done everything she could not to be like her mother, and here she was, knocked up just like her.

She picked up a branch and tossed it down the cliff, wondering if she'd thrown it hard enough that it would reach the sea or would hit the rocks and break. The light was too low for her to know.

She strolled down the headland to St Anthony. She would take the easiest option and free herself. That would be best for all of them – not just for her, but for Kit and the alien too. She let out a long, slow breath. Her decision was made. Done.

The lights were on in the farmhouse and she could see Kit sitting reading a book. She hesitated, then knocked.

He opened the door and stepped aside.

'Hi.' She shoved her hands into her pockets.

'You OK?' He closed the door behind her.

She nodded, trying to read his mood. The sitting room was

more ordered than her last visit, more settled than before. She let her shoulders drop. He wasn't running away.

'Are you worried about tomorrow?'

She nodded. 'That obvious?'

'You look like a ghost.'

She laughed. 'Feel a bit like one too, though I'm not sure why I'm worried. It's just a scan.'

'Do you want me to come with you?'

Swallowing, she thought about the feel of his hand on hers, then thought how wrong it would be to have him there looking at a scan of another man's child. 'It's probably best if I do this alone.'

He looked away. 'I'm here for you.'

'Thank you.' She reached out to him and let her fingers rest on his arm. He was tense. 'I ...' she paused, 'appreciate your support.'

He nodded.

'To be honest, I'm a bit confused, but I know I'm not in any position to keep this ... thing.'

He remained silent, then turned to her. 'If you wanted ... I would help.'

She blinked. 'Thank you.' She moved closer to him. 'But my gut says this isn't your problem.'

He looked at her, his eyes serious. 'It may not be my problem, but even if you don't want my help, I'm not going away.'

Her breath caught. Just what was he saying?

'Thanks, but I have to handle this on my own.' Not that she wanted to, but she'd landed herself in this situation and she needed to deal with it. Besides, she knew now that she loved him, and as scary as that was, she realised she had to protect him from the disaster that was her.

'Just know I'm here.'

'I do.' She let him take her into his arms and hold her close. Listening to the beat of his heart, she was almost willing to believe that they had a future. But she'd seen what havoc had been caused in the name of love.

✳ Ninety-One ✳
Lucy

6 January 2017

Just the smell of coffee drifting upstairs from the kitchen sent Lucy dashing to the loo. At least she thought it was that and not pure and simple fear. Once the heaving had subsided, she washed her face, deciding that she looked like death. All night long she had tossed and turned, Kit's and Ed's faces featuring largely in the swirl of the circling pit.

Back in her room, she dressed in trackies and her softest hoodie. She would face today like it was a pyjama day. As she looked out at the leaden sky, a big drop of rain landed on the wobbly glass, magnifying the wall of the great hall below. She was as hollow as it was; the only good things she'd done had been done here at Hell House with Hebe.

Today was just a scan to date the pregnancy, then the next step was termination. It would be fine. She sipped some water and there were no complaints from the alien. Her hand stroked her belly without her permission. This decision would have been so much easier if she'd realised what was wrong with her sooner.

Any minute now, Peta would arrive. Sarah had said that she would go to the scan with Lucy, but she knew her grandmother didn't approve of what she was planning to do. Nor did her mum, who was due down tonight. Neither had said as much; they had simply uttered the right words. It's your decision, they all told her. It was, and that might be the problem. Just months ago the toughest choice in her life was what bloody shoes to wear. How things had changed.

365

Lucy clutched the scan picture she had been given. The alien was sucking its thumb. It was eighteen weeks old and its father was a Labour MP. She'd booked an appointment for a week's time for a surgical termination. The world tilted on its axis and she grabbed a nearby signpost. Peta drove up to the kerb. Lucy turned away, hoping that for once the other woman wouldn't see her thoughts. Climbing into the car, she put her seat belt on.

'So, you made a decision?' Peta indicated and then pulled away, and soon they were into the traffic.

'Yes.'

'Relieved?'

She nodded. 'Very.'

'Good.'

Peta drove in silence but at considerable speed.

'Are we in a rush?' Lucy asked.

'I'm sensing something isn't right at Helwyn House.'

'Hebe?' Her heart stopped. Her aunt had been sleeping when she'd visited her this morning before she left.

'Yes.'

'Well at the speed you're doing, we'll know pretty quickly.' Lucy gripped the handle above her head as they roared through the lanes towards Gweek. They were doomed if they met an on-coming vehicle. Did Peta's gift include seeing through hedges? She began to pray.

Stones flew as Peta slammed the brakes on in front of the house. All the Christmas garlands were off the pillars except one that was halfway down. Peta was right. Something had happened.

Lucy bolted out of the car and raced inside, straight to her aunt's room. Everyone looked up in surprise. Rory was sitting on the bed next to Hebe, stroking her hair. Her breathing was laboured and uneven. Lucy looked at Hugh. He nodded. 'It won't be long.'

She stepped up to the bed. 'Can I have a few moments alone with her?'

'Of course.' Rory rose, and the others left as well.

'Oh Hebe. I don't know what the right choice is.' Lucy touched Hebe's cheek. 'If you could write in your diary, you would say that it was the feast of the Epiphany, and that Lucy had a difficult decision to make today. You would also say what you ate for breakfast. But this morning you didn't eat, nor last night.'

She didn't try to hold back her tears. 'Thank you for everything. I love you.' She kissed Hebe's cheek and Rory came back in.

He put a hand on her back. 'She loved you and believed in you.'

'Thank you.' She wiped her face with the back of her hand. 'I'll leave the two of you alone.' She looked up to the intricate pattern of entwined vines on the cornicing, trying to stem her tears.

He nodded. Lucy saw him climb onto the bed and pull Hebe into his arms. She heard him whisper, '*Come, madam, come, all rest my powers defy …*' She closed the door and leaned her forehead against the cool wood, feeling Helwyn House wrap itself around her.

❋ Ninety-Two ❋
Hebe

6 January 2017

Hebe opened her eyes and looked into ones filled with tears. Nothing would focus but the voice. She knew the voice. Him.

'Rory?'

He nodded.

'Hold me.'

He pulled her closer and whispered in her ear. Love. She closed her eyes, feeling him beside her.

❄ Ninety-Three ❄
Lucy

7 January 2017

Lucy's head thumped like she'd been on her mother's gin and tonics all last night rather than going to bed at seven with a cocoa. Everyone else in the house was still asleep. Hebe had died in Rory's arms not long after Lucy had left the room. Hugh had then taken over, and since then she'd avoided all the looks her mother and her grandmother had sent her.

Right now she longed to know who was the saint of the day for the seventh of January. Hebe had somehow recalled that information, but had had to write down everyday details to remember them. It was such a cruel disease. And then there was Rory. He loved her totally and she didn't know him in the end and had just walked away from him. Lucy sighed. Maybe that too was love. All she knew was that she was confused.

Rory appeared. 'Hi.'

'You look as rough as I feel.'

'Hugh's whisky.' He ran a hand through his hair.

'Ouch.'

He looked at the kettle, then turned. 'Is there tea in the pot?'

She nodded, but her brain didn't like the feeling. 'Rory, I'm so sorry.'

He took a deep breath. 'We all are.'

'I know, but you loved her.'

'I did, I do. Love doesn't go away.' He cradled his mug.

'Doesn't it?'

He pulled out a chair and sat. 'No, but right now it hurts like hell.'

369

'Yes.' She turned her mug in her hands. 'How did you forgive her?'

'For what?' He frowned.

'For leaving you?'

'She tried so many times to push me away.' He smiled. 'She was trying to protect me, imagining that the life I'd have with her would be less than what it should be.' He shook his head. 'What she didn't realise was that life without her was *never* what it should be.'

She thought of Hebe's diary. Her thinking had been clear. She had been old enough to be his mother.

'She mattered. Our love mattered.'

'Again, I'm so sorry.'

'I'm not. I had ten years with her. I loved each and every day, even though it meant hiding our love from the world. It was the only way she would let me love her, but that was enough.'

Lucy stood and hugged him 'You had something special.'

'That we did.' He wiped his eyes with the back of his hand.

❋ Ninety-Four ❋

Lucy

11 January 2017

The kitchen door opened, sending in a blast of cold, damp air. Lucy turned. Her mother walked in, followed by her father. She swallowed. It was fine to have a conversation on the phone, but here he was in the flesh. Possibly not what she needed on the eve of her termination. But her mother had made her peace with him, and Hebe's funeral was next week, so it made sense.

He stood by the table, still holding his bag. This was her moment. She swallowed. She didn't need to be emotional right now, but she had no control over it. Everything made her cry. Just when she needed to be strong, she was a bloody puddle.

'Lucy.' His voice had a catch in it.

'Dad.' She nodded, sniffling. 'Let me show you to your room.' She could have let her mother do it, but somehow this was right.

He caught up with her in the hall and touched her arm.

'I'm sorry about Hebe.' He paused. 'I know what she meant to you.'

'Thanks.' She turned to him. 'I know you didn't care for her.'

He sniffed. 'That might be because she saw what an ass I was.'

The corners of Lucy's mouth twitched.

'True.'

He laughed. 'I know I've said sorry, but I need to say it again.'

'Thank you.'

'I wasn't the father you needed or deserved.'

Lucy took a deep breath. 'The fault lies on both sides.' She tilted her head. 'I gave you hell and it couldn't have been easy to watch me self-destruct.'

'No, but I knew why.'

As they started up the stairs, Lucy went to take the bag from him. He was without his cane but still limping.

'I don't think I should be letting you carry anything heavy.' He pulled the bag back.

'Don't be ridiculous. I'm strong and well, and anyway, the problem disappears tomorrow.'

He frowned. 'Is that what you really want?'

She didn't reply. She didn't need this conversation with him of all people.

'Look, Lucy, I may have been a poor example of a parent – possibly the worst – so I won't give advice, but I will support whatever decision you make.' He placed a finger under her chin as he used to when she was small. 'Just know your mother and I are here for you.'

If he had said almost anything else, she would have hit him, and now she was left without words. The emotional roller coaster tipped and she dashed off to the loo to clear her thoughts. She didn't need people to be nice. She was a shit. She knew that.

Lucy read the email again, not sure she quite believed it. Aside from a small bequest to Michael and a large one to Rory, she was Hebe's heir. Hell House was hers. She walked the length of the loggia. What on earth was she going to do with it? She leaned against a pillar, enjoying the cool feel of the granite. Part of her had grown to love the place. She laughed. That was a turn-up for the books. She looked up to the large window in the King's Room. Kit. She could sell it to him. She smiled. What would Hebe think of Mr White Teeth owning Helwyn House? Lucy would be free then. Wasn't that what she wanted?

Fred came out of one of the downstairs rooms with a big smile on his face. 'Good news.'

'Spill.'

'Mark just texted. Planning approval has been granted by the council.'

'Brilliant.'

'Yes.' He grinned. 'Peta sends her love.'

'Send mine back. I must catch up with her when things settle down.'

'You'll see her at the funeral.'

'True.' She sighed.

He put an arm around her. 'It sucks, but it was the best thing for Hebe.'

'I know.' Tears came again and she cursed the wretched hormones; they made all emotions bigger. She had even cried at a loo roll commercial last night. But it would all be resolved later today.

'Give Peta a call.' He handed her his hankie. 'She's better with these things.'

Lucy blew her nose and gave him a wobbly smile. The sun was shining, and for a January day, it was warm. Instead of heading back inside, she walked down to the creek. The tide was high and the pair of swans swam close to the shore. She thought of Hebe and Rory, wondering if he would be able to find love again. As she walked along the lane, she hoped he would. If anyone deserved it, he did.

The sun was warm on her back. The air smelt of spring. She knew the daffodils were already out in the fields above. A heron flew low along the creek and she regretted not having her camera with her, or even her phone. That was in her bag in readiness for her appointment in a few hours' time. She shouldn't be out here walking, but she kept going. As the sun rose higher in the sky, it lifted her mood. Memories of summer holidays, good ones, rushed into her mind. Sand-covered barbecued sausages and salty crisps. She laughed, picking up a stone and skimming it across the smooth surface of the water. Three bounces wasn't bad. Looking up, she stopped in her tracks. Alice was walking along the water's edge with her jeans rolled up and her feet in the sea.

But it wasn't the fact that her feet were in the icy water that

373

shocked Lucy. It was what was on her ankle. The friendship bracelet Lucy had made for her fifteen years ago.

Alice looked up. 'Hi.'

Lucy took a deep breath as Alice shook the water off her feet and came closer.

'Cat got your tongue?' She stood two feet away. Her intense green eyes stared at Lucy, unflinching. 'Still pregnant, or have you had the abortion?'

Lucy shook her head. Had Alice just said that?

'Tough situation really. I get it.' Alice picked up a stone and skimmed it. Five hops. 'Back when we were nine or ten, you used to talk about your dreams of having a family and a cottage and all the junk that went with it.'

Lucy remembered. Just the two of them, picnicking in an empty cove. Cheese sandwiches with pickle.

'Then when you were sixteen and your periods were screwed up, you found out why and your dream crashed and burned.' Alice shook her head. 'What you didn't know, because I was too ashamed to say, was that I'd already had an abortion.' Lucy gasped and Alice threw another stone. 'There was no way I could have the baby.' She gave a short, sharp laugh. 'I wasn't going to turn out just like Mum. Pregnant at sixteen and no future.' She looked up. 'You see, I wanted a future like the one I knew you were going to have.'

Lucy frowned.

'You sure fucked that up.' Picking up another stone, Alice turned it over in her hand. 'You had everything. Family, money, education – basically everything I didn't.'

Lucy's eyes widened. How little she had known about her friend.

'You were innocent, with a wicked streak. You also had the kooky, loving aunt. Let's not forget poor Hebe.' Alice tossed the stone in her hand to the ground and selected another. 'I wanted to be in your world so badly.'

Lucy swallowed. She knew where this was leading, but she stayed silent.

'The night of the village regatta, we were both working but

374

I finished early. You were busy chatting up some cute bloke having dinner with his parents.'

Lucy closed her eyes for a moment. She had pushed everything about that night, good and bad, from her memory – or at least had tried to.

'I headed to the sailing club and got shit-faced. Your father was in the same state. The rest is history, and I learned one hell of a lesson. Shagging someone is never a way to get what you want.'

Lucy snorted.

'You've learned that now too.' Alice gave a short laugh. 'I did forgive you for dropping me in it over the fifty quid I borrowed.'

Lucy opened her mouth, then shut it.

'In a way, you did me a favour.' Alice shrugged her shoulders. 'I had to leave Cornwall. I had to have a new start. So, thanks.'

Lucy looked at the stones at her feet. Picking up a red one, she felt its contours. She had no idea what to say. She threw the stone as far as she could and watched it sink below the waters of the creek. 'Why did you tell the papers? About me being pregnant.'

Alice turned from watching the ripples circling out from Lucy's stone. 'I didn't. That was Cadan.'

'What?' Lucy drew her brows together. He couldn't have.

'He's in debt and the money on offer was good. I heard him calling them while I was outside the Shippers having a fag on Boxing Day.' Alice cleared her throat. 'Not surprised you thought it was me, but don't judge him. Not everyone was born with a silver spoon in their mouth.' She began walking away.

'Wait.'

She turned. 'What?'

'Why do you still wear the anklet?'

Alice looked down. 'Oh, I still love my best friend … only my plans to get closer to her failed.' She took a few steps down the beach, then stopped. 'If you haven't done the deed yet, think hard about it and remember your old dream. You were a sweet kid once and desperate to be a mother.' She carried on down the beach and Lucy stared after her.

Her mother was waiting for her at Helwyn. It was time. Lucy picked up her bag and followed her to the car. Kate kept looking at her, but she didn't want to talk or even to think.

As they neared the hospital, it was clear that her mother couldn't take the silence. The frequency of her glances began to concern Lucy, who wished she'd keep her eyes on the road.

'Darling, you don't have to do this alone.' Kate's hands clutched the steering wheel.

'I know, but actually I do.' Lucy covered her mother's nearer hand with her own. 'Thank you for just being here right now.'

'Oh, Lucy love.' Kate sniffled. 'I've made so many mistakes, but you were never one of them.'

'Thanks, Mum, but that's not what I need to hear right now.' She leaned over and kissed her cheek.

'I never wanted this for you ... I'd hoped things would be different.'

Lucy laughed. 'Yes, mirror, mirror on the wall, I am my mother and grandmother after all.'

'Oh dear.' Her mum stopped the car and blew her nose.

'It's not the worst thing in the world; besides, both you and Gran are all right.'

Kate smiled. 'We're not too bad.'

Lucy climbed out. 'See you in a few hours. I love you.'

'I love you too. I'll just be in town shopping, waiting for when you need me.'

'Thanks.' Lucy watched her put the car into gear and drive away. Her stomach rumbled. She wasn't sure if it was hunger or fear. But whatever it was, it would be gone soon.

She walked through the doors and checked in. While she was waiting, she read her messages.

Thinking of you. K

She closed her eyes, remembering what Alice had said, but this was the best way forward. Across the waiting area she saw her reflection in the glass covering a poster. She looked absolutely normal. Not pregnant. Not conflicted. Just boringly normal. She existed and had survived despite everything.

Her mother must have had the same moment, and even her grandmother. Lucy wasn't like sixteen-year-old Alice. She had a choice, and more importantly, she wasn't alone. Neither was she broke – quite the contrary. And most importantly, just maybe she could be a good mother. She stroked the alien, wondering what it thought. Did it want to go on this journey with her?

'Lucy Trevillion?' a woman called.

Lucy blinked and swallowed hard. Did she choose the alien and a life tied to it, or did she opt for freedom? She stood and looked in the glass. She was here and so should the alien be, even if that changed everything.

'Lucy?'

'Sorry. I've changed my mind.' She smiled, then turned and walked out into the cold January air. Somehow she would make being a single mum work. She didn't know how, but something inside her settled. Maybe it was the alien getting comfortable.

Ninety-Five

Lucy

18 January 2017

The camera strap settled on Lucy's neck. Today was Hebe's funeral and the day had arrived cold and frosty. The house was in silence as she slipped out. Crystals covered every blade of grass and a mist clung close to the fields. The creek was obscured but she knew the haze would lift as the sun rose in the sky. She wanted to capture that moment when the light broke through.

The swans were huddled together on the bank. Lucy smiled. Their down must be brilliant insulation, as the ground was cold and hard. She pulled up the zip of her coat. There wasn't enough contrast between the fog and the swans to take a decent photo. They moved in closer together as she went past.

Silence. All she could hear was her breathing and her footsteps along the road. A startled jackdaw flew out from one of the pines, climbing through the mist to the blue sky above. She smiled.

'Morning.' Kit came down the lane and stopped beside her.

'A beautiful one.'

'It is.' In the distance, the bells of St Anthony sounded the slow ring in preparation for the funeral later.

'How are you?'

She shrugged. 'Feeling a bit less sick.'

'That's good news.'

She smiled. 'And you?'

'Fine.'

She narrowed her eyes. She hadn't seen him in days. She'd

avoided everyone, needing time to think through what she had done.

'Now that's a funny word. I've always used it to avoid answering the question.'

He smiled, and her breath caught. 'I've missed you.'

'Same.' There was no point in lying.

The corner of his mouth lifted. 'I thought you might call.'

'I considered it.'

'May I ask why you didn't?'

She took a deep breath and looked him straight in his beautiful blue eyes. 'Because no matter what I feel for you, or think I do, this will be easier for both of us if we part ways.'

'Why?' The smile disappeared from his face.

'Because you're a public figure.'

'True.'

She tucked a strand of hair behind her ear, thinking how best to put this. 'I'm a shadow that would dim your light.' She pointed to her stomach. 'My alien will always be a story, poor thing.'

He frowned.

'Look, if you were Joe Bloggs who pulled pints at the pub for a living and never did anything interesting, then we might be able to make some sort of go of it.' She swallowed. 'But you're not. You're a Hollywood star and I'm posh totty that got knocked up by an MP.'

He laughed.

'It's not really funny.'

'No, it's not, but your face when you said that last bit was.' He stepped closer, leaving little room between them. It didn't make it easy to think.

'You need to shine,' she said.

'With you by my side I will.' He ran a finger down her cheek.

'No, every time I appear at your side so will all the scandal.'

'It will go away.'

She shook her head. 'Nothing in the digital age ever does.'

'That's true, but it's the same with my love.'

Her heart stopped for a second. 'I just can't do that to you.'

'Why?'

'Because …' She took a deep breath. 'Because I love you.' She tried to step back, give herself some distance, but he followed like they were dancing. 'And then there's the matter of this.' She stroked her stomach, wondering when she would begin to feel the alien move. 'I'm keeping the baby.'

His mouth lifted into a sexy half-smile, and rational thought became very difficult. 'And you're happy with the decision?'

She nodded.

'Then I am too.'

'Really?'

'Yes.'

'But it's another man's child.'

'It's *your* child.'

'Oh.'

'I love you and anything that is a part of you.' He took a step closer, but he wasn't touching her.

'You're mad.'

'I am … about you.' He kissed her. 'Marry me?'

'No.' She laughed, and he lightly touched his lips to hers again.

'Is there a compromise option?' he whispered.

'I won't marry you.' She pulled back just a bit.

'Fine.'

'There's that word again.'

'Indeed.' He kissed the side of her neck and she shivered.

'But maybe we could try having you stick around for a bit.' She linked her fingers behind his neck.

'It might work. I just turned down another film.'

She pushed him away. 'You didn't.'

'I did.'

'Not because of me?' She stepped away.

'No, because it was a terrible film.' He opened his arms and she slipped into them again. 'I will accept the right film, but only with you in my life.'

'Is that blackmail?'

'Yes.'

She pressed her lips together. 'I'm not sure if this will work.'

'I am, but you'll only know if we try.'

'True.' She leant her head against his chest and heard the beat of his heart. The church bell was still tolling.

'I think Hebe would want us to marry.' He touched the Grylls Jewel, which she'd been wearing since Hebe had died.

She laughed. 'Possibly. Ask me again in the future.'

'I will. How does tomorrow sound?' Before she could reply, he kissed her.

Ninety-Six

Lucy

18 January 2017

The funeral was over and everyone had left the reception. Lucy walked into Hebe's room, still struggling to acknowledge her absence. How could someone so important in her life be gone? Her logical brain accepted it but the other half, the bigger part, didn't.

Sitting down at Hebe's desk, Lucy began to search for something, though she didn't know what. Who was she trying to fool? She was looking for her aunt, which was crazy. She had even looked up the saint for today, not realising that there were so many. But she thought Hebe might have chosen St Day, a Cornish one.

Picking up each pen, she laid them back down exactly as Hebe left them. Then, opening the bottom drawer, she pulled out the old photo album. Hebe had been a beautiful baby. She closed the book and saw all Hebe's notebooks and diaries stacked neatly at the bottom of the drawer. Sticking out of the black notebook with *Summer 2015* written on it in silver ink was a folded sheet. She pulled it out and opened it.

My dearest love,

I've never been able to say what has been in my heart. I love you. I was too afraid. I know that loving you was wrong, but it gave my life joy. I was wrong not to celebrate it publicly. If I have regrets it was because I didn't believe in love enough. I didn't believe in us the way I should have. You made my life worth living. You brought me joy.

I want you to find love again. To have what I never gave you. Please forgive me for my fear. Forgive me for not trusting you enough. Ultimately, for not trusting in love enough.

If I could change one thing in my life, it wouldn't be you. It would be not ever telling you how much I loved you and what you have meant to me. You have been my everything.

Hebe

'Oh Rory.' Lucy turned to see if he was near. Had Hebe never told him? She put her hand to her mouth. How could she have left a love like that unspoken? He needed to know. Maybe he already did. He had loved Hebe. It had shown in everything he had done for her.

She rose, and he was standing by the door.

'Are you OK, Lucy?' He walked towards her.

She held out the letter. 'I just found this. It belongs to you.'

He frowned, but took it and opened it. His face went pale as he scanned the words. He looked up at her. 'She didn't have to say it.' He swallowed, holding the letter against his heart. 'I knew.'

Acknowledgements

I want to thank all my readers who have followed me on this incredible journey. Their enjoyment of the stories inspires me every day to keeping on writing.

The community I live in in Cornwall is fabulous and supportive. At the Helford Village Regatta in 2016, people raised funds for the RNLI and St John's Ambulance to name a character in this book. They chose Anthony Jenkin. Anthony appears as himself on the pages of the book ... or more correctly, he appears as I see him.

My lifelong closest friend Christine Moriarty has always been there by my side – whether physically for our growing-up years or in spirit for the last thirty. There is much I could say but mostly it needs to be thanks for everything.

Dr Nicola Ford provided insight into the wonders of Godolphin House, on which Helwyn House is based. Walking through the house with her and Amanda Jones gave me clues to what an archaeologist sees that your average person doesn't.

As always, my writing support comes mostly from the wonderful Brigid Coady. She cajoles, brainstorms and kicks my backside when required. I'd be lost without her support. Thanks to Julia Hayward and Sarah Callejo for their comments on early drafts of the book. Vanessa Lafaye read the beginning of the novel when I thought all was lost and helped me to see a way through to the story I wanted and needed to tell. I owe her a huge hug and am forever grateful. My intern Madeleine Inskeep has been a delightful sounding board when I couldn't see the story for the words.

John Jackson and Sarah Swan have been the behind-the-scenes

cheerleading team who have kept my spirits up during the dark days of writing. They both made the process a happier event.

Luigi and Alison Bonomi have been wonderful with support, insight and humour! All greatly needed in varying doses.

I am deeply grateful to Harriet Bourton for her understanding while I wrote this book through a difficult year when the way forward wasn't always clear.

Thanks to Kate MacEachern, Don Maass, Lorin Oberweger and all the writers and teachers of the BONI Tampa 2017 who helped in the final push to finish *One Cornish Summer*. Breakfast discussions with Kate were vital to finding the right end to the book and the missing anklet.

No writing would happen at all without the love and support of my family, but especially that of my husband Chris. His belief in me has held me together in my darkest moments … that and his ability to make me laugh.

Author's Note

Anyone who has been to the National Trust's Godolphin House will know that Helwyn House is based on it. I have always been fascinated by the building, since my first visit twenty years ago. When I toured the house two years ago, I felt stories calling to me as I walked through it. Staying there only added to that feeling. I sense that I will be using the house as a setting for several more stories. Please note there is no priest hole or skeletons to be found. However, witch marks abound!

I moved Godolphin House from its wonderful setting in the rich mining landscape near Helston to a hill above Gillan Creek. It took me ages to find the right spot to site such a house. Walking the creek, studying Ordnance Survey maps and listening to people in the pub, I eventually found it ... even if I have smoothed out the landscape a bit!

The history mentioned in the story is mostly gleaned from Mary Coate's wonderful *Cornwall in the Great Civil War and Interregnum 1642–1660*. Gear Rout has fascinated me from my earliest visit to this part of Cornwall, as we frequently drive over Gear Bridge and walk the Dennis Head. A Civil War cannon ball was discovered in our own home when the previous owners renovated in the 1960s.

I have referred to both the Civil War (as most people think of this period) and the Civil Wars, as Hebe would have done as a historian. The first war was settled when Cromwell's Parliamentary forces won at Naseby in 1645. The second part ended with Charles I's defeat at the Battle of Preston and his execution in 1649. Charles II formed an army and was defeated by Cromwell, but he ascended to the throne in 1660. Thomas

Grylls is based on no one in particular and is purely a character from my imagination.

Alzheimer's is a devastating disease at any age, but to witness it in a younger person is terrible. My heart goes out to all who love and care for people suffering with this illness. For more information, you can visit the Alzheimer's Association at https://www.alz.org/alzheimers_disease_early_onset.asp.

The poetry and works of John Donne fascinate me and have done since I first read them at university. However, I will confess that I missed much of the layered meanings when I read his words at eighteen! Through the veil of hormones only one side of his meaning was visible. Although that power is still there in them, I can now see many other ways to interpret his words.

If you loved

One Cornish Summer

Read on to discover more
about Liz Fenwick's inspiration
for the novel . . .

In Conversation with Liz Fenwick

Q *The Civil War is an important thread in the novel – has it always interested you or did you do lots of new research for this novel in particular? What is it that fascinates you about the period?*

A Living where we do in Cornwall it's hard not to be aware of the Civil War. We frequently walk the costal path around Dennis Head where the remains of one of the last Royalist forts to surrender is hidden under the bracken, and there is a 'feeling' about the place. And when we bought our home it came with a Civil War cannonball found when the previous owners renovated the house in the 1960s. Having an artefact like that sitting in your home makes you think about who has lived and died in the area.

Q *The poetry of John Donne flows through the story. Why did you choose his work to be a part of the story – when did you first fall in love with his words?*

A My affair with John Donne's poetry began in my first year of university. He seduced me with his imagery. In those years I never proceeded any further in my understanding. It was only years later, picking up my old university text book, that I reread his works and saw another layer and then another. It was a bit like watching a film you loved in childhood years later and seeing a whole new level of meaning. So when I was thinking about Hebe and Rory I saw the potential for Donne's words to pull Hebe in, and then for their nuanced meaning to offer her a reason to stay. Even as the disease progresses, taking away so much from Hebe, echoes of the words and their meanings remain with her. Insights into Donne's words can be fleeting and can change with each reading.

Q *Lucy is a talented photographer, and you write about it with a strong visual sense. Are you a keen photographer yourself?*

A I am . . . helped and aided by my husband's skill and love of photography. I'm rarely without a camera and am always playing with how light works on an image. That is my main motivator, but I watch my husband and he works with so much more . . . angle, depth of field, shutter speed . . . A photograph captures a fleeting moment and it also captures the photographer's mind.

Q *The story is packed with different kinds of writing – diaries, letters, notes – have you always known you wanted to be a novelist?*

A I have always loved stories and words. My grandfather, who was from Donegal, lived with us when I was a child. He told me stories and read poetry to me. So, from the beginning, stories – words – equalled love. All children have the gift of imagination but many leave it behind. I think most writers never do. As a child I spent hours in my head continuing stories that I didn't want to leave. That grew into my writing these imaginings down and creating my own books, complete with illustrations and

392

stapled bindings. By the time I reached high school, becoming a novelist was high on the priority list. At university I studied English literature with a focus on Medieval Studies and Creative Writing. The drive to write was strong but the ability to finish wasn't as honed. So I lived life and learned that if you truly want something you don't give up . . . *The Cornish House* was published in 2012 and I was 49 – a long journey from a child on my grandfather's lap to a persistent woman rewriting and rewriting until the story was good enough for others to read.

The Places of
One Cornish Summer

Many times I have been asked, *where do your stories come from,* or *how do you get your ideas?* The answer to that is simply, life. I have always been a watcher. As an only child I would stand to the side a great deal because I was unused to the normal tussle of kids and I was afraid they wouldn't like me. So I watched life happen around me. This has proved a very good skill for my writing life. In my opinion, writers are like magpies. We see and hear things and collect them. These things rest in the backs of our minds until one key piece pulls others to it.

One Cornish Summer was no different. I first visited Godolphin over twenty years ago with my parents-in-law. The National Trust hadn't owned it then. The wonderful Mary Schofield did, and she was doing her best to hold the place together. I knew even then there was magic in the walls. Subsequent visits didn't change my mind. The house and the garden moved to the shiny objects pile in the writer's part of my mind.

My best friend was married eleven years ago. It was a wonderful trip revisiting the places of my youth and celebrating her new life and happiness. But despite the joy and fun it was edged with sadness. Her mother was suffering from Alzheimer's and Parkinson's. I was prepared for both, but I hadn't been prepared for her elder sister in her fifties having Alzheimer's too. During the course of the weekend it was very obvious to me that this once fierce, strong, independent woman was slipping away. My heart is still broken because of it.

Fast forward to just a few years ago. Enjoying time before putting the writer Fanny Blake back on a train to London, we stopped at Godolphin House. It was one of the days when the house was open for tours. Walking through the front door, I was overwhelmed with stories. It was different, so very different from my early visits, but somehow the same. Here was a building with a past, a long one, and it had so many stories to tell. This home was a fragment of what it had once been. Depending on what you read there could have been as many as fifty bedrooms in its heyday. Step by step, through the house, I felt its history. From the big flagstones of the floor to the linenfold panelling, each part told a story of a once-great estate.

It wasn't until I stood in front of the wall that dominates the south side of the courtyard that I knew this was the location to tell the story of someone living with early-onset Alzheimer's. This wall is only a relic of the great hall. What remains of Godolphin today is beautiful, but it is only a fraction of what was once there. The lonely wall with its glassless windows speaks of a glorious history. But over the years, stone by stone, the house has diminished – leaving only a haunting impression of what once was.

And yet, thanks to the National Trust, the house has been preserved and given a new life. Albeit one I'm sure that the original family never would have imagined. It is now possible to rent the house, which I did. What an experience! I have never lived in a house so grand. Sitting in the salon I felt a proper grown-up, and seeing in the New Year dancing around the Christmas Tree in the King's Room is something I won't forget. There was so much magic and mystery in the week living there that my imagination couldn't have conjured. The reality was so much better – so much richer. One night the sky was clear and the moon hung above the house like a cut-out, and we woke to a frost so deep the world was white and the water troughs frozen. In the silence of that early morning, as I walked the deserted grounds, the stories of the house's past whispered in the stillness.

The final piece of the puzzle of this story for me was the poetry of John Donne. I'm aware that poetry is not to everyone's taste, but there was something about the way he conveys the unsayable so beautifully with words that reflected Hebe's struggle to me. I also have to confess that although I have a far greater understanding of the complexity of his words now, part of me is still the eighteen-year-old seduced by them. As Hebe says to Rory, through the power of the metaphor Donne says far more than mere words could convey. He speaks of emotions and those are the one thing that hasn't left her.

One Cornish Summer is a story of people haunted by the past they have built. One is losing hers, and the other is rebuilding her life. Godolphin to me was the perfect place to demonstrate that, even with a past as haunted as Godolphin's, we can move forward to embrace a new future.

Did you love
One Cornish Summer?

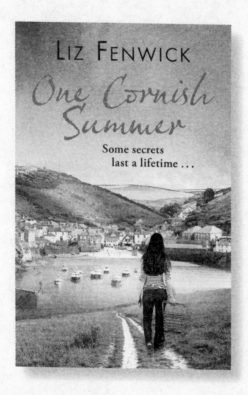

Find out more and get in touch at
www.lizfenwick.com
Sign up to her Facebook page
f/liz.fenwick.author
Or follow her on Twitter
@liz_fenwick

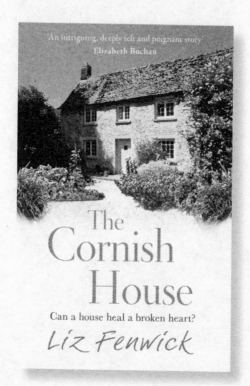

A Cornish Affair

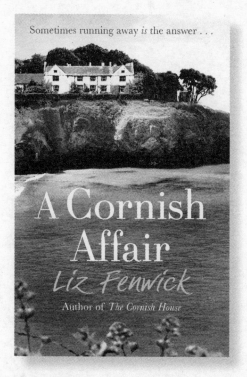

Sometimes running away *is* the answer . . .

A Cornish Affair

Liz Fenwick

Author of *The Cornish House*

Sometimes running away is the answer...

Escaping the pressure of her wedding, Jude flees
to a crumbling cliff-top mansion in Cornwall. But
when the house is put up for sale, it seems that time
is running out for Jude to uncover its tragic history,
and promise of its lost treasure...

A Cornish Stranger

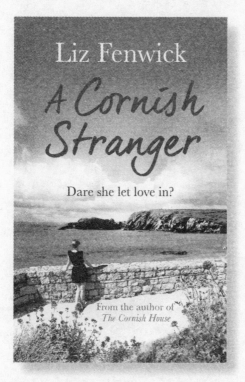

Dare she let love in?

Gabriella Blythe moves to Frenchman's Creek to care for her reclusive grandmother, but the arrival of a handsome stranger in a storm brings about the unravelling of a remarkable story of identity and betrayal.

Under a Cornish Sky

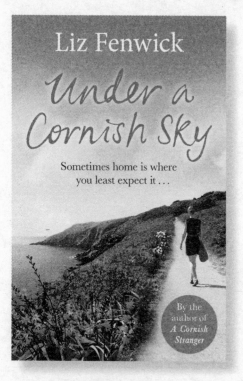

Sometimes home is where you least expect it…

Betrayed by her boyfriend, Demi has nowhere
to go but her grandfather's Cornish cottage, while
Victoria has finally inherited her family's gorgeous
estate after years of a loveless marriage. But can
two very different women find a way forward
when luck changes both their lives?